PRAISE FOR

MASQUERADE

"In MASQUERADE, Janet Dailey's latest romantic suspense novel . . . the reader never doubts that Remy Jardin will be strong enough to resolve everything for her—and our—satisfaction."
—*The New York Times Book Review*

☆   ☆   ☆

"Dailey deftly crochets together past and present as she unravels the mystery. There's something for every escape reader in this best-seller—history, suspense and romance."
—*The Wichita Eagle*

☆   ☆   ☆

"MASQUERADE has all the old Dailey charm and skill."
—*The Rockdale Citizen*

NOVELS BY JANET DAILEY

Touch the Wind
The Rogue
Ride the Thunder
Night Way
This Calder Sky
This Calder Range
Stands a Calder Man
Calder Born, Calder Bred
Silver Wings, Santiago Blue
The Pride of Hannah Wade
The Glory Game
The Great Alone
Heiress
Rivals
Masquerade
Aspen Gold

MASQUERADE

=== A NOVEL BY ===

JANET DAILEY

BOOKS

Little, Brown and Company

Boston Toronto London

Little, Brown and Company
34 Beacon Street
Boston, MA 02108

Printed in the United States of America

Published simultaneously in Canada by Little, Brown and Company (Canada) Limited
This book was originally published in hardcover by Little, Brown and Company.
First LB Books mass market paperback edition: May 1991

10 9 8 7 6 5 4 3 2 1

MASQUERADE

1

She sipped at the wine in her glass and watched with marked indifference the lewd gyrations of a short, fat man garbed in the costume of Bacchus, a wreath of grape leaves encircling his bald head and a toga stretched tautly around his protruding stomach. His partner wore a simple black cocktail dress, a collection of ribbons and bows in her hair, and festive makeup that included glittering pink eye shadow and blue stripes on her cheeks. Near them, a woman in a high, powdered wig, a fake mole, and a gown from the court of Louis XVI danced with a man in a red tuxedo with devil's horns on his head.

Turning from the sight, she let her gaze wander over the hotel's renowned rooftop garden, ablaze with light from colored lanterns strung all around, tiny fairy lights wound through the potted plants and trees, and votive candles on all the tables. Tonight it was the site of a private masked party —one of those intimate little affairs with two hundred or so guests, many in costume but some, like herself, choosing only a mask. Hers happened to be an elaborately feathered, hand-held one in amber satin that matched the dress and fur-lined stole she wore. It was lowered now, revealing the sculpted lines of her face, its expression untouched by the band's driving rock music, the laughter, the voices that filled the night air, a babble of French and Italian with a smattering of German, Dutch, Swiss, and English rising here and there—voices of people caught up in the party madness that gripped Nice, the undisputed queen city of France's Côte d'Azur, the party madness of Carnival that encouraged its revelers to celebrate all that was flesh, to don masks and shed inhibitions, to conceal and reveal.

Reveal. She finally looked at him, feeling the anger rise in her throat—along with the hurt and bitterness of disillusionment. He stood some thirty feet from her, his face partially hidden by the black satin mask he wore, fashioned to resemble a pirate's eye patch. A pirate—criminal of the high seas. My God, how appropriate, she thought. Looting, plundering, destroying in the name of—there was only one word for it—greed.

She took a quick sip of the wine, but it couldn't wash away the disgust, the revulsion she felt. Her fingers tightened on the glass's slender stem. What was she doing at this party? Why was she going through the motions of pretending everything was all right when it wasn't—when nothing would ever be all right again?

A waiter said something to him, and he lifted his head sharply, then nodded once and moved off, coming directly toward her. She took a quick step closer to the roof's edge, with its spectacular views of the gardens below and the Mediterranean beyond. She didn't want to hear any more of his explanations, his justifications.

But he wasn't walking toward her. He was heading for the entrance to the rooftop terrace to her left, a firmness in his stride that spoke of purpose. Curious, she turned and stiffened in alarm at the sight of the dark-haired man in a business suit waiting for him. What was he doing here? He belonged a half a world away. She watched as the two men met and immediately moved off to a quiet corner, away from the throng of party guests.

Why was he here? What was this all about? She had to find out. She cast a cautious glance around, then slipped closer.

"—realizes what went on that night. She's put two and two together and figured out what we did and how we did it."

"'We'? You told her I was involved?" he demanded, anger and accusation in his tone.

"I didn't have to. I told you she figured it out. That's why I called. I felt I should warn you. So far, I haven't been able to make her listen to reason."

They were talking about her. She almost stepped out from behind the concealing fronds of the palmetto plant and confronted them both with her knowledge. She wanted them to know they weren't going to get away with this. But his next words stopped her cold.

"If she can't be made to see reason, you've got to shut her up. She can't be allowed to tell what she knows. There's no place for sentiment in this. She's proved that. And you'll never have a better opportunity than now. Kidnappings, accidents happen all the time in Europe. Back home, she'll be just another statistic."

She felt her mouth and lips suddenly go dry with fear. He wouldn't agree to that . . . would he? He wouldn't hurt her. He couldn't. Not him. But his face was in profile, shadowed by the mask that covered his right eye, making his expression unreadable.

There came a sigh, heavy with defeat. "I don't see any other choice."

No! She backed up a step, moving her head from side to side in mute denial, not wanting to believe what she'd heard.

"Are you going to arrange it, or do you want me—" The wineglass slipped from her fingers and crashed to the terrace floor. Both men turned and stared directly at her. There was a split second when she couldn't move, paralyzed by the accusing look in their eyes. Then she turned and ran. "Stop her! She'll destroy everything."

She looked back and saw his familiar face, half concealed by the mask, coming after her. She brushed past a slim young man in a Degas ballerina costume and pushed through the doors to the bank of elevators, conscious of the shock, the disbelief that blurred everything but the panicked need to escape.

He reached the elevators to the rooftop terrace just as the doors to one of them slid shut. He punched impatiently at the button to summon another, gripped by his own kind of fear, the fear that came with guilt and desperation. He couldn't let her get away, or all would be lost. Why couldn't she see that? Why was she doing this? Why was she making him do this?

At the lobby, he emerged from the elevator in time to see her dart through the hotel entrance and into the street. He hurried after her. A cab pulled away as he stopped outside. He lifted a hand to call another, then saw her cutting across the street toward the Espace Masséna. If he lost her in that mob of revelers in the square—he couldn't let that happen.

But it did. The crowd swallowed her.

Where was she? The black mask cut off his peripheral vision to the right, forcing him to turn his head to scan the boisterous throng on that side of the Espace Masséna. There was a loud splash behind him, accompanied by a woman's shriek of laughter. His back was to the square's fountain, with its spectacular pillars of water shooting some forty feet into the air. He swung around, his glance briefly resting on some madcap brunette frolicking in the fountain's pool. The instant he identified the woman as a stranger, he looked away, resuming his search and unconsciously clenching his hands into tight, trembling fists.

Ignoring the tangle of confetti at his feet, he took two quick steps toward the boulevard. In one direction, only a short stroll away, was the Promenade des Anglais with its glittering casinos and palatial hotels, bastions of privacy and exclusivity for the wealthy and celebrated. In another lay the narrow, cobbled streets of Nice's Old Town section with its mélange of galleries, outdoor cafés, and *boîtes de nuit*. Beyond that were the Baie des Anges and the Mediterranean.

He hesitated, then stopped. Three-story-tall cartoon figures, garishly outlined in a blaze of colored lights, mocked him from the distinctive roccoco red buildings that flanked the square. He swung abruptly to his left, only to be met by the taunting grin of the giant papier-mâché King Carnival enthroned on the square.

For an instant, he glared at the figure, then swept his glance over the milling crowd again. How could she have disappeared so quickly? He scanned the throng, seeking the amber shimmer of her satin gown, the streaks of gold in her sun-lightened brown hair, and the gleam of the topaz brooch she wore at her throat. Again he saw no sign of her, and he felt the knot tighten in his stomach.

Someone jostled him from behind. Instinctively he turned, protectively lifting a hand to cover the slim wallet tucked inside the inner breast pocket of his black tuxedo jacket, well aware that Mardi Gras celebrations always attracted a sizable contingent of pickpockets as well as sun-and-fun-loving tourists. This time his caution was unnecessary as a fair-haired German raised a wine bottle to him in an apologetic salute and then reeled away, his arm hooked around his svelte companion.

He absently brushed at the wet splatter of wine on his sleeve and turned back. At that instant he saw her, near the sidewalk of the tree-lined boulevard, looking warily about, poised for flight. But she hadn't seen him yet.

He came up behind her and caught hold of her arm, his fingers curling into the satin of her stole. "You're coming with me—now."

She pulled back, her head coming up, her gaze clashing with his, her temper willfully set against his, stubbornly resisting him. "So you can have me kidnapped? Murdered?"

For an instant everything inside him went still. "It doesn't have to be that way. If you'd just listen to reason. Nobody got hurt in this. No one."

"What about the company? This could destroy it." She threw him another angry and challenging look, only this time it was colored by hurt and accusation. "But you don't care, do you?"

"I had no choice."

"Didn't you?"

His grip tightened on her arm, checking the pivoting turn she made away from him and steering her into the concealing shadows beneath a tree. "You've got to understand—"

"I'll never understand!" she flared, then her voice grew all tight and choked. "How could you do this? Who are you? I don't even know you anymore."

The revulsion, the distrust she showed for him broke the thin thread of his control. Seizing her high on both arms, he began to shake her, mindless of his roughness. "Don't you realize what's at stake? How can you betray me like this? If you truly love—"

"Stop. Stop it!" As her hands came up to push at him and end the violent shaking, the rodlike wand that held her satin mask struck against his upper lip, sending a needle-sharp spasm of pain through his face.

Stunned by the blow, he instinctively released her to explore the injury with his fingers and tongue. He tasted blood and realized that she'd hit him. She'd hit *him*. A sudden rage welled up in him and he lashed out, backhanding her across the face.

The force of the blow sent her reeling backward against the tree. The momentary gratification he felt vanished when he heard the cracking thud of her head striking the trunk a second before she crumpled to the ground.

"My God, no." He took a step toward her, automatically reaching out to her with his hands. "I didn't mean to, I swear—"

But she didn't move.

"Hey?!" someone shouted, the voice American in its accent. "What's going on there?"

He shot a quick glance over his shoulder, regret, fear, and guilt warring for control. He hesitated for a split second, then took off across the boulevard.

Two T-shirt-and-denim-clad twenty-year-olds ran to the pool of amber satin lying in the shadows by the street. The one with dark-rimmed glasses knelt down to check her pulse while the blond sporting a California tan started after the fleeing man.

"Let him go, Brad," his buddy called him back. "You'll never catch him anyway, and this girl's unconscious."

"Is she hurt bad?"

"I don't know, but we'd better get an ambulance."

"And the police," his friend added.

2

*B*lackness. Swirling, eddying, trying to pull her deeper —away from that distant light. She fought against it, straining toward that light, obeying some inner voice that said she must reach it. But it hurt. It hurt so much.

One last time she kicked for it. Suddenly it was there— glaring on her eyelids. She'd made it.

She struggled to open her eyes, fighting the lids' heaviness. The light—she didn't understand why it was so bright. Something was wrong. Dazed and disoriented, she looked about her in confusion, not recognizing the stark walls or the drab curtains at the windows.

A man loomed beside her, his features blurring for an instant and then coming into focus. ''Where—'' Her lips were too stiff, too dry; she couldn't get the words out. She moistened them and tried again. ''Where am I?''

''*Américaine*,'' someone said softly, very softly, giving the word the French pronunciation.

Groggily she tried to locate the source of that voice and finally saw the balding man standing at the foot of the bed, dressed in a comfortable tweed coat and a turtleneck sweater. He looked like a kindly old professor.

"You are in an hospital, mam'selle," the first man replied.

"A hospital." She frowned at that, certain there was somewhere else she was supposed to be. "I have to go." Something told her it was important. "I have to leave." But the instant she tried to lift her head, pain knifed through her and the blackness rushed back, threatening to swirl her away again. Somehow she managed to hang on, clinging to the sound of the man's voice even though she couldn't actually hear the words; they came from too far away. Finally the black pain receded to the edges.

"—lie quietly." The voice was clearer now. "Do not try to move."

She opened her eyes again, focusing on his regular features, etched with tired lines. "Who are you?" She searched without finding anything familiar about this plain-looking, brown-haired, brown-eyed man.

"I am Dr. Jules St. Clair." A faint smile edged the corners of his mouth. "And what is your name, mam'selle?"

"My name. My name is—" She frowned, not understanding why she couldn't think of it. But when she tried, there was only a confusing blankness—and a throbbing pressure in her head that wouldn't go away. "I—I can't remember it." She saw the doctor's somewhat startled look, followed by the quick narrowing of his eyes. She felt a rising sense of panic and fought it back. "What's happened to me? This pain. I—I can't seem to think."

"You have suffered a head injury, mam'selle—a concussion. I will have the nurse give you something for the pain so you can rest."

"But my name—what is it?" Even as she made the weak demand, she was conscious of the welcome promise of his words. She was tired, so very tired of fighting to hold the pain at bay, tired of struggling to penetrate this thick, bewildering mist in her mind.

"Later, mam'selle. There will be time for all your questions later," he said.

Without the strength to argue with him, she closed her eyes. Distantly she heard the doctor murmur instructions to someone else in the room. She sensed that he was no longer standing beside her, but she didn't bother to open her eyes again to see where he'd gone. She drifted instead.

At the foot of the hospital bed, Dr. St. Clair picked up her chart and began making notations on it. Inspector Claude Armand watched him in silence for several seconds, then asked, "Is it possible she cannot truly recall her name?"

"Yes," the doctor replied, without looking up from the notes he was making. "Patients with head injuries such as hers are frequently confused and disoriented when they first regain consciousness. Some memory loss is not uncommon. In the majority of cases, it is a temporary condition."

"How temporary?"

"That is difficult to say, Inspector. A few hours, a few days, a few weeks." His shoulders lifted at the impreciseness of his answer as he finished the last of his notes and retracted the tip of his ballpoint pen with a sharp click. "Your question leads me to assume that no one has come forward to identify her."

"No one."

"Personally, Inspector Armand"—he paused to hand the chart to a waiting nurse—"I find nothing unusual in our mystery lady's inability to remember her name. But she was admitted—what? —nearly thirty hours ago. How could someone forget to remember such a beautiful woman? To me, that is strange."

"Oui." But it wasn't the *how* that puzzled Inspector Armand as he left the hospital room. No, it wasn't the *how* so much as the *why*.

3

*S*unlight streamed through the hospital window, setting
agleam the shiny satin fabric the young nurse held up
for her inspection. "It is beautiful, *non?*" declared the
short, stout woman, whose olive skin and dark hair revealed
her Mediterranean origins.

She ran her hand over the gown's skirt, which lay draped
across her lap. "It is very beautiful," she agreed, then sighed,
fighting back a bitter discouragement to admit, "but I don't
remember ever seeing it before, let alone wearing it."

The nurse glanced at the balding man by the window,
dressed in a corduroy jacket of charcoal gray with a pearl-
gray turtleneck under it. A pair of glasses framed with gold
wire sat on the bridge of his nose. With a downward tilt of
his head, he peered over the top of them and signaled to the
nurse, with a slight flick of his hand, to take the gown and
its matching stole away.

Only the jewelry remained—the antique brooch and the
diamond-studded topaz earrings. She didn't recognize them
either. She pressed her fingers to her temples and tried to
lightly massage away the pressure. Earlier, a nurse had given

her something that had reduced the throbbing pain to a dull ache—an ache that kept her on edge. But she wanted nothing stronger—not now, when she needed to think.

"Is that all I had when I was brought in to the hospital?" Each time she looked at the man by the window, she had to remind herself that he was an inspector. He didn't look like one. If she had guessed his occupation, she would have said he was a headmaster or a schoolteacher—someone of authority who could be stern and benevolent by turns.

"*Oui*, you had nothing else." He removed his glasses and returned them to the breast pocket of his jacket. "No identification, no passport, no hotel key, no purse."

"Could my purse have been stolen? What happened? The nurses couldn't tell me. Do you know?"

"You were seen by two young men—Americans—struggling or arguing with a man at the Espace Masséna. They think he may have struck you—which would account for the bruise by your mouth. When they saw you fall to the ground, one of them shouted, and the man ran off. Bits of tree bark were found when the laceration to the back of your head was cleaned here in the hospital, and later, traces of blood and strands of hair the same color as yours were found at the site. From that we assume that when you fell, you struck your head on the tree, resulting in your injuries."

Those she knew about. The doctor had enumerated them for her when she'd seen him earlier—the bruise near her mouth, the laceration to her head, which had required twelve stitches to close, the hairline fracture to her skull, the concussion, and—a rare total loss of memory. Total in the sense that all details of her personal life had been lost, but not her store of knowledge.

"I know where the Espace Masséna is—and the flower market on Cours Saleya. And Nice is in France; the capital is Paris—" She broke off the spate of facts. "Why was I at the Espace Masséna?"

"I assume to participate in the Carnival festivities."

"Carnival. It comes from the Old Italian word

carnelevare—which loosely translates as a 'farewell to the flesh,'" she murmured, remembering that and so much more. "It's pagan in origin, isn't it?—a spring rite of the Greeks to celebrate the miracle of propagation, an annual event that the Romans subsequently corrupted with lewdness and the followers of Christianity eventually absorbed into their religion, making it an acceptable feasting time before the Lenten season. The custom of masking came from the French—along with the name Mardi Gras."

The inspector smiled faintly. "Nothing is ever what it seems, is it, mam'selle?"

"What about me?" she asked, suddenly intense. "What do I seem like to you?" As he hesitated in answering, she suddenly realized she had no idea what she looked like. She was trapped in the body of a person she knew absolutely nothing about. "Is there a mirror somewhere so I can see myself?"

After taking a moment to consider her request, he nodded. "I will find one for you." He left the room and returned within minutes with a small hand mirror.

A tension threaded her nerves as she took it from him, then slowly raised it to look at the reflection her face made. Her eye was first caught by the swathe of gauze around her head and the purpling near her mouth, which swelled part of her lip. She touched a lock of her shoulder-length hair, the tawny color of cognac, then noticed the paleness of her face. She wondered whether it was caused by the absence of makeup, the harshness of the light, or the drabness of the hospital gown.

Not that it mattered, she decided, and instead directed her attention to the strong refinement in her features—the good cheekbones, smooth jawline, and solid angle to her forehead and chin. Her eyebrows were a sandy shade of brown, thick at the inner corners and arching naturally in a graceful sweep. Amber flecks shimmered in her hazel eyes, and her dark-brown lashes were long and thick, tipped with gold at the ends. Her lips were well shaped, with a full curve to the lower one and a bowing arch to the upper. With the slightest lift of their corners, attractive dimples appeared in her cheeks. Except for a faintly troubled darkness in her eyes, the image in the mirror looked dauntless and proud, a hint of daring about it that seemed to eagerly seek challenge.

Was that her? In frustration she lowered the mirror. It was no use. She didn't remember that face. She didn't remember anything.

"Who am I?" she said with impatience. "Where do I live? What do I do? Don't I have family, friends? I've been in this hospital for almost two days. Why hasn't anyone missed me? Could I have come to Nice alone? The gown—" She remembered the designer label it had carried. "It was by St. Laurent. Does that mean I'm wealthy?"

"It is possible," the inspector conceded. "Though it is also possible the gown and the jewelry were gifts from a generous lover. The Côte d'Azur attracts many with income in rarefied brackets. And they, in turn, attract beautiful women to the area."

"And you think I'm one of those women."

"Perhaps." He shrugged noncommitally. "However, most—even today—are poor Bardot imitations, with tumbling blond hair, voluptuous curves, and pink, pouting lips. Few have the appearance of class you possess."

"I think that's a compliment. Thank you," she murmured with a trace of dryness.

"It was." His mouth curved with the same droll amusement she had shown. "In any case, beautiful women may arrive in Nice alone, but they seldom remain alone very long."

"Then you think I knew the man I was seen struggling with?"

"The two of you could have been engaged in a lovers' quarrel. Or—he wished to make your acquaintance, and you rejected his advances."

"But why would I go to the Espace Masséna at night, during Carnival, without an escort, and without a purse?"

she argued. "Or was the man a thief who stole my purse? That could have been the cause of the struggle—and it would explain why he ran."

"But why would he take your purse and not your jewelry?"

"I don't know." She sighed wearily, confused and frustrated by the constant blankness, the absence of any answers to the questions. "There has to be some way to find out who I am. Somewhere there has to be a room with my clothes in it, my makeup, my jewelry."

"Inquiries are being made at all the hotels and pensions in the city," he told her. "But you must remember, during Carnival people frequently stay out all night. Therefore, the absence of a guest from his or her room for one night normally would not be worthy of notice. Two nights in a row, that is another thing. If we are fortunate, I may know something tomorrow."

"I hope so. I *have* to find out who I am."

He arched an eyebrow at her curiously. "You say that with unusual urgency, mam'selle."

"I know." She heard the troubled note in her voice and tried to explain. "I have this feeling, Inspector—this vague yet very compelling feeling—that I'm supposed to be somewhere. It's important. It's more than important. It's as if something terrible will happen if I'm not there."

"Where?" It was asked quietly, almost indifferently, as if to gently jar loose a fragment of her memory.

But it didn't work. "I don't know." This time her voice was choked with the frustration and strain of trying to recall. But the more she struggled to remember, the harder her head pounded. Suddenly she didn't have the strength to fight them both. She sagged back against the hospital pillows and shut her eyes tight, hating the blankness.

"I have overtired you with my questions. I am sorry," the inspector said, his voice gentle with regret. "You rest. I will come back tomorrow."

Then he was gone and she was alone again—alone with the emptiness of her memory, an emptiness she seemed powerless to fill. With a turn of her head, she gazed out the window at the brilliant blue sky that had given the Côte d'Azur its name. If only there was something she could do, somewhere she could go—but where did a person go to find her memory?

4

From the hospital corridor came the murmur of typically hushed voices, the rustle of stiff polyester uniforms, and the whisper of white-stockinged legs brushing together in a striding walk. But no one approached her door, and no bouquets of flowers relieved the starkness of her room or sent their sweet fragrance into it to cover the sharp antiseptic smells.

Agitated, restless, and tired of staring at the walls that echoed the blankness of her mind, she threw back the covers and sat up, swinging her legs over the side of the bed. A wave of dizziness hit her. She gripped the edge of the mattress and waited for the room to stop spinning, then slowly lowered her feet to the floor and stood up. Immediately she felt a coolness against her skin where the hospital gown gaped in back. But she had no robe to cover her—no clothes at all other than the evening gown. Turning, she pulled the blanket off the bed and draped it around her shoulders Indian-style.

She was halfway to the door before she realized she was obeying that faint inner voice that said she had to leave, that she was needed somewhere. But where? Why? And why the urgency? Was she in some kind of danger? The man she'd been struggling with—had he deliberately tried to hurt her, or had he been trying to make her go somewhere with him? But where? And what was the danger? From whom? And where were they now?

Driven by the endless questions, she crossed to the window with its postcard view of Nice, the city of fun and flowers, of sun, sea, and sex, a city that sizzled softly by day and crackled with action by night.

In the distance the sunlight sparkled on the deep blue Mediterranean waters of the Baie des Anges, ringed by private beaches, crowded now with wall-to-wall sunburned flesh and languid egos. Closer were the red-roofed ocher buildings and Italianate churches of the town's old section, with its narrow streets opening to form little squares.

She hugged the blanket more tightly around her and searched the scene with her eyes, a scene so reminiscent of paintings by Matisse and Cézanne. Here the dreaded mistral that roared down the Rhône Valley twisting and turning trees was but a breeze to stir the fronds of the palm trees along the Promenade des Anglais, and the architecture was distinctly Mediterranean in character rather than French, a reminder that less than a century and a half ago Nice belonged to Italy.

Was it somewhere in Nice that she was supposed to be? Was that what had brought her here? But how could she be sure she didn't live here? The inspector claimed that she spoke English with an American accent, but she was fluent in French. The designer gown, the jewelry—it was possible she was a wealthy American living abroad, perhaps in Nice itself. After all, she knew the names of its streets, the location of a marvelous little tea shop on the Rue St. François-de-Paule, and . . . but a frequent visitor to the city might know such things too.

If she wasn't supposed to be here, though, then where?

Her head started to pound again. She turned from the window, absently massaging her temple.

Inspector Armand stood inside the doorway, his relaxed stance conveying the impression that he'd been observing her for some time. She lifted her head sharply at the sight of him, her glance quickly taking in the shiny bald top of his head, the dark-gray hair shading to white at the temples, the pleasing plumpness of his features, and the keenness of his blue eyes. She hadn't heard him come in. He had slipped in quietly—like a principal slipping in to the back of a classroom to silently observe.

"I see you are up and about today," he said, his sharp-eyed gaze continuing its assessing sweep of her. "That is good."

She took a quick step toward him, then stopped, every muscle in her body strained taut. "Have you found out who I am?"

"Regrettably, *non*. Our check of the hotels has turned up nothing. The whereabouts of all their guests have been accounted for, and no belongings have been left in any rooms, other than the normal one or two items that a departing guest might forget to pack."

She had tried to brace herself for this answer, but it was still frustrating to hear it. "And I suppose no one answering my description has been reported missing."

"Non"

She sighed. "What now, Inspector?"

"Now, we widen our search to include apartments, homes, villas, yachts. . . ."

"It will take time to check all those out." She looked down at her hands and the tight lacing of her fingers on the blanket, the tension, the turmoil, knotting them as it knotted her.

"Unfortunately, a considerable amount of time."

"I don't know if I can wait that long to find out who I am." She forced her hands to loosen their grip on the edge of the blanket. "There must be some other—quicker—way."

"When you saw Dr. St. Clair this morning, was he able to tell you anything?"

There was a wry pull at one corner of her mouth. "If you

mean other than his opinion that the laceration to my head is healing nicely, no. But he's arranged for a specialist to see me this afternoon. A psychiatrist or psychologist, I don't remember which.''

"Perhaps he will be more helpful."

"Perhaps." She sighed again. "If only I could remember something—anything."

"Maybe it is more convenient not to remember."

He suddenly had her complete attention. "What do you mean by that?" She saw the close way he was watching, observing every nuance of her reaction to this rather startling remark. "Do you think I'm faking this amnesia? Why? What would I gain by it?"

"I have asked myself that too."

She stared at him, stunned by the implication of his words. "My God, do you think I'm some criminal? Why haven't you run a check on me?"

"It was one of the first things I did—merely as a matter of routine, you understand." His mouth curved in a faint, apologetic smile that took much of the sting out of his suspicion.

"Obviously your 'routine' check didn't turn up anything, or I'd be arrested."

"The results were negative," the inspector admitted.

"You don't still think it's a possibility?"

"In my profession it is never wise to rule out any possibility until the truth is uncovered."

"I suppose it isn't. Right now I just wish I knew something. I am so tired of this endless circle of questions."

"Life is a question, is it not? And we spend our whole life trying to find the answer to it." A smile made his cheeks rounder. "But it is ironic, *non*, that many people wish they could forget their past, while you seek so valiantly to remember yours."

At that moment a small, quick man with bushy hair and beetle brows bustled into her hospital room, a clipboard and manila folder tucked under his arm. "I am Dr. Gervais. Dr.

St. Clair asked—" He stopped and blinked at the inspector. "You have a visitor."

"Inspector Claude Armand." He smoothly produced his identification.

"You are here to question the patient?" The doctor blinked at him again, with a certain vagueness in his expression.

"And you are here to examine her." The inspector smiled, but as usual, the smile didn't reach his eyes. "You have no objection to my sitting in, do you?"

The doctor seemed momentarily taken aback by the request, then lifted his shoulders in a brief, indifferent shrug. "You may stay or go, as you wish." With that settled, he turned and introduced himself to her again. "Dr. St. Clair tells me the injury to your head has caused a defect in your memory."

"A defect—that's an understatement, Doctor. I don't remember anything. Not my name, my address, or my family—assuming I have one."

"Hmmm," he said, as if he found her response most interesting, then flicked a hand in her direction. "Please make yourself comfortable, and we will talk about this."

"In other words, lie down on the couch," she murmured dryly.

He gave her a startled look, then glanced around the room. "There is no couch," he said, then the curious frown that had pulled his heavy brows together cleared in a dawning realization. "Ahh, you make a joke. It is good you have retained your sense of humor."

"It is one of the few things I've retained." Avoiding the bed, she crossed to a chair and sat down, conscious of the inspector standing quietly to one side, silently listening, observing.

The doctor sat himself down in the other chair and crossed his legs at the knee, one foot swinging in a nervous rhythm as he arranged the clipboard on his lap and opened the manila folder to leaf through the papers inside. "Shall we begin?" he said.

After thirty minutes, during which he tested her current memory retention, asked numerous general-knowledge questions, and questioned her extensively about her past, specifically her religion, her patience was exhausted.

During a lull, she demanded, "What are we accomplishing with all this, Doctor?"

He gave her a look that seemed to say the answer was obvious. "I am attempting to determine the extent of your memory impairment. Amnesia has many causes and takes many forms—senility, alcoholism, electroconvulsive therapy, acute encephalitis, brain trauma. . . . In severe cases, amnesia symptoms primarily stem from damage to such brain structures as the mammillary bodies, circumscribed parts of the thalamus, and—"

She broke in, shaking her head in confusion. "You are being too technical, Doctor."

"My apologies." There was a quick bob of his bushy head. "My initial findings tell me that you have what we call traumatic amnesia, as a result of the concussion you suffered. This is a common aftereffect of a severe head injury."

"But when will my memory return?"

"That is impossible to say. It could be today, tomorrow, next week, next month." He leaned back in the chair and pulled thoughtfully at a thick eyebrow. "It will probably return gradually, with pieces of your past coming back to you—perhaps in chronological order, from the most recent, or perhaps haphazardly, like pieces of a jigsaw puzzle that finally fit together."

"But it isn't permanent?"

"There have been cases where the patient has never recovered his memory, but they are rare." He hesitated, then added, "However, it is altogether possible that you may never remember the events that immediately preceded your injury."

"In other words, I might not remember the identity or description of the man I was seen struggling with," she concluded.

"Correct."

"You haven't said anything about treatment." And that omission bothered her. "What about drugs or hypnosis?"

"Hypnosis is frequently helpful in cases of hysterical amnesia—where there is no physical cause, no damage to the brain."

She stared at him. "Are you saying that all I can do is sit and wait for my memory to come back—if it does?"

"Essentially, yes."

"I don't accept that. There has to be something I can do." She rose to her feet and crossed stiffly to the window. "There has to be."

"You cannot force your memory to return, mademoiselle. The more you grasp for it, the more elusive it becomes. It is better to relax your mind and allow your memory to return naturally."

"It's a bitter prescription you offer me, Doctor," she murmured, unable to keep the note of frustration out of her voice.

"But it is the best one." He spent another few minutes briefly lecturing her about time and healing, then left.

She stood at the window, fighting tears and railing at her helplessness. Then a faint stir of movement intruded to forcibly remind her of the inspector's presence in the room. She threw him a quick glance then tilted her head a little higher, fixing her gaze on the colorful sails of the pleasure craft in the bay.

"The good doctor wasn't very helpful, was he?" she said.

"No, although it was apparent from your conversation with him that your knowledge of medicine and anatomy is limited. I think it would be safe to assume that you are not associated with the medical profession."

"But I must do something—have some interest." Made restless again by this blankness, she turned from the window.

"The dress you were wearing is an expensive one. Perhaps you are wealthy and do not have to work at anything."

"Maybe. But I can't imagine myself being idle—or flitting

from one fashionable resort to another, occupying my time solely with parties and charity events. A life like that would be too aimless.''

"What do you think you might do, then?"

She searched her mind for an answer, then sighed. "I . . . don't . . . know.''

"Tell me what you know about the law—the first things that come to your mind.''

"Free association, you mean?" She looked over at him, her curiosity piqued by the thought.

"Something like that, yes.''

"The law." She closed her eyes and tried to relax, letting her thoughts flow spontaneously. "Corporations, felony, fraud, writs, subpoenas, habeas corpus. . . ." She felt herself trying to grope for words, and shook her head. "That's the extent of it. Let's try something else.''

"Banking.''

"Numbered Swiss accounts, deposits, rates of exchange, interest, loans, mortgages, checking accounts, savings.''

Again the well of terms quickly dried up. It was the same with advertising, petroleum, interior design, motion pictures, computers, and the travel industry.

Refusing to give up, she insisted, "Let's try another.''

The inspector hesitated, then said, "You are fluent in both French and English. Perhaps you are an interpreter. When I begin to speak again, simultaneously translate what I say into English.''

"All right." She focused her gaze on his mouth and waited, a tension heightening all her senses despite her attempts to relax.

He began talking at a rate that was neither fast nor slow. "I was born in the Maritime Alps and grew up in Levens, a peaceful village at the entrance to the Vésubie Valley. . . .''

She was able to follow along for the first half dozen or so words, then she began to stumble, the words tangling as she struggled to listen to what he was saying while translating what he'd already said. The harder she tried, the more jumbled everything became.

"Stop—please." Laughing at her mangled translation of his words, she lifted her hands in mock surrender. "I can't do it. I can't split my concentration that way."

"It is difficult, *non?*"

"Yes," she replied emphatically, then her amusement at the abortive attempt faded as discouragement set in. "What else is there, Inspector?"

"It is always possible, mam'selle, that you haven't been trained for anything."

"Except to be beautiful and decorative, you mean."

"You say that with a touch of disdain."

"I suppose I do." But she wasn't interested in her reaction to that. "This feeling I have that I'm supposed to be somewhere—if it's true, then why hasn't my absence been noticed? Why hasn't someone missed me?"

"Perhaps when we find out who you are, we will learn those answers as well."

"But when will that be?" she demanded, all her frustration and anxiety surfacing as she turned from him and paced to the window, her arms folded tightly in front of her, her fingers curling into the blanket. "How long will I have to wait?"

After a short silence, the inspector spoke. "I have arranged for a photographer to come and take your picture today. The newspaper has agreed to print it in tomorrow's edition. Perhaps someone will recognize your photo and come forward."

"Perhaps."

When he took his leave of her, she responded automatically but didn't turn from the window, her attention riveted on the brilliant blue sky outside. Like the endless swirl of questions in her mind, it seemed to go on forever.

5

W e've located her," the man said into the telephone, studying the grainy newspaper photograph before him, transposed onto thin facsimile paper. It showed a young woman, bandages circling the top of her head and a bruise standing out sharply against the paleness of her skin. There was no hint of desperation in the eyes that stared back at him. Instead, they looked insistent, determined, demanding.

"Where?" came the sharp, quick response from the man on the other end of the line.

"At a hospital in Nice."

"A hospital?"

"Yes. I've just received a copy of an article that's appearing in the morning edition of their paper, accompanied by a photo of her." Once more he scanned the article in the French-language newspaper. Mostly it was a collection of pertinent facts, and little else, listing her height at five feet four and a half inches, her weight at one hundred and thirteen pounds, her hair dark blond, her eyes hazel, and her age estimated to be in the mid-to-late-twenties range. All of these details he already knew about her—with one enlightening addition. "My French is a little rusty, but it appears she has amnesia."

"Amnesia. My God, does that mean she can't remember anything?"

"Apparently." He couldn't keep the note of satisfaction out of his voice. "The article refers to her as the 'Demoiselle de Mystère.'"

"This is great news."

"I know."

"You've got to get to her—quickly."

"My thought exactly."

"I mean it. We can't afford for her to remember and start talking. I'm counting on you to keep her quiet. And if you can't, I will. I'm in way too deep to let her destroy me. I'm sorry, but that's the way it is."

"Don't worry." There was a sharp click, and the line went dead.

She looked at the grainy black-and-white photograph, finding it strange that she felt so detached. On second thought, she decided that it wasn't so strange, considering she didn't recognize that woman at all.

Too bad the photographer hadn't waited another twelve hours to take her picture. Dr. St. Clair had removed the turban of gauze from around her head early this morning, leaving only a small, square bandage to protect the deep cut, and her shoulder-length hair covered even that.

And the doctor had also hinted that she would soon be well enough to be released. Which raised a whole new set of problems. Where would she go? How would she live when she had no clothes, no money, and no name—other than the melodramatic one the newspaper had given her, "Demoiselle de Mystère." She suspected it could have been worse. They could just as easily have dubbed her "Mademoiselle X" or something equally trite.

Checking a sigh, she folded the newspaper shut and laid

it back down on the table in the small waiting room. As she rose from the chair and pulled the blanket-robe higher around her shoulders, she wondered if anyone would see the photograph and recognize her. It wouldn't be wise to count on that, though. No, she needed to start planning what she was going to do once she was released from the hospital.

As she passed the nurses' station and turned down the corridor to her room, she decided to ask Inspector Armand to recommend a jeweler who would give her a good price for the antique brooch and topaz earrings she'd been wearing. Once she had money, then what? Should she stay in Nice and look for work—Heaven knew what kind? Or should she leave? And go where?

Distracted by the sound of a raised voice, she looked up from her absent contemplation of the floor. There was a man standing in the corridor directly ahead of her, not far from the door to her room. He was upset about something, judging from the anxious attempt by one of the nurses to placate him. Curious to learn what the fuss was all about, she took another look at the stranger.

Dressed in a sport coat in an elongated herringbone design, a beige brown tie of woven silk, and mocha trousers, he stood easily over six feet tall. His heavy-boned features were lean and angular, with none of the carved sleekness about them that might have persuaded her to consider him handsome. It was a hard face, an unforgiving face that gave the impression that cynicism lurked just below the surface. Yet there was something compelling about his looks—something ruthlessly masculine—that she couldn't deny.

"I don't care whether you make a habit of losing patients or not," he said to the nurse, plainly unplacated. "But I suggest you find this one—now!"

"*Oui, m'sieur.*"

He turned on his heel, then stopped abruptly when he saw her walking toward them. Suddenly his eyes seemed more black than gray, with glass-sharp splinters of interest in them.

"Remy." His deep voice rumbled the name.

Who was he talking to? Was there someone behind her? She glanced back, but there was no one in the corridor. When she squared around, the man was there before her, his hands seizing her by the arms and pulling her to him, a harshness in their grip that spoke of feelings he had tried to control and couldn't. And she realized he was referring to her. She was Remy.

Too stunned by the discovery to resist, she let him gather her to him. The fine woolen texture of his sport coat against her cheek, the musky sandalwood fragrance of a man's cologne that clung to it, the faint tremors within him—those and a dozen other impressions registered on her at once. But most of all she was struck by the overwhelming feeling that it was right for her to be in his arms. It was where she belonged.

Savoring the feeling, she leaned into him and let the hands that glided with such familiar ease over her back press her even closer to him. She was conscious of her pulse quickening in pleasure when he rubbed his mouth against the side of her hair.

"I was about to turn this hospital upside down looking for you, Remy."

Remy. It was the second time he'd called her that. Was that her name? She tried to remember, but she couldn't penetrate that wall of blankness to make it familiar.

She sensed his withdrawal an instant before his hands pushed her an arm's length away from him. She caught the glimmer of anger in his hardening expression, an anger that suggested he regretted the action that had swept her into his arms. Yet the light in his eyes remained dark and bright as his gaze traveled over her face in a quick inspection.

"The photo I saw showed your head in bandages." Reaching up, he traced one side of her forehead, which had earlier been swathed in gauze, his touch incredibly light and gentle.

She should know him, but she didn't. "Who are you?"

He stiffened as if she'd struck him, then pulled his hand back to his side, his mouth curving in a humorless smile. "Obviously someone you'd rather forget."

"That isn't what I meant."

"This is Monsieur Cole Buchanan," the nurse volunteered, handing her a business card. "Your family owns an international shipping company. It is exciting, *non?*"

Before she had a chance to look at the card, footsteps approached. "It seems I have arrived late with the news," came Inspector Armand's familiar voice.

"News," she repeated blankly, still trying to make sense out of all of this.

"Oui. I came to tell you that your brother would be arriving shortly to take you home."

Struggling to hide her shock at his announcement, she quickly looked down at the card in her hand. Cole Buchanan's name appeared in bold type in the center of it, with the title of President listed directly below his name. This man couldn't be her brother. She inwardly recoiled from the thought, aware that her reaction to him when he'd held her in his arms a moment ago had been anything but sisterly. She remembered the way her body had arched in a sexual response—the gliding caress of his hands on her back—and the momentary desire she'd felt to turn her head and find the male lips rubbing so sensually over her hair.

She forced herself to look at the company name and logo that headed the card—the Crescent Line. She stared at the name, waiting for it to spark some memory, no matter how vague. But nothing came. Instead, she felt uneasy. Why?

"Is something wrong?" The deep-voiced question came from Cole Buchanan.

"No." Why was she so quick with her denial? Something *was* wrong, but what? And why didn't it feel right to ask him about it? He was her brother. "It's just that—I don't remember anything about the company or about shipping."

"You've never been involved in the actual operation of the company."

Was that criticism she detected in his statement? But a glance found nothing in his expression to suggest that. If anything, he seemed sharply alert, watchful—his look almost guarded.

"You don't remember anything, do you?" He made the observation somewhat thoughtfully.

"She suffers from amnesia—" Inspector Armand began.

"I know," Cole interrupted, a trace of aloofness in the glance he gave him. "I was informed of her condition, but I hadn't realized it was total."

"You said my name is Remy." She focused on that, compelled by a need to challenge and confront. "Who am I? What am I? Where do I live?"

"In New Orleans . . . Louisiana," he added, as if she might not remember that fact either. "You still live at the family home in the Garden district."

Images flashed in her mind, images that came and went too quickly for her to grasp and hold and discover what they meant, images of ancient moss-draped oaks, graceful wisteria arches, and scrolling iron lace railings. Were they her memories, or merely a knowledge of the place? She couldn't tell.

"Do you remember something?" the inspector asked.

"I'm not sure," she admitted, then looked at him and realized, "You two haven't been introduced. This is Inspector Claude Armand. He—"

Cole Buchanan broke in firmly and extended a hand in formal greeting. "A pleasure, Inspector. I know the family would want me to pass along their thanks for the efforts you've made in Remy's behalf." He sounded warm, sincere, and polite—but aloof. She was struck by that. Inspector Armand was a stranger to him, and she had the impression that he wanted to keep it that way. He wasn't interested in making friends, in allowing people to get close to him—just as he'd pushed her an arm's length away. Why? She was his sister. She remembered his initial embrace of her, the depth of feeling he'd shown—and subsequently regretted. Why? Distracted by these thoughts, she missed the inspector's response and discovered that Cole was speaking again. ". . . arrange for her release, we need to leave. I'm sure you can understand, Inspector, the family is very anxious to get Remy safely back to New Orleans.''

New Orleans. This time she picked up on the words, a certainty rushing through her. "That's where I'm supposed to be. That's where I'm needed. New Orleans.'' She laughed softly in a release of tension and turned to the inspector. "At last we have that riddle solved. And so simply, too.''

"What riddle?'' Cole asked.

"I've had this feeling—ever since I came to, here in the hospital—that there was some *place* I was supposed to be. It was important, I knew that, but—'' She stopped. "Why is it important?''

"I don't have any idea,'' he replied, without even the slightest hesitation. "How long will it take you to get dressed and be ready to leave?''

"Forgive me, M'sieu Buchanan,'' the inspector inserted smoothly, politely. "But there are a number of questions I must ask you first.''

"Questions—why?'' She found it impossible to tell what the inspector was thinking—or suspecting.

"We may have learned who you are, but we have yet to determine the identity of the man you were with,'' he reminded her.

"And you think—'' she began, then turned to look at Cole Buchanan, ''—he might be that man.''

"I wasn't. As a matter of fact, I wasn't even in Nice at the time.''

"And what time was that, m'sieu?'' the inspector asked, then extended a hand, palm up. "May I see your papers?''

"Of course.'' With barely disguised impatience, he reached inside his sport coat and took out his passport, then handed it to the inspector. "You will find they are all in order, Inspector Armand, and they will prove that I am exactly who I claim to be.'' Then he glanced at her. "This won't take long, Remy. In the meantime, why don't you get ready?''

"I have nothing to wear—no street clothes," she said, aware of the inspector glancing through his passport with more than casual interest.

"I anticipated that and picked up a couple of outfits for you on my way here."

"*Oui*. We left the boxes in your room," the nurse added.

The inspector nodded his acquiescence. "I would prefer to speak privately with M'sieu Buchanan. It is my job to ask questions, *non*?"

"Following the routine again, are you, Inspector?" she said, remembering the check he'd run on her to see if she had a criminal record.

"But of course." He smiled.

"In that case I will leave it in your capable hands to determine whether I should go with him or not." She said it lightly, but with an underthread of seriousness running through her voice. She didn't remember him, and she only had his word that he was her brother. Still, there was New Orleans. She had to get there. No matter what other doubts she had, that certainty remained strong.

As she entered her hospital room and closed the door, she saw the inspector return Cole Buchanan's passport, observing, "You travel a great deal."

"On business, yes." The rest of his reply was muffled by the door.

The boxes were there, exactly as the nurse had said, containing two outfits complete from the skin out—lacy lingerie, sheer stockings, shoes, and a chocolate-brown pantsuit with a blouse of cream-gold silk as well as an oversized turtleneck sweater of cranberry silk knit with a matching full skirt of silk broadcloth.

Mindful of the long flight potentially ahead of her, she chose the pantsuit. It fit perfectly, as if it had been made for her, yet it was brand-new. She wasn't sure why she felt so surprised by that. Cole Buchanan was her brother, so naturally he would know her size and taste in clothes.

Fully dressed, she sat on the edge of the bed and listened

to the voices in the corridor, the inspector's calm and low-pitched voice making its inquiries, and Cole Buchanan's deep-voiced replies, always short, sometimes impatient, sometimes angry. Finally there was a knock at her door.

"Come in."

Cole Buchanan stepped into the room, his glance sweeping over her with unflattering indifference. "You're ready, I see. I'll settle your bill with the hospital and be back to get you—" He paused and glanced somewhat cynically over his shoulder. "With the inspector's permission, of course."

"Of course." Inspector Armand walked into the room and stayed when he left. "You will soon be leaving us for New Orleans—for home."

From that she concluded that he was satisfied with the answers Cole Buchanan had given him. "Was he able to tell you anything about that night?"

"Regrettably, *non*. The case remains open." He walked over to her and took her hand. "If you should remember—*when* you remember," he corrected himself, "you contact me."

"Of course. And thank you, Inspector, for everything."

He shrugged. "It is my job."

Twenty minutes later Remy emerged from the hospital into the brilliant Mediterranean sunlight. Automatically she slowed her steps and breathed in the tangy freshness of the air, ridding her lungs of the strong medicinal smells they'd known for days.

She turned to say something to Cole and nearly collided with him, unaware that he'd been following so close behind her. His hand came up to steady her as his glance came down, lingering for only a fraction of a second on her lips—but that was all it took to spark the thought of being kissed by him and to shatter the comfortable, companionable feeling she'd had toward him since they'd left her room. She was stunned that such a thought could cross her mind, even fleetingly. He was her brother. She should never have let the inspector's questioning of him reinforce her initial reaction to him as a man.

"Sorry," she said quickly, conscious of the faint heat in her cheeks and the rare embarrassment she felt.

"It's all right. The car's over there." With a gesture of his hand, he pointed her toward a shiny gray Citroen parked in the visitors' area.

She moved briskly toward it, this time sharply aware of his footsteps directly behind her. When they reached it, he stepped ahead of her in one stride and set down the suitcase he'd provided for her clothes, then unlocked the passenger door for her. Eluding his assistance, she slipped quickly onto the seat and waited while he closed the door. In the rearview mirror, she watched him open the trunk to stow her suitcase inside. But he didn't immediately close the trunk again. When he did, she noticed that he'd removed his sport jacket. As he slid behind the wheel of the car, he reached back and laid it on the rear seat.

Instinctively she knew that despite the ease with which he wore the expensive sport coat, he was more comfortable in shirt sleeves. He hadn't always worn a suit and tie; he had learned to wear them, and to wear them well. Yet, strangely, she couldn't imagine anything but the finest cloth against her own skin. Why was that?

"Ready?" He directed the full brunt of his sharp, strong features, lean almost to the point of gauntness, at her.

She nodded and looked away, silently wishing he hadn't removed his jacket. She didn't want to notice that the muscles beneath his shirt were the hard, ropy kind that came from work, rather than the bulging perfection that came from work-outs. He had the polished look and confident air of a highly successful executive. So why did she think he'd fought his way to the top? Why did she have the feeling that despite the streak of gentleness she'd detected when he'd so lightly run his fingers along her forehead—that despite that, he could be cruel in a tight place? How did she know with such certainty that he could play the quiet game—as now—or the quick one?

And why was she so physically aware of him as a man? She shouldn't be, but the close confines of the small European car seemed to make it impossible for her to be otherwise. With each breath she inhaled the masculine fragrance of his cologne, and the sight of his tanned hands on the wheel filled her side vision, reminding her of the feel of them spread across her back. . . . Abruptly she broke off the thought, damning the sudden uneven beat of her pulse.

"How old are you?" She directed her gaze to the front.

"Thirty-five," he replied, a thread of puzzlement in his deep voice.

"How old am I?"

"Twenty-seven."

Which meant he was literally her big brother. Was it a case of hero worship? Had she always idolized him? Surely it wasn't unheard of for a sister to recognize that her big brother was sexually attractive. After all, she was a woman, and since she had no memory of their sibling relationship, wasn't it logical that she would react to him strictly *as* a woman? It was the only rationale for her behavior that made sense.

"You said you saw the photograph in the newspaper," she remembered. "Were you here looking for me?"

"No, I arrived in Marseilles yesterday on business. The company has an overseas office there," he inserted in explanation. "Frazier called me this morning about it."

She frowned. "Who's Frazier?"

"Your father."

"Is that what you call him?"

"Yes." He turned the car onto a main street.

"Do I?" she wondered.

"Occasionally."

"Frazier." She tried out the sound of it, but she couldn't summon any image of him, and stopped trying. "And my mother—what's her name?"

"Sibylle."

Still nothing. She rested her head against the seat back and tried to relax. "At least I know I have a family, even if I can't remember them. There were times when I wondered if I did—when I wondered if anyone was looking for me." She frowned again. "Why did it take so long for you to find me?"

"No one realized you were missing until almost two days ago, when you failed to return home on your scheduled flight. At first they thought you had missed your connection and would be arriving on a later flight. When you still didn't turn up, they contacted me to see if you had changed your plans and were flying back on the corporate plane with me. Of course, you hadn't—and the search for you began at that point." He paused, glancing at her sideways, his mouth twisting in something that passed for a smile. "Right after that, they discovered your clothes and your bags were still in the closet of your stateroom on the yacht. And Frazier realized you hadn't gone off by yourself for a few days, as everyone had assumed."

No wonder none of the hotels had been able to identify her as a guest. She'd been staying on a yacht. "Then originally I came to Nice with my parents."

"You joined them here. They'd been cruising the Mediterranean for a week before that. Then you and most of the family flew over for a couple of days to celebrate their thirty-fifth wedding anniversary."

"Were you here?"

"No. I was in New Orleans, nearly half a world away."

"Working," she guessed, picking up again on that charged intensity about him, the air of a man driven to succeed. "You work all the time, don't you?"

Briefly he met her glance, then gave his full attention to the traffic in front of them. "You've told me that before."

There was no amusement in his voice, which made her think she had criticized him about that in the past. She decided it was a subject better not pursued, but it brought up another question.

"What do I do? You said earlier I wasn't involved in the company. But I can't imagine myself doing nothing."

"You're heavily involved with the Louisiana State Museum. You act as a docent, and you assist in the authentication of certain items donated to it—specifically seventeenth- and eighteenth-century French porcelain, your special field of knowledge."

She suddenly had an image of an antique jardiniere with flowers and cupids painted in reserves on its sides and embellished with gold against a distinctively pink background. She knew instantly that it was a Sèvres piece done in the *rose Pompadour* color. Maybe she wasn't an expert, but she was highly knowledgeable in that field. She knew that in the same inexplicable way she knew other things.

The things he'd told her—her original purpose in coming to Nice, the reason her family had failed to miss her—all of it sounded very logical, very plausible, even believable. Yet . . . something wasn't right. None of it explained this feeling she had that she was urgently needed at home, that there was some kind of trouble.

Sighing, she turned to gaze out the window and looked blindly at the ocher buildings they passed. As the gardened boulevard made a curve, she recognized that they were traveling down the Avenue Félix Faure, approaching the Espace Masséna. Tensing slightly, she straightened in her seat, waiting for that first glimpse of it.

Then, there it was, the towering sprays of its sparkling fountains visible through a break in the row of shade trees and slender cypress, and the grinning face of the giant papier-mâché King of Carnival peering down from his alfresco throne. She scanned the stand of trees by the sidewalk, wondering which one she'd struck her head against. At the same time, she couldn't help thinking how beautifully serene the square looked with only a scattering of people strolling its landscaped walks.

Belatedly she noticed that Cole had stopped the car at a pedestrian crosswalk. A woman walked in front of them, pushing a baby stroller. Smoothly he shifted the car into drive, and they rolled forward again. A moment later she was surprised when he failed to turn at the next intersection and continued straight ahead onto the Avenue de Verdun instead.

"If you had turned back there, we could have taken a better route to the airport and avoided all this traffic."

"I know," he said, slowing the car to make the turn onto the palm-lined Promenade des Anglais.

"Then why are we going this way?" She frowned. "I thought you said at the hospital we were flying directly to New Orleans."

"We are—as soon as I eliminate the problem with your passport."

"*What* problem with my passport?"

"You don't have one . . . yet. Hopefully it will be waiting for us when we arrive at the hotel."

6

Minutes later he pulled up in front of the entrance to the Hotel Negresco. A plume-hatted doorman in a scarlet-lined blue cloak and high, shiny boots stepped forward and opened the passenger door for her. Taking his gloved hand, Remy let him assist her out of the car, then turned and waited, watching as Cole slipped back into his sport jacket, its rich herringbone wool skillfully concealing the strong build of his upper body. Idly she studied the solid, angular bones of his face, covered by skin that was deeply tanned and without a wrinkle.

With an odd certainty she knew that nepotism had nothing to do with his position as president of the family shipping business. It was his competence, his aggressiveness, his ability to lead and command that had gained him the office. Suddenly, without any effort at all, she could picture him on the wharves in his shirt sleeves, moving among the longshoremen, as tough and strong as they were. And just as easily she could see him in command of a board meeting, respected—however grudgingly—for his canny business skills. *Grudgingly*—why had she thought that?

But she didn't have an opportunity to analyze that very definite impression as she found herself now standing face-to-face with him, the rock gray of his gaze boring into her as if searching for something. For an instant the air seemed to crackle around them, charged by a tension that flashed between them. She held herself still, wondering what he was thinking. What did he want?

The whole sensation vanished as if it had never been when he said, "Shall we go in?"

"Of course." She swung sharply about and crossed to the hotel's entrance, conscious of his long-reaching stride easily keeping pace with hers.

Once they were inside, her glance swept the hotel's magnificent interior. The Hotel Negresco was typical of the many palatial hotels scattered along the Côte d'Azur, but it had a style and gloss that was all its own. It was officially listed as a historic monument, though Remy suspected that it could more accurately be called a monument to excessive consumption. Used as a hospital during World War II, it had been restored with an ostentatious hand. To the undiscerning eye, the glass-domed and marble-floored Salon Royal might resemble a gaudy if stunning piece of costume jewelry, but the one-ton chandelier was nothing less than Baccarat crystal, and the tapestry on the wall was a genuine Gobelin.

Cole's hand moved to the small of her back, the sensation of it blocking out everything else as he guided her to the registration desk. She was acutely conscious of the sudden longings that ran through her—a desire for intimacy, to touch and be touched. Why? Had it been that long since she'd been with a man?

"Am I married?" she wondered suddenly.

"No." If he found her question unexpected, he gave no sign of it.

"Divorced?"

"No."

"Have I ever been close?"

"To which? Marriage or divorce?" he asked, showing her the first glimpse of his humor.

"Wouldn't it have to be marriage?" she challenged, a faint smile dimpling her own cheeks. "I understand it comes before divorce."

"I guess it does," he agreed, then seemed to withdraw from her, a remoteness shuttering his expression. "You were engaged once."

"What happened?"

"He drowned in a boating accident on Lake Pontchartrain."

She immediately felt a sharp twinge of sadness. "What was his name?"

"Nick Austin."

Did the name mean anything to her? She couldn't tell. All she had was a vague feeling of something—someone—from long, long ago. Then the curtness of Cole's answer registered, and she looked up, encountering his glance, oddly cool and remote. "You didn't like him."

"I didn't know him."

Again he spoke curtly, as if he resented any mention of her late fiancé. Why? Surely he couldn't have been jealous, could he? Jealous that some other man had come first with her? Then another thought occurred to her.

"Cole, are you married?"

He shot her a quick look before answering, then abruptly dropped his glance. "No."

She was stunned by the relief she felt at his answer—and by the swift rise of possessiveness she'd felt just before it. She didn't follow him when he crossed to the desk and spoke to one of the clerks. She was too busy trying to come to terms with the discovery that the possessive feeling had been jealousy.

Then he was walking back to her. "He hasn't arrived with your passport, so I've arranged for a suite. I didn't think you'd want to wait around the lobby until he comes."

She stiffened at the hint of sarcasm in his remark, and its

implication that she would regard waiting in the lobby as something beneath her. She started to challenge him on it, but the arrival of a bellman deterred her—for the time being.

In silence she went up in the elevator, down the hall, and into the suite of rooms. There she crossed to the window of the richly furnished sitting room and waited while the bellman went through the ritual of showing Cole all the suite's amenities. Finally she heard the click of the door latch signal his departure, and she swung from the spectacular view of the bay's deep-blue waters.

Without looking at her, Cole locked the door behind the bellman, then loosened the knot of his tie and unfastened the top button of his shirt as he started across the room toward the telephone, which rested on an ebony secretaire. "I'm going to order up some coffee. Do you want anything?"

"Yes, I'd like to know what you meant by that remark you made downstairs. Or was that some brotherly gibe?"

"Brotherly?" he stopped, an eyebrow lifting sharply. "I'm not your brother, Remy."

Her mouth gaped open. She couldn't help it. "But . . . at the hospital . . . I thought. . . ." She stopped, trying to remember exactly what had been said—and by whom.

"I am not your brother, Remy," he repeated, his mouth slanting in a hard and cynically amused line.

"Then who are you?"

"Exactly who I claim to be—the president of the Crescent Line, Cole Buchanan."

"Inspector Armand said my brother was coming to take me home," she remembered. "If you aren't my brother, then where is he?"

"Gabe should be arriving at the hotel anytime now—with your passport."

"Then who am I? What's my name? Remy what?" she demanded, confused and angry—and making no attempt to conceal it.

"Remy Jardin."

Remembering how guilty she'd felt over her attraction to

him, she walked over to confront him, her temper showing. "You bastard!" She lashed out, striking at his face, but in a lightning-fast move he caught her wrist and stopped it short of its target. When she brought her other hand up, it was caught too, and held in the vice of his fingers. "Why didn't you tell me at the hospital you weren't my brother?" she demanded, straining to pull free of his hold but not deigning to struggle openly against it.

"I never said I was. If you assumed that, that's your problem. Not mine."

"You let me think it," she accused.

"I have no control over what you think or what conclusions you reach. If I did, then—" But he cut off the rest of that sentence. "I had no idea you thought I was your brother, Remy. If I had, I probably wouldn't have told you differently. Do you know why? Because amnesia or not, you have an incredibly strong sense of family. You might not have left the hospital with a stranger."

"The end justifies the means, is that it?"

His head came up sharply at that remark. "Believe what you like, Remy. You always do."

Looking at him, she became conscious of the harsh grip of his hands on her wrists and remembered the pressure of them when he'd pulled her into his arms, the way they had moved over her with accustomed ease, and the natural way he had spoken her name. More than that, she remembered the way she'd reacted to him. "Are we lovers?"

Slow to make her change of mood, he lowered her hands and absently rubbed at the insides of her wrists, where his fingers had dug in. "Yes."

"I should have guessed," she said, then wondered, "Why didn't you tell me?"

"You didn't remember. I thought it might be better that way."

"Why?" she asked, then immediately guessed, "Have we been arguing?"

"You could say that." His reply had the ring of an understatement.

"About what?" Was this the trouble she'd sensed? The reason for that feeling of urgency?

"Does it matter, considering you don't remember?" He let go of her hands and crossed to the window, massaging the back of his neck in a gesture that revealed strain and tension.

"Do I love you, Cole?"

He released a short, explosive sigh. "How the hell am I supposed to answer that, Remy?" She said nothing, letting her silence prod him. "You've told me you do," he said finally.

She walked over to him. "Cole." She waited for him to look at her. "Do you love me?"

His gaze locked with hers for an eternity of seconds. Then his arm hooked itself around her waist and pulled her to him as he lowered his mouth onto hers in a deep and loving kiss that had a hint of roughness to it. She remembered the familiar rightness of being in his arms, but she hadn't guessed at the powerful range of feelings it could evoke.

He dragged his mouth from her lips and rubbed it across her cheek. "You turn me inside out. You have from the first day we met," he murmured against her skin, his hot, moist breath fanning out to offer its own stimulating caress.

"When was that?" She closed her eyes, reveling in the feel of his mouth moving along her temple, into her hair, and behind an ear.

"Roughly a year ago—at a party Frazier gave at Antoine's after I came on board as the company's new CEO."

He still remembered vividly the first time he'd seen her. At that moment she'd been for him the only living thing in the room, her face softly lighted and softly shadowed, her shoulders straight and graceful, her presence creating its beauty and its imperative call. Frazier had introduced them, and he'd taken her hand, the fragrance of her nearness arous-

ing all his male interest in a reaction that was both quick and
reluctant. The glimmer of gold in her eyes had seemed to
sparkle just for him, but he hadn't been fool enough to believe
it . . . then.

"And you fell for me right off, I suppose." She raked her
fingers through his hair, flexing them almost like a cat as her
parted lips grazed along his jawline.

"Are you kidding? I swore I wouldn't get within ten feet
of you." It was a vow that common sense told him he should
have kept.

"What happened?"

"About six months ago I got within ten feet of you, and
all hell broke loose." He meant that literally. Trouble had
erupted almost from the moment they'd gotten together—
and grown steadily in the interim. But it was moments like
this, when he held her warm and cushioning body close to
him and tasted the fiery flavor of her kiss, that he could
almost convince himself he didn't give a damn.

"Now *that* is the first thing you've said that I believe,"
she murmured, seeking and finding his lips.

For her this was like the first time, because she couldn't
remember the other. That he had been her lover she did not
doubt. Her body knew him, and her heart knew him, even
if her mind couldn't recall him. This was the man she loved.

Yet the sensations of being loved by him were all brand-
new. She couldn't get enough of the feel of his hands on her
back—kneading and caressing in their foray down her spine
to her hips—or the taste of his tongue in her mouth, thrusting
and mating with her own. His chestnut-dark hair was thick
and full beneath her fingers, smooth but a little on the coarse
side, slightly rough, like the rest of him.

Wanting more, she strained to get closer to him, her back
arching, her hips pressing, her body aching to be absorbed
by him. Frustrated, she bit at his lip, inadvertently drawing
blood. She heard him stifle a faint sound of pain and rained
the spot with light kisses of apology as she brought her hands
down, encountering the muscular wall of his chest, rising

and falling with the heaviness of his breathing. She tried to run her hands over his chest to the wide points of his shoulders, but his jacket got in the way and his shirt barred contact with the flesh beneath it.

Impatiently she tugged at the loosened knot of his tie. But Cole's hand took her place, yanking it the rest of the way loose and stripping the tie away. When she pushed at his coat, he shrugged out of it. While their lips continued to consume each other with desperate greedy kisses, she set to work on his shirt buttons. But the third one defied her efforts, a thread of the buttonhole catching it and refusing to let it go. Gripping both edges of his shirt front, she pulled them apart, and the rest of the buttons snapped off one after the other. Her hands moved freely onto his bared chest, all hard, bronzed flesh over sinewy muscle, smooth and hot to the touch, like satin over sun-baked steel. But it wasn't enough to feel it; she wanted to taste it, too. She pulled away from his kiss and brought her lips down to the pulsing vein in his neck. She felt the faint tremor that shuddered through him.

"Someday, Remy—" His low voice vibrated against her hair, husky with disturbance, as his fingers curled around the collar of her jacket. "Someday you're going to pay for all the shirts you've ruined."

Openmouthed, she ran the tip of her tongue over the ridge of his shoulder, licking the hot saltiness of his skin, then lifted her head, tilting her face to him. "Make me pay, Cole," she whispered the dare, her eyes gleaming as she gazed into the darkening smoke of his. "Make me pay now."

Accepting her bold challenge, he pulled the front of her jacket apart and dragged it off her shoulders, momentarily forcing her arms to her sides before she could slip free of the sleeves. With the same impatience she had shown toward him, he ripped her blouse open, sending buttons flying into the air. Not content with that, he pushed the blouse off her, dragging the thin straps of her lace teddy with it and exposing the golden cream of her shoulders. Her blouse had barely touched the floor when his fingers took hold of the front of her teddy, indifferent to the expensive lace, and pulled it down, his large hands immediately cupping and covering her small but highly sensitive breasts.

She gasped softly at the sudden swirl of raw pleasure that swept her up, but his mouth came down to smother the sound and steal the rest of her breath. She wrapped her arms tightly around his neck and forced him closer, parting her lips to invite the mating plunge of his tongue. As his hands slipped to the sides of her waist, she arched against him, flattening her breasts against the muscled wall of his chest, needing to feel the heat that came from flesh against flesh.

She wanted him. She wanted all of him, with a fierceness that staggered her completely. What kind of passion was this that erupted so violently? The desire for him had been there all along, thrumming just below the surface. Now it had burst wide open, making her feel incredibly strong and incredibly weak at the same time.

His hands tightened on her waist and effortlessly lifted her, the iron band of his arm circling below her hips to hold her tightly against him, her feet dangling inches from the floor. He carried her that way, with their mouths locked in a kiss, to one of the suite's bedrooms. Remy didn't know which one and didn't care as she kicked her shoes off along the way.

In the room he stopped short of the bed and let her body slide slowly down his chest until her feet touched the floor. Immediately his hands were at the waistband of her slacks, seeking its fastener. Catching his urgency, she hurriedly began to finish undressing him.

Within minutes their clothes were a puddle on the bedroom floor and she lay naked beside his nude male body. At last she had time to explore at her leisure. Levering herself up on one elbow, she rolled her lips off his mouth, briefly grazing them across his square chin, then turned her head to admire that expanse of bare chest and shoulders.

There was a power and a discipline inherent in his muscled form that pulled at her and challenged her to touch him. She pressed her mouth onto the solid curve of his shoulder, then let her lips follow its ridge to the strong column of his neck before wandering down to tactilely explore the hollow at the base of his throat, conscious all the while of the caressing play of his hands over her back and ribs, stroking, teasing, stimulating, and encouraging her. Moving lower, she rubbed her mouth over the square flatness of his breast, then paused to lick at the excitingly small nub of his nipple. She heard the rumble of approval come from deep inside his chest, and she smiled. She slid her hand lower, across the flatness of his stomach, its muscles tensing at her touch, and into the silken curl of hairs at the very bottom of it. When her fingers curved around him, he groaned a muffled curse.

An instant later his fingers tunneled into her hair at the sides and grabbed a handful. She gasped a protest as he hauled her up and twisted her onto her back, letting go of her hair and catching her arms, spreading them above her head and pinning her wrists to the bed, his weight holding her down.

"No," he said against her lips, catching the lower one and lightly nipping at it with his teeth. "I've been away from you too long, Remy. And I'll be damned if this is going to be over before it's begun."

He again caught her bottom lip between his teeth and tightly nipped at it. She groaned at the action that both teased and aroused. Then she felt the satisfying pressure of his mouth on hers once more as he kissed her long and deep, drawing from her feelings she hadn't known existed. She was going soft inside and she knew it as he kissed his way over every inch of her face, then paused to sensually chew at an earlobe. When he nibbled his way down her neck, delicious shivers tingled over her.

His arms continued to pin hers to the bed, but she lay there a willing captive, trapped by the urgent need to absorb this myriad of sensations. When his tongue licked at a taut nipple, a curling started deep in the pit of her stomach. She moaned at the ache it produced and finally realized that he was doing to her all the things she had done to him. And it was wonderful. Wonderful.

She arched her back, pushing her breast at him and trying to make him take more of it. When he did, a raw sound of satisfaction came from her throat. Cole stole a glance at her, watching her head roll from side to side, her eyes closed and her lips apart. At last he could stand it no more. He had to touch her. He released one of her wrists and slid his hand down her arm and onto her body.

She was deceptively small and delicate, everything perfectly proportioned, from the narrowness of her rib cage and hips to the petite roundness of her breasts. But he knew the strength and power packaged in her delectable form. Not so much a physical strength as the mental one that came from a strong and indomitable will, a will that gave her boldness and the supreme confidence to be exactly what and who she was. And the power in her—she had the power to make him hunger, to make him ache, to make him vulnerable.

Yet none of that mattered to him as he played with her breasts—with his hands, his mouth, and his tongue. He listened to her sighs, her whimpers, and her moans, expressions of the sexuality that lived within her.

As he ran his hand up her leg to cup the soft swell of her bottom, she shuddered. "How could I have forgotten the way this feels?" she whispered achingly. "How could I, Cole?"

He didn't have an answer for that, but he drew himself up and murmured against a corner of her lips, "Does it matter? Does it matter *now?*"

"No," she groaned, and she turned to his mouth, carelessly commanding, "Love me, Cole."

He kissed her and she was all motion beneath him, her hands, her lips, her body exhorting and demanding satisfaction. He knew she didn't understand the urgency that pushed at both of them. She didn't realize this might be their last time together. But he did.

At this moment and in this place, she belonged to him and he was hers. That was the only certainty. It wasn't enough, but it was all he had, and he seized it.

She sighed his name against his neck, then raked her teeth

across his shoulder. "Don't make me wait anymore, Cole. Take me now."

He couldn't resist her—not then and not now. He felt her shudder as he shifted onto her and spread her legs apart. Her breath caught on his name when he entered her. She was hot; she was tight; she was moist. Robbed of all thought by her, he could only feel as she wrapped her legs around him, her hips driving him even as he sought to drive her. The pressure built like the approach of a summer storm, all light, wind, and heat. Then the fury of it was upon them, and release came in a torrent that buffeted both of them and left them wrapped tight in each other's arms.

7

Nestled in the crook of his arm, Remy snuggled closer and rubbed her cheek against his chest. She wondered at this dichotomous reaction of hers that had her feeling both supremely content and oddly energized.

She tilted her head back to look at Cole, then couldn't resist reaching up to trace the sharp outline of his jaw with her fingertips. "Is it always like that with us?"

"Not always." There was a sexy laziness to the smile he gave her. "Sometimes it's even better."

Mockingly skeptical, she retorted, "That is impossible."

He caught her hand and pressed her fingers to his lips, a faintly mischievous glint in his gray eyes. "You're probably right."

His response surprised a laugh from her, the admission so contrary to the typically male boast of sexual prowess that she'd expected to hear. "You amaze me."

His look turned faintly serious. "Try not to forget that." There was a brief silence in which neither of them stirred, and then Cole said, "We'd better get up, Remy."

She made a soft protesting sound. "Not yet. I'm too comfortable."

His arm tightened slightly around her, offering a silent agreement that they would remain as they were awhile longer. She closed her eyes and breathed in the musky scent of their passion, still lingering ever so faintly in the air. She wished she could hold on to this moment, never have to stir, never have to remember. She frowned at the latter thought. Why wouldn't she want to remember?

She tensed, something flashing in her mind. It had to do with Cole. She was sure of it, in that same strange way she had been sure they were lovers without being able to actually remember any part of their affair.

She lay there mentally straining to recall what it was that she should remember about him, trying to make that indistinct impression of trouble become a memory. She couldn't. It had slipped away from her.

Sighing in frustration, she was swept by a surging restlessness, her previous contentment gone. "I think we'd better—" As she started to rise, his hand slid limply off her hip. She turned and discovered he was sound asleep.

Smiling, she laid a hand on his shoulder to awaken him, but the sight of his harshly masculine features composed in the peace and innocence of sleep stopped her. Deciding it couldn't hurt anything to let him sleep a little longer, she withdrew her hand and slipped quietly from the bed.

She crossed silently to the bedroom's private bath and closed the door behind her. She showered quickly, then donned the terry robe the hotel had thoughtfully provided and slicked the wetness of her hair away from her face with her hands. Cautiously she opened the door to the bedroom and peeked around it. Cole was lying in exactly the same place and position.

She walked noiselessly over to the mound of clothes on the floor and began picking them up, remembering the haste with which they'd been stripped away. Separating the garments, she laid them out in neat His and Hers piles, then went into the sitting room to find the rest of them.

When she saw the phone on the secretaire, she hesitated and glanced toward the bedroom. On impulse she picked up the phone and dialed room service, ordering the coffee Cole had wanted when they arrived. She felt pleased with herself, knowing that when he awakened, she'd be able to serve him coffee in bed. She liked the idea of pampering him a little.

In no hurry, she gathered the clothes from the sitting-room floor and carried them into the bedroom. She laid Cole's on his stack, then took her own into the other bedroom, where the bellman had left her luggage. She opened the largest case and began sifting through her clothes, trying to decide what to wear.

The ringing of the bell to the suite's outer door interrupted her. She turned with a faint start, not expecting room service to be so prompt. Running silently on bare feet, she hurried to the door before the waiter could ring the bell again and waken Cole. She unlocked it with one hand and opened it with the other, automatically swinging it wide.

A man in a navy-blue suit stood outside, a stone-gray raincoat draped over one arm and a slim black leather brief-case clutched in the opposite hand. The tense, worried look on his face vanished, and relief sailed through his expression.

"Remy. It *is* you. Thank God." Issuing the fervent declaration, he stepped into the room and hastily set his briefcase on the floor, tossing his coat on top of it and never once taking his eyes off her.

As she stared at him, another image of that same face sprang into her mind—an image frozen in a hearty laugh, his brown eyes crinkling at the corners, a wayward lock of tobacco-brown hair falling onto his forehead.

"Gabe." She recognized her brother, and flashes of childhood memories started coming back to her—memories of Gabe pushing her in an old rope swing, racing his horse against hers along the levee, and teasing her unmercifully about her first date. Gabe, always laughing, always reckless, always carefree. No glint of mischief danced in the brown eyes of the much more mature version of her brother that stood before her now, but the ready grin was there, this time ringed with gladness and relief. When he opened his arms to her, Remy went straight to them, letting him catch her up close and hugging him back.

"I can't believe this," she said, remembering him as he briefly rocked her from side to side, then set her away from him as if needing to look at her again.

"I would have been here sooner, but—Cole had taken the corporate jet to Marseilles, and I had to catch a commercial flight. Then there was a delay for mechanical trouble, and—" He stopped and sighed heavily, happily. "You don't know how good it is to see you, Remy. Don't ever pull a disappearing act like that one again. I thought we were going to have to turn the world upside down to find you."

"It isn't something I want to go through again either."

"When I saw the photo, I knew it had to be you," he said, then chided, "You do realize that had to be the worst picture ever taken of you. I mean, the bandages around your head, the bruises . . . what happened?"

"I don't know—correct that, I don't remember."

"Then this business about the amnesia—it's true?" His expression turned serious, almost grim. Suddenly he wasn't the same—he wasn't the young, smiling Gabe she'd known. "You don't remember anything?"

"No. Just you. As a matter of fact, you're the first thing I have remembered." She paused and took hold of his hands, conscious of the strong bond she felt with him, then lifted her glance to study this new, older face of her brother. "You've changed from the Gabe I remember, though. You're not the teasing, laughing, full-of-the-devil teenage brother anymore. You've grown up and become a responsible adult." Smiling, she reached up and gave the lapel of his navy suit coat a flick. "You've even gone conservative on me."

"But it's what every well-dressed lawyer is wearing these days," he replied with a glimmer of a smile.

"You're a lawyer?"

"It was the next best thing to becoming an actor."

She laughed at that. "You always were a ham," she said, then suddenly remembered, "Your field of practice is maritime law."

"With the family in the shipping business, what else could I choose?" He paused, again sobering slightly. "We've all been so worried about you, Remy, I—Dad had almost convinced himself you'd been kidnapped or murdered or—something equally horrible."

"I wish I could remember him. . . ." She frowned at the absence of any image, any feeling, any impression evoked by the mention of her father. "Maybe when I see him," she said, trying to shrug it off. "Too bad he didn't come with you."

"He wanted to, but he couldn't."

"Why?" Seized again by that feeling of trouble, she became tense. "Has something happened to him? Is he sick?"

"No, it . . . it just wouldn't have been wise right now, that's all. Besides"—he smiled quickly, as if to cover that slight hesitation, and hugged an arm around her shoulders—"you've got your brother the lawyer here, and I'll be much more useful than Dad if we encounter any difficulties with customs or immigration. By the way, where's Cole?"

"Slee—"

"Right here." Cole stood in the doorway to the bedroom, calmly tucking the tails of a crisp new shirt inside the waistband of his mocha trousers. "I see you made it, Gabe."

"Yes, finally." Despite the easy smile her brother gave Cole, she sensed a change in his attitude, a faint, barely perceptible withdrawal. Why? Didn't he like Cole? Or had he merely been surprised to find Cole standing there?

"By the way, thanks for picking up Remy from the hospital," Gabe added.

To Remy it sounded more like an afterthought, one dictated by good manners rather than sincere gratitude. And that impression reinforced her initial feeling that her brother didn't

think all that highly of Cole. Yet she couldn't detect any
hostility from Gabe, only a wariness.

Cole shot him a look that Remy could only describe as
sardonic as he buttoned the cuffs of his shirt. "Thanks aren't
necessary, Gabe." Without a break, he said, "If you two
will excuse me, I'll get my jacket and see about rounding up
our flight crew so we can head back to New Orleans."

The instant Cole left the suite, Remy turned curiously to
Gabe. "You don't like him, do you?"

He had difficulty meeting her gaze, and briefly raised his
hands in an uncertain gesture. "You can't possibly know how
damned awkward your amnesia makes things." He stopped,
meeting her glance. "You haven't said how much you remember about Cole—if anything. But you two were—pretty
thick for a while."

"I know that much." She smiled, mostly at the memory
of the extremely satisfying moments she'd just had with Cole.

"You don't know how relieved I was when you finally
broke up with him."

"We broke up?" Somehow she hadn't gotten that impression from Cole.

"He didn't tell you that, did he?" he guessed, his very
tone making it an accusation.

"I knew we'd been arguing," she replied carefully.

Gabe shook his head in disgust, a grimness about his
mouth. "I always knew that man had no scruples, so why
am I surprised that he'd take advantage of your amnesia?"

When he looked at her, Remy glanced away, resisting—
resenting—the implication of his words. Not twenty minutes
ago she'd believed herself in love with Cole. The feelings,
the emotions had been real; she didn't question that. But could
it be that they were wrongly placed, as Gabe was suggesting?
Had Cole deliberately lied to her? Or, at the very least, told
only a half truth? But why?

"Why did we break up?"

"You never gave a reason—not to me, anyway. And I
never asked. I felt you'd tell me if you wanted to. But I do

know that as far as you were concerned it was final. You were through with him.''

"Did Cole accept that?''

"No.''

Gabe's answer confirmed what she'd already guessed—Cole wanted her back. That was why he'd been so quick to make love to her when she'd shown she was willing—eager. Had he hoped it would be the start of reconciliation between them? Did she want that? How could she know, when she couldn't even remember why she'd broken off their affair? Obviously she hadn't stopped loving him, which meant he must have said or done something that she'd found impossible to forgive. But what? And was it connected to this feeling she had that it was urgent—critical—for her to return to New Orleans?

"To tell you the truth, Remy,'' Gabe said, "I never approved of your becoming involved with him. Call it the protective instincts of a brother who wants only the best for his sister—and who knows that Cole Buchanan isn't the man for you. I always thought you'd end up regretting it. And believe me, there's no satisfaction in knowing I was right about him all along.''

"What do you mean? How were you right about him?''

He turned away, plainly uncomfortable with her questions, and walked to a window, unbuttoning his suit jacket and pushing it open to rest his hands on his hips. "I wish you could remember for yourself. I don't like being the one to say these things, but—I guess someone has to tell you.'' He stared out the window. "The man simply doesn't have the same values, the same principles as you. He comes from a totally different background, a different environment. True, he was born and raised in New Orleans, the same as we were, but on the other side of the river, in Algiers. You can't get much further removed from the Garden district than that.''

Remy nodded absently, remembering the desperately poor and crime-ridden area of Algiers, located directly across the Mississippi River from the French Quarter. The contrast between Algiers, with its dilapidated shotgun houses and scrubby yards, and the Garden district, with its colonnaded antebellum mansions, its lush, green gardens, and its tree-lined streets, was unarguably a stark one.

"And you can't grow up in an area like Algiers," Gabe continued, "without coming away with some of its hardness, its ruthlessness."

Frowning, she recalled her own impression that Cole possessed both traits to some degree, but she didn't consider either one to be something that should be held against him, as Gabe was implying. And this talk about different values and principles held criticism as well.

"You don't trust him, do you?"

He hesitated, then angled his shoulders toward her, briefly meeting her eyes. "No, I don't."

"But he's the president of the company. If that's your opinion of him, then why—"

"Look." Gabe turned from the window and raised his hand in a silencing gesture. "At the time, we thought he was the best man for the job. He had the experience, the qualifications—and a helluva reputation for turning troubled shipping lines around. As far as all the talk we heard that his methods were sometimes less than orthodox—nothing illegal, at least nothing that was ever proved—we chalked it up to disgruntled competitors. After all, every head-hunter we talked to mentioned Cole Buchanan as a solid candidate for the position. A man's name comes up that often, you hire him."

"And now you suspect him of doing something wrong."

He seemed startled by her comment, which was half guess and half supposition—startled and a little worried, as if he'd said more than he'd intended. "We're getting off the track here. We were talking about you, and why I didn't like the idea of your getting mixed up with a man whose name has been linked with some sharp—maybe even shady—dealings. As for the company, maybe it's the lawyer in me, but I don't like the employment contract he got. It ties the board's hands and puts too much power in his. In my opinion Buchanan's grabbing for power, and you were part of the grab.''

Had that been it? Logically she could see that it was more than possible. A man who had been raised in the squalor and poverty that marked so much of the violence-ridden Algiers section, and then risen from it to preside over a major shipping line, obviously had to be aggressive and ambitious. After sampling the heady taste of power, he could have decided he wanted more.

"How could I represent power to him?" She lifted her curious, troubled glance to Gabe.

"You own a substantial share in the company, and you sit on the board," he replied, studying her with affectionate patience. "And the family is not without some influence."

Remy suspected that the latter was a gross understatement, but she didn't dwell on it, her thoughts turning instead to the other things Gabe had said. With no memory of her own, she found herself seizing on every scrap of information and trying to make it mean something—specifically, something that would explain this feeling of trouble she had.

"You mentioned that Cole had a reputation for turning companies around. Does that mean the Crescent Line is in trouble financially?"

He gave a light shrug. "The company has lost money the last couple of years—nothing dramatic, certainly nothing to be overly alarmed about. All businesses experience a slump now and then."

"Then that wasn't the reason you hired him." Absently she ran a hand through her hair, which by now was nearly dry, trying to piece things together.

"No. Dad wanted to retire. He'd already put thirty years into the company, and Marc had never been involved in the operations side of the business."

"Marc—who's he?"

"Dad's brother—our uncle." He frowned at her for an instant, then his forehead cleared. "I forgot. You probably can't remember him either."

"No, I can't."

"Marc's a couple of years younger than Dad—brown eyes, dark, curly hair with just a touch of gray sprinkled through it." Gabe paused, as if trying to think how else to tell her about him. "After Grand-père died, he and Dad took over running the company. It's almost too limiting to say that Marc handles the public-relations side. He's the spokesman for the Crescent Line—the labor-relations man, the representative, the company's goodwill ambassador. The man's phenomenal, Remy. He knows even the newest employee by name. He can go down on the docks, take off his jacket and tie, and swap stories with the longshoremen over a beer like he was one of them. That same night he can put on a white tie and tails, mingle with a bunch of visiting dignitaries, and exchange views on global politics with all the ease of a diplomat. Everyone likes him. He's so charming and warm it's impossible not to."

But the only image she had of her uncle was the one Gabe had just drawn for her. She had none of her own. "Sorry." She shook her head in regret. "I still can't remember him."

"What about his son, Lance? He's the same age as me— our birthdays are just a couple months apart. He works for the company too, in the accounting end of it." He watched for some indication that his words were striking a familiar chord—and found none. "Maybe it would help if I told you that you don't like Lance."

"Why?" she asked, surprised by his assertion.

"You seem to think he's too full of himself, a little too contemptuous of women."

"Is he?"

"Probably," he conceded. "But the way they practically fall on their backs if he so much as looks at them, it's not really surprising that he doesn't have much respect for them. I used to be envious of him when we were in high school together. It was the closest I ever came to hating him. If he was around, not a single girl would look my way."

"By that I assume you mean he's handsome."

He laughed softly at that. "Actually the phrase 'handsome as the devil' could have been invented to describe Lance—dark hair, dark eyes, and a sexy, brooding look. He's the bad kind that mothers warn their daughters about and daddies meet at the door with a shotgun—and girls go crazy over."

"He sounds like a bachelor playboy." She was conscious of her teeth coming together in an almost instinctive reaction of disgust and dislike. But was she reacting or remembering? She couldn't tell.

"A bachelor? No. He's been married for three years and has a two-year-old son and another baby on the way. A playboy?" Gabe tipped his hand from side to side in a gesture that indicated that the decision could go either way.

"In other words, he's a married playboy," Remy concluded, a little acidly.

"Let's be realistic," Gabe protested, obviously coming to his cousin's defense. "If you're at a party and you keep being served up a tray of sweet, delectable morsels, are you going to have the willpower to say no every time it's offered? No man is that strong, Remy."

"And Lance is a little weaker than most, isn't he?" she guessed—or was she guessing? She wished she knew, then shook off the question as unanswerable, just as so many others were. "You said he works in the company's accounting department?"

"Yes. So you see, neither Lance nor I was interested or qualified to take over as president. Which meant we had to look outside for someone to replace Dad."

The ringing of the suite's front bell was quickly followed by a heavily accented voice announcing, "Room service."

"That must be the coffee I ordered earlier," Remy said, and automatically went to the door.

The waiter swept into the sitting room with an elaborate tray balanced on his upraised palm. He made a production out of setting the tray down, arranging the china cups and saucers, setting out the cream and sugar, and adjusting the placement of a flower vase, totally indifferent to the heavy silence stretching over the room.

He picked up the stainless coffee server. "Shall I pour, madam?"

"No thank you."

"Very well, madam." But he practically sniffed his disapproval as he presented the bill to her with a slight flourish.

Remy hastily scratched her name across it and passed it back to him. When the waiter left, she locked the door behind him, then turned back to the room.

"Would you like a cup of coffee?" She walked over to the tray and picked up the coffee server.

"Please."

Remy filled both cups with steaming coffee, then reached for the creamer. "Heavy on the cream and light on the sugar, right?"

"Right," he said. "You're starting to remember things."

"I hope so," she said, feigning a nonchalance she didn't feel.

"What happened, Remy? What caused this amnesia? I never really got the story straight. Was there an accident, or what?"

"According to the police inspector, I was seen arguing or . . . struggling with a man." She sipped at her coffee, remembering the bruised and swollen soreness of her lips. "He struck me and I fell backward, hitting my head against a tree trunk. It knocked me out. When I regained consciousness in the hospital, I had a dozen stitches in my scalp, a concussion, and—amnesia. I had no idea who I was, where I lived, or what I did, and I didn't have any identification on me."

"This man who hit you—did they catch him?"

"No. He ran off and disappeared into the crowd. The police couldn't get much of a description of him, and of course I wasn't able to remember any of it. I still don't know if he was somebody I knew, somebody I recently met, or a total stranger." She stopped. "Do you know anything about that night, Gabe? Why was I at the Espace Masséna? What was I doing? Where was I going?''

''We were all at a party that night . . . at a hotel not far from the square,'' he replied hesitantly, as if uncertain how to answer her questions. ''You, me, Marc and Aunt Christina, Lance and his wife, Julie, Diana and Kathy and their husbands—'' He caught her blank look at the last two names and paused to explain, ''Diana and Kathy are Marc's daughters, both younger than Lance.'' A rueful smile tugged at his mouth. ''They're our cousins, but—to be truthful—they're both kind of shallow and vain, more concerned with being seen with the 'right' people, wearing clothes by the currently 'in' designers, and sending their children to the 'right' schools than they are with anything else. . . . Anyway, they were there that night too. But the last time I remember seeing you, we were all at the party. Then you were gone. I assumed you'd gone back to the yacht. I wasn't surprised. After all, one Carnival party is pretty much the same as another. And when you weren't on board the next morning, no one thought anything of it. You had planned to leave that day, and we thought you had. I never guessed—none of us did—that something had happened to you. We wouldn't have left if we had.''

''I know.''

She heard the key turn in the lock and turned with a slightly guilty start as Cole walked in. He stopped, his gray eyes locking on her, but she had difficulty meeting them, no longer certain she could trust him, yet bothered by the feeling that her doubt was somehow a betrayal.

''Were you able to round up the crew?'' Gabe asked.

''They're on their way to the airport now to file a flight plan and obtain all the necessary clearances. We should be able to take off as soon as we get there.''

''Give me twenty minutes,'' she said, and she walked quickly from the room.

8

*F*rom the porthole window of the corporate jet, Remy watched the golden light of a slowly setting sun spread its color over the beaches and buildings of Nice. As the jet climbed over the tinted waters of the bay, the grand hotels along the Promenade des Anglais—those towers of luxurious elegance—diminished in size, the famed Castle Hill landmark, with its sparkling waterfall, visible from almost anywhere in the old section, was reduced to a vague knoll of ground, and the backcloth of verdant hills and distant mountains that ringed the city rose to dominance. Then the plane made its banking turn on its prescribed departure pattern, and Remy leaned back in her seat and tipped her head against the headrest.

They were going home. She was going home—home to New Orleans, to Louisiana. Yet she felt no sense of anticipation, only a kind of vague dread.

"Tired?" Gabe asked from his seat across the narrow aisle, mistaking the barely audible breath she'd released for a weary sigh.

"Not really." Though she wished she was.

The seat-belt light flicked off. Giving in to a surge of restless energy, Remy picked up her purse and got out of her seat. As she turned to walk down the narrow aisle to the lavatory, her glance encountered Cole's. He was in the cushioned chair directly behind hers, the point of his elbow on the armrest and a forefinger curved across his mouth in a thoughtful gesture.

What was in that steel-gray look of his? Remy found it impossible to tell. He had a face that revealed his inner feelings only when he chose. She hesitated an instant longer, then walked back to the lavatory and studied her own reflection in the mirror, wondering if she was that good at concealing her feelings. She doubted it. On the contrary, she suspected that she'd never bothered to learn to control her feelings or her opinions. From reviewing her own recent actions, she recognized that she was invariably blunt, even with those she liked or loved.

She freshened her makeup, touching the wand of brown mascara to the tips of her lashes, adding a few strokes of blush to the high contours of her cheekbones, and applying a fresh coat of peach lipstick to her lips. When she was finished, she ran cold water over her wrists, trying in vain to cool the agitation that pulsed through her. Giving up, she dried her hands on a towel monogrammed with the company's initials, then retrieved her purse from the sink counter.

When she stepped out of the lavatory, Remy immediately noticed Cole standing in the plane's small galley, his tall frame slightly stooped to avoid bumping his head on the curved ceiling. He had a coffeepot in one hand and a cup in the other. At the latching click of the lavatory door, he angled his upper body toward the sound, his gaze centering on her, as impassive as his expression.

"Coffee?" He lifted the pot in an offering gesture. Remy started to accept, then recalled that caffeine frequently contributed to the effects of jet lag. As if reading her mind, Cole said, "It's decaffeinated."

"Then I'll take a cup." She moved into the galley opening

and watched his hand tip the pot to pour coffee into a cup. When he passed the filled cup to her, their fingers inadvertently brushed. Her glance locked with his a second time, the memory of the way she'd felt when his hands had loved her suddenly vivid. She remembered clearly the violent harmony of their lovemaking, and the deep emotions she'd felt for him—emotions that she now hesitated to call love.

Something hard flickered over his lean features, thinning the line of his mouth before he abruptly turned away and reached into a cabinet for another cup. Had she revealed her doubt? Remy wondered. Probably. Because she did doubt—both her feelings and him.

"Why didn't you tell me we'd broken up instead of letting me think we'd only been arguing?" She wrapped both hands around the sides of the cup, as if needing the warmth from the hot coffee.

He looked at her, the line of his mouth finishing its cold-smiling curve. "I was sure Gabe wouldn't waste any time telling you that."

"Why didn't you tell me?" she challenged. "Don't you think it was slightly deceitful not to?"

"I suppose now you're regretting what happened." He raised the coffee cup to his mouth.

"Yes, I am." She watched him take a slow sip of the coffee. Instantly she recognized her mistake and lifted her glance from his mouth to his eyes, willing the uneven beat of her pulse to stop. Doubts or not, the attraction was there, strong and swift. "I wish I'd waited until I could remember our love relationship before I resumed a sexual one with you." Remy looked down at the cup and her hands, so tightly wrapped around it. "I wish—" She broke off, stopped by the futility of the phrase.

"Don't we all," Cole murmured dryly.

She looked up, suddenly and intently curious. "What do you wish?"

His gaze made a slow search of her face, a glimmer of longing in his eyes and a trace of anger in his expression that the longing was there. "I wish I'd told Mrs. Franks I was too busy to see you and never allowed you to walk through that door."

It took a second for Remy to realize what he meant by that. "That's when you got within ten feet of me six months ago, isn't it?"

"Yes."

"Will you tell me about it?" She was curious—more than curious—to learn the circumstances that had brought them together. "I need to remember. Who's Mrs. Franks?"

"My secretary." He looked at her, hearing the sharp buzz of the intercom that day and remembering his absently curt response. . . .

"Yes, what is it?" he demanded, without looking up from the operations cost report for the month of July.

"Miss Jardin is here to see you," came the reply over the speaker.

"Who?" He frowned at the intercom, which now had his undivided attention.

A short silence followed, then his secretary's voice spoke again, faintly prompting, faintly embarrassed. "Remy Jardin."

"Frazier's daughter." His frown deepened. "What—never mind." Cole flipped the report shut and leaned back in his chair, his curiosity aroused in spite of his better judgment. "Send her in."

Almost immediately the doorknob turned. Cole automatically stood up when she entered his office, the manners insisted upon by his mother too deeply ingrained to be ignored. As impossible as it seemed, Remy Jardin looked more attractive than he remembered from their one brief meeting several months before. Her hair was a fresh tawny gold in the room's artificial light, its rich color deepening the pale tan of her skin. Good breeding defined all the regular features of her face, a face made graphic by some warm, frank curiosity lying within.

As she crossed the room, the whisper of coral silk shantung drew his eye to the soft summer dress she wore, the cut of the diaphanously thin material designed to flow over her natural curves in a deliberate but subtly body-conscious style. He saw her glance make an inspection of the corner office —the standard old-world executive kind that had required the sacrifice of a small mahogany forest to panel the walls. A smile touched her lips when she noticed her grandfather's portrait hanging in its customary place, and it lingered as she stopped in front of the massive desk, the gold flecks in her hazel eyes glinting with a warmth and a touch of amusement that was oddly appealing.

Wise to the ways of her kind, he waited for the dip of her chin and the provocative glance issued through the sweep of long lashes. It didn't come. Instead she faced him with a somewhat surprising directness.

"I thought you would have had this office redecorated by now," she said. "Everything's exactly the same as when my father sat behind that desk."

"Considering the company's financial situation, I thought the money would be better spent elsewhere," he replied easily, aware that the width of the desk precluded the need for a handshake. "Please have a seat, Miss Jardin." He motioned to the two captain-style chairs with leather seats in front of his desk.

"Thank you."

He waited until she was seated, then sat down in his own chair. "I'm sure you'll understand when I say that this visit of yours, Miss Jardin, is more than a little unexpected. Just what is it you wanted to see me about?"

"I came to take you to lunch, Mr. Buchanan," she announced with all the smoothness and self-assurance of a wealthy young woman too accustomed to having her own way.

He reacted swiftly, instinctively, disguising it all behind a polite smile. "Sorry, I—"

"I've already checked your schedule, Mr. Buchanan," she

interrupted. "You don't have any appointments until three o'clock. And this is business."

"What kind of business?" He breathed in the scent of her perfume, a blend of sweet gardenia and sandalwood, as bold and feminine as the rest of her.

"Company business."

"Really? You'll forgive me if I seem surprised, but I understood you took no interest in the business—except to attend board of directors' meetings when they're called and to collect compensation of your attendance at those meetings."

She didn't bat an eye at his implied criticism, but her tone was a degree or two cooler. "You're quite right, Mr. Buchanan. I've never been involved in the actual operations of the company, but I do take an interest in who's running it. Now that you're in charge, I think it's time I found out more about you."

"Wouldn't it have been wiser to do that *before* I came on board, Miss Jardin?"

She smiled, not in the least nonplussed by his question, and he couldn't help noticing the attractive dimples that appeared in her cheeks. "You know the old saying, Mr. Buchanan—'better late than never.' Besides, you piqued my curiosity when you informed my father last week that you weren't interested in being nominated for membership in his krewe. I believe your exact words were 'I don't give a damn if the club is one of the most elite and politically powerful Carnival organizations in the state.'" Her smile widened. "Poor Daddy is still suffering from the aftershock of your refusal." She paused, considering him with undisguised interest. "According to your résumé, you grew up in New Orleans, so you must know there are people who would pay anything merely for the chance to have their names mentioned in the same breath with a nomination."

"I'm not Uptown, Miss Jardin, and I have no desire to mingle with your Uptown crowd." When he said "Uptown," Cole was referring not so much to a place as to an attitude.

"You could make some very important contacts."

"Perhaps. But these 'important contacts' didn't do your father much good, did they? They certainly haven't kept the Crescent Line out of the financial trouble it's in. That's why you brought me on board."

"So it is." She started to say something else, but the strident buzz of the intercom interrupted her.

"Yes?" He heard the tension in his voice. Dammit, why was he letting her get to him?

"I'm sorry to bother you, Mr. Buchanan," his secretary replied, a faintly worried edge to her voice. "There's a delivery man here with a package for you. He said he had instructions to bring it here—"

"Yes, I've been expecting it. Go ahead and accept delivery on it."

"But one side of it has been . . . crushed in a little. Before I accept it, maybe you should open it and see if there's been any damage—"

Cole didn't wait for her to finish as he moved out from behind the desk and started for the door, murmuring a slightly distracted "You'll have to excuse me" to Remy. As he walked into the outer office, his glance skipped over the pencil-thin Mrs. Franks and the brown-uniformed delivery man standing in front of her desk, then zeroed in on the rectangular package propped against the side of the desk. With clenched jaw, Cole surveyed the caved-in front of the cardboard container, then walked over to it and removed his pocket knife from the pocket of his trousers.

He took his time opening the package. If there was any damage, he didn't want to make it worse through careless haste. When he finally lifted the ornate, gilded frame out of the wood-reinforced box, he drew his first easy breath at the sight of the seemingly unscarred print, matted in pale blue.

"Has it been damaged?" Mrs. Franks asked anxiously.

"Except for a couple of nicks in the frame, it doesn't appear to be." But he carried it over to the couch and set it on the seat cushions, crouching down to examine it more closely. He ran his hand lightly over the surface, tactilely searching for any break in the smoothness of it and finding none. Satisfied at last, he withdrew his hand and allowed himself to gaze at the old print for the pure pleasure it gave him.

At almost the same instant he became aware of a stir of movement beside him, the soft rustle of silk whispering against silk as Remy Jardin sank down beside him. She reached out and traced her hand over the picture.

"This is an old sporting print. They were very popular between the mid-eighteenth and nineteenth centuries, before photography became widespread." She threw him a slightly surprised look. "Prints like this—especially in such excellent condition—are fairly uncommon."

"I know." His glance skimmed her blond hair, the color of dark honey, its loose windblown style the kind that invited a man to run his fingers through it.

She turned back to the picture, admiring it with keen, appreciative eyes. "It's a marvelous work—so much detail, so much genteel refinement . . . surrounding two boxers."

"Pugilists," Cole corrected. "The English regarded boxing as a noble art and a gentleman's pursuit, while Americans have tended to think of it as the sport of underclass ruffians. This particular print depicts the international match between the American John C. Heenan and the English champion Tom Sayers. The portraits of the important personages at ringside include, among two hundred others, Prince Albert, Thackeray, and the cartoonist Thomas Nast."

He straightened from his crouched position, catching her elbow and drawing her up with him, ignoring the speculating light in her eyes. But he found it impossible to ignore her. She was attractive, too damned attractive, and his reaction to her was that of any normal, healthy male. Unfortunately he'd thought he'd acquired an immunity against her type.

"Do you want me to put in a claim for damages to the frame, Mr. Buchanan?" his secretary asked.

"No, it's not worth the paperwork. Just sign for the delivery." He picked up the framed print and carried it into his office, aware that Remy Jardin was following him. He leaned the painting against the walnut credenza behind his desk, then turned to glance at her. "Was there something else you wanted, Miss Jardin?"

She smiled faintly. "I invited you to lunch, remember?"

"I remember." But he'd hoped she'd forgotten—or changed her mind.

"Surely you aren't going to refuse to have lunch with one of the directors of the Crescent Line, are you?"

He wanted to. Every instinct warned him to steer well clear of Remy Jardin. He reminded himself that he wasn't twenty years old anymore. He knew who she was and what she was—and her subtle look of class and breeding didn't impress him. He wasn't about to be taken in by her kind again.

"Where are we having this lunch?" he asked, deciding to get it over with and be rid of her.

"Galatoire's." Her smile became more pronounced. "But don't worry, Mr. Buchanan. Directors don't have expense accounts, so you don't have to be concerned about the company ultimately paying for it."

But he had a strange feeling that *he* would pay for it, somehow.

They walked to the restaurant in the French Quarter— although *walked* wasn't really an appropriate word for it. Nobody ever *walked* in New Orleans in the summer. The heat, the humidity, the languor in the air always reduced the pace to a leisurely stroll, a pace that let the sights, the sounds, the atmosphere of the city known as the Big Easy seep in.

When they crossed Canal Street, the dividing line that separated the Central Business District from the narrow streets and tightly packed houses of the Vieux Carré, Cole felt it sweep over him—the iron grillwork on the balconies, the doors leading to hidden courtyards, the clip-clop of a carriage horse, the muffled notes of a trumpet wailing to a Dixieland beat, and the heaviness in the air. He tried not to listen to the low, smoky pitch of her voice and to concentrate instead on her words. He tried, but he couldn't.

In the years when he was away from New Orleans, he'd

forgotten the sexual energy that sizzled beneath the city's surface—a sexual energy that was erotic, not the sleazy packaged kind that could be found all up and down Bourbon Street, but rather the subtle, sultry kind found in the diaphanous dress she wore and in the steamy air, thick with the scent of magnolias. Why hadn't he remembered it during the six months he'd been back? Why now—with her? Had he avoided the memory deliberately, or had he really been that busy? He wanted to believe the latter.

By the time they reached Galatoire's, the long line of people that typically stretched out the door and down the block at lunchtime had dwindled to a mere handful. A word to the maître d' and they were immediately ushered to a table in the large, brightly lit room, mirrored on all sides. The restaurant hummed with gossip, the rise and fall of it untouched by the lazy rotation of the ceiling fans overhead.

Addressing the waiter by name, Remy Jardin questioned him on which of the seafood items were truly fresh that day, treating him with an easy familiarity that spoke of a long-standing acquaintance. Cole listened somewhat cynically, aware that in her rarefied circle such relationships were frequently cultivated as a means to avoid ridiculously long waits at such places as Antoine's, where a waiter's name became a secret and very necessary password.

At the conclusion of her consultation with the plump-cheeked Joseph, she chose the oyster en brochette for an appetizer and the lamb chops with béarnaise as her main course. Cole ordered the shrimp rémoulade and the pompano à la meunière.

When the waiter had retreated out of earshot, Remy Jardin murmured, "A word of warning. If there's something you don't want the whole city to know, never talk about it in front of Joseph. As Nattie would say, he has a mouth bigger than the Mississippi."

"Who's Nattie?"

"Our cook—although she's been with us so long, she's practically a member of the family."

"I see." He had an instant image of a stout black woman—the plump-cheeked Jemima type—and withheld comment, realizing that he should have known. Her kind always had some relationship like that that they could point to to show their liberalism.

After a moment's pause, with that direct gaze of hers quietly studying him, she said, "I admit the pompano sounded good. I was tempted to order it myself. Are you a seafood lover?"

"Truthfully, my favorite dish is red beans and rice." If he'd expected to shock her with his less than sophisticated tastes, he was wrong.

She laughed, an audacious gleam lighting her eyes. "Don't tell Joseph, but it's my favorite too." She reached for the glass of crisp, dry rosé wine the waiter had brought her earlier along with Cole's bourbon and branch. "Nattie makes the best red beans I've ever tasted—hearty and creamy, seasoned just spicy enough—and serves it over the fluffiest bed of rice. And the sausage is homemade, stuffed by Nattie herself. You'll have to come to the house for dinner sometime."

"I'm afraid I'm too busy for socializing, Miss Jardin."

"So I've heard. In fact, my brother's convinced that you're a workaholic."

"Perhaps if your father and uncle had paid more attention to business and less to socializing, I wouldn't have to put in the long hours that I do now."

"I asked for that one, didn't I?" She tipped her glass to him in a mock salute, then took a small sip of wine and lowered the glass. "I don't recall seeing anything in your résumé about a family. I assume you have one."

"I do," he replied, deliberately uncommunicative.

"Any brothers or sisters?"

"None."

"What about your parents? Where are they?"

"My father died when I was eight. My mother lives here in New Orleans."

"She does? Do you see her very often, or—are you too

busy?'' she taunted lightly, a small smile taking much of the sting out of her words.

Maybe that was why he answered her instead of telling her it was none of her business. He wasn't sure. "I usually call or stop by her shop once a week or so—and occasionally I go over to her place for dinner in the evening.''

"What kind of shop does she have?''

"A small antique store.''

"Really? On Royal?''

He smiled wryly, faintly, at that. "No, on Magazine. Her shop draws the blue-jean-and-sneakers trade, not the hat-and-white-gloves one.''

The waiter Joseph returned to the table with their appetizers. When he retreated, Remy speared a bite of oyster with her fork. "What types of antiques does your mother sell?''

"They're not antiques as much as they are collectibles—period toys, lace curtains, bric-a-brac, wicker pieces, things like that.''

"What's the name of her shop?''

"The Lemon Tree. Why?''

"Just curious,'' she said with a graceful lift of her shoulders, an action that briefly drew the thin material of her dress more tightly over her breasts, momentarily delineating their roundness—something he didn't want to notice. Yet as much as he wanted to deny it, a sexual awareness of her existed in him. It had ever since their slow stroll to the restaurant, ever since she'd walked into his office—ever since he'd met her that first time, six months before.

He stabbed a piece of shrimp with the tines of his seafood fork and tried to ignore the thought. "I thought this lunch was to talk about business.''

"I never said that,'' she replied, quickly and smoothly. "I said I wanted to get to know you better.'' She paused in the act of forking another bite of oyster to her mouth. "By the way, where did you manage to find that print?''

Cole hesitated an instant, then said, ''When I was in London last month I had some time between appointments, so I stopped in at Christie's, and there it was."

"Christie's—really? That's where I took my training in eighteenth-century French porcelain." She smiled absently, as if some thought had just occurred to her. "I wonder if Jacques the jackal is still there."

"Who?" Cole frowned.

"This absolutely insufferable man—French, of course— who was an authority on *everything*. Nobody could stand him. But he had this laugh that sounded like a hyena." She paused and arched an eyebrow in his direction, her eyes glinting with amusement. "You wouldn't believe the lengths we used to go to to get him to laugh—especially if there was an important client around."

"I think I can." He nodded, imagining the conspiracies among the trainees to make the man break up with laughter.

"I thought you'd be able to." She showed him an unsettling smile of shared humor, then turned her attention back to her appetizer. "Are you a collector of sporting prints?"

Cole remembered the quiet appreciation in her expression when she'd seen the print. It would have been easy for him to talk to her about his interest—which was precisely why he didn't.

"I doubt that five—six"—he corrected himself—"prints would be considered a collection by your standards."

"Really? And what *are* my standards?" She sounded amused.

"I'm sure you and your friends generally collect original art, not prints. But that's all I can afford."

She picked up her wineglass and raised it to her lips, holding his gaze and murmuring over the rim, "You don't have a very high opinion of me, my family, or my friends, do you?"

He hesitated, then chose to be blunt. "Frankly, no."

"Why?" She studied him thoughtfully, curiously.

Finished with his shrimp rémoulade, he laid his fork aside

and coolly met the silent challenge of her gaze. "Look at the pathetic shape the Crescent Line's in now, and you'll find the answer to that. You and your family bled the life out of it, paying stock dividends to yourselves when the company couldn't afford it, when that money needed to be reinvested. You were solely concerned with yourselves and maintaining your style of living. You didn't give a damn about what might be best for the company—until it appeared that the company might go broke."

"Guilty as charged, I'm afraid," she confessed. "Although in our defense I would have to say that initially none of us realized the situation was quite so serious."

"It was—and is. Perhaps if you had studied the balance sheets and asked some questions at the directors' meetings instead of rubber-stamping whatever your father or uncle put in front of you, you would have found out."

"You're right, of course," she admitted again, untroubled by his criticism of her. "Although I felt that since I knew nothing about the business, they were better qualified than I to make decisions."

"As one of the owners, Miss Jardin, you should have made it your business to know instead of donating all your time to the museum, playing at being a docent and dabbling in acquisitions."

The dimples appeared in her cheeks again. "That sounds remarkably like a suggestion that I should be working in and for the company. Obviously you didn't intend for me to take you literally, since I can't imagine you being an advocate of nepotism."

The waiter came back to the table to remove the dishes with the remains of their appetizers and serve them their main course, his presence eliminating the need for Cole to respond to her remark and creating a lull in the conversation.

"I am curious about something else," she said when Joseph left. "Considering the company's financial problems and your opinion of us, why did you take the job?"

"Simple. You—the company—met my terms."

"Yes." She paused reflectively. "And your terms were: full and complete authority over all facets of the company; any decision you made was final; no approval required from the board of directors. If you succeed financially in turning the company around within three years, you are to receive ten-percent ownership in the company, plus some very favorable stock options."

"Then you did read my contract."

"Honestly? I read it for the first time the other day after Father told me what you said he could do with the nomination to his krewe."

"You admit that?" He was surprised by her candor.

"The truth hurts, but—yes, I do. Of course, I console myself with the knowledge that despite past mistakes, we at least had the good sense to bring you on board."

"First interest, now flattery, Miss Jardin?" he mocked.

"I don't suppose I could persuade you to call me Remy."

"What would be the point?"

"Why not say . . . in the interest of establishing friendlier relations between owners and management."

"I repeat, what would be the point?"

She laid her knife and fork down and rested her elbows on the table, folding her hands together and thoughtfully propping up the point of her chin on top of them. "You resent who I am, my background, don't you? You do realize there's nothing I can do about it. And I'm certainly not going to apologize or feel guilty because I happened to be born into the Jardin family. I had no control over it. Or—is that my problem?" She raised her chin long enough to flick a finger in the direction of his hand.

"Is what your problem?" Cole frowned.

"You prefer brunettes with short hair." She reached over, plucked a dark hair from the sleeve of his suit jacket, and held it up as evidence.

"Sherlock Holmes you're not, Miss Jardin." He took it from her and let it drop to the floor. "That happens to be cat hair."

"You own a cat?" She picked up her knife and fork and cut another bite of lamb chop.

"You've obviously had little experience with cats or you'd know that nobody ever *owns* one. You may occasionally share the same living quarters, but that's about all."

"And this cat you *occasionally* share your quarters with, what kind is it?"

"The alley variety. Its pedigree is the street."

"Does your cat have a name?"

He hesitated. "Tom."

"You're kidding." She stared at him incredulously, then burst into a laugh.

In spite of himself, he laughed with her. "Not very original, I admit, but the name suits him."

"I wouldn't do that very often if I were you."

"What?" Suddenly he found himself captivated by her gaze, unsettled and disturbed by the warmly interested glow in her eyes.

"Laugh," she said simply. "It makes you seem human."

He caught himself wanting to respond to her as a man, and immediately steeled himself against that impulse. "I'll remember that," he said, wiping the smile from his face.

"Other than occasionally sharing your digs with Tom, collecting sporting prints, and dining with your mother now and then, what else do you do? Are you interested in sports? Football? Soccer? Tennis?"

"I don't have time."

"You must do something to stay in such great shape," she said, running her gaze over the width of his shoulders and chest. "And somehow I can't imagine you working out in a gym with weights."

"Actually I do try to make it to the gym a couple-three times a week to spar a few rounds."

"You mean—you box?" She seemed uncertain that she had understood him correctly.

"Yes." Dammit, why was he telling her this? Had it been deliberate, to remind him how he'd met . . . ? But Remy

Jardin's reaction was different. There was no look of fascination for what many regarded as a violent sport, nothing that even remotely resembled an attraction to blood and gore.

"An art collector who boxes. What perfect therapy it must be," she marveled. "Personally, I can't think of a better way to get rid of frustration and repressed anger than to unleash it on a punching bag. How long have you been doing it?"

"I started boxing when I was a kid. My mother figured I'd be getting into fights anyway, so she decided it would be better if I did it in a ring under supervision, instead of with a gang in the streets."

"Obviously it worked."

"For the most part."

"I'm almost afraid to ask what kind of music you like?"

"A little jazz, a lot of blues." Too late, he caught himself and wondered why in hell he was answering these questions of hers. He knew better. She wasn't his kind. Nothing would come of it.

"Then you must like Lou Rawls. Have you seen his show at the Blue Room? From what I've heard it's drawing rave reviews."

"The tickets are sold out."

"Really." She gave him a knowing smile and a bold glance. "It so happens I have two tickets for tonight's show. Gabe was supposed to go with me, but he has a heavy date tonight—with a weighty legal brief, he claims. I can't think of a single reason why I shouldn't take you instead."

"I suppose next you'll try to convince me this invitation is all in aid of friendlier relations between ownership and management," Cole replied cynically. He signaled for the waiter to take away his plate, then ordered coffee.

"Are you suggesting that that's wrong?" The coffee arrived, the matchless New Orleans–style coffee, a blend of dark roasted coffee beans and chicory, brewed strong and black, with the option always provided to dilute it with hot milk.

Cole drank his straight, and he noticed that Remy Jardin

did too. "I'm suggesting . . . that you find yourself another escort—one suitable for a Newcomb girl."

She looked at him in surprise. "How did you know I went to Newcomb College?"

"Considering it's a tradition in the Uptown set, it was an educated guess. No doubt your mother went there, and your mother's mother—right on down the line."

"Where did you go to college?"

"I can assure you it wasn't Tulane," he replied, trying not to think about the scholarship he'd almost gotten to that university, a scholarship that was ultimately given to someone else whose family had the "right" background and a depleted bank account. "Your brother went there, didn't he? And obtained the mandatory law degree to go with the rest of his impeccable family credentials."

She propped an elbow on the table and rested her chin on the heel of her hand. "Your logic escapes me completely. What does all this have to do with refusing to go see Lou Rawls with me?"

"Some relationships between certain people are deadends from the start. This is one of them, Miss Jardin. And I don't see any reason to start something that will never go anywhere."

"How can you be sure of that?"

"It's simple, Miss Jardin. People—like water—seek their own level." It was a truth he'd learned the hard way, on more than one occasion.

She arched an eyebrow at that. "And you accept that?"

"It isn't a question of accepting it. It's reality."

"If women had that attitude, we'd still be in the kitchen."

"Somehow I doubt you have ever seen the inside of a kitchen—except maybe to complain to the cook."

"I think you'd be surprised at how well I know my way around a kitchen, but that's not the point." She shrugged idly, her eyes never leaving him. "You disappoint me, Mr. Buchanan. I thought you were more of a gambler."

"I don't play longshots, if that's what you mean."

She laughed, and the throaty sound of it worked on his senses. "I've been called many things, but never a longshot." She reached into her lap for her purse. He heard the snapping click of the clasp opening. She took something out of it, then presented it to him in a flourish, with a twist of her wrist. "Here's a sure thing, Mr. Buchanan. *One* ticket to this evening's show . . . and look." She wiggled it. "No strings attached."

He took it from her, then hesitated warily. "What's the catch, Miss Jardin? What's behind this?"

"No catch. And if it was prompted by anything, then it's probably something Nattie once told me."

"What's that?"

"A little sugar never hurt a lemon."

He smiled in spite of himself and slipped the ticket inside the breast pocket of his suit coat.

A half-dozen times that afternoon, back in his office, he took it out and looked at it. Each time, the sight of it gave him pause. And a hundred times he debated with himself whether or not he should go.

In the end, he showered and changed at his apartment, then went to the Fairmont Hotel, which, like most New Orleans natives, he continued to think of as the Roosevelt. He was shown to a table for two in the hotel's supper club, the Blue Room. The emptiness of the chair opposite him stared accusingly back. One word from him at lunch, and Remy Jardin would have been sitting there. He wondered if he could stand to stare at it all night. Finally he decided he couldn't, and he started to get up.

That was when she walked in, dramatically feminine in a high-necked two-piece dress of silk jacquard, inset with embroidered lace at the throat and with another wide swathe accenting the hem. Her hair was piled on top of her head in a crown of soft curls, a style that was both sophisticated and sexy.

"Sorry I'm late. I hope I haven't kept you waiting long," she said, as if he'd been expecting her to come all along. Had he?

"Remy." It was out. He'd said her name.

"Yes, Cole," she replied softly.

"Nothing," Ripping his gaze from her, he moved briskly to pull out the other chair at the table.

"Nothing," she mocked playfully, following after him to take her seat. Her dress was a pale shade of ivory, but the effect of it was anything but virginal, as Cole discovered when he saw the back of it. It plunged all the way down, giving him a glimpse of the tantalizing hollow at the base of her spine. "Your longshot comes in, and all you can say is 'nothing.' "

"I see you changed for the occasion." He took his own seat, rigid, tense, every instinct telling him to walk out now.

"You like my dress?"

"That isn't a dress. It's a weapon."

"Mmmm, a lethal one, I hope." She smiled, deliberately provocative.

"Just why have you set your sights on me?" He leaned back in his chair, trying to put more distance between them and negate the effect she was having on him. But he heard the whisper of silk over silk as she crossed her legs under the table.

"Frankly?" Unexpectedly, her expression turned serious, her look soberly contemplative. "Initially—as I told you before—I came to see you out of sheer curiosity. I wanted to meet the man who wanted no part of one of the most elite krewes in New Orleans. When I did, you were—at least at first—almost exactly what I expected. Then I saw the way you looked at that print. You weren't calculating its worth, as I've seen *many* collectors do, or even imagining how much it would impress others, as some do. No, it was the print itself that appealed to you—the style, the technique, the use of colors, the feelings it evoked. I suppose I recognized that look because so often that's the way I feel when I come across a Sèvres figurine I've never seen before." Pausing, she continued to look at him, seeing him, studying him. Then she seemed to realize how serious she'd become, and she quickly smiled, picking up the water glass in front of her, a faintly mocking gleam in her eyes. "Something tells me you aren't as hard, as cold, or as cynical as you may seem—not a man who's sensitive enough to understand cats."

Cole leaned forward, uncomfortable with the things she was saying. "Is the analysis over, or should I see if the management can provide us with a couch?"

"Now there's an intriguing thought."

"What? Analyzing me?"

"No—having you all to myself on a couch for an hour."

He didn't remember much of the show. He was more conscious of the play of light and shadow across her face with the changing of the stage lighting, and of the absence of any rings on her fingers when she clapped enthusiastically at the conclusion of each song. Her vitality, her zest—her passion—that was what he recalled when the show was over.

In the lobby of the lavishly decorated turn-of-the-century hotel, Cole guided her through the milling throng of showgoers, slow to disperse. "I wonder how lucky I'll be getting a taxi," Remy remarked.

"You didn't drive your car tonight?" He'd taken it for granted that she had.

"No. I had Gabe drop me off on his way back to the office to tussle with his weighty legal brief," she replied, then sent him a challenging sidelong glance. "You wouldn't happen to be going my way, would you?"

Another imaginary handkerchief had been dropped. Cole had the feeling he'd been following a trail of them all day. Each time he picked one up and returned it to her, he discovered that he'd gone a little further than he'd planned. The hell of it was that he *wanted* to be led like this.

"I could arrange to go that way," he heard himself say.

"I know you *could*, but will you?"

He answered that a few minutes later when he helped her

into his car. During the short ride to the Jardin family home in the Garden district, the fragrance of her drifted through the car, accompanied by the whisper of silk that came with her slightest movement. The intermittent glow from the street lamps along St. Charles Avenue, their light broken by the heavy branches of the old oaks on either side of the esplanade, kept her constantly in his side vision, occasionally highlighting a refined cheekbone or shadowing the delicate cut of her jaw. He had the feeling that from now on the ghost of her would always ride with him.

Following her directions, he turned off St. Charles onto a side street, then turned again and parked the car in front of one of the many old mansions that graced the district. He got out and walked around to open her door. His mother was old-fashioned in many ways, and she'd raised him to always walk a girl to her door, not to let her out at the curb and drive off. It was too deeply ingrained in him to be ignored, even though he knew it would be a mistake to walk Remy to her front door.

Beyond the delicate lacework of the iron fence and the dark shadows of the lush foliage, the white Doric columns of the mansion's pillared front gleamed wanly in the moonlight. He lightly kept a hand on her elbow as they walked up the banquette to the yard's black iron gate. She pushed it open. The hinges were too well oiled to creak—like the family that owned the property, Cole reminded himself.

The lights inside the main foyer spilled softly through the leaded glass windows that flanked the big oak door, forming pools on the hard cypress flooring of the front gallery. When they reached the door, with its gleaming brass knocker, she turned to him and held out a key. He stared at it, aware that if he reached for it, he was picking up another lace hankie.

He willed his expression to remain bland as he took the key from her outstretched hand and inserted it in the lock, silently cursing his mother for the first time in his life. He gave the key a quick turn, telling himself all the while that this was not a date. He didn't have to kiss her good-night.

He didn't have to kiss her at all. Hearing the slide of the bolt, he turned the doorknob and pushed the door inward. As he swung back to give her back the key, she held out her hand, palm up. He hesitated, then dropped the key in the center of it.

Her fingers immediately closed around it, the polished sheen of her nails flashing in the foyer light. "I enjoyed the show—and your company tonight, Cole." The golden gleam in her eyes challenged him, dared him. "Thanks for the ride."

"You're welcome," he replied automatically.

"Good-night," she said, then—to his surprise—she stepped past him into the foyer and made a graceful turn to shut the door on him. When it was half closed, she paused and said, as if only then remembering, "By the way, I met your mother this afternoon. I liked her."

Stunned, he shot out a hand, blocking the door from swinging the rest of the way shut. As he shoved it back open, she calmly turned and advanced into the foyer. He charged after her.

"You saw my mother? Where?"

"I went by her shop on Magazine after I left you at Galatoire's," she said without so much as a backward glance, and she gave her evening bag a toss onto a side table, then crossed to a set of French doors that led onto an expansive courtyard.

"Why did you go there?" He demanded to know the reason, pushed by a half-formed annoyance that rippled through him at this invasion of his private life.

She looked over her shoulder, her dimpled smile faintly mocking. "Can't you guess?" she said, and she pulled both doors open wide, then walked through them into the night-darkened courtyard.

"I don't want to guess, Remy. I want an answer." He followed her outside and immediately felt the liquid heat of the summer night wash over him.

"Very well." She stopped on a wisteria-covered walkway flanked by white columns, and turned, leaning her shoulders against one of them. "I wanted to meet the woman who gave birth to a man like you."

Facing her, he couldn't hold on to his anger. He still felt heat, but now it was part of the voluptuous ease of the night. "Why? What difference could it make?"

"Because I gambled that you'd come when I gave you that ticket this afternoon. I hoped that by seeing your mother I might get some sense of whether or not you'd show up." She paused for a fraction of a second. "When I gave you that ticket, I never once said I wasn't going. You had to know, in the back of your mind, that there was a good chance I'd be there. So . . . if you came tonight, I knew it had to mean you were interested in me, despite what you said."

"And if I hadn't come?"

There was a tiny lift of her shoulders in a shrug. "Then I would have had to accept that you meant exactly what you said. Not that it matters. You came."

"Yes—I did." And he was regretting it, too—especially now, alone with her, with this sultriness in the air.

"I know what I want, Cole. And I want to know you better." She tilted her head to one side. "Am I too aggressive for you? In a man, I know that's a trait to be admired. But some men find it off-putting in a woman. Do you?"

"No." There was a tightening in his chest—in his whole body. He couldn't get his legs to move, not backward or forward. "What exactly do you want from me? Have you become bored with your proper world and decided to find someone *improper* to liven things up for you?"

"Could you liven things up, Cole?" In a single, fluidly graceful move, she straightened up from the column, and he discovered how close to each other they were standing. She lifted her face to him. "Can you liven me up?"

She was waiting for his kiss, and he knew it. Just as he knew he was going to kiss her even before he framed her upturned face in his hands, his thumbs stroking the slender curve of her throat and feeling the heavy thud of her pulse. She looked small and delicate to him, like a porcelain figurine in a glass cabinet at his mother's shop—so very fragile, despite the directness of her eyes. Slowly he lowered his mouth onto her lips. They were soft and incredibly warm. He rubbed his mouth over them, holding himself in tight restraint. But it wasn't easy—it wasn't easy when what he really wanted was to plunder their softness, taste their heat, and make them part with his name. A second later that desire became action.

Suddenly his hands weren't steady—nothing about him was steady. He pulled back, shaken by how completely she had broken through his will. When she swayed toward him, he slid his hands onto her silk-clad shoulders, keeping her at a safe distance.

There was a radiance to her face that he didn't remember seeing before as she lifted her hand and traced the shape of his mouth with her fingertips. "Do you always kiss like that?"

"Not always." His voice sounded too husky, too thick, revealing too much of the way she disturbed him.

She released a breath of soundless laughter. "I don't think there can be any doubt: you do liven me up—in every way."

Watching him, listening to him tell of that night, Remy felt the strong pull of attraction. She could easily visualize her persistence and his resistance. "What did you say to that?" she asked when he paused in his telling.

"I didn't say anything. As I recall, we didn't need words."

The air seemed to hum between them, vibrating with a sexual tension, as it must have that night. "Did we make love?" Remy wondered.

"No. It was too soon—too sudden for both of us."

"I suppose it was." She noticed the guarded way he was studying her, the hint of wariness in his gray eyes, a wariness that suggested that he'd been hurt before. She thought back over his description of their first meeting and the remarks he'd made about the so-called Uptown crowd. "Cole, what happened to make you so distrust someone with my background—my family?"

A grim, almost bitter smile twisted his mouth. "Which time, Remy?" He turned back to the galley counter. "More coffee?"

"I—" Suddenly the plane started to shudder and buck violently, throwing Remy sideways against the counter and knocking the cup from her hand.

In the next second she was grabbed roughly by the waist and hauled against the opposite bulkhead wall, pinned there by the heavy crush of Cole's body. She found herself engulfed in the feel of him, the smell of him. The wild buffeting of the plane continued for several more interminable minutes before it settled into a mild shaking.

As Cole drew back, his hands continued to grip the hold he'd found. "Are you all right?"

"Yes." She had room enough to nod, though, like him, she wasn't sure it was over. Unsteady, shaken, she was conscious of a throbbing pain in her hip. No doubt she'd bruised it when she was thrown against the counter. But she was growing more conscious of the pressure of his hips as they held her against the wall, the hard, unmistakably male outline of him making itself felt.

"It looks like we encountered some turbulence."

Looking at him, Remy knew that the outside turbulence had moved within. "We certainly did," she said. And it increased further as the gray of his eyes darkened on her.

"Remy, are you all right back there?" Gabe called, his voice followed by the sound of his footsteps coming up the aisle to the galley.

His approach chased away the moment of awareness between them, and Cole pushed away from her, his hands moving to lightly grip her shoulders before falling away entirely.

"I'm fine," she repeated the assurance she'd earlier given Cole. But by then Gabe was already in the galley opening, his gaze immediately fastening on her in concern. Feeling the need to say more, she added, smiling, "A little shaken, but unharmed. I came to get a cup of coffee. Which now happens to be all over the floor," she noticed. "Hand me some towels or something, Cole. We'd better get it wiped up before one of us slips on it." The plane shuddered again, and Remy immediately grabbed hold of the edge of the partition to steady herself.

"I'll clean it up," Cole said. "Go back to your seat and buckle up. Get some sleep if you can. It's going to be a long flight."

She went back to her seat, not to sleep but to mull over some of the things Cole had told her. It was obvious that she'd been the pursuer. And it was equally obvious that he hadn't found it easy to trust her because of previous encounters with "her kind." He seemed so strong, so hard, that *vulnerable* certainly wasn't a word she would have used to describe him—until now. What *had* happened to make him so leery of her? Had he told her? And did it matter? Without trust, no relationship could survive. Was that what had ultimately caused her to break it off with him? Had she become tired of constantly being forced to prove to him that she cared—tired of defending her family's actions?

And that brought up another thing: according to Cole, the company was in serious financial shape. In fact, he'd blatantly accused her family of draining it of funds. Earlier Gabe had admitted that the company had been losing money, yet he'd been very definite that it was nothing serious. Which was the truth? And what could either of them gain by lying?

9

Somewhere over the Atlantic, Remy managed to doze off. When the plane began its descent to the New Orleans airport, Cole touched her shoulder. "We'll be landing in about ten minutes," he said. "Check your seat belt. There's rain and fog in the area, so it might get a little bumpy."

Groggily she acknowledged his advice and tried to wipe the sleep from her face as Cole passed the same message on to Gabe, then sat down in his own seat and buckled up.

With the dimness of the cabin lights, there was little glare on the plane's windows. Turning, Remy gazed out the window at the stars glittering before the rising moon. Below, a blanket of dark clouds hid the city. She felt oddly uneasy, unable to summon any excitement at the prospect of being reunited with her family—of returning home.

After a fairly smooth descent, the plane broke through the clouds roughly four hundred feet up. All looked black beneath them. Belatedly she remembered that the airport was located on the edge of the swamp and Lake Pontchartrain. From out of the black, the runway approach lights gleamed, twin trails of light pointing the way through the darkness and the wispy fog.

A cool, light rain fell as Remy stepped off the plane at New Orleans' Moisant International Airport. One of the ground crew ushered her to the building, sheltering her from the pattering drops with an umbrella.

After a minor delay as they went through immigration and customs, Remy walked into the terminal building itself, flanked by Gabe and Cole and trailed by a porter with their luggage. Cole tipped his head toward her, his gaze fixed on some point ahead of them as he murmured, sotto voce, "It seems the whole family turned out to welcome you home."

Following the direction of his gaze, Remy located a group of people waiting to greet them. She faltered for a moment. Strangers. They looked like total strangers, all of them. Until that moment she hadn't realized how much she'd hoped that seeing them would spark a memory, if only a long-ago one —as seeing Gabe had done. But there was nothing.

Refusing to give up, Remy focused on them individually instead of viewing them as a whole, starting first with the woman with the anxious look on her face. A soft-brimmed hat, the same teal-blue color as her raincoat, covered short blond hair that had been artfully faded to a flattering shade of platinum. Her gloved hands held a clutch purse that she gripped tightly.

When the woman saw Remy approaching, her anxious look disappeared, replaced by a glowing smile that gave a soft, Renoirish radiance to her delicate features. "Remy, my darling." Her voice caught on a happy sob as she glided forward and embraced Remy, hugging her close for a moment, then drawing back to look at her. "It's so good to have you home. You gave us such a scare, vanishing like that. What are we ever going to do with you?" She ran a gloved hand tenderly over her cheek and smoothed the side of her hair in a soothing, motherly gesture. "How are you? Are you all right? They told us you have amnesia. Gracious!" She blinked in sudden surprise. "Do you remember me? I'm your mother."

"You grow roses." She had a fleeting image of this same woman in a wide straw sun hat, with a basket of freshly cut roses on her arm and a pair of garden shears in her white-gloved hand. That was it. That was all. But it was something, a tiny piece of memory that allowed Remy to truthfully say, "I can remember that."

"Gracious, yes, I grow roses. Prize roses."

"How about me? Do you remember your kindly old father?" asked a low, jesting voice.

Less certainly, Remy turned to the man who was obviously her father, her searching glance taking in the bright twinkle in his brown eyes, the almost total absence of gray in his dark hair, and the tanned, healthy vigor of his face. "I wish I could say I do remember you, but . . . I can't." She saw the flash of stark hurt in his eyes and regretted her candor. Smiling, she reached for his hand. "Right now, it's enough to know I have a father who loves me."

She could tell that her words had pleased him as he gave her hand a squeeze. "What father could not love a daughter like you?" Then his gaze centered on the faint discoloration near her lips, his expression taking on a look of shared pain. "Remy, do you remember anything at all about what happened that night?"

"No. Nothing. And the specialist at the hospital told me the odds were I would never remember the events directly leading up to my injury. That part of my memory will probably be lost forever."

"I . . . I see," he murmured, his glance dropping to her hand.

"Now, Frazier." Her mother slipped a gloved hand under the crook of his arm. "That awful incident isn't something we should be dwelling on."

"Of course not," he agreed, somewhat hesitantly.

"Well, it doesn't matter whether you remember me or not, Remy," another voice broke in, its heartiness a contrast to her father's quietly serious tone. "I insist on having a hug from my favorite niece."

Remy turned to her uncle, a slim version of her more robust father, impeccably groomed in an Italian suit, his handsome features beaming with a smile. "You must be Uncle Marc," she managed to say before she was smoothly drawn into his arms, a dry kiss planted on her left cheek.

Then he stepped back, holding on to both her hands. "Let me have a look at you," he said, giving her the once-over, then winking. "I must say, you look none the worse for your adventure." He paused to sigh in contentment. "Ahh, Remy, you can't know how worried all of us have been about you."

"And you can't know how much I needed to hear that a few days ago, when I felt totally lost and forgotten." She smiled.

"Never forgotten, Remy," he insisted firmly. "Never for one minute."

She laughed. "Do you always know the right thing to say?"

"I try," he said, lifting his shoulders in a shrug of modesty.

"I can't imagine you could have forgotten me, Remy— your dear cousin Lance," a low voice challenged, silken with mockery. "Especially when you consider I'm your least favorite."

Turning, she forced herself to calmly meet the lazy, taunting regard of his dark, nearly black eyes. "In that case, maybe I shouldn't say it's good to see you, Lance."

He stood before her, one hand idly thrust in the side pocket of his pleated trousers, in a pose of negligent ease that smacked of arrogance. His hair was the same near-black shade as his eyes, its thickness skillfully and smoothly combed away from his face. His lips had a woman's fullness to them, yet on him it looked sexy instead of effeminate. And when he smiled—as he was doing now—there was a faintly sarcastic curl to his upper lip. Gabe was right—Lance was "handsome as the devil."

"I don't know why anyone worried about you," he said. "Your memory may be impaired, but your tongue is as sharp as ever."

Before she could show him precisely how sharp it could be, three women converged on her with effusive welcomes, hugging her and kissing the air near her cheek.

"You look marvelous, Remy," declared one of Marc's daughters, a raven-haired Southern beauty with dark, flashing eyes and a beauty queen's empty smile. "When they told me you had amnesia, I thought you'd look, well, haunted, your eyes all shadowed and your face pale and wan. But here you are—the same old Remy."

"We heard they put a dozen stitches in your head," the other chimed in, craning her neck to see where they'd been taken.

"Not a dozen," Remy corrected automatically.

"Well, however many it was, they don't show. Your hair covers it beautifully. Aren't you lucky you don't wear it short? Think how funny you would have looked with a bald spot in the middle of your head."

"She would simply have had to wear a hat to cover it, Diana," the first inserted, which meant she had to be Kathy, the older of the two.

"It's almost a pity you don't," sighed Diana, who was a less striking version of her sister. "According to *W*, hats are *in* this season."

"Is it true, Remy, that you don't remember anything?" Her aunt Christina, a plump, matronly woman who had obviously given up the battle of competing with her daughters' looks, finally squeezed in a question.

"Yes, is it true?" Kathy immediately took up the thread. "You don't remember anything? Not even about the—"

"This isn't the time to besiege Remy with questions," Marc smoothly cut across his eldest daughter's words. "She just stepped off the plane from a long and very exhausting flight. She can tell us her story later—after she has had time to rest."

"And we are all dying to hear it," Kathy put in, then added with a hint of resentment and envy, "Amnesia. Leave it to you, Remy, to come up with something so spectacularly unusual.''

"Not by choice, I assure you.'' Remy smiled, their prattle sounding vaguely familiar to her. No doubt she had been irritated by it in the past, but not tonight—not when she was standing here literally surrounded by family, embraced by a sense of belonging.

As she idly swept her glance over them, she noticed that Cole wasn't there. A slight turn of her head and she found him, standing well apart from them—alone. She was suddenly struck by the feeling that he was an outsider, he didn't belong. Unbidden came a wash of voices through her mind: ''not one of us''. . .''methods less than orthodox''. . . ''native shrewdness''. . .''not suitable at all''. . .''ruthless, cunning.''

Staring at the hard and so very cynical look on his face, Remy realized that much of that was true. Cole Buchanan hadn't been born into that uptight, Uptown New Orleans world of hers, where lineage was everything, where certain standards of conduct were quietly expected, where you were judged by the high school and college you attended and the number of Mardi Gras courts you were invited to participate in. She told herself that none of that mattered, yet . . . she felt trapped by this lack of memory that kept her from knowing whether or not she should believe in him. Part of her wanted to go to him, to include him in this moment, but she was afraid to trust her instincts—perhaps for the first time in her life.

"How much does she remember about—''

Remy recognized Lance's voice, its tone dropped to a conspiratorial level, an instant before Gabe broke in with a quick, quiet "Nothing.''

She pivoted toward them. "I remember nothing about what?''

"Gabe,'' her uncle inserted smoothly as he clamped a hand on her brother's shoulder. "I don't believe any of us have thanked you for flying all the way there and bringing her back.''

Remy started to point out that Gabe hadn't been alone, as her uncle Marc had implied, that in fact Cole had been the one to make the initial contact, but when she glanced at Cole, his back was turned to them, and he had a briefcase in one hand and a heavy garment bag slung over his other arm. Something tore at her throat when she saw him walk to the exit without so much as a backward look.

"Hey, Sweet Cheeks." Lance snapped his fingers in front of her face. "Have you lost your hearing as well as your memory?"

"I'm sorry—I wasn't listening." Still confused and troubled by Cole's abrupt departure, Remy forced her attention back to the family, looking from one to the other in a vaguely distracted way. "What did you say?"

"It doesn't matter," her father replied, his look gentle with concern. "Marc was right. That long flight has taken its toll on you. We need to get you home so you can rest." He reached in his pocket and took out a set of keys. "Bring the car around, Gabe, so we can get the luggage loaded."

Remy discovered that she was tired, more tired than she had realized. It had been a long day, a confusing day, with too much happening, too many new faces and new names— including her own. And with the fatigue, the dull pounding in her head had returned. There would be time enough to sort through everything tomorrow—after she'd slept.

10

A slowly rising sun burned through the remnants of the dawn fog and gave the air in the Quarter an unusual crystalline quality. But the damp chill remained, and Remy shoved her hands a little deeper into the pockets of her shaped double-breasted blazer of black wool, glad of the sun-gold sweater she wore beneath it and the wool slacks in a black-and-white houndstooth check covering her legs.

She'd awakened at dawn, too restless and edgy to stay in her room until the rest of the house stirred. Her first thought was to wander the house and see if familiar surroundings might arouse some memories, as Dr. Gervais had suggested. She'd roamed the lavender and plum parlor, then gone to the solarium with its cushioned rattan furniture and profusion of potted plants, but an inner tension had made her too impatient to absorb the things around her. And the emptiness of the house and the hollow echo of her footsteps had haunted her.

Finally she'd been driven outside, into the mist-shrouded courtyard, a mist thickened by the steam rising from the heated swimming pool. All the while, the urge to leave—to go—had become stronger and stronger. The compulsion seemed somehow linked to that feeling she had that she was needed somewhere.

At last she'd given in to it and left a note in her room, telling her parents she'd gone for a walk. She'd left the silent, sleeping house and set out, letting the compulsion guide her, hoping it would lead to the recovery of more memories. When the streetcar had come by on St. Charles, she'd climbed aboard and ridden it all the way to Canal, then found herself crossing the street into the French Quarter.

As she wandered down the narrow streets of the Vieux Carré, Remy was conscious of the stillness and quiet of its sleepy abandon. It was too early for the syncopated clop of the carriage horses, too early for the street musicians, the mimes, and the dancers, too early for the artists to hang their canvases on the iron fence around Jackson Square, and too early for last night's Mardi Gras revelers to be up and about. It was as if she had the city all to herself. But no, not quite all to herself, she realized as a man in a T-shirt and shorts lifted aside the curtain of a second-floor window and groggily peered out at the early morning. Then Remy saw a woman's hands slide around his middle and spread across his chest. His mouth curved in a lazy smile as he turned and let the curtain fall. Remy smiled too—a little wistfully, though, made restless again by her own longings, longings intensified by the languor of the street.

Moving on, she let her gaze absorb the old buildings that lined the streets of the Quarter, absently admiring the mellow beauty of their stucco exteriors and the rails of iron lace along their balconies. Yet there was nothing in their facades that hinted at the hidden courtyards within. Was anything ever what it seemed? This was the French Quarter, but the architecture was Spanish.

The soft, melodic notes of a clarinet drifted across the stillness. Remy paused to locate the sound. There on a balcony sat a black man, still wearing his white shirt and black suit from the night before. He had his feet propped up on the cast-iron railing and his chair tipped back on two legs while he played his song to the early-morning sun. There was no wail to it, no lively jazz melody. It was soft and sad and yearning.

And that was New Orleans too, Remy realized. For all the face it showed to the world of wild fun, steaminess, and good times, there was a subtle melancholy behind it. This was the home of jazz, but it was also where the blues had grown up. What was the French phrase? *Les tristes tropiques*.

Remy started walking again, picking up her ambling pace, needing to escape that sweetly pensive clarinet. She no longer wanted the quiet and solitude of the Quarter. There was one place that was never still, no matter the hour, day or night, and Remy headed for it, slipping down the alley between the Cabildo and the St. Louis Cathedral, with its soaring triple spires, and emerging on the cobblestoned street facing Jackson Square, its gates still locked. As she skirted the square and started past the historic Pontalba Apartments, a silver cloud of pigeons erupted in flight, their wings thrashing through the aromas of beignets and freshly brewed Louisiana coffee.

With a cup of the chicory-flavored coffee from the Café du Monde, Remy climbed to the top of the levee and faced the turgid, earth-smelling Mississippi River. The cathedral bells rang the hour and a delivery truck grumbled by on Decatur. Before her curved the crescent-shaped bend of the Mississippi that had long ago given New Orleans the nickname Crescent City.

There was always activity on the river, always something happening, always something moving. Towboats and barges, merchant ships and tankers, pilot boats and paddle wheelers. Traffic on the Mississippi was always two-way, oceangoing vessels gliding slowly along the east bank and off-loading barges hugging the west.

Remy took a sip of her coffee and wrapped both hands around the cup, absorbing the heat through its Styrofoam sides. The smells, the sights, the sounds appealed to her. She saw a tanker riding low in the water, heading downriver, the throb of its engines trailing across the morning to her. From somewhere upriver came the deep-throated blast of a whistle.

As she watched the tanker, suddenly, unexpectedly, something else flashed through her mind, passing so quickly that it took her a full second to realize that the image had been of another tanker wrapped in darkness and fog. It was so fleeting that nothing more than that registered. She stared intently at the tanker moving downriver, willing the image to return, but it didn't.

Impatient, she turned away and began to wander up the levee, drawn by the restlessness of the big river. When she reached the wharf area, Remy kept walking. Then she saw the company insignia, the same one Cole had had on his business card—the letter *C* joined by an *L* at its lower curve—painted on the side of a building. She stopped, faintly stunned. Had her subconscious been directing her to the company wharf all along? Why?

She stared intently at the building, a little weathered-looking, a little dirty, like most of the wharves along the riverfront. She tried, but she couldn't make it seem familiar to her. Was it purely an accident that she'd stumbled onto it? Refusing to accept that possibility, she walked around the long building to the dockside.

A sleek merchant vessel was tied alongside, the tall crane on its deck busy off-loading the cargo from its hold. For a moment Remy stood and absorbed the scene before her—the loud whir of the crane, the rumble of forklifts, the shouts of the deckhands and longshoremen, the lingering odor of diesel fumes, the smell of the river, and a thousand other scents she couldn't identify.

A long, low wolf whistle pierced the air, followed by a coarsely flirtatious "Hey, baby, whatcha doin' tonight?"

Out of the corner of her eye Remy saw the brawny, big-smiling dockworker looking her over. As he turned to make some remark to his buddy, another shorter, slighter man walked up, dressed in a white short-sleeved shirt, with a clipboard in one hand and a shirt pocket full of pens and pencils. He said something to the man who had whistled at her. He spoke too low for Remy to hear, but his tone was definitely angry.

Some memory suddenly flickered, distracting her. She frowned, realizing she'd almost remembered something. But what? She focused her attention again on the ship tied up to the dock, something telling her that the memory was connected to it.

She wasn't aware of the man scurrying over to her until he spoke at her side. "I'm sorry about that, Miss Jardin. That crazy Bosco, he got the head of a duck. He didn't mean no harm. He jus' didn't know who you were."

"It's all right, really."

"You be up early this mornin'. Was there something you be wanting, Miss Jardin?"

This time her ear caught the Cajun accent of his voice, but it helped her not at all. "No. I was just walking." She noticed the company insignia emblazoned on the vessel's smokestack. "This ship, what's it called?"

"She's the *Crescent Lady*, jus' come in."

Something flashed in her mind, but once again it came too quickly and passed too quickly for Remy to grasp it. She strained to recall it, oblivious of the man hovering anxiously beside her. It was something important. She was certain of it.

"Excuse me, Miss Jardin, but I got to be gettin' back to work," he said finally. "If you be needin' anything, you jus' tell one of the boys to fetch Henry for you."

"Thanks." Again she responded automatically, without really hearing what he'd said. There were more flashes, coming in rapid succession now. She stood motionless, trying not to think, letting them happen. She didn't see the man walk away. She didn't notice the looks she received or the subdued voices around her, the talk restricted to the job at hand, the rough camaraderie suppressed by her presence.

One minute, two minutes, five—Remy had no idea how long she stood there staring at the ship. Then a hand gripped her arm and roughly pulled her around.

"What the hell are you doing here?" Cole was furious. When Henry had told him she was out on the dock, he hadn't believed him. "Don't you know better than to walk along the waterfront at this hour?"

Whatever else it might be, New Orleans was a major port city. And like any port area, it attracted its share of unsavory elements. Cole knew that; he'd grown up with it. But she hadn't.

"I've been here before." She stared at him, her eyes moving over his face with a strange, faraway look—as if they were seeing him, yet not seeing him. "You brought me"— she paused, her glance drawn to the vessel lying at dockside—"to see the newest ship in the line, the *Crescent Lady*."

Cole stood perfectly still, saying nothing, recalling that afternoon clearly, vividly—everything from the warmth of the sun on his back to the way a vagrant breeze had played hide-and-seek with the jersey material of her skirt.

"What—no champagne?" Her side glance playfully chided him. "I thought you were bringing me here to christen the newest ship in the fleet. I'm disappointed."

"That ceremony is only observed when a vessel is launched for the first time. The *Lady*'s a year old." He walked her to the gangway, his hand riding on the small of her back, conscious as always of the faint sway of her hips and the natural heat that flowed from her body.

"And I suppose there's some silly superstition against christening her a second time," she said, then released a sigh of mock regret. "I've always wanted to break a bottle of champagne over the bow of a ship."

"You'll have to wait until the company can afford to commission a new ship to fulfill that fantasy."

"How can we even afford this one, considering the dire financial shape you claim we're in?"

Cole ignored her taunt. "The loss of the *Dragon* was a blessing in disguise. When the insurance company paid off on the claim, I used some of that money and raised the rest through conventional sources to buy this ship."

She shot him a quick look. "Then this is what you spent the insurance money on."

"Not all of it."

"I remember my father was upset," she said, unconcerned. "He thought there should be some distribution of dividends."

"That money belongs to the company—not to your family."

She laughed. "You love having power over my family's purse strings, don't you?"

The ship's captain was waiting to welcome them aboard, which checked any response Cole might have made to her assertion—not that he would have denied it. A part of him thoroughly enjoyed the power he exercised. And another part would have gladly traded it for some control over this— *thing*—that had erupted between him and Remy almost three months ago. They'd been seeing each other regularly ever since, meeting two, sometimes three times a week, usually at his apartment, occasionally going out to dinner or some local festival or public concert, or taking in a new exhibit at the museum or a gallery. He never went to any social function with her, flatly rejecting any suggestion of hers that he meet her friends.

Lately, though, they'd kept more and more to his apartment. He'd thought it would help. He'd thought he could handle this . . . affair they were having. He'd thought he could use her, the same way she was using him. But how many times during the day did he have to make himself stop thinking about her? How many times had he sat at his desk, staring at reports and visualizing her slender white body lying beside him, the gold flecks—like rays of sunshine trapped in her hazel eyes—glittering with desire just for him?

Yet none of it would last. He knew that—and that knowledge was his shield.

Cole introduced Remy to the ship's captain, Peder Van der Horn, a ruddy-cheeked Scandinavian with yellow-gray hair. After a brief tour of the vessel—limited mainly to the galley, the officers' quarters, and the bridge, due to the constant activity on deck as the ship was loaded with its first cargo for the company—the captain left them on the deck of the bridge for a few minutes, giving Remy an opportunity to observe the high-speed lifting cranes as they transferred the specially designed containers onto the ship to be stowed in the cellular grid of the below-decks compartments.

Alone with her, he became aware of the silence—if it could be called silence, with the noise of the cranes and the shouts of the longshoremen. He moved to stand beside her at the rail, deliberately focusing his gaze on the activity on the weather deck.

"The *Lady*'s operating costs are going to be substantially lower than those of the *Dragon*, the ship she's replacing. Not only does she require a proportionately smaller crew, which cuts our labor costs, but those containers reduce the risk of pilferage, which decreases the insurance rates. And using containers means she can be unloaded and reloaded in a matter of hours, so less time is spent in port, again lowering the cost of the crew—and she can also make more trips, which adds up to more profit for the company," he said, talking to fill the void between them. "As the captain explained when we were on the bridge, the higher-than-average service speeds she's capable—"

"Enough," Remy broke in, holding up her hands in mock surrender, then laughing and shaking her head. "It's no use, Cole. I'll never be able to tell a container ship from a tanker."

"That isn't exactly something to brag about," he chided, faintly amused.

"That's no brag—it's a fact." She turned her back to the rail and leaned her elbows on it, letting the breeze play through her hair. "Now, if you want to talk about porcelain, that's something else."

Her remark served to remind him that she was porcelain and he was ordinary river clay. Neither fact was he likely to forget, even if she pretended to. His glance strayed to the ferry in the distance, plowing its way across the swirling channel waters to the landing on the opposite bank. Cole turned from the rail to watch it.

"The ferry's making its run to Algiers." He nodded his head in its direction, pointing it out to her, then watching as she turned to look, pushing back the strands of tawny hair that blew across her face. "That's where I grew up—in a ramshackle house off Socrates."

Properly it was called Algiers Point, the origin of its name long ago lost. During French and Spanish rule, slave pens had been built there to hold newly arrived blacks from the West Indies and Africa. Although separated from it by the Mississippi, Algiers was a part of the city of New Orleans, called black Algiers by many, and not because of its origins.

"Some say Algiers is where the blues got their start," Remy said, gazing at the jutting point of land. Then she turned her head and fastened her eyes on him with typical directness. "Have you been there lately? There's some marvelous renovation and restoration work going on. In fact, it's becoming a fashionable place to live."

Cole sensed immediately that that was more than just an idle comment; it had some other overtones in it. "Are you suggesting I could become fashionable?"

"I don't know," she returned lightly, a tiny smile teasing at the corners of her mouth. "Do you think you could be a candidate for renovation and restoration?"

"No."

She laughed. "I didn't think so. And truthfully, I can't imagine you being anything other than what you are. 'Take it or leave it'—that's you." She pushed away from the rail and swung to face him in a lithe, graceful move, then slid her hands up the front of his shirt without any interference from his suit jacket, since he'd left it in the backseat of his car, along with his tie. "And I'm so glad I decided to take you."

He stopped her hands before they crept around his neck. "The question is, where do you plan to take me, Remy? Your family doesn't approve of this—affair—we're having."

The faint smile never left her face, but her fingers stopped their caressing play on his shirt as she withdrew from him and stepped back. "Has someone said something to you about us?"

"No." But he wasn't surprised by that, either. "Your father is in an awkward position. I may be good enough to run the family business, but I'm not good enough for his daughter. I can't pass the blood test—the one that checks the amount of 'blue' blood in a man's veins."

"Why do you keep bringing up this nonsense?"

He saw the anger slowly building in her expression, and ignored it. "Because it's true, whether you want to admit it or not."

"Do you want to know what's true, Cole Buchanan?" It flared hotly then, yellow fire flashing in her eyes. "It's true you were raised in Algiers and I come from the Garden district; you were poor while I had plenty; you struggled to survive, but for me, life was yachts on the lake, summer dances, and Carnival balls; you worked your way through college and I attended an expensive one; you've fought to get where you are, and I haven't! And I say, so what? My God, do you think I judge a man's worth by where he's from or what he was?"

She said it now—with the same heat, the same outrage, remembering it clearly, both the words and the emotions. Hearing her, Cole again felt that surge of feeling breaking through his restraint.

That time, those months ago, she had abruptly turned from him. But he hadn't let her stalk away in anger. He'd caught her arm and spun her around, needing to see her face, needing to see she'd meant it. Then he'd kissed her, there on the dock, amidst the whistling approval of the longshoremen, and her anger had turned to a loving passion.

The urge was in him to replay the rest of the scene to its former conclusion—and the desire was there in her eyes too. But he'd believed her then, he'd believed she was different, he'd believed—and he'd paid the price for it, a price that might still go higher. No, too much had changed, too many things had changed. He wasn't a believer anymore—and, more damning than that, neither was she.

Cole watched the light of desire fade from her eyes, and he never moved, never reached out to keep it there. Maybe he ought to. Maybe she'd forgotten. Maybe she never would remember—except he knew her family would see to it that she did.

The morning breeze blew a lock of hair across her cheek. She brushed it back, breaking eye contact with him in the process. "I remember that moment," she said quietly. "That is what happened, isn't it?"

"Yes." He sounded curt, and he knew it. Trying to cover it, he glanced at his watch. "I have to be at the office in ten minutes. You'd better come with me, and I'll arrange for a taxi to take you home."

Remy shook her head. "I can walk."

"Not at this hour, and not in this area." Taking her arm, he steered her away from the dock. She briefly stiffened in resistance, then abandoned it and let him guide her to his car.

As they drove away from the wharf area, Remy sat silently in the car. When she'd left the house this morning, she'd hoped she might remember something. She had. She'd found another piece of her memory—in many ways a beautiful memory. Yet . . . afterward, she'd had the strongest feeling that she'd lost something. Why? Why did she think that? Why did she feel it?

She stole a glance at Cole. Even in profile, his strong-

featured face wore that same cold and forbidding expression
he'd shown her on the dock. It was as if he hated her—this
same man who'd made love to her so fiercely, so desperately,
so thoroughly, only a day ago. Why had he changed? What
had she done? Or—was it something *he'd* done?

She felt herself tensing, straining to recall, and immediately
tried to make herself relax. Her memory wasn't something
she could command to return, as she'd so painfully learned.

Seeking a diversion, Remy fixed her attention on the business district of New Orleans, rising before her with its can-
yonlike streets running between lofty buildings, an eclectic
collection of architecture, with examples of nineteenth-cen-
tury styles intermingling with the concrete-and-glass towers
of the twentieth century. She waited for Cole to turn on
Poydras Street and enter the heart of it. Instead he made the
jog and turned in to the entrance to the International Trade
Mart.

"What are we doing here?" She directed her bewildered
frown at Cole when he opened the passenger door and offered
a hand to assist her from the car. "I thought you had to be
at your office."

"This is where the corporate offices for the Crescent Line
are located," he replied, waving a hand in the direction of
the thirty-three-story building as she stepped out of the car
without his help.

"I don't remember that." Why? she wondered. "Have
they been here long?"

"Since early in the sixties, shortly after the building was
completed. I understand it was your grandfather's decision
to move the company headquarters here." He took her arm
and guided her toward the entrance. "A smart move, considering that some twenty-eight foreign consulates and trade
offices are located in the Mart, as well as a number of import-
export businesses, barge lines, and other shipping companies."

She would have commented on this rare expression of
approval for something one of her family had done, but she

was still bothered by the discovery that the company offices were in this building. She didn't dispute him, exactly; she just had a vague feeling there was something he wasn't telling her—something she *almost* remembered for herself.

"There's a taxi pulling up now." His hand tightened on her arm.

When he started to steer her toward it, Remy pulled back. "No. I don't want to go home yet. I want to see the offices."

He opened his mouth as if to argue with her, then clamped it shut and swung toward the building.

When they reached the fifteenth floor, she saw the company logo on the door, gold lettering edged in black below it spelling out the name THE CRESCENT LINE. The world map showing the major ports and shipping lanes that dominated one whole wall of the reception area was too typical of a decor associated with shipping. So were the models of racy clipper ships and sleek, modern vessels.

She followed Cole down the wide hall to the executive office area. She responded automatically to his secretary's greeting but didn't pause by her desk when Cole did.

"Have they arrived yet?" Cole asked as Remy wandered restlessly around the outer office, searching for something familiar, trailing a hand over the armrest of the leather sofa, wondering if it was the one Cole had set the framed print on to inspect it for damages, then moving on when it failed to strike any chord in her.

"Not yet, Mr. Buchanan," the painfully slim secretary replied, adding, "I put a stack of letters on your desk that require your signature."

Remy paused in front of the door to his corner office, vaguely aware of Cole's saying, "Miss Jardin will be leaving shortly. Make sure there's a cab waiting downstairs to take her home."

"I'll see to it right away."

Remy's hand reached for the doorknob as she realized it was imperative that she see inside. She turned the brass knob and gave the door a push, letting it swing open. She hesitated, then walked slowly into the room, the heels of her boots sounding loudly on the hardwood floor until they were muffled by the cushion of the thick Tabriz rug.

The morning light coming through the large windows gave a lustrous glow to the paneling, revealing the mahogany's rich patina—a patina that her mind told her couldn't be achieved over a few decades. A century, perhaps, but not mere decades. The wine leather chesterfield and wing-backed chairs in the small sitting area showed the wear of many hands. And the massive kneehole desk was clearly an antique—Sheraton, she thought.

More bewildered than ever, Remy turned and found Cole watching her from just inside the door. "I don't understand. This office is . . . old."

"Yes. Your grandfather moved the company headquarters but kept his office. It was dismantled in sections—floors, walls, and ceiling," he said, thumbing a hand at the coffered mahogany ceiling above them, "and then reassembled here, with allowances made—grudgingly, I'm told—for the Mart's larger windows."

"Subconsciously I must have been remembering how very old this office was—without remembering it had been moved here." She reached down and gave an antique globe a turn in its Chippendale stand, wondering if she'd played with it when she'd come here to see her father as a child.

"If you've satisfied your curiosity, or whatever it was, I have work to do," he stated, abruptly and briskly crossing the room to his desk.

Remy looked up, well aware that he wanted her to leave and doubting that his reason was solely the press of business. "I do have one other question."

"What is it?" There was a hardness in his expression, as if he was setting himself against her, as he'd done at the docks.

"Why did you leave the airport last night without a word to me or anyone else?"

"I have a question for you: why didn't you come after me?"

"I don't have an answer for that."

"And maybe that, in itself, is an answer."

"Maybe it is." As she moved away from the globe, the light from the window glared on a framed picture, obscuring the subject and drawing her attention to it. In her mind's eye she had a fleeting glimpse of a silver-haired man, stiffly posed in a boxy jacket with wide lapels. "Grand-père." She immediately identified the brief image. "Is that his portrait?"

Without waiting for Cole to confirm it, Remy walked over to see for herself. She stared in surprise at the somewhat dashing figure in oil, dressed in a black frock coat and a silver brocade vest. His hair, far from being silver, was a deep, dark shade of red, cut fairly short, just covering the top of his ears and parted slightly off-center—the only hint of anything even slightly tamed about him. His eyes gleamed with laughter, and a smile lifted the corners of his mustache and creased his deeply tanned cheeks. The whole impression was one of a strong, vigorous man who relished challenge regardless of the odds.

"Who's the man in the portrait? Is this painting one of yours?" The instant the words were out, Remy turned with a start, paling slightly. "I've asked you that before, haven't I?" He nodded that she had, then waited, as if to see what else she remembered. But it was all blank after that. "What did you tell me when I asked?"

"It's a portrait of the company's founder. I found it buried under a hundred years of dust in one of the company's warehouses along the waterfront."

She took another look at the painting. "How strange. He doesn't look like a Jardin at all."

"That's because he isn't a Jardin," Cole stated.

"What? That's impossible. A Jardin has always been the owner of the Crescent Line."

"Not always. Certainly not in the beginning. That man— Brodie Donovan—started the Crescent Line."

"Donovan." Inwardly she wanted to reject everything Cole said, certain that he had to be wrong. But she couldn't remember. Was he right? Was this another piece of information about her family trapped behind that wall of blankness?

"By rights, Remy," Cole went on, "your name should be Donovan, not Jardin."

"What are you talking about?" she demanded, thoroughly confused.

He started to answer, then glanced at the connecting door to the outer office and paused for a fraction of an instant, smiling without warmth. "Maybe you should ask your uncle to explain."

Remy swung toward the door that had been left open. Marc Jardin stood with one foot inside the office, his dark eyes narrowed at the portrait, his mouth compressed in a tight line of displeasure. Then the look was gone, wiped away without a trace, a bland smile in its place.

"This is a surprise, Remy." He walked across the rug to her.

"Uncle Marc. Good morning." She was certain he'd overheard the statements—the assertions—Cole had just made about their family, yet he seemed to be deliberately ignoring them. Why? Did his silence mean they were true? Or was Brodie Donovan a subject he didn't wish to discuss in front of Cole? Some little voice inside her head said, *Family secrets should stay just that*. She obeyed the dictum and followed his lead, explaining instead, "I went for a walk this morning and . . . this is where I ended up."

"What brings you to the office so early, Marc?" Cole inquired with a faintly aloof indifference. "At this hour you're usually huddled with your buddies at the coffee shop of the Hotel Pontchartrain, aren't you?"

"Usually," her uncle admitted. "But with the meeting this morning—"

"There is a meeting scheduled for this morning. But what does that have to do with you?" There was a forbidding coldness in Cole's expression, which seemed to cause the temperature in the room to drop several degrees.

"I felt I should be here," Marc Jardin replied, his smile becoming a little forced around the edges.

"Why?"

A redness began to creep up her uncle's neck. "Why?" He laughed, a little self-consciously. "I am an officer of the company, Cole, as well as a director and major stockholder."

"So you are," Cole agreed. "But I think you've forgotten that *I* do the talking for the company now. And your presence isn't required."

"I see," her uncle murmured, a stiffness—a rigidity—in his expression and his stance.

Realizing there was no way he could make the graceful exit that his pride desired, Remy spoke up quickly. "If you aren't needed here, could I persuade you to give me a ride home, Uncle Marc?"

He turned, a flicker of gratitude showing in his dark eyes. "It would be my pleasure, Remy." He offered her his arm in mock courtliness. Remy took it and walked out of the office at his side.

11

Ensconced in the passenger seat of her uncle's gray Mercedes, Remy listened to the soothing sound of his voice as he drove along St. Charles Avenue, en route to her home. As he had from the moment they'd left Cole's office, Marc Jardin talked about his son and daughters and their children, telling her about the recent parades and festivities his grandchildren had attended and recounting amusing incidents concerning their reactions to them. Remy smiled at the appropriate times, but her attention drifted, her glance straying out the window to observe the morning brightness along the avenue—seeing it now without the darkness that had shadowed it the night before and without the swirling fog that had layered it in the early dawn hours of this morning.

Reminders of the current Carnival season were visible all along the popular parade route, brightly colored beads—the "throws" from the floats—winking at her from the branches of the majestic oaks lining the street, and plastic cups—the ever-popular "go-cups" that held revelers' favorite spirits—lying almost hidden beneath the azalea bushes planted the length of the neutral ground, their tightly budded blooms nearing the day when the median strip would burst into its pink glory.

And here and there Remy caught a glimpse of the official Rex flag of the elite Carnival club flying in front of a stately home in the Garden district, safe behind elaborate wrought-iron fences and guarded by towering magnolias. Seeing the insignias, she recalled that by tradition, only former rulers of Mardi Gras—the ex-Rexes and their queens—were allowed the privilege of displaying the purple, green, and gold flags in front of their homes. Purple for justice, green for faith, and gold for power, of course.

But the trappings of Carnival made her wonder all the more why Marc Jardin was deliberately steering their conversation away from any discussion of what had transpired in Cole's office. Why wasn't he telling her who Brodie Donovan was? She remembered the way he'd glared at the portrait, and she was certain he'd overheard Cole assert that this Donovan man had founded the Crescent Line. Yet he'd said nothing about it, and given her no opening to ask him. By the same token, she hadn't forced the issue. Why was she reluctant to question him?

The opportunity to correct her self-imposed silence was lost as her uncle announced, "Here we are," and swung the Mercedes between two narrow wrought-iron columns, the scrolled gates of the mansion's former carriage entrance standing open to admit them. "It must be good to be home again after the ordeal you've been through."

"If you had said that to me two days ago, in Nice, I probably would have agreed with you," Remy replied as he parked the car in front of the old carriage house, which had been converted into a four-car garage. "Now I have a feeling that the ordeal has barely begun."

Saying nothing to that, he let a silence fall between them, a silence that seemed even more pronounced after the stream of banal conversation he'd maintained during the drive here, and it convinced Remy that her statement might be more accurate than she'd realized.

When they walked into the mansion through a side entrance, she was immediately greeted by an array of tantalizing aromas. Her uncle paused and inhaled deeply in exaggerated appreciation. "Smells like that Nattie has been baking up a storm already this morning."

"It's about time you got back here." At the end of the hall stood a tall, spare black woman, wearing a businesslike white apron tied firmly around a black uniform. Her hair was cut close to her head at the sides, then allowed to pouf in a mass of pepper-gray curls on top of her head, a cut that was both stylish and practical and that showed her high cheekbones to their best advantage. Her dark eyes narrowed on Remy. "It seems to me that knock on your head took away more than your memory. It took some good sense along with it—going off for a walk before it gets light."

"You must be Nattie." Remy walked toward the woman, waiting for the sight to spark some memory.

"Considering I'm the only black woman in this house, I don't see how you could mistake me for anyone else."

Remy laughed in surprise. "Are you always this blunt?"

"If I am, I got it from you." The quickness of her retort led Remy to believe this conversation might be typical of past exchanges.

"Where's—" Marc began.

"Mr. Frazier and Miss Sibylle's in the solarium having their morning coffee," Nattie interrupted, anticipating his question.

"I'll let them know you're home," he said to Remy, then set off, striding briskly toward the white-wood-and-glass room.

"They did find the note I left, didn't they?" Remy wondered, belatedly.

"I found it," Nattie replied, "when they had me take a tray of morning coffee up to your room. Right away your momma started worrying that if you'd lost your memory, how were you going to know where you lived to find your way back?"

"I promise you I could have."

"Try convincing her of that," Nattie countered, shaking her head in a gesture of exasperation.

Despite the familiar way the black woman spoke to her, Remy noticed that she hadn't once asked her where she'd gone or why she'd left or what she'd done. She remembered that Cole had said she regarded Nattie as practically one of the family, but obviously not to the extent that she felt she had to account to the woman for her comings and goings— and it was equally obvious that Nattie didn't expect her to.

Suddenly Nattie reached up and curved a pink-palmed hand against Remy's cheek. "I'm glad you're home. I was worried about you," she declared, a little too brusquely, then quickly drew away her hand. "I don't know why I'm standing around here talking to you when I've got work to do. Go tell your momma and papa breakfast will be on the table in twenty minutes. And ask Mr. Marc if he'll be staying."

"I will," Remy promised, but Nattie hadn't waited for a response as she started for the kitchen.

Smiling, Remy turned and moved off in the direction her uncle had taken earlier. Without Nattie's presence to distract her, she found her thoughts immediately swinging back to replay the morning's events—with Cole and with her uncle. As she approached the sun-filled solarium, she heard voices and automatically slowed her steps.

"It never occurred to me that Buchanan would shut you out of the meeting," came her father's voice, its muttering tone underscored with both irritation and worry. "This complicates things."

"That's a mild way of putting it," her uncle replied. "Now we'll have to look for some other way to find out what this so-called proof is that the insurance company claims to have. Until we know that, we can't be sure which will be the best way to proceed."

"Why don't you arrange to meet privately with the representatives from the insurance company—somewhere away from the office?" The suggestion came from Gabe. "Use the meeting as a means to express the family's concern about their allegations.''

"However valid that reason is, at this stage, Gabe, I don't think it would be wise," Marc Jardin stated. "It could suggest to them that we think there might be some truth to their charges. We could lose a valuable negotiating edge that way."

"Truthfully," her father inserted, "I'm more concerned that the insurance company may carry out its threat to make this whole business about the *Dragon* public. A scandal like that would be extremely damaging."

"I wouldn't worry about that, Dad. You can bet the insurance company wants to avoid that as much as we do. But Marc's right. Before we can take any action, we have to find out what kind of case they have—if any."

"And Buchanan knows it," her father muttered. "That man is so damned cunning."

Remy used the pulsebeat of silence that followed to cross the last few feet to the solarium's open glass doors.

"Good morning." She felt the layer of tension in the room, a tension not betrayed in the smiles of its occupants—her father seated in a cushioned rattan chair, her mother at the serving cart stirring cream into a coffee cup, Gabe at the many-paned windows leaning a shoulder against the white framework, and her uncle, Marc Jardin, standing in the room's center, as if he'd halted in the act of pacing the room. "I'm supposed to inform you that breakfast will be on the table in twenty minutes—and to ask if you'll be joining us, Uncle Marc."

For an instant Remy was struck by the realization that although she recognized who each of them was, she didn't recognize any of them. They were family, yet they were still strangers—people she didn't remember. That was true even of Gabe and her mother. The childhood memories she'd recalled about her brother didn't tell her any more about the man he'd become than the fleeting image she'd remembered of her mother in the rose garden told her about what kind of woman she was. Unconsciously Remy tilted her chin a little higher and mentally tried to shake off the disturbing thoughts.

"I'm afraid I won't be able to stay for breakfast this morning—as much as I would like to indulge in some of Nattie's delicious blueberry muffins. I need to get back to the office." Marc Jardin set his cup and saucer on the serving cart.

Remy spoke up quickly to forestall his departure. "Before I came in, I overheard you talking—something about some allegations the insurance company is making against the shipping line? What's that all about?" As she glanced at each of them, she caught the quick looks they exchanged. "Is it something I'm not supposed to know about?"

"It doesn't matter if you know, Remy," her uncle declared, his smile gentle in its reproof. "They're simply taking issue with a claim we've made. You know how insurance companies are. You pay their outrageous premiums, and then when you file a major claim on a policy, they go through all the fine print to find a way to avoid paying up. Which is precisely what they're doing in this case."

Remy frowned. "But you made it sound so serious—"

"Aaah, Remy." Her uncle sighed a laugh and curved an arm around her shoulder, giving her an affectionate squeeze. "Business is always *very* serious," he declared in an exaggeratedly sober tone, then looked at her father. "Frazier, do you remember when we decided it was time to change the company logo for the Crescent Line? We agonized and worried over that for more than a month."

"Gracious, yes," Sibylle Jardin inserted as she crossed the room to give Gabe the cup of coffee with cream. "The way they carried on and argued, you would have thought the fate of the world hung on their decision."

"See what I mean?" her uncle said, then gave her shoulder a pat and released her. "I've got to be going." Lending action to his words, he walked to the doorway and paused in the opening to look back. "I'll call you as soon as I know something, Frazier."

"Right."

Remy watched him leave, wondering whether the situation with the insurance company was as forthright as he'd made it sound, or if this was the trouble she had sensed. But how could it be? She took no active part in the operations of the shipping company; both Cole and Gabe had made that very clear. Therefore, she wouldn't be needed—not in the vital sense she felt—even if the shipping line were truly experiencing a crisis. It must be something else.

"Would you like some coffee, Remy?"

Remy turned from the now empty doorway. "Please," she said in acceptance, then observed the way her mother lightly pressed a hand on her husband's shoulder as she passed his chair—and the way he reached up and absently patted it— an exchange that spoke of affection given and returned, of a bond apparently strengthened by thirty-five years of marriage.

It made her wonder if she'd observed such exchanges before—or if she'd taken them for granted.

She watched her mother pour coffee from the silver pot into a china cup, noticing the delicate look to her hands, the medium length of her clear-polished nails, and the half-moons at the base of them. The blue veins standing out along the backs of her hands were the only indication of age, their presence betraying an otherwise youthful appearance.

Lifting her glance, Remy saw that it was the same with her mother's face—the initial impression was one of youth, and only a closer look revealed the faintly crepey quality of the skin around the eyes and mouth. Yet none of it detracted from the quiet elegance, the aura of studied grace about her. Or from the inner strength Remy sensed she had—not the "steel magnolia" kind, but something gentler, warmer. She wondered what her relationship with this woman had been like. Had Sibylle Jardin been a role model for her? Had they been close? Somehow Remy couldn't imagine confiding her deepest secrets to the woman, but—she couldn't imagine quarreling with her, either.

As for her father, her relationship with Frazier Jardin was an even bigger mystery, since she remembered absolutely nothing about him. She glanced his way again, seeking some feature, some characteristic, some mannerism that might spark a memory, no matter how small. But there was nothing, nothing but the sight of his face, drawn in sober, thought-filled lines, the darkness of his eyes all shadowed with concern—or was it fear?

"Your coffee, Remy."

Distracted by the prompting statement, she looked away and took the cup and saucer Sibylle Jardin handed her. When she glanced back at her father, he had tipped his head down, and she was even less certain whether what she had detected in his eyes was fear or merely deep worry.

"Do you mind if we all adjourn to the dining room?" Gabe asked, pushing away from the window frame with a shove of his shoulder. "If we stay in here, I don't think I'll be able to resist the temptation to stretch out on that sofa and catch up on some of the sleep I lost flying halfway around the world and back."

"Tired, are you?" Remy smiled at him in sympathy, seeing the shadows, the puffiness around his eyes.

"Tired?" He raised an eyebrow, questioning her choice of words. "I feel like I need toothpicks to prop my eyelids open."

"Don't do it," she advised in mock seriousness. "It would definitely hurt."

"What's a little pain when you're numb with fatigue anyway?" he countered, walking over to her and draping an arm around her shoulders, leaning his weight on her. "I don't suppose I could persuade you to carry me to the dining room, could I?"

"As heavy as you are, I'd collapse before we made it to the door."

"I was afraid you'd say that." He straightened slightly but kept his arm around her, drawing her along with him as he set off for the dining room, followed by their parents. "Tell me, where did you get the energy to go for a walk so early this morning?"

"Easy. I was already halfway around the world; therefore all I had to do was fly back." It was a nonsensical exchange, yet Remy was conscious of how naturally she slipped into it with him. And that ease suggested a closeness between them that had transcended childhood.

"I wish I'd thought of that. Which shows you how tired I am," he said with a mock grimace of dismay. "So—exactly where did you go on this walk of yours?"

"I caught the streetcar and rode to Canal, then strolled through the Quarter. You'd be surprised how peaceful and quiet it is at that hour," she continued. "After that I stopped by the Café du Monde for coffee, then wandered along the riverfront for a while and suddenly found myself at the company wharf."

"The wharf." Beneath the shock in her father's voice, there was censure. "That area is no place for a decent young woman to be walking alone in."

"That was Cole's reaction when he found me there," Remy admitted as she turned into the dining room, a study in orchid and soft, cool blues. The long walnut table held place settings for four, the richness of the wood gleaming beneath the light from the bronze doré chandelier overhead, a twin to the one in the main salon. On the marble top of the French Empire serving table sat a tall crystal pitcher full of freshly squeezed orange juice, along with four glasses. Remy slipped free of Gabe's draping arm and crossed to the serving table with its mirrored base—a "petticoat" table. "Actually Cole put it a bit more bluntly—something like, 'What the hell are you doing here?' "

"I wondered how you came to be with Buchanan this morning." Her father sat down at the head of the table.

"That's how." Setting her cup and saucer down on the marble top, she picked up the juice pitcher and filled two glasses, one for herself and one for her waiting brother. "Afterward he insisted that I ride to the office with him and take a taxi home from there.'' She gave Gabe his glass, then picked up her cup and went over to sit down. ''But when we—''

''No, not there, Remy,'' her mother admonished when she started to pull out a chair. ''That's where Gabe always sits.''

She let go of the carved chair back as if the wood had become hot to the touch. She was stunned to discover how awkward and uncomfortable she suddenly felt. Another scene from another time sprang into her mind, a scene when she was seven or eight years old, a scene where her mother had informed her that she couldn't sit there—''That is Gabe's place''—a scene where she had childishly stomped her foot and protested, ''But he always gets to sit next to Daddy.''

Remy stared at the chair she'd almost sat in—the chair next to her father—and murmured, ''I didn't remember.''

''You can sit there, Remy.'' Gabe motioned her back to the chair. ''I don't mind.''

''No, I don't think so.'' She knew she'd be uncomfortable sitting there now. Instead she pulled out another chair, down the table from his. ''I'd rather sit here.''

''If you say so.'' He shrugged and sat down in his customary place.

Her father picked up the conversation as if the interlude over the chairs had never occurred. ''It's curious that you weren't able to find a taxi at the Trade Mart. Usually there are several around in the morning.''

''There were this morning, too,'' Remy admitted. ''But I wanted to see the company offices.''

''Why?'' He gave her a startled look, his hand halting in the midst of reaching for the glass of orange juice Sibylle had set in front of him.

Rather than attempt to explain the vague feelings that had prompted her visit to the offices of the family's shipping line, Remy said instead, ''Curiosity, mainly. I wanted to see if I would remember it.''

''And did you?'' Gabe asked.

''As a matter of fact, I remembered the portrait of Grand-père that always hung on that one wall," she replied, just as the connecting door between the dining room and kitchen swung open and Nattie walked through, a tray balanced on her upraised palm. Frazier Jardin set his juice glass down again and leaned back in his chair, a smile lifting his somber features.

"Ahh, breakfast at last," he declared lightly. "It smells wonderful, Nattie."

"Of course it does," she retorted, and put a plate in front of him, laden with the morning's fare of eggs Benedict topped by lemony bright hollandaise sauce and garnished with fresh strawberries, raspberries, pineapple, and colorful kiwi. "Whatever I make always smells good and tastes better. You know that, Mr. Frazier."

"My waistline reminds me when I forget," he replied drolly.

Nattie chuckled and continued on to serve his wife.

"By the way," Remy said as she unfolded her napkin onto her lap, "would someone mind telling me who Brodie Donovan is? Cole claimed he started the Crescent Line. Is that true?"

Her father stiffened instantly, resentment and anger in every line of his face. "In the strictest definition, I suppose he did." He sliced off a portion of his eggs Benedict. "The man was a war profiteer who made a fortune running the blockade during the War Between the States. He smuggled in satins and silks, whiskey and wines, and endless other luxuries, selling them for high dollar at a time when the South was begging for medical supplies and drugs, food for the table, and blankets to keep its people warm. The ships, the company name, may have been his in the beginning, but it was a Jardin who made the Crescent Line a respected shipping company," he concluded forcefully, and Nattie made a scornful, disbelieving sound in her throat. Frazier immediately fired a look at her. "Is something wrong, Nattie?"

"Not with me." She set Remy's plate in front of her, then calmly met his gaze. "Is something wrong with you?"

He glared at her for an instant, then Gabe spoke up. "Wasn't it Balzac who said that all great fortunes have been founded on a crime?"

Frazier Jardin turned his sharp look on Gabe as Nattie returned to the kitchen with her empty tray. "That is not amusing, Gabe."

"Sorry." He immediately lowered his head in a show of contrition, secretly directing a quick, smiling glance at Remy.

"All that's in the past, and better left there—regardless of how Buchanan chooses to look at it," Frazier stated curtly.

"Yes, but—" Remy began, wanting to ask him why Cole had said her surname should be Donovan instead of Jardin.

"It's the present we need to discuss," her father interrupted. "Specifically your amnesia, Remy, and what we need to do about it."

"Do about it," she repeated in startled confusion. "What do you mean?"

"When I learned about your condition, I called Dr. John—"

"Who's Dr. John?" The name meant nothing to her.

"Dr. John Lucius Sebastian has been the physician for the Jardin family for years. He took care of your grand-père in his final years and delivered you into this world," he explained patiently. "Even if you can't remember, I'm sure you can appreciate that he's developed a personal interest in you—a fondness for you—over these many years. Naturally he was disturbed to learn about your amnesia. Your mother and I talked with him at length about what could be done. He recommended a clinic located outside of Houston. Their staff has had considerable experience treating cases such as yours."

"Dr. John said it was very beautiful there," Sibylle Jardin inserted. "It's one of those secluded, sylvan settings, peaceful and quiet. Every . . . *guest* . . . has a private cottage on the grounds, complete with maid service and your own private chef if you wish. It's almost like a resort, really."

"Are you suggesting I should go there?" Remy looked

from one to the other, not wanting to believe what she was hearing.

"Dr. John assured us that its facilities and its staff are the best to be found anywhere. He knows we wouldn't want anything less for you." Her father calmly carved off another bite of the rich egg dish. "I thought we could fly you over tomorrow. They have their own landing strip—"

"No." Her quick and angry denunciation of his plans sounded unnecessarily loud even to her own ears.

"'No'? What do you mean?" He seemed stunned by her objection.

"I mean—I'm not going," she replied in a more controlled but no less firm voice.

"But why?" he protested. "You can get the kind of care and treatment you need there. The whole purpose is for you to regain your memory. Surely you want that as much as we do."

"Of course I do."

"Well, they can help you accomplish that, Remy."

"They can't," she argued. "The kind of amnesia I have can't be treated with drugs or psychiatric therapy or hypnosis. Believe me, I inquired about every possibility while I was in that hospital in Nice, trying desperately to find out who I was. Unfortunately my amnesia is caused by brain trauma— the kind that requires time to heal. The specialist was very definite on that point."

"I'm not prepared to accept that," Frazier said. "I think we should have a second opinion. After all, who was this specialist you saw? What were his credentials? How can you be certain he's kept up with all the latest medical advances?"

"I checked." She stabbed at a bite of Canadian bacon drenched in the congealing hollandaise sauce, feeling inexplicably angry and unsure—but at what? At her parents? Why? Weren't they merely acting out of concern for her? Or were they attempting to control her life? Had they done that in the past? Was that what she was subconsciously reacting to?

"If your amnesia is something that requires time to heal, then surely the clinic would provide an ideal setting," her mother suggested. "There you can rest and relax, have an opportunity to recuperate free of any stress."

"I can do that here, Mother," she insisted, then laid down her fork. "Why are you two so anxious to get rid of me? I haven't even been home twenty-four hours yet."

"We're anxious for you to get your memory back, Remy," her mother declared, a pained look in her expression. "It isn't that we don't want you here. We do. But we're trying to think not of ourselves, but of what's best for you."

"The best place for me is right here." Again she was overwhelmed by the feeling that she *had* to be here; it was vital. Just for an instant she wondered whether, if it wasn't for this feeling, she might have let them persuade her to go to the clinic. "I've started remembering things—Gabe, you, Grand-père's portrait. Dr. Gervais told me that familiar surroundings might revive memories for me. What better place than here, in the house I've lived in practically all of my life?"

"I have to agree with Remy." Gabe spoke up for the first time. "If she's starting to remember things, she should stay here with us. Hopefully we can help her to remember more."

"Perhaps," Frazier conceded, indicating a definite coolness toward the idea. "Personally, I'm still not convinced the clinic isn't the best place for her."

"I—" As Remy started to reassert her position, Gabe laid a silencing hand on her arm.

"Let me argue your case. I'm your brother the lawyer, remember?" He winked and gave her arm a reassuring squeeze. Grateful for his support, Remy smiled back and held her silence as he turned to their father. "What time is your committee meeting this morning, Dad?"

"Ten o'clock. Why?"

"I was thinking you could ride downtown with me. It would give us a chance to talk over Remy's situation."

"We've already talked it over."

"So?" Gabe shrugged. "We'll talk it over again. But let's not argue about it now and ruin a perfectly delicious breakfast."

"All right," Frazier Jardin agreed, albeit grudgingly.

No further mention was made about the clinic for the rest of the meal, yet the issue hung in the air with Damoclean insistence. However well-intentioned her parents might be in wanting her to go there, Remy knew she couldn't—and wouldn't. She couldn't leave New Orleans, not until she remembered why it was so important for her to be here.

12

Soon after Nattie cleared the breakfast plates, Gabe and Frazier Jardin left the dining room together. A few minutes later Remy heard the sound of a car pulling out of the driveway. She took a sip of her coffee, conscious of the silence that had fallen between her and her mother, and of her own odd reluctance to break it.

"Remy," Sibylle began in a hesitant yet momentous tone, "I don't want you to misunderstand about the clinic."

"I'm not going, Mother, and that's final."

"But we only want you to go because we truly believe it's for your own good."

She sighed, regretting her initial abruptness. "Thanks for caring, but—"

"Gracious, Remy," her mother broke in with a soft, breathy laugh. "You don't have to thank us for caring. We're your parents. We love you."

"I know." She wished she could remember feeling a similar closeness to them. She wished she could remember this house—this room.

Automatically she looked around it, seeking something

familiar in its furnishings. Her glance fell on the footed Sèvres bowl on the serving table, ornately gilded and adorned with a view of the gardens of Versailles, all on a background of royal blue. Intuitively Remy knew that the piece was from the very early 1800s, the golden age of topographical porcelains. And she knew, too, that the footed bowl had long been a family heirloom.

"Did I ever determine whether that bowl was an individual piece or part of a service?" She sensed that the question was one that she would have been lured to investigate.

"You always believed it was part of a service, but I don't recall whether you were ever able to find another piece sufficiently like it in style and design to prove it," her mother replied. "Two or three years ago, however, you were able to locate the source material for the engraving on the bowl. In fact, you obtained a copy of the original painting. It's somewhere about, I'm sure." She lowered her cup to its nesting place on the china saucer and tipped her head curiously to one side. "Why? Have you remembered something?"

She shook her head. "Only that it's been in the family for years."

Sibylle started to respond to that, then stopped. "I almost forgot. Paula called for you this morning. She'd heard you were back and wanted you to come to a little dinner party she's having tonight. Isn't it amazing how fast news travels in this town?"

"Who's Paula?" Remy tried, but she couldn't make the name seem familiar to her.

"Paula Michels. Well, she was a Michels before she married Daryl Gaylord. The two of you have been the dearest of friends since childhood. Actually there were three of you—you and Paula and Jenny D'Anton."

She shook her head in defeat. "I can't remember either of them."

"I'm sure you will . . . in time."

"Yes," Remy murmured, silently wondering how much time it was going to take. "Am I supposed to call Paula back?"

"It isn't necessary. When she told me about the party, I went ahead and made your excuses. I—I hope you don't mind."

"No, that's fine."

"I thought you'd want to spend tonight here at home with us." Something outside the window caught Sibylle's eye. "The florist's van just drove in. I hope the flowers are better than the ones he sent last week. The daisies drooped terribly, and the petals of the day lilies were turning brown around the edges. Unfortunately I was out of the house when the delivery man came, or I never would have accepted them. It was nearly six when I returned home, and by then it was too late to do anything about it. And the Girards and the D'Antons were due to arrive for dinner in less than two hours. At seven o'clock, there I was, trimming the brown off the lilies and wrapping wire around the drooping stems of the daisies, trying to salvage something so we would have a few fresh bouquets in the house. Worse than that, the roses didn't last three days. I warned Robert that if this week's flowers weren't absolutely exceptional, I was returning them en masse and taking our business elsewhere." She removed the linen napkin from her lap and laid it beside her coffee cup and saucer. "Excuse me while I inspect today's delivery."

"Of course." Remy watched her leave the room. With her own coffee finished, she had no desire to linger at the table by herself. Leaving the dining room, she drifted aimlessly across the wide central hall into the main salon.

For all the subtle grandness and the touches of antiquity in the high-ceilinged room, it had a comfortable, lived-in quality. Magazines cluttered the Louis Napoleon console, and a lap robe of white cashmere lay carelessly draped over the back of a Victorian sofa covered in a vibrant plum brocade and flanked by matching chairs. Next to the tufted easy chair, upholstered in a cream velvet material with a thin purple stripe running through it, stood her mother's petit-point frame, and beside it her tapestry sewing bag.

A walnut whatnot desk sat in the corner by a window. Remy wandered over to it and idly ran her hand over the top, wondering if she'd sat here to do her schoolwork, and stared out the full-length window instead. Briefly she touched the pale orchid sheers, then smiled when she noticed the puddling of the orchid damask draperies on the floor—a typical yet subtle display of wealth in the old plantation days, and a tradition that had once more become fashionable. Turning, she looked again at the room, noting the black marble fireplace and the Oriental rug on the floor, its strong tones repeating the richness of color in the room.

How many hours had she spent in this room? Hundreds, no doubt. Yet nothing in it stirred up memories.

Suppressing a sigh at the continued blankness, Remy crossed to the entrance hall, which was dominated by the graceful curve of the grand mahogany staircase. Her glance strayed upward to the ornate frieze that outlined the ceiling and the elaborate plumed medallion from which the bronze doré chandelier was suspended. The walls were covered with a scenic wallpaper, its blue panorama a replica of a historical design made famous by Dufour. A Brussels carpet stretched the length of the hall's cypress flooring.

Something flickered along the edges of her mind, and she closed her eyes. The image she saw was the same one before her now—except that boughs of shiny green magnolia leaves were wound around the stairs' carved balustrade. She heard the echoes of giggles and saw herself scampering down the steps, trying to reach the bottom ahead of Gabe. Papa Noël. Yes—as a very little girl, she had called Santa Claus by his French name.

From the mists of that memory came another, of the Carnival season of her debutante year, when she'd glided down the steps in her ball gown, a stunning creation in white satin and lace studded with shimmering beadwork and rhinestones—and another time in a different ball gown, adorned with snowy aigrettes and pearls. To her mother's glorious delight, Remy had been named Queen of two balls, an honor so rare as to be almost without precedent—and an indication of the power and prestige attached to the Jardin name.

Frowning, Remy tried to recall what her feelings had been toward it all. Had she enjoyed the whole social whirl of parties, suppers, and balls, or had she participated grudgingly, regarding the entire business of being presented to "society" as outdated in today's liberated world? Neither one—she'd seen it as a duty, and her acceptance of that duty as a recognition of her family . . . just as her failure to be accorded honors would have been a reflection on them.

"Certain things are expected of you because you are a Jardin." She heard the words in her mind, but she couldn't remember who had spoken them. Yet they stayed there, softly ringing, subtly applying a pressure that she felt even now.

Remy opened her eyes, breaking the spell. And the entrance hall became once again merely the entrance hall of a mansion, faintly haunted by long-ago memories. She hesitated a moment longer, then walked across the Brussels carpet, past the base of the staircase, to the double set of doors opening onto the gentlemen's study.

Pausing a few feet inside the room, Remy let the rich loden green of the walls close around her. A pair of freestanding walnut bookcases flanked the fireplace, again made of black Carrara marble artfully streaked with gray. Near the windows stood a library table of dark ebony and tooled black leather. The deep colors, the heavy solidity of the furniture, and the leather-covered sofa and chairs gave the room a definite masculine aura that appealed to her.

She wandered over to an old platform rocker, covered in dark green leather and studded with brass. On the ebony side table next to it was a well-thumbed copy of Virgil's *Aeneid*.

She ran her hand lightly over its worn cover, then caught the faint, fragrant aroma of tobacco, and her glance was drawn to the walnut pipe stand next to the book.

Images flashed through her mind like pictures caught by the shutter of a rapidly clicking camera. She tried to focus on the images and hold on to this rush of memory merging with the background. Suddenly she could see her father relaxing in the rocker, not a single strand of his dark, curly hair out of place. His somber features wore a smile of pride and approval as he reached out to take something from her.

The pipe. Unerringly Remy picked up an old briar pipe, its stem half chewed, its charred bowl scraped clean of tobacco ash and char. Beside it sat a sterling-silver tamper with his initials etched on it—the one she'd given him for Christmas when she was twelve years old. Remy looked down at the rocker, remembering, hearing the texture of her father's voice, warm with praise and affection. The love in it filled her—just as it had done all those years ago.

Her mother walked into the study, carrying a Baccarat vase filled with a spray of white tulips, their ivory color accented by lacy green fronds of maidenhair fern and delicate baby's breath. Seeing Remy, she faltered slightly in surprise.

"You startled me. I didn't realize anyone was in here." She went over to the library table and placed the vase on one corner of the tooled leather top. "Aren't these white tulips magnificent? Robert sent them as a gesture of atonement for last week's floral fiasco. I thought they'd look perfect in here, and I know your father will enjoy them."

"I remember him, Mother." She was too caught up in the wonder of the memory to care about the bouquet of rare white tulips. "I remember Dad." No longer was he a stranger to her, a face without significance, a name without personal meaning. "He used to let me fill his pipe with tobacco—and he showed me how to pack it so it would draw properly. He wouldn't let anyone else do it but me—because I was the only one who could do it right." She gazed at the pipe in her hand, conscious of the lump in her throat, a lump that came with the discovery of how much she loved him, how much she adored him. Before, she hadn't been sure what her feelings for him had been—if they'd been close. Had he cared? Or had Gabe, his son, been the recipient of all his attention? Now she knew. "This is his favorite pipe," she remembered.

"Yes . . . unfortunately. I've been wanting to throw that smelly thing away for years, but Frazier won't hear of it. Why? I'll never know. It isn't as if he doesn't have others," Sibylle declared, waving a hand at the numerous pipes in the walnut rack.

"You don't know how relieved I am," Remy confessed. "It's bothered me that I couldn't remember him."

Sibylle smiled gently in understanding. "It's bothered him too . . . as I'm sure you guessed. He was very worried about you, Remy. And he felt guilty that we'd left Nice assuming you'd gone off on your own for a few days—as you'd planned to do. When we finally realized something was wrong, he kept insisting over and over that we should have known you wouldn't have left the yacht without telling us good-bye."

"He shouldn't have blamed himself for that."

"I know, but he did. And it only added to an already stressful situation. He let it work on him. For that matter, he still is." She fussed with the floral arrangement, adjusting a tulip stem here and moving a frond there. "I'm certain that's why he was so sharp with you at breakfast."

"You mean when I argued with him about going to the clinic," Remy guessed.

Sibylle threw a startled look over her shoulder, then quickly tried to cover it with a hasty, "Yes, that too."

Remy knew immediately that she had guessed wrong. "You were referring to when I asked about Brodie Donovan, weren't you?"

After a brief hesitation, Sibylle admitted, "Actually, I was." She turned back to the flowers. "I do wish you hadn't asked your father about him—although it wasn't really your fault. That Cole Buchanan's responsible for resurrecting that whole thing. He had no right to take your grand-père's portrait down and put that other one in its place. It may be a terrible thing to say, Remy, but I hope you never remember any part of the attachment you once had for him. I was so afraid you were going to do something foolish—" She let the rest of the sentence hang unfinished.

"Like marry him?" Remy suggested, suddenly realizing that Sibylle Jardin would find it impossible to approve of a man with Cole's background.

Her mother turned from the vase of tulips. "Remy, is it so wrong for me to want to see you safely married to a good man?"

Remy had the feeling "acceptable" should have been parenthetically inserted after "good." "Mother, I could never marry *safely*," she protested with a faint laugh.

"Security is not something to be scoffed at. Marriage comes with no assurance of happiness, Remy. For a woman it's always better to love wisely."

"Is that what you did, Mother?" She found herself becoming angry.

"I am devoted to your father, and he to me. We have had thirty-five wonderful years together," she replied in quick defense. "And a great part of that is due to the many things we share in common—the same backgrounds, the same set of friends—"

"The same views on what and who is acceptable," Remy inserted. "Forgive me, but I find this conversation disgusting."

She turned on her heel and started from the room. But before she had taken three steps, her mother was there, catching her arm.

"Remy, I'm sorry. I truly didn't mean to offend you with the things I said," she declared, looking genuinely contrite. "I may have sounded like a snob, but I've seen what happens when two people from vastly different backgrounds marry. I've seen the embarrassment, the gaucherie, the stiltedness at social gatherings, and the valiant attempts to bridge the two levels. Soon it doesn't matter how exciting the marriage may be in the bedroom. In reality, the bedroom makes up only a small portion of a marriage. If it can't survive outside the bedroom, ultimately it won't survive at all. That's why I'm glad you didn't make a disastrous mistake with that Buchanan man. Do you understand?''

Remy nodded, slowly, a little stiffly. "I understand."

"I hope so." She curved her hand along Remy's cheek. "I know you're finished with him, and I'm sorry I brought up his name."

She was finished with him. Everyone was saying that, including Cole. Yet this morning on the dock, when she'd seen that container ship and recalled their previous visit to it, she'd remembered how completely she had loved him and how furious she'd been at his insinuations that his background was somehow a barrier between them. And she'd remembered, too, how his mouth had come down on hers in a claiming kiss. Even now she could feel the sensation of its lingering heat.

Afterward, when he'd lifted his head and she'd seen his dazzling smile, she'd forcefully declared, "I love you, Cole Buchanan. Nothing and no one will ever change that."

But something *had* changed it. And that part of her memory was blank.

"You look tired, Remy. It's to be expected, though, considering you were up and about before the sun," Sibylle chided gently, and she tucked a hand under Remy's arm, guiding her toward the hall. "Why don't you lie down awhile and get some rest?"

"Maybe I will." But Remy wasn't sure it was fatigue she was feeling as she let Sibylle walk her from the study to the entrance hall.

Her mother stopped at the base of the curved staircase. "You do that, and I'll go take care of my flowers. The house will be brimming with them when you come down—the way I wanted it to be when you came home."

Remy watched her move off in the direction of the solarium, then turned and climbed the winding steps to the second-floor hall. The door to her bedroom stood open. As Remy approached it, she heard someone moving around inside, humming an old jazz tune and injecting a lyric here and there. She immediately recognized Nattie's voice and smiled, entering the room as the woman proclaimed in song, " 'I got Elgin movements in my hips with twenty years' guarantee.' "

"Only twenty years?" Remy teased as Nattie reached for the remaining pillow lying at the head of the antique tester bed. "That's a shame."

Nattie shot a startled look at her, then straightened up and moved her hands onto her hips. "Have you come up here to lie down?" she challenged. "Because if you have, there's no sense in me making up this bed."

Remy glanced at the bed, all its covers thrown back and its feather pillows piled on the floor. She couldn't imagine herself doing anything but tossing and turning in it, regardless of what she'd thought when she came up here.

"No, I think I'll shower and change into something else," she replied, and she began unbuttoning her double-breasted jacket of black wool. Nattie leaned across the mattress again to pull the last pillow off the bed. "Do you do all the housework too, Nattie?"

"Me? Clean this big house?" Nattie shook and punched the plumpness back into the pillow, then tossed it on the floor with the others. "There wouldn't be enough time in the day. No, you've got dailies that come in twice a week to do all the cleaning and washing. Me, I make the beds, cook the meals, and keep things tidy."

"I wondered." Shrugging out of her blazer, Remy walked to the closet, crossing the Aubusson rug, patterned in the room's soft greens and golds. She opened the door and walked into the large closet. As she took down a shaped coat hanger, she looked around the closet and frowned. "I thought these old homes didn't have closets."

"That used to be an alcove. Back in your grand-père's day, his daddy boxed it in and made it a closet." Nattie's answer was accompanied by the sound of the top sheet being whipped over the mattress.

Remy fitted the jacket onto the hanger, fastening a button and hanging it on the rack with other tops. "How long have you worked for the family, Nattie?" she asked when she emerged from the closet.

"Come the third of November, it'll be twenty years." She smoothed the top sheet and deftly turned its hem back in a precise crease.

"The third of November. Is it so memorable that you know the exact date?" She walked over to the bed and leaned a shoulder against one of the carved mahogany posts at the foot of it.

"I know because I went to work for your family two days after I lost my restaurant, and that was on All Saints' Day." She said it very matter-of-factly, yet her long fingers hesitated in their edging of the sheet.

"You had a restaurant." Remy wondered if she'd known that.

"For six months I did. It was a fine place, too. I called it Natalie's—'course I gave my name the French pronunciation. I thought it would make a better impression on folks." She paused a moment, her expression taking on a faraway look, and then she laughed, and the laugh had a self-deprecating ring. "Why, when I opened those doors, I thought in no time at all folks would be saying Natalie's in the same breath with Antoine's and Brennan's. Which shows what big ideas I had."

"What happened?"

"I went broke, that's what happened. All that schooling I had in France in haute cuisine, all those years working in the kitchens of those other fine restaurants doing prep work when I knew I was better than those men chefs, all my dreams"—she lifted her shoulders in a shrug that Remy knew couldn't be as indifferent as it appeared—"gone."

"Why?" she protested, experiencing some of the hurt Nattie must have felt.

"It goes back to that same old thing—you put a man in a kitchen and people call him a chef; you put a woman in a kitchen and she's a cook. And when you put a black woman in a kitchen, people expect her to cook soul food. They want to see neck bones, gizzards, oxtails, and dirty rice on the menu, not potage of cauliflower with caviar, roast duck in port sauce, or feuillet of squab. There I was, broke, in debt up to my ears, with a nine-year-old girl to raise. My grandma had worked for your grand-père for nearly forty years. She got me this job here, and here's where I've been ever since."

"I'm sorry, Nattie."

Again she shrugged, pulling the quilted comforter over the sheets. "That's the way it goes sometimes."

Remy shook her head in vague bewilderment. "How can you sound so casual about it? You have to be disappointed, hurt, angry, bitter—something."

"I feel all those things and a few more," Nattie admitted. "I just don't show it like you do. People who are born poor and raised poor don't. It's been bred out of us, probably because there's too many things that can break our hearts. Having crying jags, throwing tantrums, getting all blue and low, that's for wealthy people who can afford it."

Remy immediately thought of Cole, remembering that steel control he had over his feelings—so much control that she'd wondered if he felt anything deeply. Maybe Nattie had just given her the answer to that as well as to his cynicism.

Thinking of Cole reminded her of the things he'd said about Brodie Donovan—and Nattie's reaction to the explanation her father had given. "At the breakfast table, when my father was talking about Brodie Donovan, I had the feeling you didn't believe him."

"I didn't." She took the pillows from the floor and piled them two deep at the head of the bed.

"Why?"

"Because that's not the way it was."

Remy frowned at her. "How do you know?"

Nattie looked at her and smiled sagely. "The folks who come into this house through the front door, they see the big white pillars, the mahogany staircase, and the crystal prisms dangling from the chandelier. But the folks who come in the back door, they know where the dirt is."

Unable to contest such a keen observance, Remy instead asked, "But why would my father tell me something that wasn't true?"

"Probably a case of wishful thinking." She flipped the quilted coverlet over the pillows and tucked the edge behind them. "Sometimes you want a thing to be so, and you wind up pretending it is. A lot of families rewrite their history that way. Look at what happened back when New Orleans was struggling to become a town and the men were wanting women to marry them. The French government sent eighty-eight over here, all of them inmates from La Salpetriere. Correction girls, they called them. Then, seven years later, in seventeen twenty-eight, the government started sending girls picked from middle-class families, who had some house-wifely skills. They were known as casket girls because of these little chests filled with their clothes and such that they brought with them. And today you'd be surprised how many fine old Creole families can trace their ancestry to one of them casket girls. But all of them correction girls must have been sterile—not one of them has any descendants. Amazing, isn't it?"

"Very," Remy agreed, smiling, then she became serious once more. "Tell me what you know about Brodie Donovan, Nattie. Who was he? Did he start the Crescent Line? How did the Jardins acquire it from him?"

"Let's see. . . ." Nattie picked up a throw pillow covered in the same pastel yellow-and-green floral print as the coverlet, and paused as if gathering her thoughts. "I don't know how much you can remember about New Orleans' history, or whether that's been lost along with the rest of your memory, but back in the early part of the eighteen-thirties, shortly after the four-mile-long Pontchartrain Railroad between the city and the lake was built, some businessmen from the city's new American section decided to dig a canal through the swamps so the melon schooners and other ships from Mobile could have a shortcut to the Mississippi River. Raising the money for the six-mile-long canal wasn't a problem, but finding the labor to dig it was. They couldn't use slaves, for a couple of reasons. You see, by then it was against the law to bring Negroes from Africa into the country to be used as slaves, which meant they'd have to buy slaves that were already here. Considering that they needed thousands for the job, that was too expensive—especially because they knew a lot of the slaves would likely die from working in the swamp.''

"Why would they die?"

"Well, think how miserable the working conditions were back then—the sweltering heat, thigh-deep mud, and swarming insects, not to mention the snakes and gators. And don't forget, yellow fever was the scourge of Louisiana in those days,'' Nattie reminded her. "It wasn't until after the turn of the century that they discovered that mosquitoes carried the disease. Before that, most people thought yellow fever was caused by 'effluvia' from marshy grounds like swamps.

"Anyway, they decided black slaves were too valuable to work in such a place,'' she continued. "So the next-best thing was to import laborers from Ireland. It wasn't long before ship after ship started arriving in New Orleans, crowded with Irish workers.

"Brodie Donovan was fifteen when he got here in eighteen thirty-five along with his father and three of his brothers. Like most of the Irish, they went to work digging the canal. Within a year he lost a brother to yellow fever and his father to cholera. In the seven years it took to build the canal, thousands died from cholera and yellow-fever epidemics. For a time there were so many bodies they just tossed them in wheelbarrows and dumped them in graves dug along the banks of the canal.'' Nattie paused a moment to reflect. "It's kind of ironic when you think about it, but the prevailing attitude back then was, who cared if an Irishman died? There was always another waiting to take his place.

"Brodie Donovan was an old man of twenty by the time that New Basin Canal was finally finished. He and his brothers went to work on the wharves. According to my grandma"—Nattie laid the pillow on the bed, propping it against the headboard—"Brodie Donovan first dreamed of owning his own ship during the voyage from Liverpool to New Orleans. That may be true, but I figure it stayed only a dream until he went to work on the riverfront."

A faint musing smile edged her mouth, and her eyes took on a faraway look. "The riverfront of old New Orleans must have been a sight to see back in those days. 'The master street of the world,' they called it then. Vessels of every size and kind—clipper ships, ocean schooners, river packets, cutters, steamboats, smacks, flatboats—they lined the levee for four and five miles, tied two and three deep sometimes. I think Brodie Donovan saw the steamboats arriving, with every available inch mounded with cotton bales, and he talked with rivermen, heard them tell about all the bales waiting upriver for transport to New Orleans and beyond. He saw, and he heard, and—he turned his dream into a plan.

"After about a year on the riverfront, he and his brothers left New Orleans and went upriver to Bayou Sara. There they got a contract from a local planter to clear a section of wooded land he owned; their payment was the timber from it. They used that timber to build themselves a flatboat. Then they loaded it with cotton and floated down the Mississippi to New Orleans, where they sold their cargo and the flatboat. They went right back upriver and did it all over again. After just three trips, they bought an old steamboat. Two years later they bought another, then two more each year after that. Finally, in eighteen forty-seven, Brodie got his first ocean-going ship—a schooner. And that was the start of the Crescent Line."

"It sounds like the American dream," Remy declared.

"It was." Nattie nodded in emphasis. "After a couple of voyages with his schooner, he sold off his riverboats and bought more ships, bringing his total to four within a year. A remarkable feat when you consider that less than fifteen years before that he'd been wading in mud digging a canal."

"But how did the Jardin family get the shipping line? And why did Cole tell me my surname should be Donovan, not Jardin?"

"That's because of Adrienne."

"Who's Adrienne?"

"Adrienne Louise Marie Jardin," Nattie replied. "She was one of those dark-haired, dark-eyed Creole beauties people like to write stories about. Both her parents died when she was a baby—victims of a yellow-fever epidemic. Adrienne and her older brother, Dominique, were raised by their grand-père Emil Gaspard Jardin and a maiden aunt they called Tante ZeeZee.

"Now, you gotta understand there've been Jardins in New Orleans almost from the beginning, back in seventeen eighteen. By the time Brodie Donovan met up with the Jardins, they owned a lot—real estate in the city, bank stock, a cotton plantation in Feliciana Parish, and a couple of sugar plantations south of Baton Rouge, just to name some of the larger things."

"In other words, they were wealthy," Remy inserted.

Nattie snorted. "Hmmph, they were one of the wealthiest Creole families in the city."

"You said Brodie Donovan met up with the Jardins. When was this?"

"He met *Adrienne*," Nattie corrected. "The year was eighteen hundred and fifty-two. . . ."

13

L ike a forest of barren timber, the high, proud masts of
the ocean steamers and sailing ships lined the levee,
towering against the blue sky, the gray canvas of their
sails tightly furled. Their decks and gangplanks seethed with
activity, stevedores scurrying back and forth, darky roustabouts shuffling, their bodies canted sideways by the weight
of the cargo carried on their shoulders, sea captains pacing
in impatience, more roustabouts rolling bales of cotton up
the staging and into the holds, press gangs forcing more bales
into the ships with their powerful cotton screws, and sailors
in the garb of a dozen different nations sauntering ashore or
staggering back on board. And the noise, the endless, deaf-
ening noise, a cacophony of shouts and curses, hooting laughter and challenging brag, "coonjine" songs and work-gang
chanteys, clanging bells and deep-throated steam whistles.

And the wind carried it all, a wind heavy with the ultrasweet
odor of molasses and pungent with spices, a wind that stirred
up floating wisps of cotton from the mountainous piles of
bales stacked on the levee, dotting the air with them.

From the vantage of the levee, Brodie·Donovan viewed it

all—its jostle, its din, its smells, and its energy familiar to him, more familiar than his own home. He raised a hand in a saluting wave to the captain on the deck of the *Crescent Glory,* then turned his back to the scene and adjusted his hold on the small, flat bundle he carried in his left hand.

Directly ahead of him stretched the tightly packed buildings and narrow streets of the city's old French section, still the bastion of aristocratic Creole families. Canal Street—so named for the ditch, actually a kind of moat (but never a canal), that had once run its length, when New Orleans was a walled city—was the unofficial dividing line that separated the old quarter from the brash and bustling American section, now the city's commercial center. The offices for his shipping company, the Crescent Line, were located in the American section, and most days he would have turned and headed up the levee in that direction. But not today. Today he had an errand in the Vieux Carré.

Striding easily, he went down the levee's sloping bank, past the tin-roofed shanties stocked with cheap trinkets for the sailors, past the grog-shops with their many eager customers, and past the oyster stands. The street beyond was clogged with freight wagons, the river commerce turning New Orleans into a city of drays pulled by mules in tandem.

As Brodie picked his way between them to the other side, he recognized some of the drivers and called easy greetings to them, lapsing into a heavy brogue. "Hey, O'Shaughnessy, why would you be holding your head like that? Was it too much to drink you had last night?" "Micheleen, tell your pretty missus I'll be stopping by for some of her scones— when you're not home, of course!" "Is that a black eye you got there, Dolan? Did you forget to duck again?"

And they responded in kind: "Well, if it ain't himself— or should we be calling you Your Honor now?" "Would you look at the vest he's wearing? 'Tis fancy he's getting." "What would you be carrying in that package, Donovan? Lace kerchiefs for to be blowing your nose with, maybe."

There was affection in their gibes, affection and pride for

one of their own who'd made good—and hadn't forgotten them. Like Brodie, the Irish draymen were survivors of the bloody ditch, as they called the canal.

He may have been one of them, but he wasn't like them. And the difference lay in more than the fineness of the black frock coat and brocade vest he wore, or the flat-crowned black hat on his head and the gleaming leather of his boots. The difference had been there even when he was dressed as shabbily as they.

True, Brodie felt the same strong loyalty to his own that they did, and had his moments of dark moodiness, though they were rare. He loved a good laugh and his temper could be quick. And like them he was fiercely independent, but that need for independence had directed him on a different path and turned his thinking in other directions.

Sure, he'd slogged through the ditch's muck and mire beside them, smelled the foul stench of the swamp and the rotting corpses along its banks, and fallen into his cot at night bathed in his own sweat. But never once in that swamp had he thought of Ireland's green valleys and sparkling brooks— not like they had. For him, the thought that had kept him going, that had given purpose to the sweat and weariness and death around him, was the dream that someday *his* ships would steam through the canal he'd dug . . . ships like the one he'd sailed on to America. He'd dreamed it, and the riverfront had shown him how he could make it happen. A roundabout way, to be sure—first flatboats, then riverboats, and finally his ships. But he'd learned that there was always a way, even if it wasn't a direct one.

Leaving the bedlam of the riverfront behind, Brodie entered the old quarter, his glance straying to the new triple spires of the St. Louis Cathedral, which replaced the old bell towers, changing the area's skyline—a change made even more pronounced by the recently added mansard roofs of the Cabildo and the Presbytère and the twin three-story, redbrick and wrought-iron structures built in the Renaissance style by the red-haired Baroness Pontalba, housing magnificent apartments in its upper floors. Brodie doubted they would be the last changes the old Place d'Armes would see. There was currently a lot of talk about changing its name to Jackson Square in honor of the hero of the Battle of New Orleans. It would happen. Americans now held the majority of seats on the city council, and they'd see that it did—the Creoles be damned.

Two more strides and his view of the spires was lost, buildings rising up on either side of the narrow street, their facades smoothly stuccoed and painted in mellow shades of peach or blue or pink, all of them dominated by their tall double-storied galleries, supported by iron posts set in the curb and edged by waist-high railings of delicate iron filigree in a dozen different designs. Brodie walked beneath the over-hanging galleries, shaded from the sun, which gave a spring-like warmth to the morning in place of winter's usual gray damp.

Drays rumbled and rattled over the dirt streets, occasionally sharing the muddy thoroughfare with fancy carriages pulled by high-stepping blooded horses in gleaming harnesses. Directly ahead, a white overseer with a whip supervised the rare cleaning of the street's cypress-lined drainage ditches by a gang of chained and collared slaves—runaways, most likely.

Brodie continued along the brick sidewalk—a banquette, the Creoles called it—past neat little shops and slave pens with heavily barred windows, past corner fruit stands and flower stalls, past travelers ogling the sights of the renowned city, past young, richly dressed sons of aristocratic Creole families, perhaps en route to fencing lessons with some of the many masters who ran schools on Exchange Street, or merely off to share a cup of coffee with friends, and past an ivory-skinned and incredibly beautiful mulattress—a *femme de couleur,* a free woman of color, her status declared by the brightly colored madras kerchief wrapped around her head like a turban, her eyes properly downcast, her satins and jewels closeted in her little house along the ramparts to await the pleasure of her white lover. Brodie touched a hand to the brim of his hat and nodded a *Bonjour* to a young Creole miss and her glaring chaperone, noting the quickly averted glance and smiling to himself at the hastily whispered *"Yanqui."*

To the Creoles of Louisiana, all Americans, regardless of their origin, fell into two categories: the unlettered, uncouth, and hell-roaring river crowd were all *"Kaintucks,"* and the rest—the merchants, the planters, the wealthy, and the scholars—were *"Yanquis."* To the first, the Creoles turned an icy shoulder, but as for the second—well, time, the overwhelming numbers of Yankees, and, most of all, economic circumstances had forced them to develop a tolerance of them. They did business with the Yankees, drank coffee with them, and attended the same social functions, but rarely was a Yankee invited to dine in their home. True, marriages between Yankees and Creoles had taken place, but Brodie had observed that in most cases such marriages were largely to the benefit of the Creole family, the union either bringing with it desired holdings or cementing a liaison of particular interests.

The Americans and the Creoles represented two totally different cultures. After nearly fifty years, they'd learned to coexist—warily at times, occasionally clashing, but always competing, however subtly.

Unlike most of his counterparts in the American section, Brodie had taken the time to learn the Creoles' language, though he often found it to his advantage to pretend he neither spoke nor understood it—at least not as well as he did. And he'd learned to control his impatience and not press for a decision on some business matter, instead allowing the conversation to follow leisurely lines before finally arriving at the subject—if it did at all. As a result, a good share of his business came from the Quarter, and several valuable contacts in Europe as well. Yes, he did a lot of business in the Quarter, but not all of it with aristocrats.

On the corner a blind Negro played his violin, his curly gray hair bared to the sun, his slouch hat turned upside down on the brick banquette in front of him, and a pair of black-lensed spectacles partially concealing the heavy scarring around his eyes. Brodie stopped and dropped a dollar into his hat.

"Merci." The old man bobbed his head the instant he heard the clink of the silver coin against the smaller ones.

"How goes it with you, Cado?" Brodie interrupted, addressing the old free Negro in French.

There was a quick cocking of the old man's head at the sound of his voice. *"Michie Donovan,"* he said in immediate recognition of the voice, addressing him by the Negro's gumbo contraction for *Monsieur* as he continued to saw the bow over the strings, never once missing a note. "Old Cado is fine, suh, especially today with the sun warming my old, tired bones."

"Is there any talk going around?"

"There's a lot of weeping and praying at the Gautier house on Royal. The young Michie Gautier, he took offense at some little thing said by a planter from upriver. They met at dusk under the oaks. Now blood bubbles from the young Michie's wound where the planter's rapier pierced his chest."

"A punctured lung," Brodie murmured, then asked, "Is there nothing else?"

A small grin appeared. "Michie Varnier from the Julian plantation lost fifty thousand last night in a game of brag. I think he'd sell his cotton cheap today."

Brodie allowed a faint smile to curve his mouth. "You play beautiful music, Cado." And he dropped two more dollars into the old man's hat.

"So do you, Michie Donovan. So do you." The old black man chuckled and immediately launched into a few bars of an Irish jig tune as Brodie moved away.

At the curb, Brodie waited for two heavy drays to clatter by, then stepped into the muddy street and hailed the next one. The driver hauled back on the reins and called a whoa to his mules, cussing them out in a fine Gaelic voice as Brodie climbed onto the running board and balanced himself there, tucking the bundle he carried tightly under his arm and taking a pencil and notepaper from inside his coat pocket.

"Would you swing by the Crescent Line office for me, Flannery, and give this message to my brother Sean?" He hastily scratched it on the paper, folded it, and handed it to the drayman, ignoring angry shouts and raised fists from the drivers of other wagons that had been forced to halt as well.

"Sure I'll be doing it for you, but it's a whiskey you'll owe me, Brodie Donovan," the red-headed Flannery declared as Brodie hopped down.

"Get it in Sean's hands in ten minutes and 'tis a bottle I'll buy you—and not tell your wife."

"'Tis a deal you've got, and I'll be holding you to it." He cracked the whip above the long ears of the mule team and slapped the reins on their rumps, urging them forward with shouts and curses and hollering at the wagons ahead of him to "Make way!"

Dodging the freight wagons that quickly filled Flannery's breach, Brodie crossed to the other side of the street and walked down two doors to the millinery shop of Madame Rideaux, where a small sign in the window promised the latest in styles from Paris. The fulfillment of that promise was wrapped in the bundle under his arm—the most current fashion plates from France, only two weeks old, courtesy of his ship the *Crescent Glory*.

He stepped inside and closed the door behind him, then started toward the rear of the shop, automatically scanning the front area for the henna-haired proprietress who wavered so insecurely between the unctuous smiles of a shopkeeper and the haughty airs of a customer. His eye was first caught by the shimmer of velvet the deep, rich color of garnet. It drew his glance to a young woman clad in a velvet walking dress, her back turned to him as she tried on hats in front of a freestanding counter mirror. Brodie noticed two things simultaneously: the small span of her waist, accented by the wide circle the skirt made, and the jet-black of her hair, in lieu of the typical dark-brown color of most Creole women's tresses. Obviously she had some Spanish blood mixed in somewhere.

In the next stride, Brodie saw her reflection in the mirror and halted abruptly, stopped by a sharp kick of feeling that momentarily stunned him. There was a perfection to her oval features that he could only liken to that of a cameo, her expression serenely composed yet possessing a subtle vibrancy that gave immediate life to her face. He stared, knowing he had to find out who she was but unwilling to move from this spot, for the moment content to gaze at her.

Suppressing a sigh of dissatisfaction, Adrienne Jardin laid the bonnet aside and picked up a dress cap of pearl-colored silk, trimmed with a wreath of velvet leaves, flowers, and ribbons. She slipped it on, first letting the ribbons hang, then tying them in a loose bow. As she turned her head slightly to view her side reflection, she saw another face in the mirror—a man's face. For the briefest of seconds her eyes locked with his in the mirror. A small crease appeared between his dark eyebrows, his glance flicking to the bonnet, as he gave a faint shake of his head in disapproval.

Adrienne immediately broke eye contact with him and fixed her gaze on her own reflection, stiffening in annoyance at the man's boldness, his rudeness. No doubt he was a Yankee. Did he think his opinion of the bonnet mattered to her?

To make matters worse, she discovered she didn't like the bonnet, either. She kept it on a little longer, playing with the ribbons, tucking a dark curl in here and rearranging another there, trying to make it clear, when she finally did take it off and lay it aside, that her decision hadn't been influenced by his reaction to it. All the while, she pretended to take no notice of his reflection in the mirror, acting as if her peripheral vision hadn't observed his wide and slanted brow, the slight break in his otherwise straight nose, his well-formed chin, which neither jutted nor receded, his high, broad cheekbones, and his sharply angled jaws—or the deep mahogany red of his hair beneath his black hat, and the dark brown of his

eyes. Honesty forced her to concede that he was handsome
—in that rough, raw way Yankees usually were.

As she picked up a white silk bonnet trimmed with satin
roses and white lace, Adrienne wondered what he was doing
in Madame Simone's shop. She remembered hearing the shop
door open, but she had no idea whether he had entered alone
or with another. Had he accompanied his wife, perhaps? Or
his sister? Or his demimondaine? The last seemed most likely.
There was a picaresque quality about him that would prompt
him to appear in public with such a woman.

Discreetly Adrienne scanned the interior of the shop, turning her head this way and that as if inspecting all angles of
the silk bonnet on her head, while bringing every corner of
the room into view. But *non,* there was only Tante ZeeZee
at the counter with a patient clerk, engaged in what was, for
her, an agonizing decision over which pair of gloves to purchase. As if gloves would help her appearance, Adrienne
thought with a sudden twinge of pity for the woman who had
raised her. Poor Tante ZeeZee had inherited Grand-père's very
prominent nose, a feature that on him looked most noble, but
on her . . . Adrienne understood why her aunt had acquired
such an inordinate fondness for the jade-green absinthe.

She looked again at her own reflection, discovering that
she was back to her original question: what was the Yankee
doing in Madame Simone's shop—alone? Had he business
with the proprietress? But of what kind? He was too well
dressed to be a tradesman, and he hadn't asked after the
woman, who had been called to the rear of the shop to handle
some minor emergency in the cutting room.

With rising curiosity, Adrienne let her glance stray again
to his reflection. Again eye contact was made, and again she
saw the faint frown and slight shake of his head, rejecting
the latest bonnet. And yet again, Adrienne pretended to take
no notice of him. She recognized that it would be a simple
matter to move to another mirror, but that would be an admission that she was aware of his attentions, and she didn't

want to give him the satisfaction of knowing she was in any way affected by his presence. It was always best to ignore these Yankees.

Yet sheer perversity prompted her to try on a singularly unattractive bonnet with an extra brim, reminiscent of a calash and appropriately called an "ugly." The mirror showed that it was all of that and more. She allowed the barest trace of a smile to touch her lips as she darted a quick look at the Yankee. His eyes were downcast, as if he were hiding the humor in them, while his mouth twitched with a smile, bringing into play a pair of very attractive creases in his cheeks. Again there was a shake of his head, but this time it seemed to be more an expression of amusement.

Hiding her own smile, Adrienne removed the bonnet and picked up a hat that had appealed to her earlier, of a somewhat sophisticated style, with a black lace demi-veil spilling from the brim, the effect slightly dramatic. She tried it on and liked it immediately. She felt certain that even the Yankee would approve of this choice. But when she stole a glance at his reflection to observe his reaction, he wasn't there!

Startled, Adrienne threw a quick look over her shoulder to the place where he'd been standing, but he'd disappeared. The instant she realized what she was doing, she squared around again to face the mirror, stunned by the strange disappointment she felt. A second later she was doubly stunned to see him standing before her, next to the mirror. She was extremely conscious of the quick, small beats her heart struck—from the shock of finding him there, of course. There could be no other cause.

"The hat is very attractive." He spoke in French, his accent definitely American and his voice deep-pitched. "Unfortunately it hides your eyes. And I'm certain you've been told before that you have very beautiful eyes, black-shining like the sea on a moonless night."

She made no response. Frankly, Brodie would have been surprised if she had. Well-bred Creole misses didn't address strangers, and she was unquestionably well-bred. But it wasn't necessary that she speak to him; she had a very expressive face, and what it didn't tell him, her actions did.

She had regained her composure with remarkable swiftness after initially stiffening in surprise at finding him so near. There'd been no betraying blush of discomfort, no hint of alarm in her eyes. More than that, there'd been no indignant walking away. She'd stayed—out of pique? Out of pride? Out of curiosity? Brodie didn't particularly care what her reason was. She was there, and she was listening—however much she might be coolly pretending not to be.

The hat with the veil was exchanged for a white straw bergère with a wide, soft brim, a wreath of flowers encircling its flat crown and pink satin ribbons dangling at the sides. Instead of turning her into a picture of virginal innocence, the hat made her look even more alluring, yet . . . there was nothing of the coquette about her.

This time Brodie made himself shake his head in rejection. "I admit the brim would protect your face from the sun, but it would also force a man to keep his distance. I wouldn't want you to be wearing it if you were on my arm."

Again his remark was met with silence. She removed the straw hat and replaced it with a bonnet that had plumes of white ostrich feathers sweeping down its sides. Brodie frowned in exaggerated disapproval.

"*That* would be guaranteed to tickle a man's nose and turn any whispered word into a sneeze."

The corners of her mouth deepened with the faintest suggestion of a smile, the only outward indication that his observation had amused her. Brodie didn't need any other.

When she removed the bonnet, she automatically lifted a hand and smoothed any disturbed strands of hair into place, the action drawing his gaze to the black sleekness of her hair, parted in the center and drawn back into a small knot near the back of her neck.

"In all honesty, mam'selle, your hair should never be hidden beneath a hat or bonnet. It is its own adornment, a midnight curtain gleaming with starshine," he declared softly when she reached for another bonnet. "Covering such beauty should be a sin."

Calmly she slipped her own velvet bonnet onto her head, its rich garnet color matching her walking dress. Without once looking at him, she began to secure the trailing ribbons beneath her chin with a small posy of artificial flowers.

Madame Simone emerged from the rear of the shop, took one look at Brodie, and rushed over, her expression running the gamut from horror and fury to panic and outrage. "I regret the delay, Mademoiselle," she blurted. "If this gentleman has been bothering you in my absence—"

"On the contrary, Madame Simone," she spoke at last— in flawless English, her voice round and soft and reserved. She could, Brodie thought, handle men as she pleased. "I believe it is I who have been bothering him." Brodie smiled and resisted the urge to throw back his head and laugh at this very astute and provocative observation. She had indeed been bothering him . . . in the most stimulating way. "If you will excuse me, Madame, I believe my aunt has completed her purchase."

With a graceful turn, she glided away from them. Madame Simone started after her, but Brodie caught her arm. "Introduce me."

"Nom de Dieu, you do not realize—" she whispered in frantic protest.

"Introduce me," he repeated in the same low undertone, then held up the bundle he was carrying. "Introduce me, or these drawings will end up in the muddy bottom of the Mississippi instead of in your back room. And for your information, the *Sea Star* was damaged in a storm during her crossing and limped into Havana. She'll be a week being repaired. Which means it will be more than a week before your competitor, the modiste Madame Trussard, receives *her* copies of the latest fashions."

"A week," she breathed in excitement.

"Introduce me."

She straightened, the chance of stealing a week on her

competition overcoming any reservations she had about the wisdom of granting his request. Turning, she fixed a smile on her face and walked with him over to the young woman and her chaperone, a woman of indeterminate age whose face bore no family resemblance at all to her charge's.

"Monsieur Donovan, allow me to present Madame Jardin and her niece, Mademoiselle Adrienne Jardin," the proprietress declared, then completed the reverse introductions. "Mesdames, this is M'sieu Brodie Donovan. He is the owner of the shipping company the Crescent Line."

Madame Jardin gave him a baleful look. "You are a *Yanqui*."

"Regrettably, yes. It was a tragic circumstance of birth over which I had no control. I hope you will not hold it against me, Madame, Mademoiselle." He inclined his head to each of them in turn and caught the amused, and approving, smile that curved the lips of Adrienne Jardin—and the dark glow in her eyes that revealed definite interest.

"A pleasure, Monsieur Donovan." She nodded her head, acknowledging the formal introduction.

"Yes, a pleasure, m'sieu," her aunt repeated with little conviction. "Now we must say adieu."

"Not adieu . . . *au revoir*. We will see each other again," Brodie stated, looking straight at Adrienne Jardin when he said it and realizing that his patience would be sorely tested by the careful manners and correct ways of doing things dictated by Creole society. He watched her leave the shop with her aunt, then turned to the proprietress. "Jardin. Where have I heard that name?"

"It is Emil Gaspard Jardin's name, you know. It is whispered that he owns half of the Vieux Carré and a half dozen plantations on the river. Adrienne is his granddaughter," she replied, and held out her hand. "You obtained your introduction—for all the good it will do you. I will take my package now."

Brodie gave it to her. "What makes you think it will do me no good?"

"You heard the old crow of an aunt," she said, tearing at the brown paper around the fashion plates. "You are a *Yanqui*. And Emil Jardin clings to the old attitude toward *Americains*."

"We'll see." He knew there was a way around him. There were always ways.

Leaving Madame Simone to her intense perusal of the drawings, Brodie exited the shop and paused on the banquette to gaze after the departing figure in garnet. The strains of Cado's violin came to him. He turned and crossed the street to the blind fiddler's corner.

"Emil Jardin, Cado—where does he live?"

"You want to know about him?" Startled, the old man missed a note.

"I want to know about his granddaughter Adrienne, everything you can find out. Does she assist in the marketing? If so, when? Is there a regular hour? The theater, the opera, where does she usually sit? What invitations has she accepted? What balls and masquerades will she be attending? I want specific dates and times."

"But such details—"

"The house servants will know them, and house servants can be encouraged to talk." This time he didn't drop coins into Cado's hat. Instead he slipped some folded bills into the pocket of the old man's coat.

14

Nattie moved away from the bed and picked up the satin robe Remy had tossed over the arm of the love-seat earlier that morning. "I'm sure it won't be any surprise to hear that Brodie Donovan got detailed information about Adrienne's daily activities and plans." She carried the robe to the closet and hung it on a padded hanger on the back of the door. "And during those next two weeks, he *arranged* for their paths to cross several times. Twice he was at the pillared arcade of the old French Market when she went there with her aunt to do the day's shopping. He attended Sunday mass at the St. Louis Cathedral, where her family worshiped. When he found out she had a fitting at Madame Trussard's, he waited at a nearby café until she came out, then *chanced* to meet her on the street. And there was the opera too.

"In those days," Nattie explained, "four operas were performed every week at the Théâtre d'Orléans, two *grand* and two *comique*. When he found out which operas she was going to, he got tickets to two of them, seats in the dress circle. My grandma said that between acts he visited her box.

'Course, he didn't get to talk to her every time he *accidentally* saw her.''

"But Adrienne must have encouraged his pursuit of her and guessed these weren't chance meetings." Remy curled an arm around the bedpost and sat down at the foot of the mattress, wrinkling the coverlet Nattie had so carefully smoothed.

"Sure she did," Nattie agreed quickly. "There's no doubt she was just as attracted to him. Part of it was probably that he was different from the young Creole men she knew. He dressed well, but he wasn't a dandy, like some of them were; he wasn't a quarrelsome braggart, all obsessed with honor and dueling; and he observed all the proprieties back then without acting like he was bound by them. And his being a Yankee probably added a touch of the forbidden, too. Besides"—Nattie shrugged—"doesn't every young girl at some time in her life dream of meeting a man who can thrill her—a man who's bold and handsome, who will defy anything to have her for his own? Times may change, and people with them, but not in the ways of love or our dreams of it —man or woman."

Remy couldn't argue with that.

"Anyway," Nattie continued, "after those *chance* encounters, Brodie then found out Adrienne was going to a ball at the St. Louis Hotel. That's where nearly all the fashionable balls were held—at least the ones attended by the Creoles. The Americans had their parties at the St. Charles Hotel . . . in the American section of town. This particular *bal de société*, as they called it, was a private-subscription affair. Brodie Donovan probably had to use all his contacts in the Quarter and twist every arm he could just to get his name on the invitation list. And then he had to pay dearly for the privilege of attending the ball. In a way, he was as single-minded in his pursuit of Adrienne Jardin as he'd been in building his shipping company—not minding the time, the effort, the cost, or the risk. . . .''

* * *

Tall pillars circled the famed rotunda of the St. Louis Hotel, its beige-tinged-with-pink marble floor gleaming beneath the high dome of its elaborate and ornamental ceiling. Paintings covered the walls, and a long bar of solid marble curved halfway around the room. And the patrons were as finely appointed as the decor—including Brodie Donovan. Wearing the requisite white gloves with his black tailcoat over a white waistcoat, Brodie picked up a brandy from the polished top of the marble bar and idly swirled it in its glass. With a turn of his head, he glanced again in the direction of the room's entrance and ignored the poke of his starched-stiff collar.

The cadence of the music rose as the band played a quadrille. Brodie scanned the file of dancers on the floor, doubting that he had failed to see her arrive, but verifying it all the same. Satisfied that she wasn't among the dancers, he swung his gaze to the ball guests milling about along the outside circle by the towering pillars. White satins, cream taffetas, pastel silks, gowns adorned with flowers, glittering beads, and sequined lace, but none worn by the dark-haired, dark-eyed Adrienne Jardin.

He took a sip of brandy and glanced at a group of guests entering the rotunda. He recognized a planter and his family from upriver and started to turn away, then spotted an elderly woman in a drab stone-colored gown, her headdress of lace and pink ribbons barely able to conceal the spreading thinness of her gray hair. It was Adrienne's sour and rather sad aunt.

A second later the planter and his family veered to the right, and there she stood, her black hair swept high on her head, a blood-red rose at the side, the low-cut corsage of her silk gown baring the rounded points of her pale shoulders. Suddenly every edge of the night was sharp and biting, and every scent was sweet and keen. His restlessness and impatience vanished at the sight of her.

He pushed his brandy glass back onto the bar counter, then stiffened as he saw the man at her side, lean and elegant in his black evening clothes. He had Adrienne's ebony hair and equally dark eyes, and there was a faint similarity in their features, though his were more sharply cut. Dominique Jardin, Adrienne's brother and the only grandson of Emil Jardin. Through him the Jardin legacy would live on.

Brodie breathed a little easier, but not much. According to Cado, Dominique Jardin was not a Creole dandy to be taken lightly. At twenty-five, he was a veteran of more than a dozen duels, his skill with a rapier reportedly rivaled only by that of his fencing master. More than that, he and Adrienne were exceptionally close for a brother and sister. It was said he was proud of her beauty and extremely protective of her reputation.

Thoughtfully Brodie reached for his glass of brandy and took a minute to study this new obstacle. In the past he'd had only Adrienne's chaperoning aunt to be concerned about, and she'd been relatively easy to circumvent. Her reputation for Gallic thrift was renowned in the Quarter; Brodie'd merely had to wait until she was haggling with some merchant, then he could be assured of having Adrienne all to himself. Cado claimed the old spinster used the money she saved to buy absinthe on the sly. The house servants said she was a secret tippler.

Unfortunately Dominique Jardin shared no similar failing. On the contrary, he was said to be as sharp and as quick as the rapier he wielded, a fitting heir to assume the family mantle, a man to be approached directly. Brodie took a last sip of his brandy and pushed away from the marble bar to wander slowly, casually in their direction.

As Adrienne advanced into the domed rotunda on her brother's arm, she acknowledged the waving of hands, the nodding of ornamented heads, her gaze always moving, being careful not to miss a sign of recognition from any dowager, and to maintain a composed smile of interest. The lively strains of a quadrille filled the room, rising above the bright hum of gaily chattering voices and the sweeping rustle of stiff taffetas, satins, and silks, the soft whisper of her ruched gown lost in it, the caged crinoline of her petticoat holding the circular fullness of the skirt away from her and giving her the appearance of gliding over the gleaming marble floor.

Here and there she and Dominique were detained by gloved hands reaching out to stop them. "Adrienne, if only your *mère* were here to see how beautiful you have grown."

And another declared, "Ah, *chère*, but it was only yesterday you went to sleep in our box at the opera."

"Dominique, you remember our daughter Gisette."

"Where is your grand-père? I had hoped to see him this evening."

Dominique explained that a small emergency at one of their plantations upriver had required their grandfather's presence, but that he was not expected to be away long—a day or two, perhaps. Then they moved on, strolling beneath the galleries that circled the domed ceiling.

As the last notes of the quadrille faded, Adrienne watched the dancers leaving the floor, conscious of the fine tension that had her tightly gripping the handle of her closed fan. Again she skimmed the faces of the men garbed in the mandatory black evening dress, ignoring the women with their satiny shoulders and shimmering gowns, not admitting to herself that she was looking for anyone in particular.

Before the dance floor had completely cleared, the band struck up another tune, a waltz this time. Dominique turned to the older woman on his other arm. "Come, Tante ZeeZee. Permit me to have this first dance with you."

She harrumphed in response, her expression scornful of the invitation, but her eyes warmed with affection when she looked at him. "I am too old to be whirled about the floor like a dervish. You have done your duty by asking me; now let us speak of such foolishness no more."

"Now I am hurt that you refuse to dance with me, your favorite nephew," Dominique teased, something only he could get away with.

"Hmmph, you are my *only* nephew," she retorted. "And

your feelings will recover quickly from the slight. It is better that I take my seat along the wall with the rest of the ancient tapestry. If you wish to be kind, later you may bring me a glass of absinthe.''

Leaving them, she went to join the other matrons along the wall, ensconced on seats provided for those who sat out the dancing. There she would spend her evening, listening to gossip and occasionally inserting an ascerbic comment of her own. Adrienne considered again the loneliness of her aunt's life, relegated to the role of glorified servant, the cha- telain of her father's house, dependent on him for her existence—a loneliness assuaged by two things: the jade- green liquor and Dominique.

"You almost coaxed a smile from her," Adrienne observed as she cast one of her own at her handsome brother. "She adores you so."

"Is that bad?" He drew his head back, feigning an af- fronted look.

"Very. You are adored by so many women now, one more may fill your head with conceit," she replied in jest.

Instead of maintaining the light banter, Dominique turned serious. "But it is not I who am adored by so many women so much as it is the Jardin name and the wealth it portends."

She looked at her brother, his remark reminding her of the many duties and responsibilities that would one day be solely his to bear, burdens he'd been groomed to assume almost from the day of his birth. How old had she been when she'd first recognized that no matter how much her grandfather loved her—and he'd never given her cause to doubt his love for her—she would never occupy the place of importance in his life that her brother, Dominique, held. While she was the delight of her grandfather's life, Dominique was his heir. Through him Emil Jardin would know his immortality. Through him the Jardin name would be carried on. It was the way of things, and she loved her brother too much ever to resent his position.

Studying the clean lines of his profile, she announced,

"Any woman who looks at you and sees only that is unworthy of the man you are."

"Praise from my sister?" Dominique raised an eyebrow in mock amazement. "What other surprises will this evening hold, I wonder?"

"Let us hope many." Adrienne turned again to the couples taking the floor and skimmed the host of guests crowding at the edges. Out of the corner of her eye she caught a hint of burnished red, deep and dark like mahogany. He was here. Not thirty feet away. Exchanging pleasantries with Monsieur Rousseau. She let her glance linger on him for an instant, more than a little pleased to discover how magnificent he looked in formal dress, the white silk cravat tied in a small, precise bow at his throat, the black tailcoat splendidly emphasizing the width of his shoulders. Then she looked away, her smile deepening with the sudden rush of exhilaration. "Perhaps there will even be wonderful surprises."

Although she kept her eyes steadfastly averted from him, she knew the instant he moved on—toward her—and yet she maintained the pretense of being unaware of his approach, instead watching in satisfaction as other feminine heads turned to cast curious and admiring glances his way.

She waited until his tall shape had entered her side vision, then allowed her wandering glance to encounter his. But the knowing glint in his brown eyes made her wonder if she'd fooled him at all.

"M'sieu Donovan," she said, acknowledging him first.

"Mademoiselle Jardin." He inclined his head in a show of respect, his gaze holding hers a fraction longer than propriety allowed, reaffirming his interest, and then he moved on to her brother—again showing a surface observance of convention.

"Dominique, allow me to present Monsieur Brodie Donovan." Adrienne quickly and smoothly made the necessary introductions. "My brother, Dominique Jardin."

She heard the coolness of her brother's response and witnessed the testing handshake the two men exchanged. The subtle inquiries Dominique made were what she'd expected, and the proper replies Brodie Donovan gave, she'd anticipated.

In the last two weeks Adrienne had made a few very discreet inquiries of her own about Brodie Donovan and learned that he had earned the respect of several leading businessmen in the Vieux Carré, all of whom remarked on his courtesy, his patience, and his business acumen, always adding, "If only more *Yanquis* were like this one."

But her few encounters with him had made her aware that while he may have *adapted to* their ways, he hadn't *adopted* them. He was not at all like the young Creole men she knew, never fawning in his attention like the limp-wristed ones, never swaggering with his chest thrown out expecting to be noticed like the strutting cocks of the walk, never leering like the self-styled Lotharios whose looks gave her a crawling sensation wholly unlike the excitement she drew from the quick, amused eyes of Brodie Donovan.

No, there was a directness about Brodie Donovan that he never tried to disguise, as evidenced by the way he looked at her—the way a man looked at a woman he desired and intended ultimately to have.

"With your permission, M'sieu Jardin, I would like to have this dance with your sister," he said, and fixed that look on her.

She felt Dominique's gaze on her and turned to meet it, unaware of the dark glow in her own eyes as she gave a barely perceptible nod to indicate her assent to the request. His expression immediately became thoughtful, probing, with a trace of frown appearing. But he smiled and nodded his consent to Brodie Donovan.

"You have my permission," he said, surrendering her.

When Brodie offered her his arm, Adrienne placed her hand on his sleeve and let him lead her onto the dance floor. As he moved to face her, she was confronted by the wide set of his shoulders and the white expanse of his cambric dress shirt. She felt the strong curl of his gloved fingers on her hand and the warm press of his hand on the curve of her waist, guiding her into the first steps of a waltz, the bulk of her skirt keeping a distance between them. She lifted her gaze higher—to the smoothly hewn line of his jaw and chin, then to his mouth, faintly curved in a warm, lazy line.

"You dance well, M'sieu Donovan." She met his stare, conscious of the pleasant disturbance it created within her.

"For a Yankee, you mean." The corners of his mouth deepened into a smile that brought the carved lines in his cheeks into play.

Adrienne laughed softly at the phrase he'd probably heard a thousand times, which he had now turned onto himself. "You dance well—for anyone," she insisted.

"A compliment from the beautiful Mademoiselle Jardin." He tipped his head to her in silent acknowledgment, amusement glinting in his eyes. "I can think of only one thing that would give me greater pleasure this evening."

"And what is that, m'sieu?" She matched his bantering tone, making the question half serious and half jest.

"A kiss from your lips."

Unconsciously she lowered her glance to his mouth, for an instant imagining. . . . Aloud, she wondered, "How do you have the boldness to speak to me this way?"

"How do you have the boldness to listen?" he countered, his hand tightening its grip on her waist as he whirled her into a series of concentric turns that robbed her of her breath and gave her no chance to respond. When he finally resumed their former pace, it seemed inappropriate to allude to either of his remarks.

The song ended, yet the phrase would not leave her—"A kiss from your lips," "A kiss," "kiss." The words echoed over and over again in her mind each time she met his gaze that evening, each time she danced with him, each time she thought of him.

Again he came to claim her for a waltz, and again she took

to the dance floor with him, the pressure of his hands, the length of his gliding steps, the sight of his face before her all now familiar to her.

"Do you realize, m'sieu, this is the twelfth time we have danced together this evening?" she said, aware of the speculating looks currently being directed their way.

"You've been keeping count," he observed, then smiled that slow smile she'd come to expect. "So have I."

"People are beginning to notice."

"Let them. Whatever they're thinking, it's probably true." He slowed their steps and stole a quick glance around. "Are you tired of dancing, Mademoiselle Jardin?"

"Why?" she asked, startled by the unexpected question.

"Come with me," was all he said as he calmly led her off the floor, as if to stop dancing in the middle of a waltz was the most natural thing to do. Unhurried, he guided her through the ring of onlooking guests. Adrienne saw they were heading in the general direction of the exit onto St. Louis Street. She said nothing when his fingers pressed down on her arm to check her steps, as if they were about to linger. He cast another surreptitious glance around them, then drew her toward the exit. He exchanged one conspiratorial look with her, and then they slipped from the domed ballroom and moved quickly down the long arcade of fashionable shops. Her aunt would be shocked that Adrienne had deliberately eluded her chaperoning eye, but she didn't care, not now.

Halfway down the arcade, the music and the susurration of voices became muted. Again the pressure of his hand checked her steps. She swung around to face him, feeling wonderfully wicked, especially when she saw that look in his eyes. They were near a recessed entrance to one of the shops. Adrienne wandered over to peer in its window and then turned, drawing her hands together behind her back and leaning against a corner of the entrance.

"You should not have brought me here," she said.

He rested a hand on the framework above her head. "You shouldn't have come. Why did you?"

Adrienne answered him honestly, directly. "I wanted to be alone with you."

She heard the faint sound of his indrawn breath as his gaze fastened on her lips. She watched his mouth move closer, her eyelids slowly lowering until her lashes closed with the first warm touch of his lips against hers. The initial contact was light and exploring, a brush here, a faint pressure there, her breath slipping out to mingle with his. Then his mouth came the rest of the way onto hers, covering all the surfaces of her lips in a tender yet stirring kiss.

When he lifted his head, regret quivered through her. Slowly she opened her eyes to look at him, stunned to discover that he hadn't taken her into his arms. Their lips had met, but that had been the only contact. There was still space between them. She searched his face, seeking some answer to this heady tension that held her. His eyes did their own searching of her.

"Adrienne," he rumbled her name.

Almost simultaneously his hands moved onto her, pulling her to him as his mouth came crushing down again. Some remote part of her mind noted that she hadn't given him permission to use her given name. But this Yankee wasn't the kind to wait for permission. He took what he wanted— as he was taking this kiss. She gave him all he asked for and more, her hands winding around him, her fingers curling through his hair. Heat flowed through her, but she made no effort to identify its source. There were too many other revelations claiming her attention as his delving kiss unlocked all her closely held hungers and exposed to her, for the first time, the deep and passionate values she held within.

When he broke it off, she looked at him wordlessly, conscious of the unsteady beat of her heart and of an inner trembling that had nothing to do with weakness—rather, it was evidence of the powerful effect of his kiss.

His smile seemed a little unsteady too. "I think it's time I spoke with your grandfather."

"Yes," she said in absolute and full agreement. "He is

away. We expect him to return the first of the week." Reaching up, she traced a finger over the curve of his mouth, remembering the sensation of his lips on hers. "You've had your kiss. Your pleasure in the evening should be complete."

"Yes, but now my life isn't." He caught her fingers and pressed them to his lips. "We'd better go back to the ball before I behave like a Yankee and spirit you away from here."

As they retraced their steps to the rotunda, Adrienne unconsciously held her head a little higher, secretly pleased by how womanly she felt. When Brodie suggested a glass of champagne on their return, she agreed, glad of the opportunity to have a few moments to herself to explore these new feelings. But her time alone seemed all too brief as Dominique joined her.

"You look very happy about something," he said.

"I am," she admitted. "M'sieu Donovan is going to ask Grand-père for permission to call on me."

He looked at her in shock. "Adrienne, have you taken leave of your senses? He is a *Yanqui*."

"I know."

"Grand-père will—"

"—will storm and stomp about, call upon all the saints, glower indignantly for a day or two, and then ultimately grant permission," Adrienne concluded confidently.

"How can you sound so sure of that?" Dominique shook his head, harboring his own doubts of the outcome.

"Dominique," she chided with a reproving smile. "When has Grand-père ever denied me anything I have wanted?"

"But you have never wanted to see a *Yanqui*," he reminded her.

15

The very walls of the house on Royal Street reverberated with the fury emanating from the library on the second floor—which, following the Continental style, was the structure's main story. The chandelier in the room quivered with the force of voices raised in anger. It had begun within seconds after Brodie Donovan was summarily ordered from the premises.

Emil Jardin stood in front of the library table, his silvery head thrown back—not with pride for the young woman who was now before him, but with outrage. His deep-set eyes were not bright with love for his granddaughter who was the delight of his winter years; they were burning black with ire. His hands didn't reach out to stroke her hair or caress her cheek; they flailed the air in indignation. His voice didn't croon to her in affection, each sentence punctuated with *"ma petite"* or *"ma mignonne"*; it lashed out in full Gallic temper.

Adrienne had seen her grandfather angry before, even furious, but never like this, consumed by a rage that purpled his face and made the veins in his neck stand out. She didn't flinch from him. Instead she let her own temper rise to clash with his.

"You could have had the simple courtesy to listen to him!"

"Listen to what? More of his offensive declarations of interest in you? *Non,* never! I would rather God strike me dead than hear him speak your name. *Non!*" he repeated forcefully, gesticulating with his hands. "The doors of this house are forever shut to that *Yanqui* barbarian!"

"You have no right!" she protested, just as loudly.

"I have every right. This is my house."

"It is my house too."

"And you are my granddaughter. You will do as you are told, and I forbid you to speak to this man again!"

"You forbid?! Why?" Adrienne demanded, her hands clenched in fists at her sides. "Because he is a *Yanqui?* This prejudice of yours toward the *Americains* is archaic. They are here. They have been here. Even you do business with them."

"Oui, I do business with them. And my grand-père, he did business with Indians. But he would no more have allowed them into his house than I will have that *Yanqui* enter this one!"

"You are not being fair!"

"Chut!" He demanded silence from her. "I have made my decision. There will be no more discussion on this, do you hear? Now, go to your room."

"I am not a child to be ordered to my room, Grand-père. I am a woman."

"A woman who has foolishly allowed her head to be turned by a quick-tongued Yankee. That your Tante ZeeZee allowed you to speak to this—this—man is an outrage, and that she failed to inform me is unforgivable. You will see him no more, Adrienne. This is the end of it!"

"Non, you are wrong!"

"Do not defy me in this! I will not permit it."

Glaring at him, Adrienne recognized that she was too angry

to reason with him, and he was too angry to listen. She turned sharply on her heel and stormed from the room, slamming the door behind her, the loudness of it rebounding down the side hall. She hesitated, feeling the silence of the house, its quiet reminding her of the eerie stillness that preceded a violent storm.

There was a movement at the end of the hall. Turning, Adrienne saw her black maidservant Sulie Mae peering cautiously around the corner. Hastily she caught up her skirts and ran quickly and noiselessly down the hall—in the opposite direction from her room. The young brown-skinned woman stepped out to meet her, glancing anxiously past her toward the library door. Adrienne took her by the arm and drew her into the main salon, out of sight, then whispered urgently. "Sulie Mae, when M'sieu Donovan left, did you see which way he went?"

"*Oui*, Missy." She bobbed her head in quick affirmation. "He turned like he was goin' to Canal."

Adrienne tried to remember how long ago that had been. Five minutes? Certainly not more than ten. "I want you to go after him, Sulie Mae, and bring him back here."

"Here?" She drew back in alarm. "But Michie Jardin, he say—"

"I know what he said," Adrienne cut in sharply. "But you do as I say. Bring him here. I will meet him in the carriageway. Now, go. *Vite*."

Like all the homes in the Vieux Carré, the Jardin house was built flush with the banquette, its galleries of iron lacework extending over it, but it kept its back turned to the street and faced the courtyard within. Two entrances provided access to the house. The first was a formal doorway set between half-columns and crowned by an arched fanlight, up a short flight of steps from the banquette; the second was a carriage entrance, marked by heavy double doors with a smaller opening cut into one side. Behind the doors was a tunnel-like passage paved with flagstones. At the end of it stood a pair of tall, scrolled iron gates that led into the sun-splashed courtyard with its lush greenery and weathered fountain.

In the middle of the darkly shadowed *porte cochère* there was another arched opening, and a wooden staircase that curved up to the main residence on the second floor. At the foot of the steps, within the arching frame, Adrienne waited anxiously, impatiently, hearing the clatter of mule-drawn drays in the street and listening for the creak of the small gate that would signal Sulie Mae's return.

Just as she stole a glance around the corner, the dark-green gate swung inward and Sulie Mae stepped cautiously into the passage-way, pulling her shawl more tightly around her shoulders, her head bound in a kerchief, the pointed ends poking into the air like a pair of horns. She saw Adrienne and looked back over her shoulder, motioning for someone to follow her inside. A second later Brodie ducked his tall frame through the gate and stepped to one side, letting Sulie Mae close the gate behind him. He seemed to resist Sulie Mae's attempts to hurry him down the passageway to the opening where Adrienne waited. As he came toward her, she noticed the stiffness—the erectness—of his posture, hinting at tautly controlled anger, but it wasn't until he was closer that she saw the hardness in his expression and the cold look in his eyes. She hesitated, guessing how insulting, how contemptuous her grandfather must have been when he'd ordered Brodie from the house.

He stopped in front of her, the muscles along his cheek and jaw standing out in sharp ridges. "Your Negress said you wanted to see me." His voice was as hard and cold as the rest of him.

"I do." She moved aside to let Sulie Mae scurry past her up the stairs. "You spoke to Grand-père—"

"He has refused permission for me to call on you."

"I know. He has forbidden me to speak to you." She searched his face, looking for some glimmer of the warmth she'd once seen in it. "Do you intend for this to be the end of it? Will you stay away, as he has ordered?"

His gaze bored into her, dark and angry. And Adrienne recognized that hardness as pride.

"No," he said. "Never."

Then his hands were reaching out to drag her to him, and she went eagerly into his arms, tilting her head up to receive the satisfying crush of his mouth. Again she felt shocked alive by his kiss, and more certain than ever that this was how it should be between a man and a woman.

"There's a way," he muttered against her cheek. "There has to be."

"Yes." She drew back, needing to see his face. "My grand-père is a . . . a stubborn man. But he means well. He thinks he is protecting me, and I have yet to make him understand that I have no wish to be protected from you, Brodie."

A corner of his mouth lifted in a near smile. "You make my name a melody."

"Do I?" She laughed softly, breathlessly, exhilarated by the look of desire that had returned to his eyes. Then she heard her aunt's voice coming from the courtyard, and she tensed in alarm. "You must go—before someone sees you." She cast an anxious glance over her shoulder. "I will speak to Grand-père. Not now. In a day or two, when he will be more reasonable," she said as she hurried him toward the small gate.

"Do you know the blind fiddler, Cado?" He stopped at the gate, not yet opening it. "He plays on the corner of Royal and St. Philip."

"The Negro with the violin? I have seen him," she admitted. "But I never knew his name."

"If you need to reach me, leave a message with him, and he'll see that I get it." He opened the gate, then paused halfway through it. "If I don't hear from you, I'll be back."

"A week," she promised. "No more than that."

* * *

Thunder rumbled low and ominous as rain fell in slanting torrents, filling the garbage-strewn gutters, turning the dirt street into a quagmire, and inching over the sidewalks. Only those who had to ventured out, and they hugged the buildings, seeking what little protection the overhanging galleries offered from the wind-whipped rain. The rest stayed inside and waited for the deluge to pass.

From the shelter of the covered carriageway, Adrienne watched the street, a full-length cloak of Burberry cloth covering her dress and hooding her face. Few vehicles plowed through the deep mud on Royal Street, and still fewer pedestrians scurried along its banquette. None noticed the small gate held partially ajar, or the woman on the other side, silent, calm, and determined.

A closed carriage approached, pulled by a team of matched bays, their ears flattened against the rain. The driver swung the team close to the banquette and brought the carriage to a halt next to the cypress-lined ditch. The door to the carriage swung open. Adrienne darted from the shelter of the *porte cochère* and climbed inside before the driver could alight to assist her.

With a crack of the whip, the carriage lurched forward. Inside, Adrienne pushed back the hood of her cloak and finally met Brodie's gaze. She briefly wondered why she felt no awkwardness, no anxiety, no guilt—only this calm, smooth certainty. Brodie said nothing, waiting for her to speak first.

"Grand-père remains adamant in his decision. He will not tolerate even the mention of your name."

"That doesn't change the way I feel," he said, leaving unspoken the question of whether she wanted to reconsider her position.

"Nor the way I feel," she assured him, firmly.

A small smile touched his mouth. "In that case we're left with the Yankee thing to do—run away together and elope."

"*Non.*" She had already considered that option and rejected it. "Flight carries with it the inference of wrongdoing, of guilt, of shame. I feel none of those things with you."

"I can't disagree with you. But neither am I going to allow your grandfather to keep us apart. You'd better understand that, Adrienne."

"I do."

In the last six days she'd had a great deal of time alone to think—about them, about herself, about life and what she wanted from it. She'd seen the loneliness of her aunt's spinster existence, the isolation of a single woman, her dependence upon the charity of a relative. And she'd seen the unhappiness of a loveless *mariage de convenance*, the tension, the bitterness, the resentment of young brides as they tried to pretend they didn't know about the concubines their husbands kept in those little cottages on Rampart Street. Ever since she'd been old enough to be aware of these things, she'd been determined to marry for love. She had never doubted that she could. She was a Jardin, and the Jardins had risen above the need to further their power base through marriage.

She had never guessed she would choose a Yankee to love. And she'd never guessed that her grandfather's dislike of them was so deeply ingrained.

Twice this past week she had tried to reason with her grandfather, and both attempts had ended in arguments. She hadn't tried again, recognizing that more quarrels would only harden him. And tears and pleading wouldn't work with her grandfather; he disliked weakness, even in women.

While Dominique sympathized with her plight, he wouldn't side with her against their grandfather and suggested instead that she accept that their grandfather was a better judge than she of what was best for her. As for Tante ZeeZee—she was a woman. Her grandfather would no more listen to her than to Adrienne.

Her acceptance of his demands was out of the question. She would never submit to that.

Open defiance of her grandfather was unthinkable—scandalous.

All of which left only one option: she had to arrange for her grandfather to realize that the best thing would be for her to marry Brodie Donovan.

"We will see each other, Brodie, as often as we can." She twisted sideways in the seat to face him and reached up to trace the high arc of his cheekbone. "For now, we will have to meet like this."

Irritation flickered through his expression. "Why? You can't believe he's going to change his mind."

"In time he will, yes." She smiled confidently.

He looked at her, then slowly shook his head, his mouth reluctantly curving in a smile. "Why am I agreeing to this? What kind of spell have you cast over me?"

"Brodie. Do you think you are the only one who feels this enchantment?" she asked, feeling slightly wiser than he.

"I'd better not be." He drew her hand from his cheek and carried it to his mouth, pressing an evocative kiss in the center of its palm, his eyes never leaving her face. "How long before I have to take you back to your home?"

"Not long," she said regretfully, glancing up at the upholstered ceiling of the carriage, listening to the tattoo of the rain on its roof. "Already the rain is letting up. When it stops, the streets will be crowded." She left it unsaid that that would greatly increase her risk of being seen leaving his carriage.

"You don't know how tempted I am to tell the driver to keep going—how tempted I am to kidnap you and never take you back. I want to spend more than a few minutes with you, Adrienne."

"You will. I have begun to spend my evenings alone in my room, retiring immediately after supper, refusing to attend any of the parties or the opera. Grand-père thinks I am sulking, and I have not attempted to disprove him." She paused for an instant, marveling at her own daring yet never questioning her decision. "At night there is little traffic on the street, few people to notice a carriage going by—or stopping very briefly. We would have time to be together then—perhaps two, even three hours.''

Brodie frowned in amazement, hearing her words and seeing the cleverness, the intelligence in her plan—and observing her seemingly unshakable calm. Rebellion against family dictum was so rare as to be almost nonexistent in aristocratic Creole families. That she was even in this carriage with him in the daytime, unchaperoned, showed stunning boldness. But to suggest meeting him at night—alone—for several hours. . . . It humbled him a little to think of it, especially when he considered how strict her upbringing had been. And he wondered if she wasn't putting too much trust in a gentleman's honor—his honor. Didn't she realize that if he were really a gentleman, he'd never see her again?

"Is there a place we can go when we meet? I know of none,'' she confessed, calmly looking to him.

"I do.'' He knew the requirements without asking—somewhere private where they wouldn't be seen or recognized. "My home. About three miles from here.''

There was one small flicker of hesitation, and then she smiled. "I would like to see your home.''

"When?''

"In a day or two. I will send a message to you.''

16

A waxing moon, a shimmering crescent in the night sky, joined the dusting of glittering stars to look down on the collection of elaborate homes with expansive front lawns that had sprung up in the partially wooded outskirts of the city, built by prosperous Americans on the former site of the old Livaudais plantation. Stately processions of towering columns, Corinthian and Doric in design, faced the streets, the wide galleries borrowing the lacework ornamentation of iron railings from the Creoles, and the interiors adapting to the subtropical climate of New Orleans with rooms sixteen and eighteen feet high, wide doorways, tall windows, and folding shutters that could be thrown open to admit the flow of air.

Brodie Donovan stood at a parlor window in one of those homes—his home, finished only a few short months before, its grandeur befitting the residence of a successful shipowner. Yet, looking into the mirror-black night, he had only to close his eyes and remember the unbelievable green of his native Ireland, the two-room mud house that had been his home, the meager meals that had been served on its crude table, the patched and worn clothes that had covered his back, the hunger that had been in his belly, and the smell of peat burning in the hearth. He had only to close his eyes and remember the sensation of the swamp's mire tugging at his legs, drying on his clothes and skin—the suffocating heat, the *zzzizzing* buzz of attacking mosquitoes, the trembling and aching of exhausted muscles, and the stench, always the rank, malodorous smell of the miasmal swamp.

It didn't matter that he'd left it all behind; it hadn't left him.

If Adrienne had seen him then, she would have given him a look of cool disdain and drawn her skirts aside to avoid contact with him. In all the times they'd met and talked, he'd never told her about any of it. Oh, he'd told her of Ireland, described the green of its countryside, the rocky promontories of its sea cliffs, the sparkling waters of its springs and lochs, and told her of the grand wakes—the keening and weeping in one room and the toasting and tale-swapping in another. And he'd recounted the story of how he'd started his company and built it, as well as his plans for the future.

There was a truth to all of it, but not the whole truth, not the parts that might change the way she looked at him. Did he think she wouldn't love him if she knew? Did he think he wasn't really good enough for her? Was that why he went along with meeting her in secret—because he didn't feel he had a right to be seen with her in public?

But this was America. There was no rigid separation of the classes here; a man was not forever bound to one station. He could rise—as Brodie had done. Look at his clothes, look at this house—they were as fine as anything Adrienne's family possessed.

The darkened windowpane reflected his scowling look. Brodie turned from it, irritated by the blackness of his mood. But he knew the cause of it: she was late. He glanced at the clock on the black marble mantel. The carriage had left to pick her up more than an hour ago. Had something gone wrong? Why wasn't she here? Had there been trouble? He cursed himself for not going with it and for waiting for her here instead.

He glared at the emptiness of the richly furnished parlor, the many crystal pendants of the Waterford chandelier increasing the spray of candlelight that filled it. Once he'd enjoyed this room, taken pride in its beauty. Now, when he looked at the sofa where they always sat, part of the walnut parlor set he'd bought for the room from Prudent Mallard, he always imagined her there. Sometimes, when he was alone, he'd run his hand over the curved armrest where her hand so lightly rested. And sometimes he swore the rich red velvet held traces of her fragrance.

There was no more contentment in this house for him, no more satisfaction. He remembered how proudly he'd shown it off to her the first time she'd come. Now every room was marked with the memory of her reaction—the sound of soft, indrawn breaths of admiration, the sight of a hand trailing in approval over a mantel, even the occasional carefully worded criticism offered under the guise of a suggestion.

Dammit, where was she? Brodie spun back to the window and searched the darkness beyond for a glimpse of the carriage. Would she come? Would she notice the magnolias the gardener had planted in the front lawn, or the newly laid flagstoned walk in the rear, the beginnings of the courtyard she'd thought would be attractive there?

The bright light pouring from the parlor beckoned to her. Adrienne quietly closed the rear entrance door to the wide hall and let the light guide her to the parlor, then paused just inside to face Brodie with clear-shining eyes as he pivoted from the window toward her.

"Adrienne!" Disbelief flickered across his face. He took a step toward her and then stopped, as if expecting her to disappear. "I didn't hear the carriage."

"When you were not at the door to meet me, I thought you might have given up on me." She quickly unfastened her cloak and swung it off her shoulders. "Grand-père brought guests home to dinner unexpectedly. I had to wait until they had left and Tante ZeeZee had retired to her room.''

"You're here. That's all that matters now." A smile came to his mouth.

The sight of it was all Adrienne needed as she crossed the room with no memory of her feet touching the floor. He swept her into his arms and wrapped her tightly around him, covering her lips with a fiercely tender kiss.

Almost before it had begun, he was breaking it off, raking his mouth across her cheek, murmuring a husky and rough "I've missed you."

She closed her eyes, thrilling to the emotion vibrating so thickly through his voice. "And I have missed you, Brodie," she declared just as thickly.

"It's been hell these last two days—wanting to see you, wanting to hold you, wanting to be with you."

"It has been the same for me." Adrienne rubbed her cheek against his, feeling its smoothness, its chiseled bone structure, its heat.

With an effort, he lifted his head and framed her face in his hands, looking at her with heavy-lidded need, a smolder and a sparkle in his eyes. "I was standing at the window, wondering where you were, wishing you were here with me. And when you came through that door, I thought you were a dream I was having. It's a dream you are, Adrienne—a dream most men carry in their minds but never see."

"I am no dream."

"No," he said, none too certainly, his mouth slanting in a near smile. "But I've been thinking, Adrienne—what is a man? There's stars he wants to reach, but it's the earth that restrains him. Man was meant for the earth, but he can look at the stars. When you appeared tonight, it was like I was seeing a star suddenly blaze and fall to fill the sky—to fill my night . . . and my life." He paused and deliberately lapsed into a lilting brogue, trying to lighten the seriousness of his feelings. "'Tis loving you I am, Adrienne Jardin."

She drew a small, quick breath, conscious of the sudden

soaring of her heart, and smiled. "And 'tis loving you I am, Brodie Donovan." She used his phrasing, moved by the simple sincerity of it.

Humor, warm and glinting, mixed with the desire for her in his eyes. "It's bold you are again, mocking me with my own words."

"It is no mockery." Smiling, she ran a caressing hand over the angled line of his jaw. He caught it and pressed the tips of her fingers to his lips. "I love you. You are the man I want for my husband. It is your children I want to have, your home I want to keep, your bed I want to lie in."

For an instant he gripped her fingers so tightly that she thought he would break them. Then he was murmuring her name in a groan as he smothered her lips with a kiss that was warm, hard, and demanding. Adrienne was stirred anew by the flood of sensation washing through her. She had no doubt that this was what she wanted—the heat, the need, the near desperation.

His mouth shifted, pressing rough kisses over her cheek and eye. "I want that too," came the thick words against her skin. "I want you."

She felt the faint tremors that shook him, the struggle for control. But there was no place for control in this moment of giving—this release of feelings too long held back. She knew that, as a woman knows it.

"I want you, Brodie." She drew back to look at him, taking his hand and drawing it inside the lace collar of her jasper silk walking dress, laying it against the bare skin of her breastbone, the heel of his hand resting on the top swell of her breast. "Do you feel the pounding of my heart? Do you feel the trembling within? It is for you."

He was still, so still he could have been made of stone. Only his eyes were alive to her—so very alive to her. "You don't know what you're saying, Adrienne."

A smile touched her mouth, at once warm and amused. "You likened me to a star, but I am not something to be regarded and admired from afar. I am a woman to be loved by a man—by you. The stars are outside, Brodie. We are here.''

"Aye," he breathed the word, his hand slipping lower, finding the roundness of her breast beneath her gown's corsage. At his touch, an indistinct murmur of pleasure broke from her. "We are here."

His head bent. His lips brushed hers, then came back to plunder and invade. As she tasted the hardness of his tongue, Adrienne knew that this was what she wanted—his hands on her, his mouth on her, his muscled body pressed tightly to her. It was what she had always wanted.

He swept her into his arms and carried her from the parlor, up the curved staircase to the master bedroom on the second floor. The soft glow from a lamp on the bedside table illuminated the full tester bed, with the lace baire rolled up and the bed linen turned down, the massive rosewood armoire along one wall and the pale-blue carpet on the floor. He lowered her feet onto the carpet and continued to kiss her. She felt his fingers at the fastenings of her dress, and then it was swinging loose.

Soon her clothes were in a pile at her feet. Brodie drew back to look at her standing before him, proud, bold . . . beautiful. The back-glow of the lamplight made the thin material of her chemise appear transparent. His mouth went dry. She looked small and delicate, with a narrow rib cage and a waist so small he could span it with his hands, and slender hips that were yet wide enough to cradle a man. He wondered how a form so fragile could hold so much strength—and how a pair of eyes could look at him with a desire so deep it rivaled his own.

"You are beautiful." His voice was husky as he let his gaze stray to her hair, swept back in its smooth knot. She reached up and pulled the securing pins from it, combing it loose with her fingers and drawing its length forward over one shoulder. "This is the first time I've seen it down," he said, and he ran his hand under the silken length of it, a knuckle grazing the peak of her breast, further sensitizing it.

Then the ends of his fingers were along her throat, his thumbs under the point of her chin, tilting it up. "You have such full and giving lips."

He lowered his head and she closed her eyes, anticipating the hard demand of his kiss. She was startled—wondrously so—when he caught her bottom lip between his teeth, the light nibbling sensation arousing a whole new shimmering ache within her. A sigh whispered from her as he brushed his mouth over her parted lips, saying against them, "It's sweet they are too—like wild honey."

He tasted them, his tongue tracing their outline, then stroking their inner softness. She swayed against him, her hands clutching at his middle as the world spun behind her closed eyes at this excitingly evocative kiss that was not really a kiss at all. An instant later she discovered that his fingers were no longer at her throat. Instead, they were at the front of her chemise, undoing its fastenings with a deftness that surprised her.

Only a moment later, when she stood naked before him, her chemise joining the rest of her clothes on the floor near her feet, Adrienne felt no self-consciousness, no awkwardness. She knew by the soft hiss of his indrawn breath that the sight of her more than pleased him, and the look in his eyes confirmed it.

Needing no invitation, Adrienne moved against him, the fine texture of his linen shirt brushing against her bare skin as she curved her hands behind his neck and drew his head down, urging his mouth to take its fill of her lips. When he did, her tongue began a slow and silent seduction. His hands glided down her spine, the faintly rough feel of them somehow stimulating to her as they pressed her hips against him, then roamed free over her waist, her ribs, her breasts, in even more stimulating play.

Swept by a desire to touch him as he was touching her, she tugged the hem of his shirt free and ran her hands under it and onto his hard flesh, reveling in the sudden contraction of his stomach muscles. Abruptly he gripped her arms and pushed her back, then pulled off his shirt, baring his torso to her.

His sun-bronzed skin gleamed in the lamplight, lean muscles rippling in his chest, shoulders, and arms as he unfastened the fly-front of his trousers, then hesitated. "Do you want me to turn the lamp down?"

"No." If there was color to her cheeks, it was not from embarrassment as she watched him strip off the rest of his clothes. When he stood before her, she was stirred by the magnificent breadth of his chest and shoulders, the tapered trimness of his hips, and the long columns of his legs. "You are beautiful," she said.

Succumbing to her fascination with the innate power of his body, she spread her hands onto his shoulders, rubbing her palms over their hard, coiled muscles. But the feel of him only whetted her appetite for more as she pressed her mouth to his chest, running her lips and tongue over its lean ridges and the tiny nubs of his male nipples, tasting the warm, salty flavor of him and inhaling the earthy and invigorating scent of his skin.

Before she could protest, he scooped her up into his arms and strung a trail of hungry kisses across her cheek, jaw, and lips as he carried her to the tester bed. He lowered them both onto it. Neither of them needed its relative narrowness to force them to lie close together, facing each other, their lips joined in an intimate kiss, their hands alternately caressing and pressing. There was no sense of urgency, only a desire to pleasure each other to the fullest. It incited a passion stronger and hotter than lust.

Adrienne felt consumed by heat—the furnacelike heat of his body that seemed to envelop her from head to toe, the moist heat of the kisses he burned over her face, lips, and throat, and the curling heat from within that spiraled through her with such a pleasant ache. His hands lifted her higher, with a strength and an ease that she'd come to expect. Then his lips brushed her breast, and she gasped at the fresh explosion of sensation. His hands had fondled her breasts and teased her nipples into erectness, but never his lips, his mouth, his tongue. When he drew a nipple into his mouth, Adrienne shuddered.

Brodie felt her tremble with pleasure—the pleasure he gave her as he tasted, tempted, and teased. He had never known such power or such humbleness as he heard her breath catch on his name. She was small, delicate, and fragile but more than strong enough to hold him—to move him. For all the lust, all the passion, all the desire that coursed through him, he was driven by a need to cherish and protect her. She belonged to him, and he was determined to show her how beautiful it could be for them, no matter the ache that grew hotter and hotter within him. He waited until her hips rubbed against him in eager insistence, until her hands pressed and urged in desperate demand, until the sounds coming from her throat revealed the intensity of her longing. Only then did he ease himself onto her, the caress of his hands subtly positioning her body to receive him.

She had a moment of making the small discovery that he wasn't too heavy for her. Nor did his greater height cause any awkwardness. They fit together naturally, the way God had intended. Then she could think of nothing but his hard body, the damp earthy smell of him, the wild taste of his mouth—and the kiss that swamped her, drawing her into some dark, secret place where there were only the two of them.

"I'll not hurt you, Adrienne." His voice rumbled against her skin. "I'll never hurt you."

But she knew he was wrong. It was inevitable that he would hurt her. Three years ago she had gone to her aunt with stories she'd heard from other girls in the convent about the horrible agony a woman was expected to endure on her wedding night when she was impaled by her husband. Tante ZeeZee had explained that a woman would feel pain when her maiden veil was torn by a man's entry, but she said the discomfort would pass in a little while and not return. Knowing that, Adrienne had no fear.

Yet the pain never came. She could feel him inside her, the slow and lazy, oh so very satisfying stroke of him, but each time she felt the beginnings of discomfort, the pressure was withdrawn. Then it would begin all over again, invading a little deeper.

She didn't understand, and she didn't care, not when it felt so good and the ache inside only became wilder and sweeter. Suddenly she felt a sharp pinch, followed by the incredibly wondrous sensation of him filling her. Her tiny gasp became a shuddering sigh. They were one, rising together in a harmony of rhythm that was its own form of beauty.

17

"The magnolias." Remy stood at the French doors leading onto the second-floor gallery, staring at the towering trees with green, leathery leaves on the front lawn. She turned to Nattie, faintly stunned by the realization. "Brodie Donovan built this house. I never thought . . . I assumed . . . even though I remember that the Garden district was originally established by wealthy Americans, it never occurred to me this house was built by anyone other than a Jardin. I should have known that the Jardins, being Creole, would have lived in the Vieux Carré."

"This was Donovan's house, all right," Nattie confirmed with a nod of her gray head.

"Then we got not only the shipping line from him but this house as well. How?"

"I'm getting to that." Nattie waved a hand at her, demanding patience. "Anyway, there's no doubt Adrienne knew exactly what she was doing when she went to bed with Brodie. By that I'm not saying that she didn't give herself to him for the same reason any young woman gives herself to the man she believes she loves. But she had other reasons."

Remy frowned. "What other reasons could she have?"

"Don't forget, in those days a woman was compromised merely by being alone with a man for an extended amount of time. And Adrienne always intended for her grand-père to find out that she'd been secretly meeting Brodie—at the appropriate time, of course—*and* she wanted her grand-père to know without a doubt that she'd been irreparably compromised. There was even a good chance she was going to have his baby. She figured her grand-père not only would have to accept Brodie Donovan, but he'd also insist that they get married." She paused briefly. "I think Adrienne had images of the two of them reigning over both American and Creole society, living a life still cushioned by the wealth and prestige of the Jardin name."

"Obviously that didn't happen," Remy guessed as she wandered over to an old rosewood prie-dieu, suddenly wondering who had knelt on its padded knee-rest to pray. Had it belonged to Adrienne? "Why? What went wrong, Nattie?"

"She didn't think about what might happen if her brother found out she was seeing Brodie. Which is exactly what happened," she replied. "By that time she'd probably been meeting Brodie secretly for almost a month, no oftener than twice a week. Now, when she came back from seeing him, she never used the stairs; she always came through the courtyard and entered the house that way. She figured if she was seen she always had the ready excuse that she hadn't been able to sleep and had gone outside to take some night air. . . ."

Adrienne moved along the cool, dim passage of the *porte cochère* to the scrolled iron gates at the end of it. She paused there and listened to the receding clop of hooves and the muted clatter of the carriage as it departed on Royal Street. She hesitated a minute longer, letting her ears adjust to the new silence and her eyes to the uneven darkness of the courtyard beyond the tall wrought-iron gates. The silvery glow from the moon highlighted the shininess of the magnolia's green leaves and gleamed on the central fountain's bronze statue, of a woman balancing a basin on her head, over which water flowed in a melodic whisper. But there was no sound, no movement other than that. And no light shone from the *garçonnière,* the narrow wing that extended from the main house and provided private quarters for the unmarried males in the family as well as for the occasional guest. The Lenten season had arrived, bringing an end to the winter's lively social season, so there were no guests, and the absence of any lights in the windows assured her that Dominique had retired for the night.

Carefully, Adrienne opened one side of the double gate and slipped through into the garden patio, closing the gate quietly behind her, then pushing back the hood of her cloak. Deliberately holding her pace to a wandering stroll, she moved along the brick walk that circled the fountain and its reflecting pool. The night air was scented with the fragrance of the shrubs and trees that were planted in abundance throughout the courtyard—honeysuckle vines entwining with the ivy to cover the high brick wall in the rear, sweet olive and fig trees shading the rosebushes, and crepe myrtles, gardenias, and camellias crowding the edges of the informal parterre.

By the time Adrienne reached the outside steps to the second-floor gallery, all her tension was gone. It wasn't necessary to feign insouciance as she climbed the stairs, thinking back on the pleasurable two hours she'd spent with Brodie and savoring the stimulating memory of their moments of lovemaking, warmed anew by it.

As expected, her room was dark, but her black maidservant Sulie Mae wasn't hovering at the French doors, waiting to unlock them and admit her, a necessity forced upon them by the nightly check her grandfather made before retiring to insure that all the doors were securely locked. Adrienne tapped twice on the glass. Almost immediately the familiar shape of the round-bosomed Negro woman appeared on the other side of the glassed doors. She fumbled briefly with the lock, then swung the door inward. Adrienne glanced down the length of the deeply shadowed and empty gallery and then stepped into her room, unfastening the front of her cloak, preparing to remove it and hand it to her servant.

A voice came out of the darkness, low and ominous—her brother's voice. "You may go now, Sulie Mae."

As Adrienne stiffened in alarm and swept her eyes over the black shapes in the darkened room to find him, a lamp-wick that had been no more than a faint speck of light was turned up, throwing a bright glow over the room. Dominique stood beside it.

"Michie Dominique, he say I gots to let him in," Sulie Mae murmured, her eyes round and dark with apprehension as she met Adrienne's accusing look. Then she hurried from the room.

Adrienne turned to face her brother, unconsciously tilting her chin a little higher at the sight of his cold and forbidding expression. "Dominique," she began with forced lightness.

"You were with the Yankee—and do not add to your shame with lies of denial."

She was stunned that he knew. How had he found out? Had Sulie Mae betrayed her? Recognizing that the answers were irrelevant, Adrienne dismissed the questions from her mind and admitted, "I was with him, yes. I love him, Dominique."

"And what of Grand-père?" he challenged in a voice that was all ice, his stare raking her. "How could you betray his trust? How could you bring this dishonor to him, to the family?"

"My love for Brodie is no dishonor, but Grand-père has refused to see that," Adrienne asserted. "He left me no choice."

"And you have left me no choice."

As he came toward her, Adrienne instinctively took a step back, intimidated by this man who seemed so unlike the brother she knew. "What do you mean by that?" she demanded, belatedly realizing that he wasn't approaching her

—instead, he crossed to the gallery doors, which Sulie Mae had left standing open. "Are you going to tell Grand-père?"

He paused in the doorway. "I would never deliberately say or do anything that I knew would hurt him—as you have done." He stepped onto the gallery and quietly closed the door behind him.

She believed him. He wasn't going to tell Grand-père about her assignations with Brodie Donovan. She felt momentarily weak with relief, aware that it would have ruined all her plans if her grandfather had found out from Dominique—but now she would have to alter those plans. She couldn't count on Dominique's keeping silent for long.

She realized she had to talk to her brother, make him understand the reasons for her actions. Not now, though. Tomorrow, when he was not smarting so from what he considered to be her betrayal.

Not for the first time in her life did Adrienne rail at society's duality of standards, which demanded strict observance of rigid moral codes by women but imposed no such inhibitions on men, leaving them free to drink, gamble, carouse—and install café-au-lait-skinned concubines in little cottages on Rampart Street.

When Adrienne entered the dining room the next morning for breakfast, only her grandfather and her aunt were seated at the table. Dominique's chair was empty. She murmured a greeting to her grandfather and nodded to her aunt, who was always sour-tempered in the morning, quick to speak sharply to the servants at the least clatter of dishes.

"Dominique is late this morning," Adrienne observed, taking her customary seat on her grandfather's left.

"*Non*, he arose early," her grandfather replied as he slathered raspberry sauce over a flaky pastry.

"Then he has left?" Adrienne asked, frustrated that she was being denied the chance to speak to him privately.

"He had his horse saddled more than an hour ago," her

grandfather confirmed, then added vaguely, "He made some mention of an appointment."

"Did he say when he would return?"

"Not until evening."

All through breakfast, Adrienne debated her next move. Before she'd left Brodie last night, she had arranged to meet him again tomorrow evening. Now she decided that until she reached some type of understanding with Dominique, it wouldn't be wise to keep the appointment. But to cancel it without a word of explanation—she couldn't do that, either. No, she had to advise Brodie of this new situation, and she could do that only in person. She couldn't run the risk of having a note fall into the wrong hands.

The instant she returned to her room, Adrienne summoned Sulie Mae. "I want you to take a message to the old fiddler Cado. Tell him, 'She will meet him at the market this morning,' " she said, deliberately not mentioning Brodie's name and trusting that the mere fact that she would risk a daytime meeting would lend an urgency and importance to her words.

The black woman drew back, shaking her head vigorously. "No, Missy, I can't do that. If Michie Dominique find out, he have Michie Jardin sell me."

In no mood to be opposed in this, Adrienne retorted, "You must, or *I* will have him sell you."

Two hours later Adrienne lagged behind her aunt, scanning the throng of shoppers and merchants gathered under the pillared arcade. The din was ceaseless, with hens squawking in their crates, merchants shouting out proclamations of their wares, parrots screeching from their cages, customers calling greetings to this person or that, and all of it abrasive to her as she kept watching for Brodie.

Stall after stall of fishermen proudly displayed their morning's catch, gray-blue bodies of fish gleaming in the sunlight, hard-shelled oysters piled in mounds, crayfish wiggling and brandishing their claws, dingy gray shrimp spread in layers six or seven inches deep waiting for a spiced boiling pot to turn them a delectable pink, and lazy crabs stirring reluctantly. But none of them tempted Adrienne's aunt as she continued on to the fruit and vegetable section to inspect the prickly pineapples for freshness. While she haggled with the vendor, Adrienne surreptitiously looked for Brodie. But he wasn't here either.

Nor was he among the butchers busy carving cuts of meat to order from fresh carcasses—nor among the huddle of flower merchants or the roughly clad bayou hunters with their assortment of wild fowl, turtles, and alligators. Worried, Adrienne looked around openly. Hadn't he got her message?

The clinking of foils echoed from the fencing room, followed by a well-modulated voice proclaiming, *"Bien.* Let us try it again." Again there was a ring of steel as rapiers met.

With ill-concealed restlessness, Brodie rose from his chair in the academy's austere office and crossed to the window, clasping his hands behind his back, fingers gripping each other tightly. He stood there—for how long, he didn't know—his tension mounting at the sound of clashing blades.

Then it stopped. There was a polite murmur of voices and then he heard footsteps approaching the door. Brodie pivoted from the window as the door opened and the academy's master walked in, a lean-visaged man with a deceptively warm and pleasant look. His fencing mask was tucked under one arm, and his other hand loosely held a tipped foil. Yet there was ever an alertness about him that spoke of well-honed instincts, muscles, and senses trained to react in fractions of seconds.

"Brodie, how good to see you, my friend. I regret that I had to keep you waiting. It was a rare morning lesson, you understand." Each movement was lithe and supple as he laid his fencing mask and glove on the writing table and placed the rapier beside them. "May I offer you coffee, or perhaps a glass of wine?"

"No," Brodie refused abruptly, and came straight to the point of his visit. "I need your advice, Pepe," he said, familiarly addressing the renowned fencing master José Llulla by his more common name. A Spaniard by birth, José "Pepe" Llulla was unlike most of the fifty or so masters with fencing schools strung along the flagstoned Exchange Alley. He did not dress extravagantly, affect the manners of a dandy, or try to enter the ranks of Creole society. More than that, he saved his money and invested it in various businesses— a sawmill, a grocery, a slaughterhouse, a barroom. It was through his many ventures that Brodie had first met this man who had lived the life of a seaman before becoming a *maître d'armes*, considered by many to be the finest swordsman ever to draw a blade in New Orleans.

"You seek my advice? I am flattered, Brodie."

"I have been challenged."

Merely saying the words recalled the coolness of Dominique Jardin's expression when he'd confronted Brodie outside the offices of the Crescent Line an hour earlier—and brought back the flicking brush of the man's glove against his cheek. There'd been no display of anger, no hot words. The challenge had been delivered in the precise, courteous manner dictated by the duello, the dueling code.

"You have been challenged—this is wonderful, *mon ami!*" the *maître d'armes* declared, smiling in delight. "Congratulations."

"Wonderful?" Brodie snapped. "I see nothing 'wonderful' in it."

"But of course it is wonderful," Pepe insisted with an expansive wave of his hand. "You have been accepted at last. A challenge cannot be issued to one who is not an equal. Tell me, who is your opponent?"

"Dominique Jardin."

A black eyebrow arched sharply. "A formidable rival, and a veteran of many duels—all of which he won with his blade. You are fortunate that he challenged you. The choice of weapons becomes yours. I suggest that you choose pistols."

"I'm not going to fight him."

The Spaniard stiffened, his look turning hard and cold. "You must."

"Dammit, I can't, Pepe. That's why I'm here. That's why I needed to see you. You know the proper procedures. There has to be some way this can be avoided, something within the letter of that damnable dueling code."

"If Monsieur Jardin chooses to accept an apology from you for whatever it is you have said or done over which he has taken offense, then there is no need for a duel to take place, and there is no loss of honor for either party. However, the apology must be tendered within the prescribed time. Once you meet on the field of honor, it is too late."

"You can forget the apology," Brodie said with a sigh. "He wouldn't find it acceptable."

"Then you must meet him."

He shook his head. "I can't."

"Then I advise that you get on one of your ships and leave, M'sieu Donovan. To refuse to meet him is tantamount to cowardice. You would be finished here in the Vieux Carré. And I suspect your American associates would lose their respect for you as well."

"I'm not leaving."

"You came here for my advice. I have given it to you. Since you are afraid—"

"I'm not afraid of him, Pepe. If there was no one else involved, I would meet him with shotguns at a handkerchief's length. But that isn't the case."

The Spaniard looked at him with new curiosity. "Someone else is involved? Who?"

"His sister, Adrienne. I intend to marry her, Pepe. Now do you see how impossible this situation is? No matter what choice I make, I lose. If I refuse to meet him, I'll be branded a coward. I'm not sure I could live with it, even knowing that it wasn't true. And I doubt Adrienne could bear the shame of it even if she knew I'd done it for her. As you pointed out, I'd be finished in this town, and if she married me, she'd be finished too. On the other hand, if I accept his challenge, she'll never agree to marry the man who killed her brother.''

'' 'Killed.' '' Pepe Llulla laughed easily, lightly. ''You Americans and your notion that every duel must mean the death of one. Honor is satisfied with the mere drawing of blood; a scratch on the cheek or the hand is enough. I myself have been in numerous duels, and regardless of the stories you may have heard to the contrary, the occasions when I have inflicted a fatal wound were few. Most are still walking around, sporting the scars from their encounter with me.'' He came over to Brodie and clamped a friendly hand on his shoulder, smiling broadly. ''Accept Monsieur Jardin's challenge. Meet him on the field of honor. Shoot to wound and pray to Le Bon Seigneur that his bullet does not strike a vital organ. Then allow the beautiful mademoiselle to nurse you back to health, let her be angry with you for dueling, let her fuss at you and love you all the more.''

Brodie hesitated, then slowly smiled. ''I knew there was a way.''

''It is not without risk, *mon ami*,'' Pepe reminded him.

''But it's a risk worth taking.''

''Have you chosen your second?''

''My brother Sean, I guess. I would ask you, Pepe, but I'd rather not draw you into the middle of this.''

''Perhaps that is wise,'' he conceded indifferently. ''Have you considered the time, the place, the weapons, the distance?''

Brodie gave him a dry look. ''Pepe, I've been spending the last hour trying to figure how to get out of this duel, not how to carry it out.''

''May I suggest you arrange to meet him late this afternoon—at four or five o'clock? It is never wise to allow yourself too much time to think about what is to come.''

''If you say so.'' The haste suited him. But his own thought was that he wanted this duel over with before Adrienne could find out about it. It was her nerves he wished to spare, more than his own.

"The oak grove on the Allard plantation is the common choice of sites. Everyone knows it. You may as well meet him *sous les chênes*." The Spanish master began slowly to pace the room, thinking, planning, deciding on details. "As for weapons, I have a fine pair of Navy revolvers. Have you handled one before?"

"Yes." Brodie nodded, remembering his river days. Only a fool traveled the Mississippi on a flatboat unarmed.

"You may have the use of mine, then. I suggest you set the distance at thirty paces." He allowed a brief smile to show. "After all, it is not your desire to kill your opponent, *oui?*"

18

The afternoon's warmth lingered over the courtyard, ignoring the long shadows of twilight that stretched across it. Adrienne betrayed none of her inner agitation as she wandered along the bricked walk. Pausing, she pretended to admire the perfection of a red rose while mentally she screened out the musical fall of the fountain's water and listened intently to the muted sounds coming from the street beyond the thick walls that enclosed the courtyard.

Where was Dominique? Already lights gleamed inside the house. If he didn't return soon, she would have no opportunity to speak to him privately before it was time to dress for the evening meal. Then what would she do? Postpone it until tomorrow? She doubted her nerves could stand it; already they felt brittle from the strain.

Again she resumed her apparently idle stroll along the parterre. Then came the groan of the tall wooden carriage gates swinging open, and the noise from the street grew louder. Adrienne turned to face the courtyard's scrolled gates, tense, expectant. She heard the clop and clatter of a horse and carriage in the flagstoned *porte cochère* and almost turned away, realizing that it couldn't be Dominique returning; he'd left on horseback, not in the family carriage. But who would be coming to call so late in the day?

A black groom hurried from the stables to hold the horse's head when the open carriage stopped before the flight of stairs. Drawn forward, Adrienne saw a short, slightly pudgy man alight from the carriage. She recognized Victor Dumonte, a contemporary of Dominique's and one of his closest friends. How oddly disheveled he looked, she thought, his cravat all askew, the front of his shirt stained. As he turned back to the carriage, he saw her and froze.

"Victor." She went to greet him and welcome him to the house, manners permitting her no other choice. Leaving the private patio, she passed through its wrought-iron gates and approached the carriage. "It is good to see you. But if you have come to speak with Dominique, he is not here. He left early this morning and has yet to return."

"I know." He took a quick step toward her and stopped again. Adrienne was struck by how unusually pale he looked, with no pink-cheeked glow to his face. He took her hands and she felt the clamminess of his skin, the sensation eliminating any further doubt that he was ill. Even his eyes had a sick look to them. "I—" Victor started to say something more, then stopped and looked back at a second man now stepping down from the carriage.

"Dr. Charron." Adrienne glanced at the gray-goateed man in surprise. His tall beaver hat sat firmly on his head, and a pair of spectacles rode the high break of his nose. He carried a walking cane but not his black medical bag. Adrienne saw it sitting on the carriage seat. "This is unexpected. I—"

The doctor wasted not a breath on a greeting, his expression stern, his manner grim. "Where is your grand-pére?"

"He is inside," she began, then frowned in bewilderment when he brushed past her without a word and hurried up the stairs. She turned back to her brother's friend, feeling the first glimmer of apprehension. "What is it? What is wrong, Victor?"

He looked down at her hands, his grip tightening on them. "There was a duel, Adrienne," he said in a low, choked voice.

She stared at the sickly pallor of his face, suddenly remembering how many times Dominique had called on Victor to act as his second—and how frequently Dr. Charron had served as the attending physician. "Dominique?"

When he lifted his head, there were tears in his eyes. "He was shot, Adrienne."

She made a small sound of protest, her eyes racing to the carriage as the driver and the family's Negro groom gently carried her brother's motionless form from it. For an instant she stared at Dominique's face, noticing how very white it looked against the black of his hair—the moment filled with a strange unreality.

She shook it off. "We must get him inside at once. The doctor will need his bag—"

"*Non.*" He checked her attempt to pull away. "Adrienne, he is dead."

"*Non,* it is not true!" She glared at him, furious that he had dared to make such a claim.

"I swear it is."

Ignoring his earnest plea, she twisted free of his hands. "I do not believe you. It cannot be." She moved immediately to her brother's side, his still body cradled in the arms of the liveried black driver and the old groom. She saw no wound of any kind—the front of his linen shirt showed not a trace of blood. But when she laid a hand against his smooth cheek, she was shaken by the coolness of his skin. "It is a mistake. It must be!" She leaned over him, sliding her hand around his middle—and stopping abruptly when she felt something damp and sticky.

A pair of hands gripped the points of her shoulders. She didn't resist them when they pulled her back, away from Dominique. She looked at her own hand, seeing the dull red stickiness on her fingers and palm. It was blood, but it wasn't warm, it wasn't bright—it wasn't . . . life.

From somewhere behind her came a moan of pain that sounded more animal than human. Turning, Adrienne saw her grandfather on the stairs, leaning heavily on the wooden rail. He seemed to become an old man before her eyes, his proud shoulders bowing, his stiff back hunching, his face turning as ashen as his gray hair as he stared at the body of his grandson.

Slowly, as if each step required all the strength he possessed, he came the rest of the way down the stairs and halted in front of the body. With eyes as dead as the man before him, he looked at the doctor.

"Who did this?"

"A *Yanqui*."

Adrienne stiffened.

"Who?" her grandfather persisted.

"Brodie Donovan."

"*Non*," she whispered in protest.

Her grandfather lifted his head at the name. "He lives?" The doctor nodded. "A shoulder wound. Nothing more."

Adrienne tried to be glad, but she was too numb. Over and over again she kept remembering the statement Dominique had made the night before in her room: "And you have left me no choice." She should have known what he meant by that. She should have remembered his inflexible code of honor. But never once had she considered what her brother's reaction might be to her activities. No, her whole attention had been concentrated on placing her grandfather in a position where he would be forced to accept Brodie.

"Dominique." A rasping sob broke from her grandfather as he said the name. Bending, he kissed a colorless cheek and murmured softly, brokenly, "Blood of my blood. My life."

She saw his shoulders shake with sobs more wretched for their silence. The first of her own rose in her throat. *Nom de Dieu*, what had she done?

*   *   *

"I don't understand," Remy said in confusion, pushing herself off the bed to pace the room. "If Brodie intended only to wound him, what went wrong? Was his own aim thrown off when he was shot?"

"No. It was one of those freak things nobody could have expected," Nattie replied. "Brodie's shot struck Dominique in the arm, but the bullet hit a bone and glanced off, entering his body and going right through his heart, killing him instantly."

"Then it was an accident, a horrible accident."

"It was that, all right."

"Surely Adrienne knew."

"Brodie told her."

"Then he saw her again." For some reason, Remy'd had the feeling that Dominique's death had meant the end of their affair.

"Briefly—at the St. Louis Cemetery, when her brother was laid to rest in the family tomb. . . ."

The sky was blue and cloudless, the sun warm and bright, its rays spilling between the leafy branches of the oaks and magnolias to cast their light on the whitewashed stucco of the cemetery's many "mansions" of the dead, built close together in a precise pattern that reminded Brodie of the houses standing shoulder to shoulder along the narrow streets of the Vieux Carré. Here too—in death as in life—many generations slept under the same roof.

Absently he adjusted the black sling that held his left shoulder immobile, his eyes never leaving Adrienne's veiled face. The filmy black net shaded her features but didn't hide them. From this distance they appeared to have been carved out of white marble, so cool and blank did they look, not a tear falling to glisten on her cheek.

Not so her aunt. Her weeping hadn't slackened since they'd arrived at the cemetery. Now that it was time to leave, it grew worse. Brodie watched as both Adrienne and her grandfather helped the grieving spinster to her feet. Emil Jardin himself bore little resemblance to the autocratic patriarch Brodie had faced a little more than a month ago; his eyes were dull and haunted, his firm stride reduced to a shuffling gait.

He stared at the three of them for a moment, huddled together in their black mourning dress yet unable to draw comfort from each other. Then Emil Jardin signaled to Adrienne that her assistance was no longer necessary. She stepped back, letting him lead her aunt away from the mausoleum. She started to follow, then hesitated and looked back, tilting her head to gaze at the family name, JARDIN, carved above the temple's bronze door, ornamented with laurel leaves and seraphim. She was frozen there for a timeless second. With an effort, it seemed, she dragged her glance away and trailed after her grandfather and aunt, staying a few paces behind and letting her grandfather deal with the mourners who had lingered to offer their condolences in person.

It was the chance Brodie'd been waiting for. He'd come hoping he'd be able to speak to her, even though he knew there was nothing he could say that would enable her to forget what he'd done. But he needed to talk to her—he needed to tell her how much he regretted it, he needed to say the words for his own sake.

He glanced at her grandfather's gray and tear-wet face as he passed by, then stepped out from between two temple-shaped tombs to intercept Adrienne when she approached. She faltered for an instant, then stopped.

"I had to come," he said. "I swear it wasn't deliberate on my part." In his mind's eye he saw again the grove of old oak trees dripping with gray moss, that moment when he'd brought the barrel of his revolver to bear on Dominique's long, lean shape thirty yards away, sighting on his arm and squeezing the trigger, that instant of relief he'd felt when he'd seen Dominique's arm jerk even as a bullet slammed into his own shoulder, the force half turning him so he never even saw Dominique crumple to the ground, the glimpse of everyone running to the limp form lying on the spring-green grass, the shock of hearing someone cry out, "He's dead!" and his own disbelieving protests insisting that his shot had been true, that Dominique had been wounded in the arm, without knowing the bullet had ricocheted off a bone and into his heart. "I'm sorry," he finished tightly.

"We each have our cause of deep regret." Just for an instant she let her own intense pain show. "My brother is dead. My family is dead. Everything is dead."

As she walked away, Brodie knew exactly what she meant. He felt dead inside knowing he'd never see her again. The steady beat of his heart was a lie.

"Of course, Adrienne didn't know how wrong she was," Nattie declared from her perch on the arm of the bedroom's overstuffed chair. "Not then."

"'Wrong'? What do you mean?"

"I mean she was pregnant, but she didn't realize it until a couple weeks after the funeral."

Remy sat down on the loveseat, all the pieces starting to fit together. "And even though she was pregnant with Brodie Donovan's child, her grandfather refused to let her marry the man who had killed her brother. And that child is the reason Cole said our name should be Donovan instead of Jardin."

"That's true, though there's one thing wrong with what you're saying. You see, the question of Adrienne marrying Brodie was never raised—not by old Emil Jardin, and definitely not by Adrienne."

"Why not? I would have thought—"

"You're forgetting the guilt she felt," Nattie broke in. "As far as she was concerned, she was the one who'd killed Dominique. Brodie had merely been the instrument of his death. Considering how much she loved her brother, that alone would've been a heavy load of blame to carry, but she had the added guilt of knowing that the family name had died with Dominique. That's why when she learned she was with child, instead of that knowledge filling her with deep despair, it gave her hope. That's why she wouldn't let her grandfather arrange a marriage for her even though she knew the scandal, the shame, the disgrace she would face by having a child out of wedlock back then."

Remy slowly shook her head. "I can't imagine Emil Jardin agreeing to that—not with his pride, his sense of family honor. However much he may have wanted the family line to continue, he couldn't have tolerated the humiliation of a bastard child continuing it—especially Brodie Donovan's. He did know Brodie was the father, didn't he?"

"He guessed. It wasn't too hard. . . ."

"This bastard you carry comes from the seed of that *Yanqui*, is this not true?" The glitter of loathing was in his eyes, a loathing born of disgust, a match to the pain that rasped his voice. "The same *Yanqui* who killed my Dominique. It is why he challenged him."

"*Non*," Adrienne denied that, her calm like an armor that not even his trembling rage could penetrate as she stood before him in her brother's darkened bedroom, the drapes pulled against a world that continued to go on. The room was exactly as it had been on the afternoon of his death—a change of clothes for dinner neatly laid out on the bed, his shaving things arranged on the bureau, the basin of water kept full and fresh by a servant. The only alteration was the tapers that burned in his memory on the prie-dieu. For it was here that her grandfather came to pray. In the days and weeks since Dominique's death, he had divided his time between this bedroom and the family tomb, isolating himself with his grief and sharing it with no one. And in all this time he'd hardly spoken a word to anyone, sitting in silence at meals, staring at the plate before him, and rarely touching the food on it. "Dominique knew only that I was meeting . . . him in secret." She deliberately avoided referring to Brodie by name, and spoke quickly to make her case. "It matters not who the father is, Grand-père. My child will be born a Jardin and raised a Jardin. He will know no other name, no other past. Through him, our family will live.''

''Through a bastard.'' The words were spoken low, thick with the disgrace inherent in the phrase.

''*Non*, Grand-père.'' She smiled faintly, serenely. ''This life that grows within me is God's will. He has taken Dominique from us, and He has given us this life in return.'' She moved toward him, lifting her hands, but he drew back stiffly. ''No one can take Dominique's place—in your heart or mine. I know that. But God in His wisdom has allowed me to conceive this child.''

''To punish you for your sins,'' he said bitterly.

''*Non*, Grand-père. It is so I may atone for them,'' Adrienne replied with a certainty of heart. ''My son's origins need never be known. Your friends are aware that we have distant relatives in France. In May, when the fever season approaches, we will sail for France to visit them. After my son is born in November, we can return home . . . to raise the baby of a Jardin cousin, orphaned at birth.''

And that would be her punishment, her pain—the knowledge that she would forever have to deny to the world and to her own child that she was his mother. It could be no other way. Just as she would have to live the rest of her life knowing she had killed her brother, as surely as if she'd pulled the trigger herself.

A knock at the door broke the thick silence in the room. In response, her grandfather snapped an impatient ''*Entrez*.''

The bedroom door swung open under the push of his black manservant's hand. ''Michie Varnier is here,'' Gros Pierre announced. ''I told him you don't want to see no one, but he say he gots to talk to you. He say there's an emergency at the old Clinton plantation.''

''See him, Grand-père,'' Adrienne said, quietly urging him to speak to the man who served as his secretary and assistant, handling the details for the family's many and varied business interests. After Dominique died, her grandfather had ceased to care about any of it and had let the full responsibility fall to Simon Varnier. "You have reason to care about the future. When you think on what I have said, you will see I am right." She held his look an instant longer, then turned and left the room.

"Is you going to see him, Michie Jardin?" the black asked, then added, "He sure was powerful upset."

Emil Jardin gave no sign that he'd heard him, his gaze lost on some distant point. Then he roused himself and nodded absently, *"Oui,* I need to see him."

"Finding out about the baby gave old Emil Jardin reason to go on, all right," Nattie declared. "But it was never the reason Adrienne thought she'd given him."

"What do you mean?" Remy asked, even as she guessed at the answer.

"I mean he set out to destroy the man who had taken his grandson's life and ruined his granddaughter."

"The Crescent Line." She had a sudden, sinking feeling that she knew how her family had acquired the shipping company.

"You've got it." Nattie pointed a long finger at her in affirmation. " 'Course, it wasn't something he could do overnight. And it wasn't something he could do without placing some money in the right hands—and as successful as Brodie'd become, that meant a considerable amount of money. Her grandfather ended up selling his sugar and cotton plantations to raise it. While he was doing that, he had his man Simon Varnier find out who Brodie was doing business with, both here and abroad, where he was getting his cargo, who was working for him, who he owed, and how much. After a couple months—about the time Adrienne and her Tante ZeeZee left for France—he put his plan in motion."

"And there was nothing Brodie could do to stop him, was there?" Remy mused aloud, recalling the power and influence

Emil Jardin had possessed through connections long established.

"At first he didn't even realize what was happening.
You've got to remember, he loved Adrienne. He'd taken it
hard, losing her that way. For a while he lost interest in
everything, including the Crescent Line. When things started
to go wrong for him—his captains leaving him to command
other ships, his crews going off on shore leave and not coming
back, mysterious fires breaking out aboard ships, cargo spoil-
ing on him or getting damaged, the insurance companies
hiking the premiums on him—he thought he was having a
run of bad luck. Within a year, nobody wanted to sail with
him, nobody wanted to ship their goods on his vessels, and
nobody wanted to sell to him. And the last was the part that
ended up making him suspicious. The others he could understand. People tend to be superstitious; if they thought his
ships were jinxed, they'd steer clear of him. But not to sell
to him—that didn't make sense. . . ."

An overcast sky spread a premature gloom over the Vieux
Carré, the black clouds hanging low and heavy as Brodie
made his way along a narrow street. In the far distance,
lightning danced, but the clatter of drays and the street noise
masked any faint rumble of thunder. Casting a weather eye
at the approaching spring storm, Brodie judged it to be another
three or four hours away. He welcomed its coming, wanting
a release from the charged tension in the air.

As he neared the corner, he found his steps slowing. He
rarely came to the Quarter anymore, not since. . . . It still
hurt to think of her, to see the places where he'd met her, to
remember her smile and the shining black glow of her eyes.
A year, and the pain was still as fresh as if it had been
yesterday, especially here in the Vieux Carré, where she
lived.

He spotted the old blind fiddler at his customary place on
the corner. Brodie stopped and almost turned around, not

wanting to talk to the black man who had relayed so many messages from her, afraid he wouldn't be able to keep from asking about her. He forced himself to think of the Crescent Line and the trouble it was in—and of his suspicions about its worsening situation, suspicions that it was more than bad luck.

He walked up to the fiddler and dropped a silver dollar in his hat. "How have you been, Cado?"

The old man stiffened at the sound of his voice and stopped playing, something he'd never done before. Startled, Brodie watched as the man bent down and fished around in his hat, then straightened up and held out a silver dollar.

"Your money ain't no good no more, Michie Donovan."

"What the hell are you talking about, Cado?"

Centering on his voice, the black man pushed his hand against Brodie's middle. "Take your money and go. Leave old Cado alone."

For an instant Brodie warred with his anger, torn between ripping the coin from the man's hand and smashing his fist into that cold black face.

"You've turned against me too, have you, Cado?" he muttered, seizing the black man's wrist, taking the silver dollar from his unresisting fingers, and flinging it into the gutter.

When he started to shove past him to cross the street, the old man murmured under his breath, "Four o'clock. The shoemaker's shop on Dumaine."

There was only one shoemaker's shop on Dumaine, a narrow hole-in-the-wall affair. A hand-painted plaque by the door identified the owner as Louis Germaine, F.M.C.—a free man of color. The door was propped open, letting in the heaviness of the storm-laden air. Promptly at four o'clock, Brodie walked into the shop, which was redolent of leather and polish.

An ebony-skinned man in a leather apron sat at a cobbler's bench. When Brodie walked in, he looked up, hesitated, and darted a quick glance at the open doorway, then nodded his head in the direction of a curtained opening in the rear of the shop.

When Brodie approached it, Cado's voice came from behind the thin curtain. "There's some boots on the counter to the right of you. Look 'em over, Michie Donovan, and don't give no sign you can hear old Cado. There's eyes everywhere."

Brodie did as he was told. "What's going on, Cado?"

"You made yourself an enemy," came his low reply. "I knew you'd be coming to old Cado. I been listening and I been hearing. The word's out: a man does business with you and he be finished in this town."

"Who put the word out?" Brodie picked up a boot and pretended to examine it, his fingers digging into the soft leather.

"You mean you ain't got that figured out?"

"I have my suspicions."

"If you're suspicioning old Emil Jardin, you'd be right," Cado said, and Brodie swore under his breath. "Ain't no use in that, Michie Donovan. You got more troubles coming your way. Talk is he bought up the notes on the ships and your house. I figure he's jus' waiting for the right time to say you gotta pay."

Brodie hung his head, knowing Jardin would pick a time when he was certain he couldn't scrape the cash together. "All because that damn bullet had to ricochet," he murmured to himself, realizing that the bullet had taken away more than Dominique Jardin's life, more than Adrienne from his side. Now it was going to cost him the Crescent Line. A part of him didn't care—and hadn't cared since he'd lost Adrienne.

"I'm suspicioning it's more than that, Michie Donovan. He ain't after you jus' cause you killed his grandson in a duel."

Adrienne. The old man was getting back at him for meeting her in secret, Brodie realized, but he said nothing, feeling too sick inside.

Cado began talking again. "When they come back from

France last December, they brought a baby with them, a little boy child. Claimed he didn't have no momma and no papa.''

"I heard.'' Brodie nodded indifferently.

"The house Negroes say Missy Adrienne love that boy like he was her own,'' Cado declared, then paused for several seconds. "The house Negroes, they say that boy got red hair. Real dark red hair . . . about the color of yours.''

In the heartbeat it took for the implication of those words to sink in, Brodie reacted, whipping back the curtain and stepping into the back room to grab the blind man by the collar of his gray shirt. "What're you saying? Speak plain. Is the boy my son?''

"Ain't no one can tell you that for certain sure but Missy Adrienne, her aunt, or Old Emil. It's a fact, though, she was feeling poorly before they left. And when they come back, they didn't have none of their servants with them—gave them all their freedom and left 'em in France. That says to me old Emil didn't want them to come back here and do no talking. Then there's that red hair of his. Where would a Jardin get red hair? If you ask old Cado, there can only be one place —and that's from his daddy.''

Brodie loosened his hold on the blind man's collar, never having wanted to believe anything so much in his whole life. "His name,'' he said thickly. "Do you know it?''

"Jean-Luc Étienne Jardin.''

"Jean-Luc. Luc.'' He liked the sound of that.

But was he his son? The question drove Brodie from the shop and up the street. He turned on Royal and didn't stop until he reached the Jardin home. A cool breeze brought the smell of rain to him as he hesitated briefly, then went directly to the pedestrian gate cut into the tall wooden carriage doors. He opened it and stepped through into the tunnel-like passageway of the *porte cochère*. He moved briskly to the stairs and took them two at a time, then paused at the top. The second-floor gallery was empty, the French doors leading onto it from the house standing open to admit the fresh breeze.

The indistinct murmur of voices came from inside, their

tone and texture definitely feminine. Brodie paid no attention to them and listened instead for another sound. When he heard the gurgling laughter of a baby, he followed it to a pair of open doors and walked in.

He paused a moment to let his eyes adjust to the deeply shadowed interior, then looked around. It was a bedroom, the set of silver brushes and combs on the rosewood vanity table telling him it was a woman's bedroom. He heard the happy coo of laughter again, coming from a corner of the room. He spotted the tall crib, draped in lacy mosquito netting. There was movement behind it, a waving of arms.

The last few steps to the crib seemed long. Almost hesitantly, Brodie lifted the netting to look at the baby inside, conscious of the quick beating of his heart and the tightness in his throat.

A baby, sitting up by himself, looked back at him with wide, startled eyes. His hair was dark and thick, with a telltale glint of red showing in it. He scowled at Brodie as if expressing his annoyance at being surprised, then grabbed at the silk hem of a blanket and flailed the air with it.

Brodie hooked the netting over the bar, freeing his hands so he could trail a finger over that smooth cheek. "It's a fine-looking lad you are, Jean-Luc." As he drew his hand away, the little boy grabbed for it, squealing with delight when he caught hold of it. As the child tried to pull himself upright, Brodie could feel the straining of his small muscles, and he smiled. "You're a bit young to be standing, aren't you?"

But he reached under the boy's arms and set him on his bootied feet. Then, having gone that far, he picked him up —a little awkwardly, his hand momentarily tangling with the long linen gown the baby wore before he managed to smooth it over his long, chubby legs.

"Somebody should tell your mother you look like a girl in this thing," Brodie murmured, receiving another scowl in reply. "As hefty as you are, there's no doubt you're a boy."

The scowl faded into a look of fascination as Jean-Luc stared at Brodie's mouth and chin, his hand coming up to investigate, little fingers curling onto his lower lip. Brodie caught at his hand and freed his lip from the boy's fingers, then chucked him under the chin with his own little fist. Jean-Luc gurgled a laugh, breaking into a wide smile. Brodie wanted to laugh too, but the pleasure he felt was too deep, too intense; it choked him instead. Just for an instant, he hugged the boy to him and pressed his lips against his temple, breathing in the baby-cleanness of him.

Suddenly, unexpectedly, he had the sensation of being watched. He looked over his shoulder at the door to the hall. Adrienne stood inside it, dressed in black, just as she'd been the last time he'd seen her, at the cemetery. The color suited her, bringing out the darkness of her hair and eyes and the luminous whiteness of her skin.

For a long moment, words wouldn't come to him. He had the feeling she'd been standing there for some time. He turned slightly, and her gaze went from him to the baby in his arms, then back to his face.

"I wanted to see my son."

She said not a word, her expression remaining serenely composed, yet there was a shiny brightness to her eyes, the shiny brightness of tears—happy tears, proud tears. Her look eliminated any vestige of doubt that the child was his.

A jagged bolt of lightning flashed from the dark clouds, lighting up the late-afternoon sky. It was followed immediately by an explosive crash of thunder that shook the glass panes in the French doors. Jean-Luc whimpered, his lower lip jutting out in an uncertain quiver. With the second clap of thunder his whimper became a full-blown wail, and he stiffened in Brodie's arms and turned, stretching out needing hands to his mother. When Adrienne came over, Brodie reluctantly surrendered him to her, watching those small arms cling to her and listening to the shushing croon of her voice.

The wind and the rain came next, driving across the gallery and sweeping through the open doors. Brodie knew he should leave, but he continued to stand there, gazing at the two of them, a thousand *if-only*'s going through his mind, his heart twisting with each of them.

"Adrienne?" Footsteps and the rustle of layers of silk swishing together came from the hall. "Is that Jean-Luc crying? What is wrong?"

Adrienne took a step toward the hall door, calling, "The storm has frightened him, Tante ZeeZee." She looked back at Brodie, her eyes begging him to go.

He hesitated, then reached out and stroked Jean-Luc's silken hair and let his fingers run lightly over her hand as it cupped the back of the boy's head, feeling the softness, the warmth, of her skin. Suddenly he didn't trust himself to stay. He turned abruptly and went out the way he'd come.

When he left the shelter of the *porte cochère,* closing the gate behind him, he paused, oblivious to the sheeting rain. He remembered the sensation of holding the baby in his arms, the little fingers pulling at his lip, the softness of him, the strength of him. A son. He had a son. He walked down the street smiling, tears mingling with the rain that streamed down his face.

19

The carriage rolled across Canal Street and entered the brash and raw American section of the city. Emil Jardin sat stiffly erect on the tufted leather rear seat, his gaze fixed on some distant point, not deigning to glance around him. Usually his eyes had a flat, dead look to them, coming alive only when Brodie Donovan was mentioned. They were alive now.

His gloved hands adjusted their grip on his silver-handled cane. "This attorney, this—" He lifted a hand to gesture, searching for a name.

"Horace Tate," Emil Jardin's ever-precise, ever-fastidious secretary, Simon Varnier, supplied the name.

"*Oui*, Tate." His hand returned to its resting place atop the cane, which he carried more out of habit than out of necessity. In his youth Emil Jardin had carried a *colchemarde*—a sword cane. Everyone had, back then. Although he was too old and too slow for such a weapon now, he liked the reassuring feel of a cane in his hand. It was his gavel, tapping the floor for attention; his pointer, directing that attention where he wanted it to be; his rod, administering sharp raps of reprimand; and his scepter. He took strength from it. "This Tate, he told you nothing about this information he claims to have on Donovan?"

"He said he had information on the Crescent Line, not Donovan," Simon corrected, with his customary insistence on exactness. "Information he was certain would be of enormous interest to you. He refused to tell me what it was. In fact, he was most adamant that he would speak to no one but you."

"What of this warning he issued?"

"*Warning* is my word. M'sieu Tate *strongly advised* that you make no further move against the Crescent Line until you had spoken with him. He indicated that you may wish to take a different course of action once his information is in your hands."

"What could this mean, I wonder?" Emil Jardin murmured, his gray eyebrows drawing together to form a thick, solid line.

Simon Varnier took him literally and responded with his own speculation. "We know Donovan has been trying to sell three of his ships. Perhaps he has found a buyer for them. Or perhaps he has obtained financing from some unknown source. If he has, then it would not be wise to demand payment at this time for the notes you hold."

"What do you know of this Tate?"

"Very little. He landed in New Orleans on the first of March, barely a month ago. He says he is from St. Louis, but he arrived not by riverboat, but on one of Donovan's ships that had stopped in Boston. I suspect that is how he came to know about Donovan's situation."

"But how did he discover my interest in him?"

"He refused to disclose his source."

"He will disclose it to me before this goes further." He didn't like the idea that someone new to the city had learned so quickly that he was the force behind the move to crush Brodie Donovan—to crush him slowly, to make him suffer, to make him feel the pain, the grief, the humiliation and shame that he, Emil, knew. The man had destroyed lives—his, Dominique's, and Adrienne's. It was only right that he be destroyed, and only fair that a Jardin be the instrument of his destruction.

As the carriage slowed, Emil Jardin lifted his head and took note of his surroundings, looking down the prominent length of his patrician nose at the string of hastily constructed clapboard buildings. On only two other occasions in his life had he found sufficiently strong reason to venture into the *Yanqui* section. Both times he'd sworn that nothing would induce him to repeat the experience of being in the midst of those jostling, crude, loud-talking *Americains*, always hurrying, always demanding, always greedy.

"If this attorney was so anxious to share his information, why could he not have come to the Vieux Carré?" Emil grumbled when the carriage rolled to a stop in front of one of the clapboard buildings splashed with whitewash. "Why was it necessary for us to come to *this* place to meet with him?"

"I explained that," Simon Varnier said patiently. "Horace Tate is a cripple. A childhood injury left him without the use of his right leg. He has great difficulty getting in and out of a carriage, and he could not have walked the distance from his office to yours."

"I cannot think what information this man could have to give us that would be of any value." But he had to find out, and he stepped down from the carriage.

Horace Tate's office was as spare and inelegant as the building's exterior. A collection of worn law books occupied crude shelves of bare, rough wood, and more sat in a trunk waiting to be unpacked. There were scratches and gouges in the oak panels of the large kneehole desk that dominated the room. Emil Jardin walked straight to it, looking neither to the left nor to the right, his gaze fastened on the man behind it—though he seemed hardly a man, with his dusting of freckles and thatch of hay-colored hair. His quick smile had the eagerness and innocence of a boy's. He reminded Emil of a young man who had barely reached his majority, coming to the city fresh from the river bottoms, whose view of the world had been obscured by the back end of a mule pulling a plow—an impression reinforced by the ill-fitting suit and poorly tied cravat he wore.

"Mr. Varnier, it's good to see you again," he greeted them, speaking in English with a thick country drawl. "And you must be Mr. Jardin. Forgive me if I don't get up, but this leg of mine makes it mighty awkward." Emil observed the limp and crooked sprawl of the attorney's right leg under the desk, and the pair of sturdy canes propped against the plaster wall behind his chair. "Have a seat." Horace Tate waved a hand in the direction of the three chairs crowded in a semicircle in front of his desk.

Emil ignored the chairs and the invitation, choosing to stand, certain, now that he'd seen Horace Tate, that their meeting would be an extremely brief one. "Let us not waste time, M'sieu Tate."

"I agree." The voice came from somewhere behind him to his left. Emil turned and stiffened in shock.

Brodie calmly met his thunderstruck look and raked his thumb-nail over the lucifer, then held the flame to the tip of his cigar. "Surprised?" he queried between puffs.

Purpling, Emil Jardin swung back to the attorney. "What is the meaning of this? It is an insult. An outrage." He stamped the floor with his cane. "Come, Simon. We are leaving."

He turned and flashed a look at Brodie, as if expecting him to try to stop him. Brodie merely shrugged his indifference. "You can stay or go. It doesn't matter to me. But you might want to take a look at the documents Mr. Tate has for you. They could make for some interesting reading."

Emil glared at Brodie for a long moment, then thrust a hand at his assistant. "Let me see these documents."

Horace Tate silently passed them to Simon Varnier, who

gave them to Emil Jardin as Brodie wandered over to the far side of the desk. "Pull out a chair for him, Simon. I think he'll want to sit down."

Emil had barely got past the first paragraph when his hand began to tremble and the color drained from his face. "What is this?" He sank into the chair Simon had pulled out for him.

"Exactly what it says," Brodie replied. "You seem so anxious to destroy the Crescent Line, I thought you might like to know I don't own it anymore."

His fingers curled into the papers, crumpling their edges. "You cannot do this!"

"It's done—all legally signed, sealed, registered, and recorded," Brodie waved the cigar at the papers. "You don't have to let them stop you, though. You can still go through with your plans to ruin the Crescent Line. Of course, it will be interesting to see how you'll go about demanding payment on those notes from your own great-grandson. But I forgot. You refer to Jean-Luc as your ward, don't you? Then as his legal guardian, you should know that he's now the owner of a shipping company and a house. If you'll read further, you'll see I've named Mr. Tate here, Father Malone, and Adrienne as the administrators of his properties until my son turns twenty-one."

"How—" Emil choked off the rest of the question.

"How did I find out Jean-Luc was my son? It was a good job you did of muffling my sources of information, but you failed to silence all of them."

"You cannot prove this."

"I can't prove it, not legally. But he is my son. I know it and you know it." Brodie moved to the corner of the desk, dropping his air of coolness and seeking the confrontation he'd arranged.

Emil Jardin rose from his chair and hurled the documents down on the desk. "I will see you in your grave for this."

"Maybe you will. But my death—whether by your hand or by God's—won't change the one thing that matters: Jean-

Luc is my son. He may carry the Jardin name, but he has Donovan blood.''

On that note Emil Jardin stalked from the room, his cane pounding the hardwood floor with each stride.

The honking of a car's horn somewhere outside jarred Remy into the present. "Then Brodie gave the Crescent Line to his natural son,'' she murmured. "Emil Jardin didn't steal it from him.''

"It wasn't for lack of trying,'' Nattie declared as she pushed off the armrest of the stuffed chair.

"And Brodie? What happened to him?''

"He died in August of that same year.''

She remembered the threat Emil had made, swearing he'd see him in his grave. "How? Did Adrienne's grand—''

"No one knew for sure—except Brodie and old Emil. They say he died of yellow fever. Old Bronze John, they called it back then. Maybe he did. That summer of eighteen fifty-three saw one of the worst yellow-fever epidemics ever to hit New Orleans. Somewhere around fifteen thousand died from it, although some claim the figure was more than twenty thousand. Upwards of sixteen hundred died the same week in August that Brodie did. There were so many bodies needing to be buried, officials didn't bother with death certificates. Which is why there's none showing the cause of Brodie's death. And by then there weren't enough gravediggers to keep up with all the work. Coffins were stacked up like crates in a warehouse. The situation got so desperate they dug trenches and dumped the bodies in common graves. That's where Brodie ended up—in an unmarked grave. It was a terrible, terrible time.''

"And Adrienne?''

"She and her family escaped it. Like always, they left the city the first of May, before the fever season arrived. She knew what was going on here. The whole world knew. People from all over the country sent gifts of food and money,'' Nattie said, then paused. "Adrienne never married. Wore black the whole of her life—for her brother, folks claimed, but I think she wore it for Brodie too. Every All Saints' Day, she went around and placed flowers on the common graves of the yellow-fever victims—because she didn't know which one Brodie was in. Old Emil couldn't have liked that, but I guess by then she didn't care whether he did or not. Old Bronze John took Father Malone too. And five years later Horace Tate was killed when the boiler on a riverboat exploded. He'd been on his way to visit his family in St. Louis.''

"And Adrienne ended up as the sole administrator for her son.''

"That's right. And that's how Emil Jardin ended up running the Crescent Line—and the Union blockade during the Civil War. Made a fortune at it, too. Why, it wasn't nothing for one of his ships to net almost a half a million dollars in *one* round trip. And the war went on for four years, with the ships making anywhere from five to ten trips a year. Most Southerners lost everything they had in the war, but old Emil Jardin got rich—or Jean-Luc did, since it was really all his, and old Emil didn't live long enough to enjoy much of it. He died in eighteen-seventy, after Jean-Luc turned eighteen.''

"Then the Jardins were the war profiteers,'' Remy mused absently, and she leaned against the curved back of the love-seat. "I wonder how Cole found that out? I suppose if he went far enough back in the company records he would have found a copy of the document transferring all Brodie's interest in the Crescent Line to Jean-Luc. Maybe there was even some mention of his death in eighteen fifty-three—long before the Civil War started.''

But it didn't explain why he had dragged Brodie Donovan's portrait out of storage and hung it in place of her grandfather's. He had to know it would upset her family, especially her father—which meant it had been a deliberate act. Why would Cole want to deliberately antagonize him?

"Are you still going to take that shower and change?'' Nattie wanted to know.

"Yes.'' She nodded, still preoccupied with her thoughts.

"I'll lay you out some clean towels, then."

As Nattie headed for the adjacent bathroom, Remy rolled to her feet, restless again. She crossed to the French doors, unlocked them, and stepped onto the front gallery. Like twin sentinels, the two magnolia trees stood guard over the front lawn, magnolia trees that Adrienne had suggested Brodie plant.

Remy paused for a moment, then walked to the railing, its delicate ironwork a tracery of leaves and flowers. She let her gaze wander over the lawn, the wrought-iron fence that surrounded it, and the quiet street beyond.

Catty-corner across the street, a navy-blue sedan was parked at the curb. Remy noticed the driver sitting behind the wheel, her eye drawn by the incongruity of his dark hair and neatly trimmed salt-and-pepper beard, which looked more salt than pepper from this distance. He appeared to be writing something. She guessed he was a salesman. At that moment, he looked up. Realizing that he'd seen her, Remy turned from the railing and walked back to her room, not wanting her presence to be taken as an invitation for him to come pitch his wares.

As she entered the room, she glanced at the antique tester bed and stopped, suddenly wondering if Adrienne and Jean-Luc had lived in this house after Emil Jardin died. She was certain they must have. How else could it have become the family home? And if it had been haunted with memories for Brodie, how much more haunted it must have been for Adrienne.

A pink-palmed hand waved in front of her face. Startled, Remy blinked and focused her gaze on Nattie's high-cheeked face. "Sorry, I didn't see you."

"I guessed," she said dryly. "The towels are all laid out for you, and your robe's hanging on the back of the door."

"Thanks."

"What's wrong?" Nattie frowned at her in puzzlement. "You looked like you were in some kind of a trance."

"I was thinking about Adrienne, remembering how much

she liked the social life back then—and how much she pitied her Tante ZeeZee. Yet she ended up just like her, a spinster—alone. I wonder where she found the strength to do it.''

''Honey,'' Nattie said, offering another one of her sad and sage smiles, ''a woman is like a teabag—you never know how strong she is until you get her in hot water.''

Remy laughed, yet she had the feeling that somewhere nearby, trouble seethed. Where and of what kind, she couldn't remember. But she needed to be there. Why? To prevent what? To stop whom?

20

The museum complex on Jackson Square wasn't the place. At least her visit to it hadn't given her any indication that it was. Remy stood at one of the desks in the museum's office area, closed to the public, and absently twined the telephone receiver's coiled cord around her forefinger.

Gabe's voice came over the line. "If you're calling to tell me you're too tired to go to the museum this afternoon, I'm not surprised—considering how early you were up this morning."

"Actually, I'm calling from the museum."

"You're there?" She could hear the frown of surprise in his voice. "I thought you were coming to my office at two-thirty so we could go together."

"I was." After spending all morning wandering the house, she'd been on the verge of going crazy from inactivity. Then her brother had called around lunchtime to let her know he'd talked their father out of sending her to that clinic outside of Houston. In passing Remy had mentioned she was thinking about going to the museum later on, and Gabe had immediately insisted on going with her. At the time, she'd agreed. It wasn't until later that she'd known she would prefer to see it alone—with no one to distract her with talk—so she could be open to any impressions, any memories, any sense of trouble. "I was too restless sitting around the house, so I left early and came here to look around on my own."

"Then you've already been through everything."

"Yes." She couldn't keep the dispirited tone from her voice.

"You seem . . . discouraged. Weren't you able to remember anything?"

"Unfortunately, no," she said on a sigh. Nothing had been familiar to her—not any of the layouts, not a single exhibit, not one member of the staff, nothing.

As she idly scanned the bank of television monitors, part of the museum's security system, on the opposite wall, she noticed an older man standing near the traveling exhibit. With his dark hair and distinctively whitish beard, he looked exactly like the man she'd seen in the car in front of her house. Obviously she'd been wrong to assume he was a salesman. He must be a tourist. It was odd, though, that he was wearing a suit and tie. Most of them dressed much more casually, especially in the daytime. And he certainly wasn't very interested in the exhibit. The way he was looking around, Remy had the impression he was searching for someone.

"What are your plans now?" Gabe asked, distracting her attention from the black-and-white monitors. "Are you going to stay there for a while, or head home?"

"I don't think so. I'll—"

"Don't tell me. I think I can guess," he broke in. "You're going to Canal Place and see if you can buy out Saks and Gucci's this time."

He sounded so certain that Remy frowned. "What makes you say that?"

"Because you always go on a shopping binge when you're depressed."

"I do?"

"You do," he declared, with an undertone of amusement. "I'd offer to carry your purchases for you, but I've got some paperwork I should catch up on. Why don't we meet at La Louisiane for drinks at, say . . . about four-thirty? That'll give you almost three hours to shop."

"All right," she agreed, though she had no desire to go shopping.

There was a hesitation on the other end of the line, as if Gabe sensed her reluctance. "Remy . . . you aren't going to get yourself lost or—wander down to the docks again, are you?"

"No. I promise." She smiled at the phone.

"Good. I'll see you at four-thirty, then."

"At La Louisiane," she confirmed, then hung up the receiver when the line went dead. "Thanks," she said to one of the staffers, who nodded in response.

As Remy started to leave the museum's administrative offices, a young woman in her early twenties came bounding up to her, her dark hair cut in a short, sleek bob with a full fringe of bangs. She stopped abruptly, exclaiming in delight, "Remy! When did you get back?"

"Last night," she replied, silently wondering who this girl was.

"How was the Riviera? I expected you to have a gorgeous tan that would make all of us poor working girls green with envy," she said, scanning Remy from head to toe. "That's a gorgeous outfit. Did you get it in France?"

"It was in my closet." She had no idea where she'd bought it.

"I wish I had your closet," she responded, casting an openly admiring eye over the hunter-green paisley jacket and blouse that Remy had paired with a navy skirt and red belt. "Have you got time for a cup of coffee or something? I've got about an hour before my tour gets here, and I'm dying to hear all about Mardi Gras in Nice. It can't possibly be as crazy as it is here."

"I'd love a cup—" Remy began, then stopped, a wry

smile curving her mouth. "This is awkward. I'm sure I know you, but—I can't remember who you are. You see, I . . ." She hesitated, but there was no way to say it except straight out. "I have amnesia."

The girl gave a jaw-dropped look. "You're kidding."

"I wish I were."

"Oh my God, you're not kidding," she declared. "For heaven's sake, what happened? How? Oh, Remy, you've got to tell me all about it." She reached out to clutch at her hand, then laughed self-consciously. "I forgot. You don't remember me. I'm Tina Gianelli. We both started working here at about the same time."

With that, she caught at Remy's hand again and practically dragged her back to the employee area, sat her down at a table, and demanded again to know all about it. Remy briefly filled her in, keeping to the basic facts and concluding with, "I came to the museum today hoping something would be familiar, but when I wandered through the various exhibits, I felt like a stranger looking at things I'd always known about."

"In a way, you *have* been something of a stranger around here lately," Tina stated, combing her fingers through one side of her hair and giving it a flipping toss. "You're hardly ever here more than two or three times a week, and then only for a couple of hours. It's certainly not like it was in the beginning. Of course, the circumstances were different then."

" 'Different'? In what way?" Remy studied her curiously.

"You came to work here shortly after your fiancé drowned. I think you wanted to lose yourself in something, and the past probably seemed safe—without a lot of constant reminders of him, if you know what I mean," she said, then added quickly, "By that I'm not implying this was nothing more than distraction. You seemed to really enjoy working here. Heavens, when you weren't helping with the tours, you were persuading some family friend to either loan or donate an item to the museum—especially things for the eighteen-fifties house and the Mardi Gras exhibit.''

"But you're saying that lately I've lost interest in my work here," Remy guessed.

"It isn't that you've lost interest, exactly. I've just had the feeling there isn't enough challenge here for you." She paused and cast a rueful smile at Remy. "I'm afraid I'm putting this badly, but—it's like you enjoy this as diversion, but it's not satisfying enough to be your life's work. Am I making any sense?"

"Possibly more than I realize," Remy murmured thoughtfully, then lifted her shoulders in a light shrug. "Who knows? This amnesia might turn out to be a good thing and make me take stock of my life and decide what it is I want—and don't want—to do with the rest of it.''

"Wouldn't that be something? Truthfully, I've always wondered why you never got involved in your family's shipping business, but I suppose when you live with your family, you don't want to work with them every day, too," she said. Then she suddenly brightened. "I've got an idea—why don't you tag along on this tour with me? It might be just the thing to help you remember.''

Remy glanced at the large wall clock. "I'd better not. I'm supposed to meet my brother for drinks at four-thirty—''

"You are! That's nice. Although I'll never understand why it takes some sort of crisis to shake a family up and make them pay attention to each other. I guess we get too caught up in our own lives. I remember when my mother was in that terrible accident last summer and my brother flew home. We sat down and talked—I mean really *talked*—for the first time in years. I learned so much about him that I never knew.''

"Hey, Gianelli," a voice called from the doorway, "your tour's here.''

"Already," she protested and flashed a look at the clock. "Wouldn't you know, they're early? Look, I've got to go,'' she said, pushing to her feet. "Give me a call, OK? And don't use amnesia as an excuse. My number's in your address book —under *G* for Gianelli."

"I'll remember," Remy said, and followed her out of the room.

Outside the sun was bright and warm, the weather atypical of the gray and damp dreariness of a New Orleans February. Yet Remy couldn't bring herself to appreciate it.

At the corner, while she waited for one of the city's many mule-drawn carriages to roll by, she looked back over her shoulder at the museum that had been another dead end in her search, her glance falling on the entrance just as the man with the grizzled beard emerged in some haste, stopping to quickly scan the street. Guessing that someone had failed to meet him as planned, Remy briefly empathized with his anxiety and frustration. She felt those things too, only in her case they were colored with discouragement as she crossed to the other side of the street.

She was beginning to doubt this feeling she'd had that she was desperately needed somewhere. It didn't appear that she was *needed* anywhere. And she was beginning to suspect that this inner compulsion was really only a desire to give meaning to her life. It made sense—a good deal of sense.

Yet there was that man in Nice, the one she'd been struggling with. Why? Over what? Who was he? The description from the witnesses was so vague that it could have fit almost anyone—including the bearded man.

Remy sighed and a second later realized how fast she was walking. She slowed her steps and looked around to get her bearings. She was on St. Ann. She glanced at the old buildings, noting the smooth plaster covering on them, chipped here and there to reveal powdery red brick beneath. Cars were parked along the curb, lining one whole side and turning the narrow thoroughfare into a one-way street. As she neared a pair of tall wooden gates, the entrance of an old *porte cochère*, she idly wondered if a courtyard could still be found on the other side.

Garbage cans and black plastic trash bags were piled in front of one of the scarred doors. A scruffy long-haired cat rummaged through the contents. He saw her and crouched low, as if to flee, regarding her with suspicious green eyes. Except for a patch of white at his throat, he was all black— and big, weighing at least twenty pounds. The tip of his left ear had been chewed off, and Remy guessed that his long hair hid even more scars.

She started to smile, then stopped, realizing, "You're Tom, aren't you? You're Cole's cat."

When she took a step toward him, the cat flattened his ears and showed his fangs in a silent hiss, then lashed the air with his tail and bounded to the top of a metal garbage can. Stunned, Remy watched as the black cat hurled himself at the old wooden carriage gates and clawed his way over the top with an alacrity a boot-camp trainee would have envied.

Was he really Cole's cat? Cole lived in the Quarter, didn't he? She was almost certain he'd told her that. And she had a vague memory that his apartment was located somewhere on St. Ann. She looked again at the old carriage doors the cat had disappeared behind. Was this the building?

A few feet away, a recessed doorway marked the entrance to it. Remy hesitated momentarily, then walked over to it and pushed it open. A wide cool hall stretched away from the door. French doors, their glass panes grilled and barred for security, stood at the opposite end. On her right, a curved staircase led to the second floor.

When she stepped into the hall, she noticed the row of mailboxes. Pausing, she stared at the first one, the one marked 1A, the one with the smudged lettering that read C. BUCHANAN. Remy hesitated again, then crossed to the side door near the end of the hall.

There was no bell, only a large brass knocker cast in the shape of a roaring lion with a heavy ring suspended from the corners of its mouth. She studied it for a long second, then reached up. Of their own volition, it seemed, her fingers slipped inside the lion's mouth—and touched a key hidden in a hollow at the back of its mouth. As she slipped the key into the lock and gave it a turn, she told herself that she wasn't really trespassing—she only wanted to see if his apartment was familiar to her, if it would spark some memory.

The well-oiled door swung silently inward. She walked in and quietly closed the door behind her. The living room was a masculine mix of heavy, solid furniture and large over-stuffed sofas and chairs, rough-textured tweeds, and smooth leathers, all in deep earth tones of brown, tan, and burnt red.

In her encompassing gaze around the room, Remy noticed a framed sporting print hung at eye level on the cinnamon-glazed wall near her. The scene depicted a boxing match held amidst an unspoiled landscape, with a throng of well-dressed spectators crowded around an alfresco ring, turning it into a sea of top hats. In the center of the ring two pugilists in tight-fitting breeches, their hair neatly combed, faced each other in the old-time upright stance. She knew immediately that it was the print that had arrived that day she'd gone to his office to take him to lunch.

She swung around to look at the other framed prints on the living-room walls. There was a foxhunting scene hanging above the heavy-beamed mantel, the scarlet red of the riders' jackets against the gleaming coats of their mounts catching her eye. And near the hallway on her right was a Currier and Ives print of a harness race.

The hallway. It led to the bedroom. Suddenly, in her mind's eye, she could see the golden gleam of brass accents on the lustrous black iron bed, the mixed blue of the striped spread, the clutter of men's things on the dresser—and Cole lying on the bed, cushioned by propping blue pillows, bare to the waist, the coverlet down around his hips.

Abruptly she turned from that image and found herself facing the far door in the living room. What was behind it? She couldn't remember. Curious, Remy walked over and gave the door a push, then swung it open wider to see more of the kitchen, with its heart-of-pine cupboards, beamed ceiling, and gleaming array of copper pots. Tucked in a corner of it was a small dining alcove with windows facing the courtyard without.

More images came to her—vague at first, then sharpening with clarity. Cole standing at the stove stirring something in a copper pot, steam rising from it, a towel wrapped around his waist. Then she was there, moving to his side, offering him some morsel and ordering, "Taste."

Obediently Cole lowered his head and let her feed it to him. "Mmmmm, good," he said, with a faint trace of surprise and a quick licking of his lips to savor every bit of it. Then, still stirring the pot with a long wooden spoon, he arched his arm and let her duck beneath it to fit herself to his side.

"I told you I knew my way around a kitchen," she chided.

"Know something else?" he said, dropping a playful kiss on the tip of her nose. "I think you know your way around the cook too."

Suddenly a noise—a scraping of metal, a click, something—shattered the image. Remy swung away from the kitchen, letting the door shut on it as the front door opened. A pulsebeat later, Cole filled the doorway, his suit jacket slung over his shoulder, his shirt unbuttoned at the throat, his tie draped loose around his neck. He saw her and stopped, still holding the door open, the key still in the lock. A sudden brightness leapt into his gray eyes, erasing the tired, drawn look. Just as quickly, it was shuttered again.

"What are you doing here?" The tightness in his low voice gave it a husky quality.

"Tom was outside. I recognized him." She felt his tension—her tension. "Then I found the key in the lion's mouth."

"I always left it there for you. You used to come here and wait for me to get home from the office." He stopped, a muscle working convulsively in his jaw. "You don't know how many times these last couple of weeks I've wanted to see you waiting for me when I walked through this door."

There was a rawness in his look and his expression, an

ache that suddenly made him appear . . . vulnerable as he stood there, holding himself so stiffly, so rigidly.

"What was it like between us, Cole?" Remy took a step toward him, then halted, realizing she needed to keep the room between them. "What did we do? We shared more than the bedroom, didn't we?"

"We did, yes." His reply was clipped, almost as if he didn't trust himself to say more.

"Tell me about us, Cole," she insisted. "I need to know. I need to remember. Did we stay here in the apartment? Did we go out? Where? What did we do?"

Turning from her, he pulled the key out of the lock and pushed the door shut. "Sometimes we stayed here and tried out our culinary skills on each other," he replied with a touch of wryness as he walked over to the leather recliner, tossing his jacket over the back of it and pulling his tie from around his neck to lay it on top. "Other times we went out for the evening and had dinner at some restaurant."

"Which one? Did we have favorites?" Remy asked, pushing for a more specific answer, not at all surprised that the evening's entertainment had consisted of no more than dinner. New Orleans was a great food town. For most natives, dining out was neither a prelude nor an acillary activity, but an event in itself—something to be not hurried but relished.

"Mr. B's, Cafe Sbisa, L'Eagles—"

"L'Eagles—that was one of your favorites," she remembered, visualizing the interior of the small, classy restaurant with its deep coral walls and European country decor. "You always claimed you liked to go there for the cold crawfish fettuccine they served, but it was really the collection of antique prints that you went there to admire."

Some of the remoteness left his expression, replaced by warmth as he conceded, "It was probably a combination of both."

"Where else did we go for dinner?"

"Every now and then we'd venture uptown and eat at the Garden Room in the Commander's Palace or else at Brigsten's. Or when we got the urge for a good po'boy or a meal of red beans and rice, we usually went to Mother's Restaurant on Poydras. And of course there was always Galatoire's.''

"Where we had lunch that first time." Remy smiled.

"Yes," Cole nodded, then continued, "Other than that, some evenings we'd go to a concert. Or if someone one of us wanted to see was playing at the Blue Room, we'd go there. Other nights we'd wander down to Preservation Hall and listen to them jam." He looked at her, a faint smile slanting the line of his mouth. "After the first time you heard the wail of Kid Sheik's trumpet, you became a die-hard jazz fan."

Preservation Hall—that aging and tattered building with its doors thrown open on most nights to let the unamplified music within spill onto St. Peter and Bourbon streets. Remy could almost hear the gritty notes of the trumpet growling its song in the old club's smoky atmosphere, yet—oddly—it was Cole's face she could see, "feeling" the music, "grooving" to it, letting it speak to him, move him, lift him. As she strained to recall more, it all began to fade.

Frustrated by these near memories that were little more than impressions, Remy pressed on to something else. "What about the weekends? Did we do anything special? Go anywhere?"

His eyes were on her, a reflective quality in their gray depths. "You were always dragging me off to flea markets, hoping to find some treasure among the junk. Or if you saw a notice for an estate auction in one of the outlying parishes, we'd go to it—especially if they listed porcelains among the items."

"Did I ever buy anything?"

"Once. You discovered a Meissen vase, then felt so guilty because you'd paid only fifteen dollars for it that you gave it to a charity to be sold at their benefit auction. Actually"—he paused briefly—"it usually ended up that you did the browsing and I did the buying."

"The statue of the horse," she said suddenly. "I

remember—it was that plaster of Paris kind with glitter sprinkled over it, like the ones they used to give away at carnivals for prizes." But there was more, and the memory of it drew her closer to him. "When you were a little boy, your father took you to a carnival and won you a horse like that at one of the booths on the midway. That's why you bought it, isn't it? For sentimental reasons."

"Yes."

Seized by the feeling that she was on the verge of remembering more, she didn't let him continue. "There was something else we often did on the weekends. What was it?"

Cole frowned slightly and shrugged, as if he wasn't sure what she might be referring to. "If the weather was nasty, we'd rent some movies at the video store and watch them here."

Remy took an eager step toward him. "What kind of movies?"

"*East of Eden*—"

"*On the Waterfront,*" she remembered as another scene flashed before her.

It had been a damp and drizzly Saturday afternoon in November, the misty rain gathering on the panes of the doors to the courtyard and trickling down the glass. She and Cole had been encamped on the sofa in front of the television, reclining in each other's arms, their feet propped up on the coffee table, which was already crowded with a pair of bottles of Dixie beer and a bowl of popcorn dripping with butter.

When Cole had shifted her out of his arms to get up and change the tape, he'd given her a playful swat on her behind. She had instantly retaliated with a kick in the pants and had then bounded to her feet, assuming a fighting stance, dancing around on the balls of her feet, bobbing and weaving like a boxer and throwing jabs at Cole's arm.

"Whatsa matter, tough guy?" she taunted. "Am I too much for ya?"

She threw two more quick punches that Cole fended off with the flat of his hand, his gray eyes regarding her with open amusement. "That'll be the day, kid. You've got lousy footwork."

"Lousy, eh?" She danced back, sniffled loudly, and brushed her thumb across the end of her nose. "I'll have you know—I coulda been a contender," she declared in her best Brando imitation.

"You could have been a contender, all right—for the role of Funny Girl."

"Oh yeah?" she challenged, and she hunched her shoulders, crouching down and rubbing her thumb over her nose again, "Why do boxers do that? Do they all have runny noses, or what?"

"Wouldn't you if yours kept getting bopped all the time?" His hand snaked out and sharply tapped the tip of her nose. Grinning, he immediately caught the fist she aimed at him. "Come here, you idiot."

When he pulled her into his arms, Remy pretended to resist, protesting, "Foul. Clinches aren't allowed."

"Can you think of a better way to feel out an opponent?"

"I think you mean feel *up*," she said in mock reproof as his hand cupped her bottom. "Or is that called going below the belt?"

"That's *hitting* below the belt."

"Like this?" She punched him low in the stomach.

He grunted, more in surprise than in pain. "Now you've done it."

When he caught her up to him, she smiled in satisfaction, but a second later she was squealing with laughter. "No! No! Don't tickle me! Don't!"

She twisted, turned, pushed, trying to elude the tickling fingers that had her convulsing with laughter, but there was no escape from them, not even when she collapsed on the chocolate-colored shag rug, too weak to stand. They rolled around on the floor until she was laughing so hard she could barely breathe.

"I give up," she cried between shrieking giggles. "Uncle. Uncle!" Mercifully, he stopped, and she drank in air, each breath a sigh as she relaxed against the floor, gradually becoming conscious of the pinning weight of his leg hooked over hers, an arm propping him up alongside her. She saw his grin and accused, "You don't fight fair."

"Who's fighting?" he countered softly. "I think I went down for the count at your hands weeks ago."

She caught her breath at the simple declaration so freely made, and lifted a hand to run her fingers through one side of his thick hair. "Are you as happy as I am, Cole?"

The laughter went out of his gray eyes, a sudden and serious intensity claiming them. "Every time you walk into a room, Remy, every time I see you, you"—he seemed to momentarily hesitate over the words—"you make my heart smile."

"It's that way for me too," she said, his words describing exactly the swell of buoyant, happy feeling inside her each time she saw him. She ran a finger down the side of his cheek to his lips. "Who was she, Cole? The one who hurt you— the one you always think I might be like?" She felt the tensing of his muscles, that move to withdraw from her both physically and mentally, and slipped a hand behind his neck to prevent him from rolling away. "You were in love with her, weren't you?"

"I was nineteen. I was in love with who I thought she was."

She ignored the curtness of his answer, recognizing that he used it to hide an old hurt. "Tell me about her, Cole."

"There's nothing to tell." This time he succeeded in pulling away from her as he rolled over and sat up, his back to her.

"I think there is." She sat up too, but made no attempt to touch him. "How did you meet?"

There was a long pause, and she thought he was again going to refuse to discuss her, but then the words came . . . grudgingly, tersely. "She liked boxing—the blows, the blood, the bodies glistening with sweat. To her it was primitive and exciting. She saw me box. Afterward—she was outside waiting for me. . . . She had so much class—not like anyone I'd ever met—I guess I was blinded by it."

"You started seeing each other," Remy said, quietly prompting him to go on.

"Not all that often. I was going to college, holding down a full-time job to pay for it and boxing on the side to earn some extra money. I didn't have a lot of free time for dating. Mostly she came to see me work out at the gym. Then afterward we'd go somewhere for a beer. Correction—I'd have a beer; she'd have a glass of wine. She didn't seem to care that I didn't have the money to take her out to Antoine's for dinner. It was enough that we were together—at least, that's what I thought."

"But you found out differently, didn't you?" Remy guessed. "How?"

"I made the mistake of going to her house one afternoon to see her—one of those cozy little mansions uptown near Audubon Park," he added with more than a trace of sarcasm, then paused again. "The shock on her face when she saw me standing in the foyer—I'll never forget that . . . or the anger that followed. I remember she said, 'How dare you embarrass me by coming to my house!' I turned every shade of red there is, and walked out." He tipped his head back and gazed at the ceiling. "It's funny, but the thing that hurt the most was knowing I'd told her about my father. I'd never been able to talk to anyone about it before. I . . ." He shook off the rest of it and lowered his head.

"Your father?" She frowned curiously. "He died when you were eight, isn't that what you told me?"

"Yes." Again his answer was clipped.

"How?"

With a turn of his head, he looked at her, something hard and unforgiving in his expression. "In a head-on collision with another car, driven by a very eminent—and very drunk—former state senator from *your* district."

Remy breathed in sharply, realizing that she knew exactly who he meant. The senator had been one of her grandfather's closest friends, a man whose political career had been cut short by an automobile accident that had left him paralyzed.

She'd heard the story a dozen times as a child. "But I had always understood—"

"—that my father was the one who'd been drinking?" Cole inserted. "That was a lie. I know. I was there."

"You . . . were in the car?"

"Yes."

She stared at him, remembering the shock, the panic, the terror she'd felt that day on the lake when she'd seen her fiancé, Nick Austin, overturn in his speedboat. She'd waited with her heart in her throat for him to surface and wave that he was all right. He hadn't. And the search had begun, a search that lasted four agonizing hours before his body was recovered. The shock of witnessing the accident, of discovering how tenuous life was, how insecure—she'd had trouble coping with it. It was part of what had driven her back to the family home—the solidness, the security it represented. That was three years ago; she'd been twenty-four. How much harder it must have been to lose someone you loved at the age of eight.

"Cole," she murmured, feeling the fear and pain he had to have experienced.

"He'd taken me to the zoo. My mother was working. She couldn't come with us. We were on our way home. It had started raining. Suddenly there was a glare of headlights right in our eyes. I remember my dad yelled something. Then his arm was across me, pushing me back against the seat. Then there was a lot of noise of glass breaking and metal. . . ." He paused and drank in a trembling breath. "My dad was lying on my lap, and there was blood all over. I knew he needed help, but I couldn't get the door open, so I had to climb out the side window. The police came and I grabbed one of them and took him back to the car to help my dad. Then his partner calls to him—'Jesus Christ, Hudson, get over here quick! You aren't gonna believe who's driving the other car!' The cop grabs my hand and shoves a bloody handkerchief in it and tells me to hold it against my dad's neck to stop the bleeding. I remember hearing the cop say,

'My God, it's the senator,' and the other cop said, 'Yeah, and he's drunker than a sailor.' After that all I can remember is crying and holding that handkerchief on my dad's neck, but I couldn't make the blood stop. It was all over my hands . . . on my arms . . . I was too little. I couldn't do it, and the cops never came back to help me. They were too busy saving the senator.''

And Remy knew that along with the senator's life, they'd saved his reputation, placing all the blame on the other driver, the one who wasn't alive to deny it.

She didn't say anything. She simply put her arms around Cole and held him tight.

Reliving the scene in her mind, Remy felt the same pain all over again. She released a long sigh and discovered she was gripping the back of the sofa. As she lifted her head, her gaze happened to fall on the television's blank screen. Instantly she stiffened.

"We watched television another time, but it—it wasn't a movie." Frowning with the effort of recalling it, Remy turned to Cole, then remembered in surprise, "It was you! You were interviewed by one of the local news stations. Why? Wait—" She broke into a smile as it came back to her. "It was because of the annual Christmas party for the company employees. You'd arranged for it to be held on board one of our ships. And you had Christmas lights strung on all the decks all over the ship. The whole thing was so unique that the television station sent its anchorwoman out to cover the story.''

Remy turned to stare at the television again, seeing the interview—Cole standing on the deck of the ship, casually dressed in a turtleneck and navy blazer, a breeze playing with the ends of his hair, the camera gentling his hard-edged features and imbuing them instead with a quiet strength and character.

"This is festive and fabulous, Mr. Buchanan," the anchor, a stunningly attractive black woman, had declared. "What gave you the idea of holding your employee Christmas party on board one of your ships?''

Cole flashed her one of his rare smiles. "With as many attractions as our city has to offer, it's easy to lose sight of the fact that the port of New Orleans is second in activity only to that of New York City. And there are years when our export tonnage has surpassed New York's. The company has always been proud of the fact that New Orleans has always been the home port and the headquarters of the Crescent Line, ever since its founding more than one hundred and fifty years ago. Ships and shipping have always been our business. But when you spend most of your time behind a desk in an office, you tend to forget that. Recently I realized how few of our employees—not to mention any of their families—have ever had the reason or the opportunity to set foot on the deck of one of our ships. . . . When it came time to plan our Christmas party this year, I saw this as the perfect chance to correct that situation and remind everyone what the Crescent Line is all about.''

"Approximately three months ago, you lost one of your ships. Did that play any part in your decision?''

"It's true one of our tankers sank in the Gulf during a storm—fortunately with no loss of life or any damage to the environment. Which means we have that much more reason to rejoice in this holiday season.''

With that statement from him, the reporter concluded the interview, and Remy turned on the sofa to hug Cole in delight. "You handled that question perfectly. But how quick and clever you were to brag about New Orleans' status as a port *and* work in a plug for the company at the same time. And here I always thought Uncle Marc was the expert at dealing with the media,'' she said, then poked him in the ribs. "But I'm not sure I liked the way you flirted with that reporter.''

"I wasn't flirting—merely turning on the charm," he replied, with a faintly smug smile. "In all business, there's a time to play hardball—and a time to play it soft.''

"You've never played it soft with me," she retorted in mock complaint.

"I should hope not," he chuckled, the glint in his eyes giving an entirely different meaning to the word *hard*.

She poked him again. "That isn't what I was talking about."

Remy couldn't remember what had happened next, though she could guess. But it didn't matter; the memory had prompted her to wonder about something else. "Did we spend Christmas together?"

"Christmas Eve," Cole replied.

"What did we do?" She crossed to the leather recliner where he stood.

"We drove up to St. James Parish and watched them light the bonfires along the levee—"

"To light the way for Papa Noël," Remy inserted, recalling the tradition, allegedly begun by early settlers in the area, of building giant bonfires along the Mississippi River to help Papa Noël find his way to their new homes. She smiled to herself, remembering the little boy—no more than seven years old—who had scoffed at the whole proceeding.

"Don't you believe in Santa Claus?" Cole had asked.

"No!" the boy had responded emphatically.

Cole had crouched down to the boy's level. "It doesn't matter . . . because Santa Claus still believes in you. He always will."

When Cole had stood up from the boy, she'd marveled aloud, "You still believe in Santa Claus, don't you?"

"Of course," he'd replied with a perfectly straight face. And she'd suspected he really did.

Realizing that Cole was talking, Remy forced herself back into the present.

"—came back to the apartment and exchanged our gifts, then we went to midnight Mass together."

"What did you give me?" She had the feeling it had been something special.

"An antique brooch."

Remy frowned, certain there'd been some sentiment attached to it. "Had it belonged to your mother?"

"My grandmother."

She breathed in sharply and unconsciously pressed a hand to her throat. "It was set with topaz, wasn't it?" Even before Cole nodded affirmatively, she knew it was the brooch she'd been wearing that night in Nice. "Cole, why did we break up? What did we argue over?" It was suddenly imperative that she know.

"The same thing we always argue about—your family and their destructive greed. Now—" He cut off the rest of it, a grimness thinning his mouth. "Look at you. You're already bristling."

It was true. She didn't try to deny the flash of temper his words had sparked. "What do you expect, Cole? They're my family."

"And we're at another impasse," he observed curtly.

"That wasn't your attitude when we were in Nice, at the hotel," she reminded him. "Why? Why have you changed since we came back? This morning at the dock—and later, at your office—it was like you were pushing me away from you. Why?"

He studied her for a silent moment. "Last night . . . at the airport . . . seeing you wrapped again in the bosom of your family, I realized you'll never love me enough to trust me and believe in me over them."

"How can you say that? I love you."

"In your way, yes."

She covered his mouth with her hand, wanting to cut off the things he was saying. "That isn't true. I love you in *every* way."

He dragged her hand from his mouth, his fingers gripping it. "Don't make this any more painful than it is, Remy. You don't know how much I want to believe you."

"But you can," she insisted. "I was wearing the brooch you gave me the night I was hurt. Don't you see? I wouldn't have been wearing it if I was still angry at you, if I didn't want us to be together again.''

With a throaty groan, he pulled her to him. As his mouth moved over hers with a pressure that was urgent, his tongue delving, filling, Remy discovered that nothing had changed from the hotel room in Nice—she felt the same immense shock, the same feeling of deep need satisfied.

In the bedroom, Cole undressed her. He wouldn't let her help. This was something he wanted to do himself. He peeled off her clothes, layer by layer, touching, stroking, caressing as he went. She was beautiful, with her high, firm breasts sized perfectly to fit the cup of his hands, and her hips, thighs, and legs with their silky, woman-soft curves, and the warm smoothness of her body beneath his hands. He looked at her —into the gold-flecked glitter of her hazel eyes—and saw the deep, bright glow of love for him.

Reaching out, he pulled down the blue-striped coverlet and the sheet, then lifted her and laid her gently in the middle of the bed. He stepped back and shed his own clothes while she watched with half-closed eyes, resting on her elbows. He had a magnificent body, muscular and flat, but she'd thought that from the first moment she'd seen him. She lay back against the pillows, languid with anticipation as his eyes grew needy and dark and his final nakedness gave away his rising desire—his bold desire.

His knee touched the bed, and the mattress caved in beneath his weight. Leaning over, he pressed a warm kiss against her belly, and she felt the curling sensation of it deep inside. Her arms reached out for him, drawing him to her, his length stretching out alongside hers, as his mouth came down.

He intended to be gentle, to make the kiss sweet and lasting, but he'd been too long without her, he was too hungry, too starved. He tore his mouth from hers and pressed another hard kiss against her jaw, then into her neck, the fragrance of her surrounding him. His mouth found hers again, her lips parting, seeking and eager in accepting the deep strokes of his tongue.

Gripped by the fierce need to touch, to kiss, and to taste, he held her to him with both arms and legs as they tumbled together on the bed, her belly straining against him and the twin peaks of her soft breasts flattened by his chest. The sweet woman smell and the sweet woman taste of her drove him on.

His hands slid into her loose hair. He loved the silken feel of it, the silken length and the scent of flowers that clung to it. He stroked her body, cupped her breasts, and probed the petal-like folds of her until she arched against his clever fingers. He kissed her breasts, his mouth gently suckling, his teeth gently nipping, and she writhed beneath him, her fingers digging into his hair to keep him there. She reached down to touch him, her hand encircling, stroking. He heard his own grunt of raw pleasure. "Love me, Cole," she whispered into his ear.

A cheek muscle flexed as he realized she was killing him slowly, softly. Then he was inside her, thrusting deep, his moans lost in hers. He wanted to make love to her slowly, completely. He wanted her to belong to him again, and this time to make it last. He braced his weight with his hands, the muscles in his arms trembling with the strain of holding back, but she arched her hips against his. It wasn't his restraint she wanted, but all of him.

He plunged into her, then plunged again and again, the tempo rising, the pressure building, the pleasure sharpening until it broke over and through them, disseminating and decimating them in a thousand white-hot shards of sensation.

21

Remy slipped on the paisley patterned jacket of silk charmeuse and fastened its one button, then glanced at Cole sprawled over half of the pale-blue bed sheets, for a moment watching the even rise and fall of his bare chest in light sleep. She smiled faintly, still warm inside with the feeling that she had been well and truly loved. She moved to his side of the bed and sat down on the edge of the mattress, then slowly, quietly she leaned forward—with every intention of disturbing his slumber—and nuzzled his ear, lightly breathing into its shell.

"You fell asleep on me again," she accused softly, feeling him stir a second before his hand glided onto her back, the silk of her jacket sliding over the matching blouse at his touch.

His hand stopped. "What is this?" He turned his face into hers, seeking and finding the corner of her mouth. "What are you doing with clothes on? I didn't take them off for you to put them back on, you know."

"I know." She let her lips brush over his mouth, eluding his attempt to claim them in a kiss as his hand resumed its caressing foray, now joined by the other. "But I have to go."

"Oh no you don't," he said in a lazy denial, his encircling arms tightening to keep her with him. "You're going to stay right here with me . . . in my arms . . . in my bed." He punctuated each pause with an evocative nibble on her neck.

"I'd love to." She closed her eyes, strongly tempted to take off her clothes again and crawl back under the covers with him. "But I can't." Sighing her regret, she spread her hands over the hard plane of his chest and used them to lever herself partially away from him. "I'm supposed to meet Gabe at four-thirty, and it's going on four o'clock now."

"That's no problem." His hand moved onto her hip, rumpling the navy wool of her skirt. "Call him up and say you can't make it. Tell him something's come up. It would be the truth," he said somewhat wickedly, tipping his head far to one side to pointedly look past her at the very noticeable protrusion of the sheet around his hips.

Remy looked too, and smiled mockingly back at him. "You know what they say—what goes up must come down."

"Ahh, but it's the *come* part of 'come down' I'm interested in," he said.

She pretended to be critical. "Once is never enough for you, is it?"

"Not with you, it seems."

And she understood exactly what he meant. No matter how well their bodies might know each other, it didn't seem that either she or Cole had exhausted the mysteries they discovered each time they made love.

"I really do have to meet Gabe," she said with reluctance.

His gray eyes lost their teasing look and turned needing and dark. "Stay with me, Remy."

"It's my first night back. I need to spend some time with my family."

His hands ceased their wandering and simply held her. "You're running true to form, Remy. Amnesia or not, your family still comes first with you."

"Let's not argue about this." The potential for it was there; she sensed it in the dead quiet of his voice.

"You're right. It would be useless anyway," he said dryly, then forced a smile.

Another kiss and a few more whispered words and she left, retrieving her purse from the living room on her way out.

On the banquette outside his apartment, Remy breathed in the air, scented with the thousands of aromas of the Quarter, everything from the mustiness of the past to the Cajun spices of today. The long slant of the sun's rays cast a mellow light over the old buildings. It was, Remy decided, an absolutely gorgeous day. She started walking.

As she rounded the corner onto Bourbon, a hand hooked her elbow. Reacting instinctively, Remy switched her clutch purse to the other hand and threw her weight into the would-be purse snatcher rather than away from him. Her shoulder connected with something solid, drawing a grunt of surprise and causing him to loosen his hold. She pulled her arm free, and at the same instant caught a glimpse of a heavily grizzled beard in her side vision. The man in the car outside her house—and at the museum!

She swung around to confront him. "Who are you? What do you want? Why are you following me?"

A dozen impressions registered at once: the neatly trimmed beard, heavily streaked with white, that failed to hide the thickness of the man's neck; the top-heavy quality of his build, with massive shoulders and chest tapering to boyishly slim hips; and the keenness of his pale-blue eyes, a keenness that immediately reminded her of Inspector Armand's.

"I'll ask the questions, if you don't mind, Miss Jardin," he said, unsmiling. "You are Remy Jardin, aren't you? I guessed it was you I saw on the balcony this morning."

"I repeat, who are you?"

"Howard Hanks." With two fingers, he produced a business card from his breast pocket and offered it to her. Remy glanced at it, then at the wallet that he flipped open to his identification. He was a licensed investigator—according to the card, working for an insurance company.

Remy looked at the business card again, conscious of the odd churning in the pit of her stomach and of the alarm bells going off in her head, warning her not to tell him anything. It was crazy—she didn't even know what he wanted from her. Whatever it was, why did she feel she needed to conceal information? What information?

She took the card from him, stalling for time until she could decide what to do. "Do you normally accost people on the street, Mr. Hanks?"

"Only those who refuse to accept—or return —my phone calls and claim to be indisposed when I come to their houses." He gestured toward the entrance of a nearby bar, a gold signet ring flashing on his left hand. "May I buy you a drink or a cup of coffee?"

She hesitated. "I have an appointment at four-thirty—"

"This shouldn't take long."

"All right—coffee, then." But it wasn't the quiet insistence in his voice warning her that he wouldn't take no for an answer that convinced her to accept—rather, it was the realization that she had to know what this was about, had to discover the reason for this feeling of danger she had.

Her low heels made a hollow sound on the dirty and old hardwood floor as she walked into the bar ahead of the investigator. The place smelled of beer, bourbon, and old cigarette butts; its atmosphere consisted of its lack of any pretension of class—with its dingy smoke-stained walls, round wooden tables with initials and dates carved into their tops, sturdy but cheap wire-backed chairs, and an old bar that was probably mahogany under its layers of grime.

Remy crossed to the table by the corner window. She sat down in the chair facing Bourbon Street, with her back to the view of Cole's apartment building. The bearded Howard Hanks sat down opposite her, on a seat still warm from his last occupation of it.

He held up two fingers to the bartender. "Coffee."

She laid her purse on the table and lightly clasped her

hands together on top of it. "For your information, Mr. Hanks, I was out of the country until yesterday, so I wasn't avoiding your calls—as you implied. I simply wasn't here to accept them. I'm sure you were told that."

Remy was careful not to admit that she hadn't been informed of his calls. She could only guess that in all the anxiety and the relief of having her home, her family had simply failed to mention them. As for this morning, it was possible that she'd been in the shower when he came to the door. Nattie would have known that, and her mother might have heard the water running. But that didn't explain why she hadn't been told that he'd been there to see her.

"There was some mention of your being in France, but everyone was very vague about your exact whereabouts."

She could have told him that they hadn't known, but she was reluctant to say anything about her hospital stay or her amnesia. The bartender arrived with their coffee. Remy moved her purse aside as he set two mugs in front of them.

"Cream or sugar?" Hanks asked, holding up a hand to keep the bartender from walking off.

"Neither, thanks," she directed her answer to the bartender, who immediately returned to his station behind the bar. She wrapped both hands around the thick stoneware mug. "You said you wanted to ask me some questions, Mr. Hanks. What about?"

"The sinking of the *Dragon*."

The *Dragon*. She'd heard that name before. Marc Jardin had mentioned it this morning in the solarium. What had he said? Something about fearing the insurance company might go through with its threat to make this business about the *Dragon* public. Later, when she'd asked him about it, her uncle had dismissed it as a typical hassle with an insurance company over a claim they were attempting to get out of paying. But . . . at the wharf, when she'd remembered the previous time Cole had shown her around the container ship, he'd said that the loss of the *Dragon* had been "a blessing in disguise''—that he'd used the insurance money to buy this ship. Had the insurance company paid the claim, or hadn't it?

"What about the sinking of the *Dragon?*" she asked, and took a sip of the chicory-strong coffee.

"What do you know about it?"

"Why should I know anything about it?"

"You are a stockholder and director of the Crescent Line, aren't you, Miss Jardin?"

"Yes."

"Then tell me what you know."

"About what?"

He shot her a look that was both tolerant and wryly amused. "Spare us both the dumb-blonde act, Miss Jardin. I know you graduated cum laude from Newcomb College."

"If you've checked on me to that extent, Mr. Hanks, then you must know that my role as a company director is basically a titular one. I have very little knowledge of the company's operations. I've simply never bothered to involve myself in the family shipping business."

"In other words, you want me to believe you don't know anything about the *Dragon.*" The skepticism in his voice was as thick as river fog.

"I'm aware that we lost a ship, and I'm also aware that the insurance company has been causing trouble over the claim."

"Wouldn't you, if you discovered that someone had fraudulently collected on a cargo that didn't exist, after deliberately sinking its container ship in deep water to conceal that fact?"

Stunned by the charge, she blurted, "That's ridiculous. Why would anybody do that?"

"Why, indeed, would anybody try to collect twice for the same cargo?"

"Collect twice?" She frowned, her mind racing at the implication of his words as she feigned confusion. "I'm afraid you've lost me, Mr. Hanks. Exactly what is it that you're saying?"

"That tanker was empty when it went down, Miss Jardin. At some point, between the time it was loaded here in New Orleans and when it sank in the Gulf, that cargo of crude was off-loaded. Once the tanker ran into the storm and heavy seas being reported in the Gulf of Mexico, it was sunk— probably with the aid of some strategically placed explosive charges."

"But you don't know that for a fact, do you?" The conversation she'd overheard in the solarium —she remembered that her father, Gabe, and Marc had been talking about finding out what proof the insurance company had, if any.

"Miss Jardin, there are basically only two ways to scuttle a ship—open the sea cocks and flood her, a process that could take as long as twenty-four hours, or blow out her bottom with explosive charges and send her to the sea floor within minutes."

"And you think that's what happened to the *Dragon*?" she managed to challenge him before taking a slow sip of her coffee, wondering if it was true and telling herself it couldn't possibly be. So that was why her family had sounded so worried. These were serious charges.

"I'd bet on it."

Remy shook her head in denial. "I'm sorry, but your theory doesn't make good sense—or good business. Why would we deliberately sink one of our ships simply to collect on a cargo that you claim wasn't on board?"

"The *Dragon* was an old tanker, Miss Jardin. I doubt she could have had more than a few voyages left in her before she would end up in a scrap heap. You probably collected more from the insurance company for the ship than you could have got if you'd tried to sell her . . . not to mention the tax losses the company will get out of it."

"But if she was that old and in such bad shape, then she could easily have broken up in the storm and gone down *with* her cargo of crude oil."

"Then why wasn't there any oil slick?"

"Maybe her tanks—or whatever you call them —weren't

ruptured," Remy argued, then lowered her cup to the table, lacing her fingers tightly around it. "In any case, these charges against the Crescent Line are preposterous. My family would never involve itself in such dishonest activities."

"What about Cole Buchanan?" His quiet question hit her like a fist.

"Cole," she repeated dumbly, then tried to laugh off her shock, conscious of the sick feeling in her stomach. "Don't tell me you suspect he's behind this so-called insurance scheme?"

"Why not?"

"Because it's absurd. What would he have to gain?" At the moment Remy was too stunned to think it through for herself. She needed the insurance investigator to provide the answer.

"Money, of course."

"How? Where? Not from the insurance company. The claim money would be paid directly to the Crescent Line . . . unless you're about to suggest that he's stealing funds from the company."

"Not directly. But he could have sold the shipment of crude oil, off-loaded it onto barges waiting downriver—or into a pipeline—and pocketed the money himself. Your company wouldn't be losing anything, since it would be collecting on the shipment from the insurance."

"I don't believe that." Yet she found herself remembering the comment Gabe had made about Cole's name being linked with some shady dealings in the past.

"Why not?"

"Because I don't." She loved Cole. How *could* she believe that about him?—but then she wondered if it wouldn't be closer to the truth to say that she simply didn't *want* to believe it. She went on as if she had no doubts. "If that's what you think, you should confront Cole with your suspicions, not me."

"I have. Naturally, he denies everything."

"Then why are you talking to me? I've already told you I have nothing to do with the comp—"

"But you do have something to do with Cole Buchanan." He smiled. At least Remy thought he did. With that thick, silvery growth of whiskers above and below his mouth, it was difficult to tell. "I think it's safe to say you know Cole Buchanan quite well—certainly well enough to visit his apartment."

"It's no secret that Cole and I have been seeing each other, but I don't see what that has to do with this."

"I thought perhaps he might have said or done something unusual in the past few months—bought you an expensive present or been a little freer with money, maybe received some unusual phone calls . . . anything out of the ordinary."

"Nothing that I can remember." Which was the truth. Of course, she didn't tell him she could remember almost nothing about her past, including these last few months.

"Think about it. Maybe something will come back to you. If it does, my phone number's on the card. Be sure you call me. I wouldn't want to see you get into trouble over this."

"That almost sounds like a threat, Mr. Hanks."

"I'm sure you've heard the term *accessory*." He stood up, took a money clip from his pocket, peeled two one-dollar bills from it, and dropped them on the table. "I appreciate your time, Miss Jardin. Let's stay in touch."

Alone at the table, Remy let in the wash of questions she hadn't dared think about with the investigator looking on. Was it true? Was there an insurance fraud? Was this the trouble she'd sensed? Was Cole a part of it? Had she known that? Was that the reason she'd broken off with him? Had she seen something or heard something, as the bearded Mr. Hanks had suggested? Was that why it seemed so imperative that she be here?

"More coffee, Miss?"

Startled, she glanced at the stained glass pot in the bartender's hand and quickly shook her head. "No—thank you," she said, breaking free of the questions whirling about in her mind and gathering up her purse.

By the time she reached La Louisiane, the shock of the information had worn off. She swept into the lounge and spotted Gabe at the large mahogany bar, the gleaming centerpiece of the elegantly appointed room. He'd obviously been watching for her. The instant he saw her, he picked up two drinks and gestured to a quiet corner table. She met him there.

"It's about time you got here," he said. "I was starting to worry about you. You realize you're almost fifteen minutes late?"

"I was detained."

"I gathered that."

She opened her purse, took out the investigator's business card, and laid it on the small cocktail table in front of her brother.

"What's this?" Idly he picked it up, then went still. "Where did you get this?" he asked, too casually.

"Mr. Hanks gave it to me personally."

"You've seen him?"

"Yes. He had some questions to ask me"—she closed her purse with a sharp snap—"about insurance and fraud—and the sinking of the *Crescent Dragon.* That was what you and Father and Uncle Marc were talking about this morning, wasn't it?" she said stiffly. "Why didn't you tell me about it then? Why did all of you pretend there was nothing to worry about, when you knew better? When you knew this man—"

"Remy, you've already been through enough this past week. We all agreed there was no need to tell you about this. And we were right. Look at the way you're trembling."

"It's because I'm mad," she said, and tried to cool the angry tremors of her hands by wrapping them around the cold, moisture-laden sides of the iced drink. "You should have told me."

"Maybe we should have, but you don't have any involvement in the company—"

"But I *am* involved with Cole—as Mr. Hanks was so quick to point out."

"What exactly did he say?"

"He all but accused Cole of being the one behind this fraud scheme, and he suggested that I might have seen or heard something suspicious."

"What did you say?"

"What could I say? The little I can remember might as well be nothing." An olive was impaled on a red plastic saber in her glass. Remy seized the miniature sword and began stabbing at the ice cubes.

"Is that what you told him?"

"I said I didn't remember anything unusual happening. I didn't tell him why."

"Is that all?"

"Why all the questions, Gabe?" she demanded. "Am I being cross-examined by you now?"

"Of course not." He smiled at her so gently that she felt churlish for having snapped at him. "I was curious, that's all. I hate seeing you all tense and upset like this. It's what we were trying to avoid."

"Is it true, Gabe?" She turned to him, earnestly, seriously. "Was the *Dragon* deliberately sunk? Is it fraud? Is Cole a part of it?"

"To tell you the truth, Remy, we don't know. Obviously we don't want to believe it, but . . . I can't imagine that the insurance company would throw around accusations without having some proof of wrongdoing, though we haven't been able to find out what it is. And Cole's not talking." He paused for a fraction of a second. "Hanks didn't happen to reveal anything to you, did he?"

"No," she said, and sighed. "Unfortunately, I didn't ask whether he had any proof. . . . The more I think about it, though, most of what he said sounded like conjecture."

He absently rattled the ice cubes in his glass as if considering the possibility, then shrugged. "It could be they're just fishing," he conceded, taking a sip of his drink.

"Fishing? Why?"

"Insurance scams involving old—and supposedly fully loaded—ships on the high seas happen more frequently than any insurance company cares to admit, and they're next to impossible to prove with the evidence 'twenty thousand leagues under the sea,' so to speak. The *Dragon* might fit what they see as a pattern."

She didn't believe that, and she didn't think Gabe did either. He was only trying to play down the situation for her benefit. It wasn't working.

"What if Hanks is right, Gabe? What if I do know something?"

"About all this?" His glance was openly skeptical. "You would have told us, Remy. If not me, then Dad."

Maybe not. She might have kept silent—not necessarily to protect Cole, but to give him a chance to quietly rectify the situation. Maybe she had even threatened that if he didn't, she'd go to her family with what she knew and give them grounds to demand his resignation—or to break the contract and vote him out of office if he refused to resign. Yes, she could think of a dozen reasons why she might initially have kept silent. It might have been why she'd planned to go off by herself for a few days in France—to give herself time to think and decide what was the best thing to do.

"You're worried." He reached over and covered her hand with his, giving it a squeeze. "Don't be."

"Why don't you tell the Mississippi to flow backward?"

"I mean it, Remy. In the first place, there's nothing you can do. And in the second, you need to concentrate your energies on getting better and not get all worked up over this. Let us handle it. OK?"

If he'd patted her on the cheek and told her not to worry her "pretty little head about such things," his message couldn't have been plainer: leave it to the menfolk to handle.

Southern chauvinism, in its place, could be nice; it could be sweet. But this was life, her life, and her business—as much as it was theirs. But Gabe would never see it that way. He couldn't.

"You will tell me what's going on, won't you? I'm in the dark about so much now that I don't think I could stand not being kept informed about this."

"The minute we have some hard facts, I promise I'll tell you."

Which meant that he'd only tell her things that would reassure her. If she wanted something more than a watered-down version of the truth, she'd have to find it herself.

22

The minute her mother left the next morning to keep her standing Thursday appointment at the hair salon, Remy headed for the public library, a drab concrete and glass example of fifties architecture located at the intersection of Tulane and Loyola avenues.

She scanned the newspaper article printed on the computer screen. The account on the sinking of the *Crescent Dragon* had been relegated to page 3 of the paper's front section, running only slightly more than half a column in length and obviously not deemed newsworthy enough to rate a follow-up story.

Why should it be? she thought. There'd been no loss of life, no daring rescue at sea, no harrowing days spent in lifeboats by the crew, and no major oil spill, and no one in the crew had been from the New Orleans area—or even from Louisiana. If it hadn't been for the fact that the tanker was owned by a local shipping company and went down in the Gulf of Mexico, Remy doubted the newspaper would have devoted more than a paragraph to the story—if it had covered it at all.

She read the article again. According to the captain—one Titus Edward Bartholomew from Cornwall, England—the combination of the vessel's age and the heavy seas had caused a structural failure in the tanker's hull. At approximately 10:00 P.M. on the night of September 9, the ship had begun taking on water. Twenty minutes later, with the pumps unable to handle the flow and the tanker foundering badly, the captain gave the order to abandon ship. Twelve hours after that, a passing freighter saw the distress flare fired from the lifeboats and picked up the crew. A search of the area by the Coast Guard yielded some debris, but no evidence of oil spillage.

The only thing Remy found in the entire account that was even remotely suspicious was the tanker's failure to issue a distress call, or Mayday—evidently the ship's radio had chosen that moment to quit working. In fact, problems with the equipment had been reported earlier—perhaps conveniently?

What had she hoped to find? She wasn't sure. A clue, maybe—something that would lead her to look somewhere else. If there was one in the article, she didn't see it. Just the same, she asked for a hard copy of the story and waited while a word processor printed it out.

Where did she go from here? Would the company files have more information? They would definitely contain the names and addresses of the rest of the *Dragon*'s crew. But how was she going to get to see them? She'd never taken an active interest in the shipping business before, so she couldn't just walk in and ask to see the files without drawing attention to herself—and her search. *That* was the last thing she wanted to do—especially after last night.

By the time she'd gotten home the evening before—after somehow, somewhere making a wrong turn and not knowing it until she discovered she was on the River Road and had to double back—Gabe was already there. She'd walked in to hear him and her father locked in another debate over her.

"I'm not even going to guess how that Hanks character managed to track her down. But as far as I'm concerned, this changes things. Remy is going to that clinic. I want her safely away from here—away from all these questions and charges.''

''That isn't the way to handle this, Dad,'' Gabe had protested. ''She needs to be here with us, where we can keep an eye on her—not three hundred miles away.''

''The clinic is the best place for her. I don't care what you say.''

''Dad, she's already said once that she won't go. If you try to make her, she'll fight you—especially now. Is that what you want? To be at odds with her? I don't think so.''

''Frazier,'' her mother had inserted tentatively. ''Maybe he's right.''

A long and heavy sigh had come from her father. ''I don't know. I just don't know.''

''Where is Remy?'' her mother had asked worriedly.

''I don't know. She left before I did. I walked her to her car—''

At that point Remy had taken her cue and walked in. ''Would you believe I was halfway to the airport before I realized where I was? I guess I thought the car knew the way home, so I didn't pay attention.''

There'd been no further mention of the clinic or of Howard Hanks—not in front of her, anyway. But what she'd heard was enough. Her family was determined to protect her, to shield her from this ''unpleasantness'' over the *Dragon*—for her own good, naturally.

Maybe they'd always treated her like this, but this time she couldn't let them. These allegations of fraud had to be the trouble she'd sensed. She knew something, she was certain of it—maybe something that would either clear Cole or convict him. She had to find out what it was. She couldn't sit back and twiddle her thumbs, waiting for her memory to return—if it ever did.

Assuming that the charges of fraud were true, more than one person had to be involved in it. Somewhere there was proof of that. Maybe the company files could provide it.

But once again, the question was, how was she going to

get to them? That was her next problem. She paid for the
hard copy of the newspaper article and left, arriving home a
good twenty minutes before Sibylle returned from the salon.

The newspaper print blurred. Not that it mattered, Remy
thought. She'd read the article so many times she practically
had it memorized. She lowered the copy to her lap and let
her gaze drift restlessly around her bedroom. The blackness
of night pressed against the glass of the gallery doors and
threw back a fuzzy image of the room. Remy couldn't help
noticing how relaxed she looked, lounging on the loveseat
clad in a jade satin robe—the proverbial lady of leisure. She
knew a closer look would have revealed her tension.

She glanced at the digital clock on her bedside table and
sighed. The minutes were ticking away with all the speed of
stampeding snails. She considered going through the drawers
of the small escritoire again, but she'd already spent the
afternoon doing that, and had found little more than bank
statements, blank checks, a sheaf of embossed stationery with
matching envelopes, an odd letter or two from what she
presumed were girlfriends of hers—letters she obviously
hadn't gotten around to answering—and an address book
filled with names and phone numbers of people she couldn't
remember, with two pages devoted to family birthdays and
anniversaries. There was a date calendar for the new year,
but the notations in it were few, limited to the month of
January and containing mostly reminders of dinner engage-
ments, somebody's party, museum meetings or tours, and a
dental appointment, and concluding with the time, airline,
and number of her flight to Nice.

Cole's name didn't appear anywhere. Remy didn't know
whether that meant that she'd already broken up with him by
the time the new year started or that she hadn't needed to be
reminded of her dates with him.

The drawers had yielded no diaries or journals—not that
she had expected any. Even now she had no compulsion to
commit her thoughts to paper. And there hadn't been any

lists of things-to-do. If the contents of those drawers were a reflection of her life, she obviously led a very carefree existence—no responsibilities, no demands, no obligations.

Had she always let others do things for her? Like Nattie, who cooked the meals, made her bed, tidied her room, and saw that she had clean towels for her bath. And the dailies, who cleaned the house and did the laundry and the ironing. And her mother, who planned the meals, managed the household, arranged the dinner parties, and kept fresh flowers in all the rooms. And her father, uncle, and cousin, who ran the family shipping business that provided her with an income—though it wasn't her only income. According to some papers she'd found in the desk, she had a trust fund of some sort. Set up by her grandfather, she thought.

But what had she ever contributed—except to put in her appearances at the board meetings? Had she always let others provide for her needs, let them have the work and the worry of the shipping line while she breezed through life—until now? But it couldn't have taken until this minute for her to realize what she'd been missing. No, it had to have happened earlier, or she would have never been nagged by this feeling of trouble at the hospital in Nice when she hadn't known anything about herself. Had she been jolted into awareness by the insurance company's charges of fraud and her own now-lost knowledge of it? Or had it started before that? Maybe with Cole's criticism of her ignorance about the company's financial situation?

My God, how horribly and painfully ironic that would be, she thought, and then she heard footsteps and muffled voices in the hall outside her door. Hurriedly she snatched the latest issue of *Harper's Bazaar* off the floor next to the loveseat and sandwiched the copy of the newspaper article between its pages. A second later there was a light rap on her door.

"Come in."

As she'd expected, her parents walked in, her father in white tie and full evening dress, her mother gowned in a soft chiffon cloud of deep rose pink, a silver fox stole around her shoulders. They were off to another gala event, one of literally dozens strung in multiple strands through the Carnival season, which began on the sixth of January—Twelfth Night—and ran all the way to Mardi Gras, gathering momentum all the while.

"We wanted you to know that we're leaving now," Sibylle Jardin declared, casting her a concerned smile. "Are you sure you'll be all right here alone?"

"I am twenty-seven." Remy automatically smiled, then caught herself and remembered not to look too bright, too cheerful—or too anxious for them to leave. "I think that's old enough to stay home alone at night, don't you?"

"Yes, but . . . with you being ill and all—"

"I have a slight headache . . . probably from fatigue. It's nothing more serious than that. I promise."

"Just the same, we'll give you a call later and make sure you're all right," her father said.

"No, don't. You'd be alarmed if I didn't answer, and I wouldn't," she said, thinking fast. "I was planning on disconnecting my extension so I wouldn't be disturbed if the phone rang."

"I suppose that's sensible," he conceded. "You know where we'll be if you need us."

"I do. Has Gabe left already?" She thought she'd heard his car, but she wasn't sure.

"About ten minutes ago."

When her father made a move toward the door, Remy quickly encouraged it. "You two enjoy yourselves tonight, and don't worry about me. I'll be fine."

After a few more flutterings of concern from her mother, they left. Remy waited until she heard the Mercedes pull away and let another ten minutes drag by for good measure, then ran silently across the second-floor hall to the master bedroom. For an instant she stared at the solid brass doorknob, conscious of the hard thumping of her heart and the nervous churning of her stomach, and then she closed her hand around it, gave it a turn, and slipped inside. She felt exactly like a thief sneaking into her parents' bedroom—but she hadn't come to steal, only to borrow.

She flipped on the lights and went directly to the bureau. There, on top of it, in the oval tray that held her father's loose change, an empty money clip, and a pocketknife, was a key ring with some half-dozen keys looped on it. Smiling in triumph, Remy scooped it up. The smooth fall of his trousers—with no jangle of keys when he walked—had earlier encouraged her to believe that he was carrying only his house and car keys, leaving the rest behind. What they all went to, she didn't know, but she was counting on the fact that when he'd resigned as president of the Crescent Line, he hadn't returned his key to the office.

Back in her room, Remy pulled on a pair of navy-blue slacks and a matching raw-silk sweater, grabbed a fawn-colored suede jacket from the closet, and left the house.

Thirty minutes later she was inside the International Trade Mart, standing in front of the entrance to the corporate offices of the Crescent Line. Neither the first nor the second key fit in the lock. Remy flipped past the next two, which bore the Mercedes logo—possibly spare keys to her mother's car. She tried the fifth key. It slipped right in. She gave it a turn, and the lock clicked open.

The office lights were on. For security reasons? Or had someone forgotten to shut them off before leaving? Or—was someone here? Remy stepped partway into the reception room and listened intently for some creak of a chair, a rustle of paper, the faint click of computer keys, a cough—anything. Silence. Not trusting it, she inched the door closed and moved stealthily forward to investigate, in the process discovering how loud the sound of cloth brushing against cloth was, how dry her mouth could be, and how acutely tense her muscles could become.

But there was no one about. She was alone. She drew her first full breath and began her search for information. She glanced at a computer terminal. A touch of the right keys would call up all the information she wanted—assuming she could figure out the access codes. But it was the documentation for the computer entries that she really wanted to see.

She went to the file cabinet. Locked. She started down the row, pulling at drawer handle after drawer handle. Locked, locked, locked—they were all locked. She sagged against the last cabinet in frustration and combed a hand through her hair, trying to think.

The file clerks had to have keys to them. Did they take them home? Drop them in their purses or pockets to get buried in the bottom or sent to the cleaners—or left on the kitchen table? They wouldn't take that risk; they'd leave the keys in their desks. She found a set in the first drawer she looked in, and went to work.

It took Remy fifteen minutes to figure out the filing system, and another twenty-five to gather together all the paperwork relating to the tanker's final voyage. Armed with the names of the crew from the ship's manifest, she shifted to the payroll records, pulling each man's file.

Unwilling to take the time to study all the documents now, Remy turned on the copy machine and glanced through the papers while she waited for it to warm up. All of them appeared to be simple and straightforward—a list of the stores and their associated invoices, a bill for the cargo of crude oil and a copy of a check representing payment in full for the same, charges for fuel and marine services, copies of some kind of licenses or permits, employee rate cards and personal information. Yet something bothered her. She had copied all the documents and was halfway through the crew's records before she realized what it was.

Hurriedly she copied the rest, stuffed the copies into a blank folder to take with her, returned the originals to their proper files, and began going through other employment records to see if maybe—just maybe—she was wrong. She wasn't.

The crew that had sailed aboard the *Crescent Dragon* on her last and final voyage—from the captain to the lowliest seaman—had never worked for the Crescent Line *before* or *since*. Judging from the records, it wasn't uncommon for a seaman or a first mate, or even a captain, to work for the company only one time. But an entire crew? No, that was too coincidental to be anything other than suspicious—very suspicious.

Remy stared at the crew names, mãny of them Oriental, possibly Korean, and thought how funny it was—a twisted and bitter kind of funny—to realize that this was just the kind of thing she had hoped to find. And now that she had, she wished she hadn't.

Where were they now, she wondered. Probably scattered to the four winds—or in this case the seven seas. More than likely with a considerable amount of extra cash in their pockets in return for keeping quiet about what they knew . . . or what they'd seen. And if Howard Hanks was right, what they'd seen was the tanker off-loading its cargo of crude oil onto waiting barges or into an offshore pipeline.

The crew had to have known what was going on—at least the officers definitely did. And the seamen would have recognized that it wasn't normal to off-load cargo within a day or two of leaving port, and then continue on empty.

And Remy understood that her chances of tracking down any of the crew were virtually nil. Maybe Howard Hanks had succeeded in talking to one of them. Maybe it was even where he'd gotten his proof of fraud. Or maybe he hadn't talked to any of them. If he had, surely he would have known whether the crude had been off-loaded onto barges or into a pipeline. He wouldn't have held out both as possibilities.

Maybe Gabe was right. Maybe Hanks didn't have anything more to go on than suspicion. Maybe he was trying to scare somebody into making a mistake . . . somebody like Cole.

She turned away from the thought and walked to the window, the night's darkness a mirror for the sudden desolation she felt. She looked out, directly at the glittering lights of Algiers. Below was the Spanish Plaza with its lighted fountain. And in between, the wide, black ribbon of the Mississippi made its sweeping crescent curve, outlined by the lights on both banks.

Then, on the river itself, she saw lights moving. At first she thought they belonged to the ferry that ran from the foot of Canal Street across the river to Algiers Point. Then she realized they were the running lights of a ship crawling steadily upriver, the vessel itself almost invisible from this distance—a black shape on a black river.

Suddenly she was seeing another darkened ship—close to her—enveloped in swirling fog, two men silhouetted at the rail, thick lines stretching toward her. It was a full second before she realized the image of the ship was in her mind. There was white lettering on the bow—white lettering that spelled out the name of the ship.

"Please, God, let me read it," she whispered.

CRESCENT DRAG—

"I don't care what you say." A woman's voice, bitter and accusing, broke over Remy, shattering that fragment of a memory. "She was dancing so close to you, it would have taken a crowbar to pry the two of you apart. It was disgusting."

She spun away from the window and stared at the open door to the corridor, for a fraction of a second frozen by the sound of footsteps. Someone was out there! Who? Why?

"What did you expect me to do? Shove her away?"

That voice—it was Lance's. Dear God, she couldn't let him find her here. She looked frantically around the lighted room for some place to hide. That side door—it had to lead somewhere, if only to a closet.

"You didn't have to look like you were enjoying yourself."

"Dammit, Julie! Do we have to go through this every time we go out for the evening?" Lance protested angrily as Remy ran to the desk. At the moment speed seemed as important as silence. She grabbed her purse off the top of the desk, slinging the strap over her shoulder and hugging the folder against her, hoping their voices would cover any sound she made.

"You should be flattered that after seven years of marriage I still care enough to be jealous."

Their voices were closer; they were coming this way. She darted for the side door. Just as she reached it, Remy heard a low, steady hum. The copy machine—it was still on.

"I have never liked green eyes, Julie."

Remy dashed over and turned the machine off, the click of the switch sounding much too loud. She raced back to the door and forced herself to turn the knob slowly, to ease back the latch. When the door gave, she opened it only wide enough to enable her to slip through. But when she tried to glide noiselessly through the narrow opening, her purse thwacked the frame.

"What was that?"

"What?"

Remy closed the door and flattened herself against it, shutting her eyes, longing to drink in great gulps of air, yet too afraid to breathe.

"I thought I heard something." Lance's voice moved along the corridor, accompanied by the sound of firm, long-striding footsteps. Right behind them was the tap-tap-tap of high heels.

Remy's eyes flew open. The file cabinets. She'd forgotten to lock them. It was too late. He was too close. Would he look? Would he notice? Would he blame it on a careless file clerk?

Dear heaven. Remy looked around her, suddenly realizing she wasn't in a closet. She was in somebody's office. Lance's? It couldn't be—could it? She spotted the door to the corridor and darted to it, pressing herself against the wall next to the hinges so the door would hide her if it was opened.

"Hello? Is somebody here?" He was directly outside; only the wall separated them. Remy sank her teeth into her lower lip, biting down on it hard to keep from betraying herself with a sound, a breath.

"It's probably the cleaning people, Lance," replied the woman, obviously his wife. "Nobody else would be working this late."

He was walking past the office door, continuing on toward the file room, his steps a little slower now—as if he was listening. Somehow she had to get out of here. If he started looking around, he'd find her. There was no place to hide.

"Lance—"

"Shut up."

Remy snuck to the other side of the door and very, very carefully turned the knob, then opened it, not a crack but a sliver. When she peered out, the corridor was empty—in both directions, as near as she could tell. They must be in the file room. Then came the metallic sound of a file drawer gliding that last inch before it shut. She must have left one partially open. How long did she have—maybe seconds?—before he opened the connecting door to this office?

She had one chance, and she took it, slipping out the door into the corridor and running swiftly and silently toward the reception area, totally exposed and expecting at every step to hear his shout of discovery. But it never came. As she rounded the corner, she threw one quick look down the hall. It was still empty. She dashed across the reception area to the door. He'd left it unlocked! She couldn't believe her luck as she banished the image of fumbling with the keys from her mind.

She opened the door and slipped outside, taking care this time not to hit her purse on the frame. She closed it as quietly as she could, then turned, glancing from the elevators to the door to the emergency stairs.

Not the stairs—they were too open, too exposed, too noisy; the slightest sound would echo. She ran to the elevators and punched the Down button, then waited, watching for an arrow to light up above one of them.

"Hurry, hurry," she murmured under her breath, then caught the faint whir of one coming. Suddenly it hit her—

the bell, the damned bell would ding when it reached this floor!

It did—twice—as loud as any alarm to her ears. Remy cast one last glance over her shoulder at the office door, then darted inside the cage and pushed the Lobby button, and then the one marked Door Close.

In their own good time, they slid shut. She made her first-ever white-knuckle descent in an elevator, her hands holding the shoulder strap of her purse and the file folder in a death grip as she wondered whether Lance had seen or heard her —and whether security would be waiting for her when the doors opened.

But no uniformed guard was standing outside when the elevator reached the lobby. Remy hesitantly stepped out and was immediately engulfed by a laughing, loud-talking group streaming out of another elevator. One of them, a man, accidentally bumped into her.

"Oops, sorry," he said, as Remy noticed the security man at the desk—on the phone. With Lance? "Hey, you're a cutie, you know that?" The man draped an arm around her shoulders, his breath reeking of whiskey.

Remy saw the security guard glance at the group, and she carefully withheld any objections to the man's overt attentions. "Thanks," she said, letting the man draw her along with him as the group headed in the general direction of the doors.

"Whatcha been doing? Working late at the office?" he asked, looking at the folder she was carrying.

"Sort of."

"That's too bad. We've been partying."

"Really."

"Yeah, we been at the bar up on top."

"The Top of the Mart."

"Yeah, that's the name of it." He leaned closer and giggled. "Agnes lost her purse. She laid it down on the ledge, and the next minute it was gone. Did you know that bar revolves? About an hour later, there was her purse."

"How nice. I'm glad she got it back." They were directly level with the security desk.

"You wanna go party with us?"

"I don't know. Where are you going?"

He frowned. "Hey, Johnny!" He called to one of the men at the front of the group. "Where're we going?"

"Pat O'Brien's!"

"Yeah, Pat O'Brien's. I'll buy you one of those tornado drinks."

"Hurricane."

"What?"

"Never mind." They were out the door, walking into the sharp, cool night. She slipped free of his draping arm, offering a quick, "I've been to Pat O'Brien's before. Maybe another time."

She had to force herself not to run to the parking lot, recognizing that she was almost safe and that this was no time to draw undue attention to herself. As she neared the sleek bronze Jaguar, she hastily dug through her purse for the keys. She unlocked the driver's door and quickly slipped behind the wheel, depositing her purse and the folder on the passenger seat, then sinking back against the tawny leather seat. Safe. It was over. Or was it? Wasn't it just beginning?

"What have I gotten myself into?" she murmured. "I must be crazy."

But she wasn't crazy, and she hadn't gotten herself into anything. On the contrary, she'd probably been involved from the onset—perhaps knowingly, or perhaps not. One thing she was sure about: she had seen the *Crescent Dragon* tied up to a dock—in the mist and darkness of night. But what else had she seen? Or was the operative word *whom*?

She sighed in frustration and inserted the key into the ignition.

23

"Good morning." Remy breezed into the dining room, encompassing all at the table in her greeting.

"You seem remarkably chipper this morning," Frazier observed, from his chair at the head of the table.

"I had a marvelous night's sleep, that's why," she said as she crossed to the serving table and poured orange juice into the one remaining glass beside the crystal pitcher. "How was the party? I have to admit I didn't hear any of you come in."

"It was—" Gabe started to answer.

"Remy, what are you doing in those clothes?" Sibylle looked at her with something akin to concern for her sanity.

Remy plucked at the fawn-colored jodhpurs. "Isn't it obvious? I thought I'd go horseback riding this morning." Actually, she didn't know if she could ride a horse, but the jodhpurs, riding boots, and chocolate-brown corduroy jacket with fawn-colored suede patches at the elbows had been in her closet. Judging by the signs of wear on the inside of both the boots and the pants, she assumed she'd worn them for the use they were intended for and not simply for appearances.

"At Audubon Park, I suppose," Gabe said.

"Is that where I usually go? I wasn't sure." She walked over to sit beside him, her juice glass in hand.

"Remy, have you looked outside?" her mother protested.

"Yes." But she glanced over her shoulder again at the bleak gray overcast beyond the dining-room windows, then scooted her chair up to the table. "Depressing, isn't it? I decided it would be better to go out in it than stay in the house and have that gray gloom get me down."

"But it's cold."

"I prefer to think of it as 'brisk.' " She unfolded her napkin and laid it across her lap. "And I'd much rather go riding when there's a nip in the air than when it's warm and muggy. Besides, I'm dressed for it," she said, indicating the black ribbed turtleneck sweater she wore under the heavy corduroy jacket.

"What if it rains?"

"Mother," she said in a laughing voice. "I may have lost my memory, but I still have enough sense to come in out of the rain." But she mentally crossed her fingers, hoping the rain would hold off until later in the day.

"By that I take it you mean you haven't been able to remember anything else," Gabe said, studying her with a sympathetic look.

She hesitated, then deliberately hedged the truth. "Not really. A few times I've had vague déjà vu feelings that I've seen or done the same thing before, but I can't honestly say they were memories."

"You're home and safe with us again—that's what counts," Gabe assured her.

"I know." She took a sip of her juice, then asked, dividing the question between Gabe and her father, "Have you been able to find out anything about the *Dragon*?"

"Not yet," Gabe replied.

"I thought Uncle Marc might have learned something."

"He didn't." Her father's answer was curt, his expression

closed and tight, making it clear this was not a subject he wished to discuss.

She would have dropped the matter, but another question occurred to her. "Has anyone come right out and asked Cole what his meeting with the insurance people was about? It seems to me that regardless of how strong his contract is, he's still accountable to the board."

She saw Gabe and her father exchange a quick glance, and then Gabe smiled at her. "Out of the mouths of pretty babes," he murmured, then shrugged. "I suppose we've all been so worried about you that we overlooked the obvious. It's definitely an option we should consider."

"I'll mention it to Marc at lunch today," her father stated.

This time the subject was closed for good as Nattie walked in with their breakfast. Remy breathed in the aroma coming from the tray and immediately guessed, "Pecan waffles."

"With honey butter, brown-sugar syrup, and sausage," Nattie announced, setting the first plate in front of Remy's mother. "It should stick to your ribs and give you some cushion when you fall off that horse."

But Remy had no intentions of going horseback riding. It was nothing more than an excuse to be absent from the house.

Remy parked along the edge of the levee road and stepped out of the Jaguar, the road's oyster-shell surface crunching beneath her riding boots. A few feet from the opposite shoulder, the levee's grassy eight-foot bank sloped away to level out beside the River Road, which followed the Mississippi's twists and bends.

She closed the car door, then glanced in the direction of the tank farm and pipeline terminal on the other side of the road. Some one hundred tanks, resembling giant steel cans painted a dull white, stretched away from her in orderly rows, the whole area enclosed by a towering chain-link fence. A sign on the gate identified it as the property of the Gulf Coast Petroleum Association, a name that meant nothing to her.

A commercial jetliner rumbled in the distance, making its

departure climb from nearby New Orleans Airport. Remy watched it for an instant, then noted the hard, cold look of the clouds overhead and hoped again that they reflected only the gray of winter and not the gray of rain.

Turning, she faced the Mississippi River and the trio of petroleum docks that stood in the muddy brown waters some three hundred feet from the bank. Low, flat barges were moored to the downriver dock, but the middle one—the nearest one—had an oceangoing tanker tied alongside.

Was this the dock where the *Crescent Dragon* had taken on its last load of crude? Was this where she'd seen the tanker? She couldn't remember, and she'd found nothing in the company files that identified the location of the vessel's last berth—or, at least, if the information was there, she hadn't recognized it as such. And heaven knew, there were literally dozens of petroleum docks scattered along the Mississippi River, stretching all the way to Baton Rouge. Most of them, like this cluster, were located upriver or downriver from the city itself, away from thickly populated areas—or so the Port Authority had told her when she'd called them from a phone booth.

Unfortunately, that was about the only useful information she had been able to obtain from them. The man she'd spoken with had claimed he didn't know how to go about finding out where a specific vessel had been berthed more than five months before. He wasn't even sure the commission kept a record of such things, especially when there was no requirement for a vessel to notify them when it left port. He'd told her that the dock agent probably kept track of that type of information.

Which left her back at square one—which dock, and which dock agent?

With no crew available to question, the dock was her only starting point. If she'd been there when the *Dragon* was loaded, as she believed, she might have been seen by one of the dockworkers. If she could locate the men on duty that night, talk to them, maybe one of them could tell her what had happened, who'd been there, and what she might have seen.

It sounded possible . . . even logical. Remy smiled to herself, fully aware that it wasn't logic that had selected this particular petroleum dock as the place to begin asking her questions—it was simply the second one she'd come across. The entrance to the first had been locked up tight, with no one on duty at the gate, and she'd been forced to drive on. She tried not to think about how many more like that she might encounter, and concentrated instead on this one.

A ramp, wide enough to allow the passage of a motorized vehicle, led out to the middle quay. Ignoring the sign that read AUTHORIZED PERSONNEL ONLY BEYOND THIS POINT, Remy walked onto the ramp and continued past the NO TRES-PASSING and NO SMOKING signs posted at frequent intervals along the entire length of it.

The reek of petroleum fumes grew stronger as she neared the tanker. Stout mooring lines ran from the vessel to the bollards on the concrete dock, securing the ship to its berth, and a gangway stretched from the dock to the ship's weather deck. There was no sign of activity on the tanker itself, except for the three chick stands that connected the dockside pipe-lines to the ship's holding tanks.

Catching sight of two men on the dock, Remy angled toward them. For some reason she'd expected it to be busier than this, with more of the bustle she'd observed on the cargo wharves.

"Hey, lady!" a voice barked, directly behind her.

Remy stiffened, suddenly and unexpectedly feeling the cool breath of the river fog on her cheeks, smelling the damp-ness of the mist, and seeing darkness all around her—the darkness of night, that night. In that instant she knew she'd been surprised by someone that night—just like this.

She whirled around and stared at the bejowled bulldog of a man facing her. Not by him—she was oddly certain of that. He wore a plaid-lined jacket in a dark navy twill and a pair of pants in the same fabric that rode precariously low on his hips, the waistband dipping under his big beer-belly.

"What're you doing out here? Didn't you see the signs?" He jerked his thumb in the direction of the NO TRESPASSING placard behind him. "No one's allowed on this dock without authorization."

"I know. I was looking for someone who could give me permission. Can you?" She gave him her most winsome smile, but he didn't bat an eye.

"You'd have to see the director of operations, Tom Hayes, and he ain't here today."

"What about you? What do you do?"

"I'm in charge of loading and operations."

"Then maybe you can answer a few questions for me—"

"Look, lady. We don't give tours and we don't allow visitors. You'll have to leave now."

"At least you can tell me whether you're loading or unloading this ship," Remy persisted.

"Loading it," he said, and he pursed his lips and teeth to emit a loud, ear-splitting whistle. He followed it with a shout and motioning swing of his arm. "Charlie! Come over here!"

Both men on the dock turned at the sound of the shrill whistle, but it was the shorter of the two who broke away to answer the summons. As he trotted over, the jaunty tilt of his billed cap, the natural spring to his step, and the litheness of his build all gave a deceptive impression of youth. When he stopped in front of them, Remy noticed the deep lines that age and the elements had carved into his face, and she realized he was a great deal closer to sixty than to thirty.

He darted a curious, bright-eyed glance at Remy, then averted his gaze to the man beside her. "What'd ya want, Mac?"

"This lady needs an escort back to her car."

"My pleasure."

Remy started to protest, then recognized that she'd only

succeed in antagonizing Mac further. As stubborn as that man was, he'd probably have her bodily carried off the dock if she refused to leave voluntarily.

As the man walked off toward the tanker's gangway, Remy glanced at her escort. "I'm sorry about this, Mr.—"

"Just Charlie," he insisted, grinning. "Everybody calls me that. And don't mind him. He snaps at everybody when he's under the gun to get a ship out. At times like this, he's our version of a Big Mac Attack."

She smiled wryly. "I do feel like I've been pounced on and chewed a bit." She saw the tanker's captain step to the rail of the bridge deck. Mac cupped his hands to his mouth and yelled something at him. The captain responded with an acknowledging salute and went back inside. "What was that all about?" she asked, and reluctantly moved toward the ramp.

Charlie lifted his shoulders in a light shrug. "Mac was probably letting the captain know he could go ahead and call for a river pilot."

"A river pilot." She looked at him with quick interest.

"Yeah, all ships on the Mississippi have to carry a river pilot licensed by the state, someone who knows the river, the locations of its shoals, the tricks of its currents, everything. The ships have to give the Pilots' Association a three-hour advance notice of their departure. Which is about how long it's gonna take us to finish loading this tanker. By then, with luck, the crew will have reported for duty, the pilot'll be on board, and down the river she'll go."

"Then a river pilot takes a ship all the way to the mouth." Unconsciously, Remy slowed her steps, forcing Charlie to shorten his loping stride to stay abreast of her.

"There's always a pilot on board, but not the same one. A Baton Rouge pilot gets on here and takes her down to around Chalmette. A Crescent River pilot gets on board there and helps guide her to Pilot Town. Another pilot takes her from there out to the sea buoy. From this dock, a tanker like that's got about a hundred and forty miles of river to navigate before it reaches the open waters of the Gulf. Kinda amazing, isn't it?''

''I don't think I realized it was that far,'' Remy murmured, thinking as well that no matter where the *Dragon* had been loaded, it must have had well over a hundred miles of river to navigate. And somewhere along that hundred-plus-mile stretch, the bearded Mr. Hanks claimed, the tanker could have off-loaded its cargo of crude onto waiting barges. If it had, the river pilot would have known about it. ''Charlie . . . how long does it take to unload a tanker like that one back there?''

''We can do it in less than twenty-four hours.''

''It takes that long.'' Remy stopped in surprise, twenty feet short of the end of the ramp.

He chuckled. ''It wasn't that many years ago when we thought we were doing good to turn a tanker around in three days.''

''Would it change any if you were unloading onto barges instead of a pipeline?''

''Not really. Your rate of discharge is the same.''

''What about these river pilots?'' These river pilots who were bound to keep some kind of log on the ships they guided. These river pilots who obviously lived in the area, who could tell her where the *Dragon* had been docked and whether she'd made any stops in her journey downriver. ''How would a person get hold of them?''

''You just call 'em up.''

''You mean they're listed in the phone book?'' She nearly smiled at the fact that the answer could be so simple as they made the turn off the ramp toward her car.

''Yep. All you gotta do is look in the Yellow Pages under the Pilots' Association, and the office numbers for all three of them are there.''

''Which means I can let my 'fingers do the walking' instead of me,'' Remy murmured to herself, this time letting the smile come, aware that she was no longer faced with the daunting and time-consuming task of going to all the petroleum docks, trying to locate the tanker's last berth. A couple of phone calls should tell her that—and give her the names of the pilots who had been on board the *Dragon* on her downriver trip.

"Sorry—what'd you say? I couldn't hear," Charlie said, flicking a hand at a small Toyota pickup truck that was accelerating to make the sloping climb onto the levee road.

"Nothing." She paused in front of her car to let the pickup go by. As the small white truck drew level with her, it suddenly applied its brakes, the tires digging into the shelled surface and skidding to a stop a half a length behind her.

The passenger door immediately swung open, and a man dressed in a dark business suit and tie, wearing a pair of attractive gold-rimmed glasses, stepped out and turned his frowning look on her. Judging by the deep perpendicular creases between his eyebrows, Remy suspected that he frowned a lot more than he smiled. She mentally braced herself to receive another lecture about unauthorized visitors.

"Remy. I thought I recognized you. What are you doing here?"

My God, she thought, he knows me. She hadn't expected that, and made another quick study of him, trying to find something familiar. He looked to be somewhere in his late thirties or early forties. His hair was dark and combed straight back from his face—a sternly pragmatic face, with no particularly distinguishing features, unless it was the thinness of his lips.

"This is a surprise. I didn't expect to run into you here," she declared, pretending to know him—a decision she hadn't been conscious of making.

"And I didn't expect to see you. So what brings you here?" He tried to smile, but the expression was foreign to him. Remy briefly thought that it was a shame; he could have been a good-looking man if it weren't for the permanent scowl etched in his forehead.

"What brings me here?" she echoed his question, certain

that she couldn't tell him the truth. If he knew her, he must know her family, and she couldn't have him telling them what she was doing. She had to come up with some other reason—something innocuous. "A friend of mine is writing a book, and I offered to help her with some of the research. One of her characters is in shipping, and she thought I'd know about it."

"A friend of yours? Which one?"

"I don't think you know her. She works at the museum."

"I see." Was he convinced? Remy couldn't tell as she tried to conceal how uncomfortable she felt under his penetrating study. "Did you get all the information you needed?" His glance flicked to Charlie, as if guessing that he'd provided it.

"I think so." She produced the car keys from her jacket pocket and glanced pointedly at the pickup, its motor idling. "I won't keep you. I know you have things to do, and I have a date with a horse to keep."

"See you around, Remy." He hesitated a moment longer, then turned and climbed back into the cab of the pickup.

Remy waited until the truck pulled away, then looked at Charlie. "I hate it when that happens."

"What do you mean?"

"My mind's an absolute blank. I know him, but I can't remember his name."

"Him? That's Carl Maitland."

"Of course." She pretended to recognize the name. In truth, it was vaguely familiar, but she couldn't remember why or how. She held out her hand. "Thanks for escorting me to my car, Charlie—and for your patience in answering all my questions."

"No problem." His calloused hand briefly gripped hers, then released it. "And if your friend needs any more help with her book, tell her to call me. I got some stories about things that have happened on the docks that she wouldn't believe. They'd make a good book."

"I'll tell her."

As she walked around the car to the driver's door, he called after her, "Last name's Aikens. I'm in the phone book."

"Got it," she said, and waved a final good-bye.

Leaving the tank terminal and the petroleum docks, Remy followed the River Road for a short distance, then turned off and made the jog to intersect with Airline Highway. She stopped at the first pay telephone booth she saw. In the directory, just as Charlie Aikens had promised, were the numbers for all three river-pilot districts. She called the Baton Rouge district first and simply asked if someone could tell her which pilot had been aboard the tanker *Crescent Dragon* when it had left port in the early part of September last year. Within minutes a man came back on the line and said the pilot had been Pete Hoskins—no, he wasn't there right now. He was on a Russian grain ship and probably wouldn't be back for another five hours.

Her second call was more productive.

Thirty minutes later Remy was sitting in a booth in a Mid-City coffee shop with the *Dragon*'s Crescent River pilot, Gus Trudeau, a tall man of imposing proportions with a full head of sandy hair tinged with gray. She watched him take a long drink of the scalding-hot coffee, secretly convinced he had an asbestos-lined mouth.

Amazingly, he didn't breathe out fire, smoke, or steam when he set his cup down on the Formica-topped table and looked her squarely in the eye. "So you're a writer, eh?"

"That's right. I'm writing a follow-up piece on the *Crescent Dragon*, a retrospective story from the viewpoint of various people like yourself who had some involvement with what turned out to be her last voyage." Remy thought the cover was a good one—one that would arouse the least possible amount of suspicion about her interest in the tanker. "So tell me, Mr. Trudeau, what do you remember of her? Were there any problems? Did anything unusual happen?"

"No, it was pretty routine. When I took over from Pete Hoskins, the Baton Rouge pilot, I remember he told me that she answered pretty sluggish, so I kept that in mind on the trip down to Pilot Town. And I talked briefly with the captain, too, about the storm brewing in the Gulf.''

''Then there weren't any stops—any delays along the way?''

''None.''

''That was almost six months ago, Mr. Trudeau.'' Remy eyed him curiously. ''How can you be so sure about that?''

''Like I told those other two who came around asking—''

''Other two?'' She frowned. ''What other two?''

''I don't remember their names, but one was a heavyset guy with a beard who came around asking questions about the tanker—musta been two weeks ago. Then a couple days before that, I talked to another guy. He was younger, probably in his thirties, tall, brown hair.''

Gabe. She should have known her brother would do some checking of his own. ''I'm sorry. I interrupted you. What was it that you told them?''

''Just that when a ship goes down in a storm three days after you've been on her, you remember that ship *and* that trip—*well*. You go over the trip in your mind, compare notes with the other pilots, and try to remember if there was something—anything—that might have indicated the vessel wasn't really seaworthy.''

''And you did that. You talked with the other two pilots,'' Remy guessed.

''I did. And it was routine all the way.''

''Did they have any stops or delays?''

''None. And I know that for a fact, because I saw copies of their log sheets.''

She took a small sip of the still-hot coffee and wondered whether she should take his word for it or talk to the other pilots herself. ''You don't happen to know where the tanker was docked, do you?'' she asked curiously.

''Pete told me he picked her up at the old Claymore docks.'' He hesitated, then nodded. ''That's right. She was berthed in the upper one. I remember Pete told me the current takes a funny twist there and can sometimes be a problem when you're pulling away from the dock. That's when he discovered how slow the tanker was to maneuver.''

"Where are the Claymore docks?"

"Let's see." He leaned against the booth's red-vinyl back, a thoughtful, searching frown claiming his expression. "What mile marker are they located on?"

Remy immediately guessed that he was talking "river" miles. "No, I was wondering how I could reach them from land."

"I don't know if I can tell you how to get there by land," he said, absently scratching his head. "They're on the east bank, north of Kenner a ways. I'm sure you could get to 'em by the River Road."

She realized that she must have been close to them earlier that day. "How far are they from the tank farm and docks owned by Gulf Coast Petroleum?"

"Those *are* the old Claymore docks."

"What?"

"Those *are* the Claymore docks," he repeated.

She'd been there—at the very place where the *Dragon* had been berthed—and not known it, not recognized it, not remembered. "Wait. There are three docks there." And she'd been on the middle one. "Which one did you say the tanker was at?"

"The upper one."

She shook her head in confusion. "Which one's that?"

"The upriver one—that's why it's called the 'upper' dock."

She hadn't been on the right dock. Was that why nothing had seemed familiar to her? She didn't dare go back and risk running into that Carl Maitland again. And she doubted that "Bulldog" Mac would be any more cooperative the second time around. Then she remembered Charlie—dear, wonderful Charlie Aikens, so friendly and free with information. Was he one of the men who had loaded the *Dragon?* Had he seen her there that night? Wouldn't he have recognized her if he had? His number was in the phone book, he'd said. All she had to do was call and ask. And if he hadn't worked that shift, maybe she could persuade him to find out who had.

With an effort, she brought her attention back to the booth. "You said the trip downriver was routine, but—was there anything about the *Dragon*'s voyage that raised questions in your mind? In other words, when it went down, was it way off course? Or had it not traveled as far as you thought it would? Anything like that?" Even though the pilot had eliminated the possibility of the tanker off-loading its shipment of crude oil onto river barges or a pipeline downstream, there was still a chance it had hooked onto an offshore pipeline.

"No. According to the Coast Guard report I read, it went down about where you'd expect, given its course and speed and the strength of the storm. It sunk just a mile or two off the sea-lane. Fortunately, it's a well-traveled route, and the crew was able to signal a passing ship. And before you ask, no, we didn't run into much barge traffic."

"I beg your pardon?"

"The bearded guy asked a lot of questions about the barges that ply the Delta waters south of the city. But like I told him, about the only barges you meet downriver are the ones hauling trash and garbage out into the ocean."

"I see," she said, and went back to something he'd said just before that. "The Coast Guard issued a report on the sinking?"

"Yes"

She wondered why she hadn't found a copy of it in the company files. Had it been there, and had she somehow overlooked it?

She was still bothered by the question when she arrived home. She walked into the house and immediately caught the distinctive aroma of bay leaves and spices stewing in a gumbo pot. Her father was in the entrance hall, holding the telephone receiver to his ear. He hung up when he saw her.

"I was just dialing the stables to see if you'd left."

Remy faltered an instant in midstride, then recovered and

smiled at him in mock reproof, trying not to think how close she'd come to getting caught in a lie. "Why would you be doing that? I told you I'd be home in time for lunch, and here I am," she said, then chided him as she paused to pull off her gloves. "I have the distinct feeling you're keeping closer track of me now than you did when I was a teenager."

"That's not true."

"Isn't it?" she challenged lightly.

"If it is, it's only because it's natural for us to worry after the way you disappeared before."

"I promise I'm not going to disappear again, so stop worrying."

"Remy." Her mother came out of the dining room. "I thought I heard your voice. I was just telling Nattie I didn't think you were going to make it back for lunch. How was your ride?" She inspected her daughter's appearance with a slightly puzzled expression. "I expected you to come back chilled to the bone, with your nose and cheeks all rosy-pink from the cold, but you look . . . fine."

"The Jaguar *does* have a heater. I warmed up on the way home." Remy glanced toward the dining room and deliberately sniffed the air. "Is that shrimp gumbo I smell?"

"Yes. I'll let Nattie know you're here. You'll want to change out of those riding clothes—"

"I'll do that later. Right now I'm starved."

Food was actually the furthest thing from her mind, but exercise was supposed to make a person hungry, and if she wanted to maintain the pretense that she'd spent the morning horseback riding, she had to feign an appetite.

An hour later, fresh from the shower, Remy sat in the middle of her bed, swathed in her satin robe, a towel wrapped turban-style around her wet head, and the folder containing copies of the documents from the company files lying open in front of her. Her first rifling search through the stack had failed to turn up a copy of the Coast Guard report. She started to go through the papers again, one at a time.

Two quick raps were the only warning she had. Frantically, she pulled the towel off her head and dropped it over the files to conceal them as the bedroom door swung open.

"Nattie," she declared in relief when the tall, spare black woman walked in. "You startled me." She laughed self-consciously and nervously combed her wet hair away from her forehead with her fingers.

"I knocked first."

"I know."

"Where're your boots?"

"In the closet. Why?" Frowning, Remy slid off the bed when Nattie immediately walked in that direction.

"'Cause I'd better get 'em cleaned before they stink up the place," she said, opening the closet door and walking inside.

"You don't need to." Remy took a quick step after her, then stopped as Nattie emerged from the closet, boots in hand. Except for some white dust from the levee road's oyster-shell surface, the soles and heels of her riding boots were dry and unstained—as Nattie quickly saw. "I already cleaned them," Remy asserted.

Nattie shot her a skeptical look, then walked over and picked up the dark-brown corduroy riding jacket that Remy had laid over the back of the loveseat. "Just like you already brushed all the horse hairs off this jacket, I suppose."

"That's right." Why was she lying? Nattie didn't believe her, not for one second. But she couldn't tell her the truth. She wasn't even sure what the truth was. "Nattie, I—"

Nattie held up a hand to stave off the rest of her words. "Lies and rabbits both have a way of multiplying. I'll just put these boots back in the closet and hang up this jacket and leave it go at that."

"Thanks." Remy smiled a little in relief.

"I just hope you know what you're doing," Nattie muttered as she walked back into the closet.

"So do I," she replied over the faint rustle of clothing and hangers.

As soon as Nattie left, Remy lifted the covering towel off the open folder and began going through the individual copies again. Suddenly a name leapt out at her—Maitland. She stared at the invoice from Maitland Oil Company for the tanker's shipment of crude. Maitland Oil Company—as in Carl Maitland, the well-dressed man in the white pickup who'd addressed her by name? They had to be one and the same. Which meant that not only did he know her family, he also did business with the Crescent Line.

What if he ran into her father or her uncle? What if he mentioned seeing her at the docks—and the research she was supposedly doing for a friend? But she couldn't worry about that now. She'd deal with it when and *if* it happened. Maybe by then she would have found out something—or remembered something.

Right now she needed to look for that Coast Guard report. Later she'd call Charlie Aikens and see if he knew or could discover anything for her. She idly wondered what time he'd be home from work, then continued going through the sheaf of papers.

After the fourth ring, a familiar-sounding voice came on the line. "Yeah, Charlie here."

"Charlie." Remy glanced at the digital clock on her bedstand. Seven thirty-two. "I was beginning to think you were going to work all night."

"I stopped by Grogan's for a couple of beers. Who's this?"

"Remy. Remy Cooper." With the Crescent Line and the Jardins virtually synonymous to anyone on the waterfront, she'd realized that she'd have to use a different name. "I'm the one Mac had you escort off the dock today."

"Oh, sure," he said, as it dawned on him. "I remember you. How're you doing?"

"Fine. Listen, I was wondering if you could help me with some more information my friend needs for her book."

"I'll try."

"Do you remember the tanker the *Crescent Dragon*? She

was loaded with a shipment of crude from your docks last September, probably the fifth or sixth.''

"Hell—excuse my language, but we service so many barges and ships off those docks, I lose track of the names of 'em all.''

"Yes, but this one went down in the Gulf during a storm.''

"Yeah, there was a tanker that sank last year," he said slowly, thoughtfully. "And now that you mention it, I think I do remember hearing some of the guys talking about how she'd loaded out from our docks. But I didn't work on her.''

"Could you find out who did? My friend would like to talk to them.''

"No problem. I'll ask around tomorrow when I go in. Somebody's bound to remember something. Ships don't take up residence in Davy Jones's locker every day. What's you're number? I'll give you a call tomorrow night and let you know what I've found out.''

"I'd better call you. I'm not sure where I'll be.''

"Carnival goes into full swing tomorrow, with wall-to-wall craziness, doesn't it? I steer clear of it myself these days. It's not like when I was young—not with all those gays strutting around dressed up like fancy showgirls. It used to be a wild time; now it's just plain crazy,'' he declared, then said, "You give me a call tomorrow night . . . 'bout this same time.''

"I will.'' Remy said good-bye and hung up. With that in motion, the next thing on her agenda was to locate a copy of that Coast Guard report.

24

S he's started snooping around asking questions."

He gripped the telephone's black receiver a little tighter and sat down in the chair behind the desk. "I don't believe you."

"I'm telling you she is. I know it for a fact," came the low, accusing reply. "Right now she's asking the wrong people the right questions. It's got to stop there."

He frowned, stunned, confused, and troubled. "But she can't remember anything. I know she can't."

"Maybe not, but she's damned well trying to. That insurance investigator Hanks can't cause us half as much trouble as she can, and we both know it. The last thing we need is somebody else going around asking questions. Do you hear me?"

"I hear you." The room suddenly seemed very stuffy. He reached up, loosened the knot of his tie, and unfastened the top button of his dress shirt. "Just let me handle it."

"I let you handle it the last time, and look what almost happened."

"But nothing did happen, did it?"

"And I'm not going to take the chance of something happening this time. I've gone too far, come too close. I'm not going to lose everything now."

"You won't. *We* won't."

"You're damned right we won't. Because I'm having her watched every time she leaves that house—and if I find out she's opening her mouth to anybody else, I'll persuade her to shut it."

"We agreed, going in, that there'd be no violence—no one would get hurt. You—"

"The ground rules have changed. Remy's changed them. No one's going to ruin me—not her, not you, no one. Do you understand?"

"Of course."

"Then do something about her, or I will."

There was a sharp click and the connection was broken. He held the receiver to his ear a second longer, then slammed it down and leaned back in his chair to stare at the ceiling, and not at the darkness that loomed outside.

Crowds lined St. Charles Avenue and filled the neutral strip in the middle. Small children sat perched atop stepladders in seat contraptions specially designed for the occasion. More youngsters were on the ground, gripping bags brought to hold the afternoon's booty. Some wore masks, others didn't, but all—young and old and everyone in between—stood with eager hands outstretched to the parade of riders in spangled costumes and the maskers on mountainous papier-mâché floats and screamed, begged, and cajoled—"Throw me something!" "I want the pearls!" "Over here!" Occasionally Remy heard someone erroneously call out, "Throw me something, *mister!*" as the all-female krewe of Iris, which by tradition always paraded on the Saturday afternoon before Mardi Gras, rolled by, launching the start of what amounted to a four-day weekend.

Carnival parades in New Orleans were never a spectator sport. The fun, the thrill, the excitement of them was in catching the prizes thrown from the floats—the plastic beads, the coasters, the toys, the aluminum doubloons. It didn't matter that today's treasure invariably became tomorrow's trash, not when the mask of adulthood was shed to reveal the child in everyone. But Remy didn't join the throng that surged against the barricade to catch the trinkets hurled at them by an obliging masker. Instead, she took advantage of a brief open space along the outer fringe and quickened her pace. During the mad scramble to retrieve necklaces that had fallen through ensnaring fingers to the ground, she reached the corner and turned, heading toward the river.

Away from the parade route, the congestion lessened along the sidewalks, if not on the streets. Traffic going into the city proceeded at a crawl when it moved at all. As Remy walked past cars inching their way along, she knew it would only get worse the closer she got to Canal Street and the Vieux Carré. There was no doubt in her mind that she'd made the right choice in leaving the Jaguar in the garage.

When she entered the doors of the International Trade Mart twenty minutes later, the quiet of the building was a welcome shock after the ceaseless din of the parade crowds, marching bands, blaring car horns, and tooting kazoos. She smiled at the security guard on duty at the desk and went straight to the elevators. She hadn't realized she was on edge until she felt the tension falling away as the elevator whisked her to the fifteenth floor and the corporate offices of the Crescent Line.

She stepped out of the elevator and glanced at her watch, mentally giving herself an hour to locate the Coast Guard report. From a zipper pocket in her purse, she took the shiny new key that an all-night locksmith had made for her, copied from her father's set, and inserted it in the lock. It turned easily under her hand. She stepped inside and locked the door behind her. She paused long enough to drop the key in her purse, then crossed the reception lobby and turned down the corridor toward the file room.

Voices. She heard voices. She stopped to listen, telling herself it was ridiculous—no one would be here on a Saturday, especially not the Saturday before Mardi Gras. She was probably hearing the shouts from the parade crowd on Canal Street—or a band. On the fifteenth floor? No, the voices seemed to be coming from the wing of executive offices at the opposite end of the hall. There was definitely someone there—more than one "someone." Remy started to quietly retreat, then paused near the opening to the reception area.

That voice—its pitch, its rhythm—it sounded like Gabe's. That was impossible. He and her father had left the house about ten minutes before she had—to go to the krewe's float barn, they'd said. Then she heard the deep rumble of a second voice, and she frowned. Gabe was with Cole? Why?

Curiosity overcame caution as she slipped down the hall, hugging the wall, intent on getting close enough to hear what they were saying. Remy caught the sound of a third voice— its tone smooth, charming, disarming. Then Cole interrupted, and it was a full second before she realized that the third voice belonged to Marc Jardin. Her uncle was there too?

Farther along the corridor, a door stood partially open. She saw the ice-blue fabric on a side wall and instantly pictured the rest of the room. It was windowless, the expanse of cool color relieved by a single impressionistic painting of the New Orleans waterfront with the triple spires of St. Louis Cathedral rising in the background. A long table of pale pecan and eight chairs with seat cushions covered in a matching ice-blue fabric filled the rest of the room—the boardroom.

They were all in the boardroom. Remy stiffened, sharply recalling her conversation with Gabe at the breakfast table the day before, when she'd suggested they should ask Cole about his meeting with the insurance company instead of wondering what had transpired. Gabe had indicated that they'd consider it.

But they'd done more than consider it; they'd acted—acted and deliberately excluded her from the meeting, without even telling her one was scheduled.

Damn them, she thought, yet she wasn't at all surprised, only irritated at their overly protective attitude.

"The insurance company has you scared, Frazier. Why?"
So her father was with them!

When Remy heard Cole speak, his words now as distinct as his deep voice, she discovered that she'd moved closer without even realizing it.

"The reputation of this company happens to be at stake," her father responded in a clipped and angry voice.

"Then you should want me to defend it, instead of insisting that I capitulate to their demands," Cole fired back, equally curt, and Remy immediately sensed the hostility in the air, a hostility that neither man seemed to be attempting to conceal.

Marc Jardin attempted to inject a measure of calm and reason. "I don't think you understand, Buchanan, how very damaging it would be for these accusations of fraud to become public."

"Damaging to whom? To you, Marc?" Cole challenged. "Are you afraid all the publicity might make your political friends decide you aren't the most likely candidate for governor in the next election? I don't know why they should mind—corruption and fraud aren't new to Louisiana politics."

"I won't pretend that isn't a concern of mine," her uncle asserted stiffly. "But it is hardly my only concern. Like the rest of the family, I'm thinking not only of myself but of the good of the company. There is no reason for any of this to become public. An amicable and *quiet* settlement with the insurance company can be negotiated."

"The Crescent Line is not repaying one dime of the claim. If you're all so anxious to hush this thing up, then I suggest you dig into your own pockets and buy them off with the money you've been siphoning from the company for years," Cole retorted. He paused and then added in a harshly amused and cutting voice, "Of course, if you did that, then you wouldn't have the funds to buy your election, would you, Marc? As I understand it, between the problems in the oil patch and Wall Street's Black Monday, you've taken a financial bath, Frazier. As for the good counselor and our genius with figures—the thirty-six-twenty-four-thirty-six kind—it must be hell not to be able to get your hands on all that money your granddaddy socked away in a trust fund for you.''

''All of that is irrelevant and immaterial, Buchanan,'' Gabe spoke up. ''The insurance company isn't looking to any of us. They're looking to the company for their money.''

''They can look and threaten all they want. The company lost a ship that was fully loaded with a cargo of crude paid for in advance. We collected for that loss legally. And we both know, Counselor, that an anonymous phone call claiming there was no oil on board when the tanker went down and a signature on a receipt for plastic explosives hardly constitute incontrovertible evidence that a crime was even committed. And I'm not about to jeopardize the financial stability of this company simply because the board of directors is afraid of bad publicity. Look at the balance sheet.'' There was a thump on the table, accompanied by a whisper of paper. ''To pay back even a portion of the claim would destroy the progress the company's made this past year and cripple it for the next five, if not longer.''

''And if that happened, you wouldn't be entitled to the ten-percent ownership share your agreement calls for in the event that you succeed in turning the company around in three years, would you?'' Lance inserted, his voice heavy with sarcasm. ''You accuse us of having selfish motives, but you aren't looking out for the company's interest—only your own. You've always hated us, Buchanan. Half the reason you signed on was so you could show a bunch of rich bastards you were better than they were. Only you found out you weren't the wonder boy you thought you were, didn't you? That's why you came up with this insurance scam, isn't it? It brought in the working capital the company so badly needed before it could even hope to turn the corner. Plus you probably sold that shipment of crude on the black market and salted away six or seven million dollars in some Swiss account. There's no doubt, Buchanan, that you had the motive, the means, and the opportunity. Sooner or later that insurance investigator will prove that. And it galls me that by settling with the insurance company, we'll be saving your ass.''

Stunned by the brutal logic of Lance's indictment, Remy discovered she was holding her breath, waiting for a quick, angry denial from Cole. But it didn't come. Instead, there was a long and heavy silence.

When Cole did speak, it was with a deadly calm. ''That's the family line, is it? I figured it would be something like that.''

''On Monday morning,'' her father began, ''you will contact the insurance company and set up a meeting with them. Marc will handle the settlement negotiations—''

''No.'' Cole's flat, quiet refusal cut him off in midsentence.

''What?''

''No,'' he repeated, in an even firmer tone. ''I'm still running this company, Frazier. There will be no settlement talks.''

''I don't think you understood Lance. Either you work out a deal with the insurance company, or this board will be forced to demand your resignation.''

''You can demand till hell freezes over,'' Cole snapped.

''I strongly advise you to reconsider,'' Gabe said quietly. ''The insurance company's allegations and limited evidence of attempted fraud are sufficient cause for this board to question your conduct. If you refuse to resign, this board will remove you from office for malfeasance, and will terminate your contract.''

''Try it,'' came Cole's quick and cold challenge, followed by the sound of a chair being pushed back. ''You try it, and I'll file so many charges and countercharges of malfeasance against this board that the Jardin name will make headlines every damned day. If it's a fight you want, Frazier, you've got it.''

''You can't win.''

''Maybe not. But if I go down, you'll all go with me.''

Without warning, the door was yanked the rest of the way

open and Cole came striding out—not in a business suit and tie, but in a pair of soft, washed-out jeans and a bulky pullover of ecru that made him look rougher, tougher. There was the smallest break in his stride when he saw her in the corridor. Hostile gray eyes washed over her, their coldness a shock to her numbed senses.

"I assume you brought your rubber stamp," he muttered as he swept past her.

Realizing that he thought she approved of their decision, Remy whirled around to tell him that she'd had no knowledge of this meeting, then stopped. The things she'd heard—Lance's accusations, Gabe's warnings, Cole's threat—what did she think? Were they right?

"He's bluffing," she heard Marc say.

"Don't kid yourself," Lance snapped. "The bastard means it."

"Damn him," Gabe swore, and slammed a hand on the table. "Why can't he see it makes more sense to settle with the insurance company than to get involved in a long and costly legal battle? That was a perfectly sound argument, and he didn't even listen to it."

"You can't reason with a man like that," her father murmured tightly just as Remy heard Cole go out the front door.

"We've got to do something," Marc insisted. "Dammit, Frazier, we can't let him ruin us. My God, you know what will happen if any of this gets out."

It suddenly hit her what they were saying. They weren't solely concerned with whether Cole was guilty or innocent, or even with whether the fraud charges were true or false. Their approach was much more pragmatic: find a solution that would have the least damaging effect on the company overall. In their opinion, that solution was to negotiate a settlement with the insurance company before any further action was taken. Wasn't that the sensible thing to do? Couldn't the rest come later? Remy went after Cole.

When she reached the street, she caught a glimpse of him crossing Canal, heading for the Quarter, then immediately lost sight of him. The parade was over, and the crowds that had gathered to watch it pass along Canal Street now flooded onto the narrow streets of the Vieux Carré. She hurried after him, joining the streaming mass of revelers, tourists, and college kids as they sauntered along, a look of anticipation on their faces, searching for something—they weren't sure what, but they were confident they'd know it when they found it.

Impatiently Remy threaded her way through the throng, trying to catch up to Cole. She barely glanced at the prom-enading drag queen in a gold-sequined body stocking complete with feathery tail plumes or at the couple in matching satin jackets with DETROIT AUTOMOTIVE written on the back, who nudged each other and gawked at her-him-it, unaware that it was only the first of many elaborate and outrageous costumes they would see as Carnival turned the Quarter's narrow streets into a bizarre bazaar indeed. At this point, the families who had earlier lined the parade route were nowhere to be seen.

A one-man band worked the corner of Chartres and Conti, blowing, strumming, and drumming an unusual rendition of "Mardi Gras Mambo." Remy spotted Cole as he shouldered his way around the crowd that had gathered to watch because it seemed the thing to do. She shouted his name, but he didn't hear her. Finally the cross-flow of strolling people on Royal slowed him down long enough for her to close the distance between them.

"Cole, wait!" she called, and she saw him look back, his eyes locating and then narrowing on her. For an instant she thought he was going to keep going, but he stopped, letting the crowd break around him. She pushed her way to his side, murmuring hasty excuses as she went.

"What do you want?" he said, and brushed off a hawker selling an assortment of gorilla, Dracula, and plain or se-quined Lone Ranger-style masks.

"To talk." She felt his impatience, his rigid anger, and wondered how she was going to reach him.

"If you've come to repeat the family position, I've already had a bellyful of it."

"You don't understand—"

"I understand better than you do," he snapped, and he swung away to plow his way through the living stream to the other side of the intersection.

Remy was right on his heels, following in his wake. There was a slight thinning of people on the side street, enough to allow her to draw level with him as she quickened her steps to a running walk to keep pace with his long strides.

"Cole, my family's only thinking of what's best for the company."

"Like hell they are." He kept walking.

Now angry herself, she grabbed at his arm, feeling the hard bunching of muscles beneath the bulky knit of the sleeve. "Dammit, Cole, will you stand still and listen to me?"

He halted so abruptly that she shot past him and had to swing back to face him. "Listen to what?" he demanded. "More phony declarations that they're only thinking about what's best for the company? They're only worried about mud getting thrown on the Jardin name—and maybe leaving a stain that won't wash out."

"That's not true. Once the insurance company goes through with its threat to file both civil and criminal suits, the Crescent Line will spend a fortune in attorneys' fees fighting it. All they want to do is spend the money now to settle it before it gets to that stage. Big companies do it all the time. It isn't an admission of guilt on anyone's part. It's simply good business."

There was a sudden and sharp narrowing of his eyes. " '*Once* the insurance company goes through with its threat'? Why didn't you say '*if*'? You're assuming that the claim was fraudulently collected. Why?"

"I don't know why I phrased it like that," she replied uneasily, aware that it had been an unconscious slip on her part, made because she believed she knew something.

"Don't you? What proof could there be?"

"You mentioned something about plastic explosives."

"Which doesn't mean anything unless the insurance company can find someone who can swear he saw them on board the tanker. And I was talking about the crude, not that. How could the *Dragon* have been empty when it went down?" he challenged, watching her closely. "I saw her being loaded at the docks. Roughly ten hours after she left the dock, she was at the sea buoy—that's within the normal range of trip time during low water. And the river pilots all swear the water was lapping at her Plimsoll line, indicating that the tanker was running fully loaded. Her course didn't take her close to any offshore oil rigs or drilling platforms. And the Coast Guard found her wreckage floating less than two miles from her anticipated course. How could she have been empty when she went down? What happened to the crude oil? Do you know?"

"Of course I don't." But the facts he'd set forth bothered her too. Everything seemed to indicate that it was impossible for the tanker to have been empty. It was what made her doubt the insurance company's accusations.

"Then why is your family so anxious to get rid of me? Why are they setting me up to take the fall for this?"

She looked at him, seeing the bitterness and anger in his harsh features. He sounded paranoid. She remembered how much he despised her family and all it stood for. *Uptown.* How many times had he thrown that word at her? Why? Because he felt insecure? Inferior? Or was he asking her all these questions to make himself appear innocent?

"They only threatened to remove you from office when you refused to cooperate."

"Is that why you're here—because their threats failed and now you hope to persuade me to accept the family line?"

"I'm trying to persuade you to be reasonable," she argued.

"No." He shook his head, disputing her claim. "You don't want me to be reasonable. You want me to be the patsy."

"That's not true."

But he wasn't listening. "I was a fool to believe I meant anything to you," he muttered thickly. "And I have the feeling you and your family played me for the fool all along. But not anymore, Remy. Not anymore.''

When he walked away, Remy didn't go after him—but she wanted to. That was the crazy part. She ran a hand over her face, feeling confused, bewildered, understanding only a part of what was going on—the part that dealt with facts, not emotions, reactions, or relationships.

Was she overreacting? Was she seeing shadows that weren't there? What were the facts? A tanker had sunk in a storm, a tanker owned by her family's company. Had it been deliberate? Had it been loaded with crude oil when it went down? Or had the crude been off-loaded? Where? How?

Blindly she turned onto Bourbon at the corner and headed uptown, buffeted by the human current flowing in the opposite direction. Laughter, rebel yells, carefree voices swirled around her, occasionally competing with the wail of a jazz clarinet, the driving beat of a rhythm-and-blues tune, or the deep-voiced chanting from a group of rollicking college kids patiently urging a likely-looking wench at a gallery rail above them to "show us your tits," an echo of the very phrase scrawled across her T-shirt, offered all in good fun, if in questionable taste—proof that a trace of the pagan rites of spring lingered in the Vieux Carré during the ninety-six-hour day of Mardi Gras.

Remy walked around a barker posted in front of the open door to a topless bar, mechanically reeling off his spiel to the passersby. Heads turned to peer inside, but nearly everyone kept walking. On impulse Remy walked into the next bar she came to. Typical of most bars during Carnival, it was quiet, uncrowded. All the action was in the street, and bars were merely a place for revelers to buy another go-cup.

She went directly to the pay phone in a back hall by the restrooms. With a quarter in hand, she dug in her purse, found the number, and dialed it. There were too many answers she didn't have, too many questions that led her in circles, too many things that didn't make sense—especially Cole's part in all this. If there was a scam and he was involved in it, then why hadn't he immediately jumped on her family's recommendation to work out some kind of settlement with the insurance company—*before* their investigator came up with incriminating evidence? Why was he playing hardball?

"This is Remy Jardin," she said quickly, before she could question the wisdom of what she was doing. "I need to talk to you. Can you meet me in . . . twenty minutes at La Louisiane, in the lounge?"

The reply was affirmative

In the quiet, softly lit lounge, Remy sipped at her whiskey-laced coffee and glanced over the rim of the cup at the burly man with the salt-and-pepper beard seated across from her, watching as he peeled off a ten-dollar bill and gave it to the bartender. When the bartender walked away, the insurance investigator lifted his Scotch and water in a toasting gesture.

"To surprise phone calls?" he suggested. Remy didn't respond. He noted her silence with another keen glance, then took a quick sip of his drink, barely moistening his lips. "You said you had some information for me."

"No. I said I wanted to talk to you." She set her cup down on the small cocktail table, keeping her voice calm and controlled. "I've come to the conclusion that the insurance company's charges of fraud are totally false."

"Is that right?"

"I think you know it too, Mr. Hanks. You must have learned that it takes roughly twenty-four hours to unload a tanker of the *Dragon*'s capacity. Given the time it sailed from the Claymore dock, the distance it traveled, and the location where it went down, it was physically impossible for the shipment of crude to be unloaded anywhere en route. And you have to agree that there isn't any percentage in deliberately sinking a fully loaded ship simply to collect the insurance. Hence there's no scam, and no fraud. You're on a wild-goose chase."

"Am I?" He regarded her thoughtfully. "I'm afraid I don't see it that way."

"What other way is there to see it?" she retorted. "You can't change the facts or the laws of physics. That crude couldn't have been off-loaded into pipelines or onto barges, as you suggested. There wasn't time."

"I admit that's bothered me some."

Remy laughed at that, sounding just a little brittle with nerves. "It should have bothered you more than 'some,' Mr. Hanks."

He looked at her, his mustache and beard moving near the corners of his mouth, obviously with a smile that she couldn't see for all the hairy growth. "You claim I'm on a wild-goose chase, Miss Jardin, but I think you're on a fishing expedition."

She hesitated a split second, then admitted, "I am. I honestly can't believe those charges are anything but false. Yet—you seem to believe otherwise. How can you, given the facts?"

"Have you ever seen a magician make an elephant disappear?"

Remy leaned back in her chair, impatient and a little irritated. "Please don't try to convince me it was all done with mirrors."

"Magic—it's all an illusion. The only time the hand is quicker than the eye is when you're watching the wrong hand. It's called misdirection. Football coaches design entire plays around that concept."

"I'm not in the mood for riddles." Especially when she was living one. "Say what you mean."

"I'm saying, what if it was all an elaborate hoax? What if that tanker never sank at all? What if the debris the Coast Guard found was nothing but a smoke screen? What if the *Crescent Dragon* is in some faraway port with a different name painted on her sides and fake registry?"

"But the crew abandoned ship," she protested in a stunned voice.

"*Did* they abandon it? Or was that another smoke screen so a different crew could take their place and sail off in the tanker?" he countered. "While everyone's looking in one place, the tanker is really somewhere else."

Remy shook her head, bemused and skeptical. "It's a very interesting theory, but I think you're reaching. If that's all you have to go on—"

"It isn't," he said, and he reached inside his tweed jacket.

"Yes, I've heard about the receipt for plastic explosives," she said as he pulled a square of paper from his breast pocket. Then she noticed there was more than one item in his hand. "But a receipt doesn't prove the explosives were ever taken aboard the tanker."

"Do you recognize this man?" He placed a black-and-white photo on the cocktail table, facing her.

Remy drew the picture closer and studied the man with his wide, staring eyes and thick, bushy brows. He had dark, slick hair, a swarthy complexion, and a sweeping handlebar mustache waxed to points at the ends.

She shook her head, answering honestly, "I don't remember seeing him before."

"What about this one?" He laid a second photo down beside the first.

The man in the second picture laughed out at her, his strong white teeth gleaming in the center of a dark, closely trimmed full beard. His hair was dark too, a little on the long side, and definitely curly. Remy stared at his thick, full eyebrows, then looked again at the man in the first picture.

"I don't know him, either, though I can see a similarity between the two—the eyebrows, the forehead, the swarthy complexion. Are they related?"

"This"—he tapped the first picture—"is Keith Cummins, the first mate aboard the *Dragon*. And this is Kim Charles," he said, indicating the second photo. "A Eurasian and known demolitions expert with one conviction for arson. A handwriting expert has examined the signatures of both Keith Cummins and Kim Charles. He insists they were written by the same hand."

"I see," she murmured.

"We have our link between the explosives and the tanker,

Miss Jardin," he said, sweeping up the photos and tucking them back into his breast pocket.

"And where is this . . . Mr. Charles?"

"That's a curious thing about the *Dragon*'s crew. After they were rescued and their statements were taken, they all —every last one of them—disappeared, vanished, poof . . . like magic," he added deliberately. "Another curious thing—the last time Kim Charles, alias Cummins, was seen was approximately a week ago . . . in Marseilles, France. And who do you suppose was in Marseilles that same day?"

"Who?" Remy asked, even though she already knew the answer.

"Buchanan. He claims he was there on company business. The strange thing is that he arrived the night before, but didn't come into the branch office until late in the afternoon. And like our explosives man, he was seen on the waterfront in the morning. What do you suppose he was doing there? Meeting his cohort in crime, maybe?"

Why *had* Cole gone to Marseilles? The question was a hammer that kept pounding at Remy as she walked along Iberville, moving slowly but steadily away from the boisterous throngs that packed Bourbon and Royal streets. Until the bearded Mr. Hanks had tossed out those questions, she hadn't realized how desperately she had wanted to believe that Cole wasn't mixed up in this insurance fraud. She'd secretly been hoping that he'd say something different—something that wouldn't implicate Cole.

She sighed and lifted her gaze to the rosy afterglow the setting sun had painted on the sky, remembering Cole's warmth, his smile, his gentleness—and trying to forget the coldness that could come into his eyes, the almost obsessive dislike of her family, her friends, and the damning things that had been said.

It could have been just a coincidence that he was in Marseilles at the same time as that Kim Charles. Or he could have been trying to find him—to question him about the *Dragon,* as she would have done if she'd known the man was there. Remy sighed again, aware that she was attempting to justify his presence there.

And again she wondered why he was so adamantly opposed to settling with the insurance company. Was it greed, as Lance had suggested? Cole had said himself that returning any portion of the insurance money would jeopardize the company's profit potential for the next several years—and therefore his bonus of 10 percent ownership in the company as well. Was he trying to hold out for that? Wasn't the money he'd made from selling the crude oil on the black market enough?

Why would he have done it at all? Lance had said it was because he'd seen that he wouldn't be able to turn the company around without it. Was that it? To save his pride? His ego? Or was it solely for the money? Why, when he had nothing but contempt for her family and its wealth? Or . . . had he done it for her? Had he felt so insecure that he thought she couldn't love him unless he had a lot of money? Didn't he realize how much she loved him?

Yes, that was the problem—she loved him. Even knowing that he might have committed fraud, she still loved him. That was why the thought hurt so much. Right or wrong, guilty or innocent, she loved him. It was staggering to discover that she cared that deeply, that strongly for him.

She felt a tear on her cheek and hastily wiped it away, glancing around to see if anyone had noticed. But the few tourists strolling up the relatively quiet side street weren't paying any attention.

She heard footsteps quicken behind her. Automatically she tightened her grip on her purse and started to look back, angling closer to a stuccoed building.

Suddenly she was grabbed from behind, both arms seized by a pair of hands that jerked her to a stop. As she tried to cry out, a sweaty palm clamped itself over her mouth, smothering the sound. She felt the painful wrenching of her shoulders as her arms were pulled together behing her back, pinned by a hooking arm, and trapped by the solidness of a man's body.

There was a man in front of her, too, in a blue plaid shirt and faded jeans, a Halloween mask covering his face—a mask of a pig, with mean dark eyes and tusks protruding from the sides of its ugly snout. Remy had only a heartbeat's time to wonder why she'd never noticed how frightening a pig's face could be.

Then a voice growled in her ears, "This is the only warning you're going to get, little gal. Stop asking questions, and keep your mouth shut."

That voice. She'd heard it before. That night on the dock. This was the same man who'd grabbed her then, hurting her arm and calling her "little gal."

As she tried to see the face that was pressed so close to her ear, something slammed into her stomach. The pain—she couldn't breathe. The other man had hit her. She realized that as his fist slammed into her again. She tried to twist sideways and elude the third blow, but it struck her, causing knife-sharp agony.

There are people on the street, her mind screamed. Why don't they see? Why aren't they coming to help me? The hand was no longer covering her mouth, but she couldn't make any sound come out—she couldn't draw a breath. It was like a nightmare—trying to scream, wanting to scream, but having only silent screams come out.

She had a hazy glimpse of a blurred hand coming toward her face, then there was just the roaring in her head when it struck her jaw—again and again. Suddenly the ground seemed to drop out from beneath her. She felt herself sinking onto the sidewalk and tried to catch herself.

The man from the dock had let her go. They were both gone. Dizzily she looked up and saw them hurrying down the street. And she saw the other people, too, staring at her in frozen shock. She couldn't know that her eternity of terror had lasted no more than twenty seconds. She tried to stand up . . . but God, it hurt so much.

25

With each careful breath she drew, Remy smelled the sharp, antiseptic odors of the hospital. The pain had subsided to a throbbing ache in her face and stomach—as long as she didn't move too much or breathe too deeply. She focused her eyes on the cubicle's hospital-green curtains, which partitioned her bed from the rest of the emergency room.

"Is there anything else you can tell me about these two men? The color of their hair? Their eyes?"

She swung her gaze toward the uniformed policeman standing next to the bed and gave a very small shake of her head. "All I can remember . . . is the pig's face," she said slowly, her face stiff from the swelling along her jaw and cheek, "and how mean it looked with those big tusks sticking out —like a wild boar's, but the mask was painted pink . . . like Porky Pig." She made a weak attempt at humor. "Somehow I have a feeling I'll never think of Porky Pig as cute or funny again."

The officer nodded absently and went back to his questions.

"What about the man who grabbed you from behind? You said he put his hand over your mouth. Was he wearing a ring?"

Remy closed her eyes, trying to remember if there'd been any sensation of metal. "I don't think so." She started to sigh, then winced at the sudden stab of pain that stole her breath. "His palm was sweaty, I remember that, and his fingers were rough—calloused."

"What about the second man, the one in the pig mask? Was he wearing rings, watches?"

She pictured that blurred image of his right hand coming at her face. "I'm almost sure there wasn't anything on his right hand, but . . . I don't know about the left."

He made a note of that, then flipped his notebook shut. "If you think of anything else, Miss Jardin, just call the station."

Again Remy gave a barely perceptible nod of her head in agreement, saying nothing about the warning that had preceded the beating. She couldn't—not without telling him about everything, including the insurance company's allegations of fraud. The first people to come to her aid afterward had been from out of state. They'd automatically assumed they'd witnessed a mugging—after all, this was big, bad New Orleans, and things like that happened here. By the time Remy had recovered enough to speak for herself, she'd realized it would be better to let everyone believe it *was* a mugging. And everyone had . . . without question.

As the green curtain fell back in place behind the departing policeman, Remy heard her mother's anxious voice demanding, "Is she all right? Where is she? I want to see her."

A second later the curtain was swept aside and Sibylle Jardin stepped quickly into the cubicle. If she'd been the hand-wringing type, her fingers would have been twisted in a knot, but she wasn't. She faltered briefly when she saw Remy lying there, one cheekbone red and swollen, a purpling under one eye, a bruise coloring the skin above her jaw. But her hesitation lasted only a fraction of an instant, and then she moved to Remy's side and lightly ran smoothing fingers over the top of her hair.

"Remy, my poor darling," she murmured, biting at her lower lip.

"I'm all right, just sore." Remy reached for her hand and gave it a reassuring squeeze.

Then Gabe was there, hovering on the other side of the bed, his look intense, angry, his face white under its tan. "Who did this, Remy? What'd they look like?"

She heard the tremble of rage in his voice, a brother's rage. "I don't know. They wore masks."

He half turned from the bed, then swung back. "What the hell were you doing in the Quarter, anyway? You said you were going to stay home and lie around the pool. Why didn't you? Dammit, why'd you have to go out?"

"Gabe." Sibylle silenced him with a look, giving her a reprieve from his questions, but Remy knew it was only a temporary one. Sooner or later she'd have to answer them.

"I'm sorry. It's just—" He raked a hand through his tobacco-brown hair, something helpless in the gesture.

"I know," her mother murmured.

"Is she going to be all right, Dr. John?" Her father stood at the foot of the bed, looking pale and shaken.

Remy glanced at the white-haired man standing beside him. She'd expected someone old, short, and irascible, but Dr. John was tall and proud, exuding competence—a Southern version of Marcus Welby, right down to the vacuous smile.

"I've consulted the resident who examined her when she was brought in. Her injuries, for the most part, are minor. The bruises on her face you can see, and we do have a cracked rib."

Remy heard that and observed dryly, "If *we* had a cracked rib, Dr. John, *you* wouldn't be smiling." He chuckled, and she added, "Or laughing."

"Listen to her. I think that proves my diagnosis, Frazier,"

he declared. "By Mardi Gras the bruises will have faded enough for makeup to cover them, and she'll be dancing at the ball—at least to the slow songs."

"Does that mean we can take her home?" Sibylle asked.

The doctor hesitated a full second before answering. "I'd like to keep her here overnight—strictly for observation. There is her recent ordeal in France to consider."

When she heard his announcement, Remy felt oddly relieved. She didn't want to go home and face a barrage of questions—not tonight, when she ached all over and just breathing was an effort. Tomorrow. She'd tell them about the warning tomorrow. She knew there'd be an argument, and she simply wasn't up to it.

"Yes, I think it's best for Remy to stay here tonight," her father agreed.

"I'll arrange for a private room," Dr. John said, then winked at Remy. "And one of our gowns—a Charity exclusive, guaranteed to repel muggers."

"Just what I need," Remy murmured, not at all amused.

An hour later she was in a private room, far removed from the hustle and bustle of the emergency room with its dinging bells and rattling gurneys, its urgent voices and moaning injured. She lay in the regulation hospital bed with eyes closed, not sleeping or resting, just aching, but aching undisturbed, without her mother offering to fluff her pillows to make her more comfortable or Gabe asking if she wanted something to drink. As long as she kept her eyes closed, they left her alone.

Her mother sat in a chair beside her bed. Remy could hear her idly flipping through the pages of a magazine. Gabe was at the window, alternately pacing and stopping, pacing and stopping. Her father had stepped out of the room several minutes before, maybe longer. She was losing track of time, and silently wondered how much longer it would be before visiting hours were over. They'd have to leave then.

What a contrast this was from Nice, when she'd been so

desperate to have her family around her. Now they were here and she wanted to be alone so she could rest . . . no, that wasn't true—so she could think.

"Stop asking questions, and keep your mouth shut," the man had growled. Asking questions of whom? Who'd sent those men to beat her up? Not Cole. He wouldn't do that. She was sure of it. Did that mean she'd been wrong to think he was behind this fraud?

She heard footsteps in the corridor, approaching her room. Not the quiet, rubber-soled squelch of a nurse's shoes, but the firm sound of hard leather soles. They entered her room and paused.

"How is she?" The low question came from her father.

"Sleeping, I think." Gabe moved away from the window. Remy heard his footsteps stop somewhere near the door.

"Good. I spoke with Dr. John just now." His hushed voice was barely above a whisper, and Remy had to strain to catch his words. "He's making all the arrangements to have Remy flown by air ambulance to the clinic tomorrow morning."

She stiffened in instant protest, then breathed a little easier when she heard Gabe reply, "She isn't going to like that."

"She isn't in any condition to argue. She's lying to us, Gabe, and I don't like it. Something's wrong. We can't watch her every minute. She needs to be in a place where she can be monitored at all times."

"I agree," came Gabe's soft, hope-killing reply.

She wouldn't go. She *couldn't* go—not now. But how could she stop them? They'd override any protest she made. If she told them about the warning and the few things she could remember about the tanker and that night on the dock, they'd be more determined than ever to protect her and get her out of harm's way. And if she became too vocal in her objections, they might persuade Dr. John to give her something—and then when she came to, she'd find herself in the clinic, with the doctors there convinced that she'd lost her mind as well as her memory.

Dear God, what was she going to do? She had to think of something. She couldn't let them send her away.

She remembered the pig mask with its small, mean eyes and vicious-looking tusks. The man had said this was the only warning she'd get. If she stayed, if she asked more questions, if they found out. . . . Remy shuddered and immediately felt a stab of pain from the fractured rib.

"Remy." Her mother's voice reached softly out to her an instant before she felt the touch of a hand on her arm. Slowly she let her eyes open. "We're leaving now, dear. We'll see you in the morning."

She made a faint sound of understanding, then pretended to drift back to sleep.

Silence. Remy unconsciously held her breath and listened for the faintest whisper of sound in the hospital corridor outside the darkened room. Nothing. She could hear nothing. She hadn't heard any movement in a long time.

She folded back the thin blanket and the bed sheet, then used her hands and elbows, propping them under her, to carefully and gingerly ease herself into a sitting position. She wondered if she dared turn on the small wall-light above the hospital bed's metal headboard, then decided against it. She groped for and found the telephone on the stand next to the bed, picked it up, and set it on her lap.

There was just enough light from the window to allow her to see the numbers on the dial. Directory Assistance gave her the number, and she dialed it.

"It's Remy," she said quietly, softly, keeping one eye on the closed door to the corridor. "I need a place to stay tonight, and I didn't know who else to call." She almost sighed in relief, but she knew it would hurt too much. "Can you come get me? I'm at Charity. . . . I'm fine," she insisted. "Just bruised up some. I'll explain when I see you. . . . No, don't come in. Wait for me outside."

She put the phone back on the stand, then half rolled and

half slid out of the high bed, gritting her teeth against the waves of pain that every movement seemed to bring, despite the stretch bandage that bound her rib cage. She found her clothes in the closet, but changing into them was agony.

Once she was dressed, Remy leaned against the wall to gather her strength, then moved to the door and listened for footsteps and the stiff whisper of polyester uniforms. Nothing. Cautiously, she opened the door a crack and peered out. The corridor outside her room was empty. She opened the door a little wider to check the nurses' station. There were three of them there, talking softly among themselves, none of them looking in her direction. But to reach the elevators, she had to go by them, and she knew she didn't have a hope of accomplishing that unseen. Then she spied the fire stairs and silently blessed the architect who had unwittingly placed them so close to her room.

She counted to three and slipped out the door, pulling it almost shut behind her, unwilling to risk a sharp click of the latch. Not a single head turned in her direction. Cradling her right side, Remy darted across the corridor to the stairway door.

Five minutes later she walked out the front door of the hospital. She spied the car parked at the curb, its engine idling. She hurried to it, never once doubting her decision, which had been prompted by one single question: if she remembered what she'd seen on the dock, would she be safe anywhere?

26

The clanging crash of the brass knocker had been replaced by a fist pounding at the door, the racket
drowning out the sound of the cathedral bells ringing
out their summons to morning Mass. "I'm coming!" Cole
shouted a second time, padding across the living room in
bare feet, fastening the snap of his jeans as he went. The
hammering didn't let up. He threw the night bolt and started
to jerk the door open, but it exploded inward and Gabe Jardin
charged through, with Lance at his heels.

"Where is she? Where's Remy?" He looked wildly around
the room, fury and desperation in his face.

"Remy?" Cole frowned. "What makes you think she's
here?"

"Because she's disappeared from the hospital—as if you
didn't know." He glared at Cole as if he were a roach to be
crunched underfoot, then just as quickly waved a hand at the
door to the kitchen, ordering, "You check in there, Lance.
I'll look back here."

"Hold it." Cole grabbed Gabe's arm as he started toward

the hall that led to the bedroom. "What was Remy doing in the hospital?"

"You mean she didn't tell you?" he jeered and tried to shrug off Cole's hand.

But Cole tightened his grip, easily outmuscling him as he surged forward to growl in his face, "Listen, bastard, you don't like me and I don't like you, but you're not taking one step in any direction until you tell me what Remy was doing in a hospital."

Gabe eyed him uncertainly but held his ground. "She was mugged yesterday afternoon in the Quarter. A couple guys in masks worked her over."

"Why?" Stunned by the announcement, Cole loosened his grip.

"How the hell should I know? Maybe they were a couple of crazies high on crack." He pushed past Cole as Lance came swinging out of the kitchen.

"She's not in there, Gabe."

"Come on. We'll look back here."

When the two of them headed toward the bedroom, Cole made no attempt to stop them. Instead, he turned away in troubled silence.

"Where is she?" He had a stranglehold on the black receiver, his hand—like his voice—trembling with fear and rage. "What have you done with her?"

"Who?"

"You know damned well I'm talking about Remy."

"Isn't she in the hospital?"

"No," he admitted. "She disappeared from there . . . sometime in the night." He gripped the phone even tighter. "Leave her alone—do you hear? If you touch one hair on her head, I swear I'll—"

"—kill me?" the voice taunted with contempt. "Don't make threats you can't keep."

"Dammit, I—"

"Don't give me any of this noble shit! You won't do a

damned thing, and we both know it. You're all greed and no guts. You always have been."

"Where's Remy?"

"I don't know. But you'd better find her before I do."

Fog. A menacing white mist swirling thick and cool around her. Out of the night fog came an eerie yellow glow, dancing, wavering, coming closer and closer. Remy wanted to run from it, but her feet were rooted to the ground. The yellow light kept moving toward her, flaring, separating into two, three, then four towering columns of flame. Black faces loomed from beneath the dancing fire, black faces on black bodies wrapped in white rags, bodies dancing, gyrating, high-stepping, holding aloft their flaming torches, grinning at her, and rattling their tin cups in her face.

Flambeaux. Remy laughed in relief. It was a parade, a night parade, complete with black torchbearers to light the way. Riders emerged on snorting, sidestepping steeds, their rich costumes, knightly in design, all with plumed helmets and hooded faces, glittering in the mist. Then came the float, a dazzling display of bright, shining paint and sparkling glitter. Riding atop it was the god Comus, the chosen ruler of the parade, a silver and white specter of rhinestones and blinding white stones. He raised his jeweled goblet to her, and Remy clapped her hands together in delight, seeing gray eyes smiling at her from behind the full mask. Cole. Comus was Cole, the god ruler of—

Suddenly the mask changed shape, sprouting a snout and huge, gleaming tusks. Remy recoiled from the image. No—Cole couldn't be the man in the pig mask. She backed away, shaking her head in denial, as he kept pushing the goblet toward her.

Then she remembered that Comus was never the true ruler, not in the arcane society of the krewe. No, the true power in the krewe lay with the captain—one of the riders who had preceded Comus's float. She turned and ran through the thick fog after the disappearing riders. But her legs moved so slowly, so very, very slowly, that she couldn't catch up with them. She could see the streaming tails of the horses and the gleam of their polished hooves as the mist started to gradually swallow them.

"Wait! Wait!"

A rider stopped and turned in his saddle. Gone was the shimmering hood that concealed his face. In its place was a pig mask. Mean, glittering eyes fixed their accusing gaze on her.

Remy froze and whispered, "Who are you?"

"I told you to stop asking questions!"

All of a sudden the mist around her dissolved and she was surrounded by riders, riders in pig masks. In unison, they chanted, "You were warned. You were warned," and walked their horses toward her, tightening the circle.

"No! No!" She was screaming, but no one was listening. She could see the parade crowds along the street, their arms outstretched to the riders, but they weren't looking at her.

She felt hands on her and she struck out wildly, feeling the pain again, stabbing, slicing. . . .

"It's all right, girl," a voice crooned. "Sssh, now. You're safe here. Do you hear? You're safe."

She came awake with a rush, aching and disoriented, still half in the grip of the dream. She stared into Nattie's face, the dark and gently knowing eyes looking back at her.

"Nattie," she murmured, trying to swallow the fear that still choked her throat. "I—" She glanced around, seeing the rose-flowered paper on the walls, the white woodwork, the chintz curtains at the windows, and the old chiffonier against the wall, the top of it cluttered with framed family photographs and crystal atomizers. The spare bedroom at Nattie's house—that's where she was. She remembered now—Nattie had picked her up the night before at the hospital and brought her home to her small cottage-style house in the Channel. She felt the pressure ease from her shoulders and realized Nattie had been holding her down. ". . . I was dreaming, wasn't I?" She saw she was clutching at the sleeves of Nattie's chenille robe, and she let go of them to run a hand lightly over her cheek, feeling its soreness, its ache.

"The way you were thrashing around, I'd say it was more like a nightmare," Nattie declared as she rose from the edge of the bed.

"It *was* a nightmare." She relaxed against the feather pillow and felt the last of her terror drain away. "Has it only been five days that I've been home, Nattie? In some ways it feels like a lifetime." Nattie didn't comment as she walked over to the window and raised the shade, letting in a bright glare of light. Remy winced at it and lifted a hand to shield her eyes. "What time is it?"

"Going on eleven o'clock."

"It can't be." Remy started to sit up, but her injured rib raised an immediate and painful objection.

"Maybe it can't be, but it is," Nattie stated, then laid a brightly patterned velour robe over the spindled foot of the bed. "The bathroom's across the hall and the coffee's in the kitchen."

Ten minutes later Remy walked into the living room, a cup of black coffee in hand, wearing the caftan-style robe over the cotton shift Nattie had loaned her the night before. Nattie sat curled up in a colorful chintz armchair, the Sunday edition of the *Picayune* on the floor beside her, the section with the crossword puzzle folded open on her raised knees.

Nattie gave her an inspecting look, then said, "As soon as I get this puzzle finished, I'll get you some witch hazel for those bruises on your face. It'll take some of the swelling down and ease the sting."

"Thanks," Remy said, then hesitated. "I'll need to use your phone to make a call."

"If you want some privacy, there's an extension in the kitchen, or you can use the one in here." With a nod of her head, Nattie indicated the beige phone on the end table next to the sofa.

Remy glanced at the phone and wished she could wait until she'd drunk her first cup of coffee before making the dreaded call. But she knew that postponing it wouldn't make it any less of an ordeal. She crossed to the end of the sofa and sat down carefully on its hard cushion, then picked up the receiver and dialed the number from memory.

"Hello?"

"Mother, it's Remy—"

"Remy! Where are you? Are you all right?" she rushed the words then turned away from the mouthpiece and called, "Frazier, it's Remy. She's on the phone." Then she was back. "We've been so worried about you. We didn't know what to think when the hospital phoned us this morning and said you were gone."

"Remy, is that you?" her father broke in with the demand.

"Yes, it's me. And I'm fine—"

"Where are you? We'll come get you."

"No." This time it was Remy who broke in. "I'm not coming home—not now. I'm only calling to let you know I'm fine and I'm perfectly safe where I am."

"But where are you?"

She hesitated an instant, then replied, "I'll talk to you later." And she hung up. She stared at the phone for several more seconds, then looked at Nattie. Her dark eyes regarded Remy with open curiosity, but she asked no questions—she hadn't even asked any the night before, when she'd picked her up at the hospital. Beyond telling Nattie that two men had beaten her up and flatly stating that she wasn't going home, Remy hadn't offered any other explanation—and Nattie hadn't demanded one. But she was entitled to know. "I'm sorry to draw you into the middle of this, Nattie, but they want to put me in some clinic outside of Houston. They were going to have me flown there this morning. That's why I snuck out of the hospital last night. I didn't know how else to stop them."

"That must be the same clinic they were talking about sending you to when you first came back," Nattie guessed.

"Yes. There's more, though, Nattie," Remy said, then briefly told her about the insurance company's claim of fraud over the sinking of the tanker, her belief that she'd witnessed something that night on the dock, and her attempts to find out what it was.

"Are you sure you should be telling me all this?" Nattie frowned warily.

"I have to. You see"—Remy paused and cradled her coffee cup in her hands—"before those two men beat me up, they warned me to stop asking questions and to keep my mouth shut."

"And you don't plan to do either one, do you?" Nattie folded her arms across her chest in a gesture that indicated both resignation and challenge.

"How can I? Somehow I have to find out what or who I saw that night. Until I do, how will I know whom to trust? Whom to believe? Obviously I'm a threat to somebody." She stared at the black coffee in her cup. "And the more I think about it, Nattie, the more convinced I am that there's a connection between the man I was seen struggling with in Nice and the two men who worked me over. Maybe they aren't the same men, but they must have something to do with the *Dragon*. It's too much of a coincidence for it to be anything else."

Nattie swung her feet to the floor and laid the crossword puzzle aside. "You're saying you think somebody followed you all the way to France and cornered you there?"

"It makes sense, Nattie. Whoever doesn't want me to talk now couldn't have wanted me to talk *then*. Maybe that's what we were arguing about when he struck me and I hit my head on that tree." She sighed at the irony. "He must have thought he was home free when I ended up with amnesia."

"And he couldn't have been too pleased when he found out you were asking questions."

"I know." She combed a hand through her hair and glanced at the room's small fireplace, framed in metal stamped with a design of entwined morning glories. "He probably thinks I'm close to remembering what happened. Who knows? Maybe I am."

"Or maybe you were just getting close to the truth with your questions."

"But I haven't talked to that many people. I met with one of the river pilots who guided the *Dragon,* and I talked to Charlie—Charlie. I was supposed to call him last night," she remembered, reaching for the phone.

"Who's Charlie?" Nattie frowned.

"Charlie Aikens. He works on the dock where the tanker was loaded. He was going to find out who was working the night the shipment of crude was loaded—or at least try to." Unfortunately, his number was in her purse, which the hospital had locked away somewhere for safekeeping when she was admitted. She had to get his number through Information.

On the fourth ring, a woman answered; Remy hadn't expected that. Somehow she'd gotten the impression from Charlie that he lived alone. Of course, that didn't mean he couldn't have company.

"Is Charlie there?"

"No, he isn't."

She caught the stiff, almost defensive tone in the woman's voice. "I'm Remy Cooper, and Charlie was getting me some information on shipping for a friend of mine's book. Do you know when he'll be back?"

"He won't . . . not ever." There was the smallest break in the woman's voice. "Charlie's dead."

Remy froze, every muscle contracted in shock and alarm. "When? How?" They were the only words she could get out.

"Yesterday. They told me there was a section of the dock that had been damaged a while back, and he was checking to see if it'd gotten worse. They think he got dizzy or slipped. He fell in the river."

"Are you sure? Did anyone see it happen?" She felt sick, sick with fear and guilt. She didn't even look at Nattie when she took the coffee cup from her hand and set it on the end table.

"They heard him cry out when he fell, but there was

nothing they could do. The current swept him away.'' The woman kept talking, as if she needed to say all these things to believe them herself, her voice flat and thin with grief. ''Charlie's my brother, the only family I had left. They recovered his body this morning. The funeral home said I should bring them a suit to bury him in. I thought he had one. Why does Charlie have to be buried in a suit?'' she protested in a sudden burst of anguish. ''He hated them—called 'em 'monkey suits.' Momma always used to make him wear one to go to church, and he'd argue with her. 'God don't care if I'm wearing a suit,' he'd say. Do you think I have to get a suit for him?''

''No. No, I don't think so,'' Remy murmured. ''I'm . . . I'm sorry.'' Numb, she hung up the phone and turned to Nattie. ''That was Charlie's sister. She says he's dead. If that's true—'' She stopped and fought off the sudden surge of panic. ''Was there anything in the paper about a drowning yesterday?''

''I think there was something, but I didn't read it.''

They both got down on the floor beside the chair and went through the newspaper, section by section, page by page. Remy found the paragraph-long write-up on a back page of the B section. It gave the same account Charlie's sister had, with the added detail that it had happened in the morning, and said the search was continuing for his body. Remy sat back on her heels and stared at the article.

''I know exactly what you're thinking,'' Nattie announced.

''What if it wasn't an accident?'' Remy finally said it out loud. ''What if he didn't fall into the river? What if he was pushed? He was asking questions for me, Nattie.'' Still holding the folded page with the article, she got to her feet and started to pace, automatically hugging an arm to her bandaged ribs. ''I already know that the man who grabbed me that night on the dock was the same man who held me while his buddy hit me. I recognized his voice. He could have found out that Charlie was asking questions—and made sure I didn't find out his name.'' As another thought occurred to her, Remy stopped and swung back to face Nattie. "They had to know I'd find out about Charlie. Maybe they even wanted me to. Maybe they thought if the beating didn't scare me into shutting up, this would."

"It scares the hell out of me," Nattie said. "Just what could you have seen that night?"

"I don't know." Remy shook her head in frustration. "When I talked to Howard Hanks, the insurance investigator, yesterday afternoon, he had this theory that the tanker had never gone down at all—that it was an elaborate hoax to collect the insurance money. He thinks the *Dragon* is sailing around out there somewhere under another name. The debris the Coast Guard found, the crew in life-boats—that was simply to make it look like the tanker had sunk in the storm. Instead, another crew came on board and sailed off in it."

Nattie's mouth gaped open in shock as she sagged back against the chair. "The man's crazy."

"I thought it was farfetched, too."

"It's more than farfetched; it's downright stupid," she declared in disgust, and clambered to her feet. "Do you realize how many people it would take to pull off a stunt like that? I don't know how many are in a crew, but let's say there's fifteen. With two crews, that makes thirty people. And how did that second crew get on board the tanker? A helicopter wouldn't have flown them out there—not in a storm. Which means they'd have to have gone by boat, and now you got more people involved. What happens if one of the thirty-five or forty people decides he doesn't like the split he got? Do you realize how many chances you've got of being blackmailed? And believe me, silence is golden, especially if you're the one paying somebody to keep his mouth shut. No." She shook her head. "If you're going to commit a crime, the fewer people who know about it, the better."

"You're right," Remy murmured, faintly stunned by the logic of it.

"Of course I am." Nattie sat back down in the armchair

and laid both arms on its curved armrests. "If there were any switches pulled, it had to be at the very beginning. That's what you must have seen. Exactly how much do you remember?"

"Almost nothing," she admitted in frustration. "I saw the tanker moored to the dock, and then a man grabbed me. That's it. That's all I've been able to remember."

"Didn't you say it was foggy that night?"

"Yes—"

Nattie held up her hand. "If you've overlooked that detail, what others have you omitted? Think about it, picture it in your mind, and describe every thing you can recollect."

She started to say it was a waste of time, but—what if it wasn't? "All right." She closed her eyes. "It was dark and very foggy. The *Dragon* was tied up to the dock. I remember seeing the mooring lines and the gangway. There were two men at the rail—"

"What'd they look like?"

"It was too dark. All I could see was their silhouettes. One of them had a cigarette—" She opened her eyes with a snap. "He was smoking. There're No Smoking signs all over the place."

"I don't imagine smoking is one of the smartest things to do when you're loading crude oil on a tanker," Nattie remarked drolly.

"Then why was he smoking?"

"Maybe the tanker was already loaded."

"But it would still be too dangerous to smoke on deck."

"We'll get back to that later. Tell me what else you can remember."

Remy tried, closing her eyes again, but all she could picture was the black shape of the tanker in the mist and the two men at the rail. "Nothing." She shook her head impatiently. "It was too dark."

"Dark?" Nattie frowned. "The ship was dark? Weren't there floodlights? Ships loading at night are usually lit up like Christmas trees."

"Not this ship," Remy stated. "It was mostly dark, except for a few lights on the bridge deck." She breathed in sharply, suddenly remembering more, and instantly grabbed at her ribs as pain shot from them, nearly doubling her over.

Nattie was immediately at her side, curving a supporting arm around her shoulders. "When are you gonna learn you can't be doing things like that? You better sit down." She helped her to the sofa.

Remy clutched at Nattie's hand, drawing her onto the hard sofa cushion beside her. "I remember Cole was standing on the bridge deck with Carl Maitland and a man with a handlebar mustache—the man Howard Hanks said was a demolitions expert." She stared at nothing, the memory of that night coming back in a jumbled rush. "I'm not sure what happened next—after I saw Cole. I think maybe . . . I waved to him. That man grabbed me and said something like . . . 'Not so fast, little gal.' Then . . . something about snooping around. The walkie-talkie." She curled her fingers around Nattie's hand. "He had a walkie-talkie hooked to his belt. A voice came over it—a valve had broken, it said, and there was water all over the deck. Water, Nattie. That's it, isn't it?" Turning, she searched the woman's face—not with excitement or relief at remembering, but with a cold feeling. "That's the switch. The *Crescent Dragon* had no crude on board when it went down because its tanks had been filled with water." She laughed briefly, softly, in harsh remembrance. "And Maitland explained it away by convincing me they were loading fresh water for bathing and drinking. I believed him."

"You probably did that night," Nattie said. "More than likely you didn't recognize the significance of it until later —when the insurance company started making all that noise."

But it was the bitterness of that memory that she was tasting—the bitterness and the ache it caused, not its significance. "Cole was there. He was with Maitland, watching the tanks being filled with water. He was part of it."

No matter how many times she'd considered the possibility of his guilt, she'd resisted believing it. Now she couldn't any longer. The memory of Cole on the bridge, his faced bathed in full light, with Maitland at his side, was too vivid, too clear.

"I know it hurts." Nattie patted her hand in comfort. "Every woman wants to believe her man is good. They seldom are, but that never makes it any easier to accept."

"No." Had Cole been the man in Nice? He'd claimed he was in New Orleans at the time. But she only had his word on that. She'd never checked. She could imagine how upset she must have been when she realized what he'd done—how hurt, how angry, how disillusioned. She would have argued with him, lashed out with the hurt and confusion of betrayal—a betrayal of both her trust and her family's. But the men who'd beaten her up—she couldn't believe he'd sent them. "Maitland. He saw me at the docks the other day. He saw me with Charlie. He sent those men to give me this warning." She touched the bruises on her face, oddly relieved to be able to shift the blame for them away from Cole.

"It wouldn't surprise me a bit if he had," Nattie responded. "Whenever he came to the house for one of your momma's dinner parties, that Maitland always reminded me of a barracuda, lurking in some dark pool, looking all small and innocent until you saw his teeth."

"Wait a minute. This doesn't make sense." Remy painfully pushed herself off the sofa again. "It's obvious why Maitland did it. He could sell the same oil twice. But what would Cole get out of it? The Crescent Line paid for that crude in advance. I've seen a copy of the cashier's check."

"You certainly don't have a criminal mind, Remy," Nattie said with a shake of her gray head. "He got money from Maitland. They probably worked out some percentage deal to share in the proceeds of that second sale. More than likely he got his money right out of that cashier's check."

"More than likely," she agreed, then sighed tiredly. "But how do we go about proving that?"

"An audit of Maitland's books would probably turn up some sizable checks written to companies nobody's heard of. The money might even have passed through a couple of those dummy companies before it got to Cole's hands." Nattie paused, then asked gently, "What are you going to do?"

"I don't know." Remy walked over to a window and lifted the rayon sheer to look out at the quiet Sunday morning. "I'm not sure. First I want to find out whether Charlie's death was an accident. Tomorrow I can check with the coroner's office and see what they can tell me." A little black girl skipped along the banquette in front of Nattie's house. She was wearing a pink ruffled dress and a dainty hat that was perched atop her braided hair and tied to her chin with ribbons. Remy wanted to go outside, take her hand, skip down the street with her—and feel again that innocent and carefree. Sighing, she turned from the window and met Nattie's gaze. "I have to know if this has gone beyond fraud, to murder."

27

Silence echoed through the house, a silence that said no one was home. Remy blinked sleepily and glanced around the living room, then crossed to the doorway into the kitchen, Nattie's pink scuffs slapping at her heels with each step. More silence waited for her in there, as the cat clock on the wall, with its moving eyes and swishing tail, chided her for sleeping late. Ignoring the hands pointing to nine o'clock, Remy headed toward the coffee maker on the counter, fighting the grogginess that came from too little sleep too late.

A note was propped against the glass carafe:

> Remy,
>   *Since you had to leave your purse at the hospital, I thought you might need some walking-around money.*
>   *Gone to work,*
>   Nattie

Paper-clipped to the back of it was a twenty-dollar bill. Remy slipped the bill into the slash pocket of the velour robe, also loaned to her by Nattie—like the slippers on her feet, the cotton nightgown she wore, and the new pancake makeup and mascara waiting in the bedroom to cover up her bruises. She smiled to herself as she poured a much-needed cup of coffee, but the smile faded when she saw the newspaper on the counter, folded open on the obituary notices. The very first one was for "Aikens, Charles Leroy, age 57."

She sighed, not really needing to be reminded of the cause for this flat feeling she had. Absently she combed her tousled length of hair away from the side of her face and reached for the paper, only to be distracted by the sound of a car pulling into the drive. Frowning, Remy lifted her head. Nattie wouldn't be coming home at this hour. She must have been mistaken—the car must have actually pulled into a neighbor's driveway instead.

But the slam of a metal door sounded close. Remy moved to the window above the kitchen sink and peered out. If there was a car in Nattie's drive, though, it hadn't pulled far enough forward for her to see it from the kitchen window.

The doorbell rang twice, in rapid succession, and she whirled around to face the living room. A salesman—it had to be. Nattie wouldn't have told her family she was here. She wouldn't. The doorbell chimed again, something strident and insistent in the sound. Another short interval of silence followed and Remy waited, poised, tense. Whoever it was would give up soon.

She nearly jumped out of her skin at the sudden pounding knock that replaced the chiming bell. She told herself he probably thought the doorbell didn't work. *"He"?* It had to be a he; a woman wouldn't knock that loud or that long— would she? Whoever it was, he couldn't be a friend of Nattie's, or he'd know she was at work.

Hearing the demanding rattle of the doorknob, Remy stiffened. Somebody wasn't taking "nobody-home" for an answer. She threw a look at the back door. Should she—silence. No rattling, no pounding, no ringing. For how long? Was he leaving?

She ran swiftly, lightly, to the living-room doorway, keeping to one side so she wouldn't be seen by anyone looking through the windows on the front porch. She snuck a glance at the front door, the glassed top of it curtained with gathered sheers. There was no dark shape on the other side of it—and nothing at the windows. And no sound of a car door opening and closing or an engine starting, either.

Then she saw it—her unstructured raspberry cardigan sweater lying in plain sight on the arm of the sofa. Anyone peering in the window would have seen it—and anyone who knew what she'd been wearing on Saturday would know she was here, or would at least be certain she'd *been* here.

She heard the telltale creak of the screen door behind her. My God, he'd come around back! She bolted out of the kitchen and ran for the front door. It was locked. She threw the security bolt and reached again to try the doorknob.

"Remy!"

She threw a half-panicked look over her shoulder. Cole halted inside the living-room doorway, his gray eyes narrowing sharply at the bruises on her face. Frozen by her memory of that night and her now-certain knowledge of his guilt, Remy stared at him, conscious of the throbbing in her side and the hard pounding of her heart. He looked nonthreatening in his double-breasted suit of navy wool and patterned tie. Had she thought he would be threatening?

Cole raised his hands in a calming gesture. "It's all right, Remy. It's me. I didn't mean to frighten you."

Frighten her. Had she been frightened? Of course she had. The specter of the pig mask was always there, hovering at the edges of her consciousness. She hadn't let herself think about it. She hadn't let herself think about the beating, the pain, the fear. She hadn't let herself imagine how they must have watched her, stalked her, then swooped on her without warning—in broad daylight, with people around, silently telling her she wasn't safe from them anywhere.

She felt the trembling start, the trembling of delayed reaction. Cole took a step toward her, his hands still raised, and Remy shrank against the door.

"I won't hurt you, Remy."

She wanted to scream at him that he already had—he'd cheated, he'd lied, he'd betrayed her belief in him, her love. But as if in a bad dream, she couldn't get any sound to come out.

"I swear I won't hurt you. I'd never hurt you." He sounded as if he were talking to a frightened child.

My God, that was what she felt like. She turned from him and leaned against the door, feeling the facade of bravery fall away as the first tears rolled down her cheeks. Those two men had forever shattered the illusion that she was inviolable. They had proved that she was vulnerable, that her status and the Jardin name were no protection. She hadn't wanted to face that. She'd denied it. But the seed of fear had been planted, and with Charlie's death it had taken root.

She felt his hands move onto her shoulders and stiffened in instant resistance. "No," she choked out the word, and tried to shrug away from them. "Don't touch me. Don't."

But his gentle grip persisted in turning her away from the door and toward him. Remy brought her hands up to keep from being drawn into his arms, struggling with all the proverbial weakness of a woman—knowing it and hating it.

"Sssh, it's all right," Cole murmured. "You're safe. I won't let anyone hurt you." The crazy part was that she did feel safe in the circle of his arms, with his shoulder right there waiting for her to cry on it. She tried to swallow a sob, and his hands pressed her closer. "Go ahead and cry, Remy," he urged softly. "After all you've been through, you need to. Only a fool wouldn't be scared. And you're no fool."

She stopped fighting the tears and sagged against him, weeping softly, brokenly, vaguely conscious of the comforting stroke of his hands on her back and her hair, mutely reaffirming that everything was all right. But she cried because nothing was all right, and never would be again—not her own feelings of security, not their love, and . . . not Charlie.

How long she cried quietly she didn't know. At some point

she became conscious of Cole rubbing a lean cheek against the side of her hair, of the wet smell of wool from his jacket, and of the drained feeling of tears being used up.

"How—" Her voice sounded so choked and husky that Remy stopped and started over. "How did you know I was here?" She kept her head down, not ready to look at him, not ready to face him.

"I'd looked everywhere else." His voice was strained with emotion. "On my way to the office this morning, I remembered your endless Nattie-isms, and I took a chance." He turned his mouth to her hair, his arms tightening slightly around her. "When I told myself that it was over for us, that we were finished, I spent all Saturday convincing myself I didn't want you, I didn't need you . . . I didn't love you. Then your brother came charging into my apartment Sunday morning, thinking you were there. Why, Remy? Why would he think that? Why did you come here? Why aren't you at home with them?"

But she just shook her head, unable to answer him.

In the next second his mouth was near her ear and he was murmuring thickly, "It doesn't matter. I want to grow old and cranky with you, Remy. Do you understand what I'm saying?"

"Yes," she whispered, and she wondered, was it possible? Could they survive this? Unsure, she drew back from him, her hands resting on the lapels of his navy suit coat, her gaze fixed on them.

He tilted her head back and tactilely examined her bruises, first with his fingers, then with his lips. So light was the graze of his mouth that she wanted to cry again. It wasn't lover*like*—it was pure loving.

She shut her eyes. "Cole . . . I remember. I remember that night on the dock. I know how it was done."

She felt the stillness of his hands, his body. She couldn't bring herself to look at him—not yet.

"What are you going to do?" His voice was low, his tone cautious.

"I don't know."

"Will you help me?" His hands tightened their grip on her arms in silent demand. "I need you, Remy."

She opened her eyes to stare at the knot of his tie, hesitating as she thought of Charlie. If Maitland had had him killed—and she was convinced that Maitland was the one, not Cole—maybe he'd acted without Cole's knowledge. But what did that change? Charlie was still dead.

Pushing away from him, she stepped free and shook her head. "I can't help you, Cole."

"Dammit, why not?" The explosion of anger instantly dissipated in a gusty sigh. "I know the answer to that, don't I? The family. I meant what I said. I'm not going to let them destroy me—even if it means I have to destroy *them*," he said—without the rancor she'd expected.

"Cole, you're destroying *yourself*," she protested, finally looking at him. "Why can't you see that? Maybe if you'd cooperate, it would go easier for you. If you'd just tell them—"

"I can't, Remy—not even for you."

"I don't want this, Cole. I love you. You've got to believe that."

His gray eyes made a slow search of her face, something sad and yearning in his expression. "Oddly enough, I do. But it's gone too far now. I can't turn back."

Charlie. He knew about Charlie. "Neither can I."

"Then there's nothing left to be said, is there?"

"No"

He held her gaze an instant longer, then opened the front door and walked out. He didn't look back to see her standing in the doorway.

The taxicab rolled to a quiet stop at the curb. Remy handed the driver the ten-dollar bill that was all she had left from Nattie's loan. "Keep the change," she said, and climbed out. She crossed the grassy verge to the scrolled iron gate, then stopped to study the white-pillared house and the two perfectly proportioned magnolia trees guarding its front lawn.

She pushed open the gate and stepped through, then closed it behind her and made the long walk up the banquette to the front door. As she'd expected, it was locked. She lifted the heavy brass knocker and dropped it twice, then waited.

Nattie opened the door, clad in her black uniform and snow-white apron. She took one look at Remy and sighed grimly. "You've been to the coroner's office. I was hoping you were wrong."

"So was I." Remy stepped inside and paused while Nattie closed the door. "Where are they?"

"In the solarium," she said with a nod of her head in its direction. "Mr. Marc's with them. They're beside themselves wondering where you are and what's happened to you."

"I know." She could hear the low, worried murmur of voices, yet she hesitated, unable to shake the feeling of dread. But it had to be done, and she had to do it. She was the only one who could.

Before she was halfway to the solarium door, Gabe saw her. "Remy!"

It was as though a torrent was being unleashed as their voices rained on her, sharp with anxiety and reproof, gentle with relief and concern. She let them wash over her, not listening, not letting them sidetrack her from the thing she'd come to do. That would be too easy.

"Do you have any idea how worried we've been about you?" Gabe led her to the sofa and gently sat her down on the soft cushions, sitting beside her and curving an arm around her shoulders.

"Where were you?" her father demanded. "And what was the idea of taking off like that? Don't you realize—"

"Don't scold her, Frazier. Can't you see how tired she is?" Her mother pressed a cup of tea into her unresisting hands. "Drink this."

She didn't. Instead, she stared at the amber-brown tea, watching the shimmer of its surface and the dark leaves at the bottom of the cup. "I remember being on the dock the night the *Dragon* was loaded." Her statement shocked them all into silence. "There was never any crude oil loaded onto the tanker. They filled it with water."

"Are—are you sure, Remy?" Gabe asked cautiously.

"Yes." She shot a quick glance at her uncle, standing stiffly near the end of the sofa. "Lance was right. Cole was part of it—he and Carl Maitland."

"Cole. . . ." Her father sat down rather abruptly in a side chair. "How do you know that?"

"Because I saw them on the bridge, watching the tanks being loaded with water. It was quite clever, really." She was surprised at how cold her hands felt. "Maitland gets paid for a nonexistent shipment of oil, then turns around and sells the same oil and shares the proceeds with Cole. Meanwhile, a demolition charge sends an aging tanker to the bottom, and the Crescent Line collects from the insurance company for the crude it paid for but never received and for a ship that had seen better days."

Marc whistled thoughtfully, then murmured, "I'd say it was damned clever."

"And you knew this." Gabe looked at her. Remy nodded reluctantly. "Why didn't you tell us before?"

"I don't know. Maybe I wasn't sure. Maybe I didn't want to believe Cole was mixed up in it. Maybe that's why I planned to go off by myself for a few days when we were in France. Maybe I was trying to decide what to do. I honestly don't remember." She tipped her head back and gazed at the high ceiling, fighting the rawness in her throat. "Now . . . I find myself wondering if Cole could have been the man I was arguing with. He says he was in New Orleans—"

"He told you that?" Gabe frowned.

"Yes." She felt suddenly confused as Gabe got up off the sofa and stalked over to the decanter of whiskey on the drink cart. "Wasn't he?"

"He was in Marseilles." There was a loud and brittle clink of ice cubes in a glass. He removed the crystal stopper and cast Marc a challenging look. "What's that—maybe a twenty-minute flight to Nice? Hell, he could have been there and back in the company jet without any of us ever knowing it—except Remy, of course.''

''Maybe.'' She touched the purpling mark on her left cheek-bone—the puffy swelling was gone, but the extreme tenderness remained. ''But *this* was a warning from Maitland.''

''Maitland.'' Gabe turned from the drink cart. ''I thought you said you didn't know the two men who beat you up.''

''Not by name. But I recognized the voice of one of them. He's the same man who surprised me that night on the dock. I'm sure he works for Maitland.''

''What makes you think that?''

She told them about her recent visit to the dock area, about Maitland seeing her there with Charlie, and about Charlie's offer to obtain the names of the men who'd loaded the tanker and his subsequent ''accidental'' drowning. ''Only it wasn't an accident. I saw the coroner's report this morning. He had a bruise on his cheek, like mine . . . like he'd been hit by something . . . like a fist. Of course, the coroner theorizes that he was struck by an object in the water. But I know he was knocked unconscious—or at least dazed by a blow—and thrown into the river.''

''That would be difficult to prove,'' Gabe observed. ''If there weren't any witnesses.''

''There were two. But one saw him only *after* he was in the water, and the other was probably the man who hit him.'' She blocked out all emotion. It was the only way she could get through this.

''You *assume* he hit him, but you don't know that for a fact, do you?'' Gabe said.

''Of course not.''

''That's what I thought.'' He walked over and sat down beside her again, fitting his palm to hers and linking their fingers together. ''Look . . . let us handle it from here. Stop trying to be a one-sister show.''

She managed a smile of sorts and nodded, but she had to know. ''What are you going to do?''

''To start with,'' Marc inserted, ''you've given us the leverage we need to force a resignation from Buchanan. We can have him packed and gone before the day's over. Which will leave us free to negotiate a settlement with the insurance company.''

"Wait a minute.'' Remy turned to her father and Gabe. "You aren't going to let them get away with it, are you?''

"You think we should file charges against them,'' Gabe guessed.

"Don't you?''

"In principle, yes. In reality, it would be a waste of time.'' He held her hand a little tighter, not letting her pull away. "It's a white-collar crime. There'd be a lot of headlines, a lot of scandal, but the chances of either one of them ever going to jail are slim to none.''

"As much as I hate to admit it, Gabe is right,'' her father declared with a heavy sigh. "And then too, we can't overlook the fact that the Crescent Line would be drawn into any charge of insurance fraud. We would end up being a defendant— and we'd be found guilty.''

"That kind of notoriety wouldn't be good for anyone,'' Marc put in. "There's nothing this town loves more than a scandal. It's something like what happens at the scene of an accident, with people driving by slowly, wanting to see how much blood there is and to watch somebody writhe and twist in pain so they can feel alive.''

"But what about Charlie?'' Remy protested.

"We'll look into that,'' Gabe said in reassurance. "But I'll be honest, Remy. The mere fact that he agreed to get some information for you isn't sufficient cause to file a murder charge against anyone, not without some corroborating evidence. A bruise isn't enough, especially when the coroner reached the conclusion that he was struck by an object in the water. A defense attorney wouldn't have to be F. Lee Bailey to get a man off with that kind of testimony. I'm sorry, but—''

"—that's the way it is,'' she finished the sentence for him, pulling her hand free of his entwining fingers and pushing the teacup onto the glass-topped coffee table, then rising to her feet in barely controlled agitation.

"I'm afraid it is."

"Remy, I have the feeling you're blaming yourself for this man's death," her father said gently as she moved toward the windowed wall, a confection of white wood and glass. "You're thinking he'd still be alive if you hadn't asked him to help you. But that's something none of us can know. Whether his death was an accident or a deliberate act, you're not responsible."

She wanted to challenge that, but instead she just stared at the shafts of sunlight piercing the canopy of an oak to shine in a broken pattern on the rosebush skeletons in her mother's prize garden. "And Maitland, what are you going to do about him?" She wrapped both arms around her middle. Not because her ribs were hurting, but because she felt vaguely sick.

There was a lengthy pause before Marc responded to her question. "Maitland . . . is a slightly different situation. However, he does live—and work—within our community. There are certain *subtle* pressures that can be brought to bear. We can promise you that, Remy."

"We know how to handle this problem," her father asserted. "You've done more than enough. It's our turn now."

"Of course." She turned from the window, avoiding their eyes. "If you'll excuse me, I think I'll go to my room. I feel like I've been living in these clothes. I need to change."

"You look tired, darling," her mother observed. "This has been such an ordeal for you. Would you like me to have Nattie bring a lunch tray to your room? I'm sure you'd like to rest."

"Yes, thank you," she murmured absently, and she left the room, sickened by her silence and by the token objections she'd raised to their plans to hush up this whole messy affair very quickly and very quietly. It was wrong, she knew that —even though common sense told her they were right. Even if Cole and Maitland were tried and convicted of fraud— after lengthy delays, postponements, and appeals—they'd probably get off with a suspended sentence and probation. And the insurance company would still look to the Crescent Line for restitution, and possibly even damages. All that scandal, all that publicity—for what? A slap on the hand.

Her family was merely following a common business practice by dealing with the problem themselves, in their own way. But she was going along with them for a much more selfish reason: she didn't want to see Cole punished. She was glad there was another way to handle it, a way that wouldn't dirty his name and brand him a criminal.

"Forgive me, Charlie," she whispered as she climbed the mahogany stairs to her room.

A breeze, chill and sharp, blew strongly through the open French doors onto the second-floor gallery. Remy hesitated, then set the tray bearing the remains of her lunch on the low table by the love-seat and walked over to close them. As she drew them together, a car pulled up out front and a man charged out of the driver's-side door.

Cole. Remy froze for an instant, staring as he swept toward the house with long, rigid strides. What was he doing here? The wide gallery quickly blocked him from view, and Remy turned, hearing the squeal of brakes from a second car as she started across the room, leaving the French doors partially closed and the lunch tray on the table.

The clangorous pounding of the brass knocker shattered the quiet of the house, and Remy broke into a running walk, reaching the top of the stairs just as Nattie arrived at the front door. Nattie barely had a chance to open it before Cole shoved his way inside.

"Where the hell is she? I want to see her—now!" His voice was like a distant and ominous roll of thunder.

"Cole—" Remy stopped halfway down the steps, stunned by the anger in his expression when he swung toward her, his jaw clenched, all the muscles in his face contracted, making him appear even more gaunt-cheeked and hard-edged.

As Cole moved toward the staircase, Marc charged through the door, looking all flustered and upset. He grabbed at Cole's arm. "Buchanan, I told you—"

"And I told *you* I wanted to hear her say it." Cole shook off his restraining hand and continued to the foot of the stairs, fixing his silver-black stare on her. "I want to hear it from you."

"What are you talking about?" Remy glanced uncertainly at her uncle.

"He doesn't believe—"

"Don't you put words in her mouth," Cole snapped. "Let it come from her."

"You mean—" she began.

"Tell me what you told them," he demanded, pushing the words through his teeth.

She closed her eyes for an instant, then opened them to meet his gaze, hurting for him and for herself. "I'm sorry, Cole, but I saw you with Maitland that night on the dock when you were loading the tanker with water."

"That's a goddamned lie!"

She flinched at the rage in his voice even as her uncle spoke, reminding him, "Buchanan, you've already admitted you were there with Maitland."

"Yes, dammit, I was, but—"

"Cole, stop," Remy protested. "Don't make this any harder than it already is."

He turned back to her, harshly demanding, "Was it hard this morning? You said you loved me. And was I supposed to believe that?"

"It's the truth. I do love you—"

"Save it for one of your Uptown friends," he said harshly. "Someone used to a woman saying she loves him in one breath and then stabbing him in the back in the next." He pivoted to face Marc. "You wanted my resignation—now you've got it. Tell Mrs. Franks to clean out my desk and drop my things by the apartment."

"Cole, wait." Remy started after him as he crossed to the door, but Marc caught her.

"Let him go, Remy." The door slammed shut. "It's better this way."

28

Mardi Gras night, and the interior of the Municipal Auditorium had been transformed into a splendorous setting worthy of the ball considered by many to be *the* social event of the year. Gleaming, swagged, and valanced draperies formed an elaborate backdrop for the dais of the ball's god-ruler and his court. Overhead, chandeliers glittered, the prisms dripping from their many tiers catching and reflecting the light. And below, a dazzling white carpet covered the floor of the dais, spilled down its steps, and spread over the entire stage. A stage that was now empty—the expectancy in the air growing.

Remy sat in the special "call-out" section near the dance floor, reserved for ladies, wives, mothers, friends, and debutantes of the members of the Mistick Krewe of Comus. She wore her hair piled atop her head in soft, smooth waves. Layers of artfully applied makeup completely concealed her bruises and created a kind of mask of calm composure, a mask that she was certain would crack if she smiled—though that was hardly a concern, since she found nothing to smile about.

She turned her head to catch something her mother said, the long multistrands of emerald and blue beads of her earrings brushing the shoulder of her long-sleeved top, which was covered with teal-blue sequins. Sibylle's remark didn't require a reply, and Remy made none as she turned back to watch the opening of the gala event.

In the ancient tradition of the Old World *bals masques,* it began with a glittering processional led by last year's court in evening dress, followed by the members of the exclusive Carnival club in their beaded and plumed costumes. Remy sat through the mimed welcome by the hooded captain and managed to appear interested when this year's debutantes, in de rigueur white gowns, were presented.

During the tableau that followed, she absently played with the clunky jeweled pendants on the gold chain belt she wore around the waist of her emerald-colored taffeta skirt, then forced herself again to pay attention to the introduction of important guests to the masked god-ruler Comus, seated on the ornately gilded dais with his queen.

At the conclusion of it, the ''call-out'' dances began. Remy sat through the first one while her mother danced with her father and Gabe danced with his date for the evening. Her name was called for the second, and she took to the floor to dance with her father, her sequined top concealing her tightly girdled ribs. Her brother partnered her on the third. Then it was back to her chair. Shortly after that, the general dancing began—restricted to the krewe and their ladies only, of course.

She watched the swirl of taffeta, satin, chiffon, and silk, beaded, bangled, and rhinestoned in coral, saffron, azure, plum, turquoise, and naturally, white, and longed to hear the band strike up ''If Ever I Cease to Love,'' the official song of Mardi Gras, which signaled the meeting of Rex and Comus—and the end of the ball, a song played slowly and oh so very seriously. Thinking of it, the lyrics sprang into her mind:

> *If ever I cease to love,*
> *May sheepsheads grow on apple trees*
> *May the moon be turned into green cheese*
> *May oysters have legs and cows lay eggs*
> *If ever I cease to love. . . .*

This time she couldn't summon a smile at the incredible, forgettable lyrics.

She contained a sigh and sipped at the white wine Gabe had brought her, surrounded by music, laughter, and the susurration of gay voices. What was she doing here? she thought, then wryly wondered how she could have forgotten. Her family had insisted that she attend—to maintain appearances.

In the space of time between Rex's arrival by riverboat on the previous evening, Lundi Gras, and the Zulu parade on Mardi Gras morning, word had gotten out: Cole Buchanan had been ousted as president of the Crescent Line, the very man who had formed a liaison with Remy Jardin that had shown every indication of becoming a permanent one. If she failed to attend the ball, only one possible conclusion could be drawn by the family's very important friends: there was a severe split in the family over the decision.

Surely by now "appearances" had been satisfied. She'd been seen by everyone who mattered. Was it necessary to maintain this charade to the end? What difference could it possibly make if she went home early?

She left her seat and went in search of Gabe or her father—not to *ask* them, but to *tell* them she was leaving. Neither was on the dance floor, or among the chatting clusters at the edges. Remy guessed immediately where the two of them were—at the backstage bar, talking business, power, and politics in between comparing golfing, football, and hunting notes with some of their colleagues. An invitation to have a drink at the backstage bar was a privilege offered to few, but at the moment, Remy didn't even give a damn that it was off-limits to her sex. She was tired of their secretive, cliquish, little-boy rules and this endless concern for appearances.

She was stopped at the entrance by a krewe member. "Sorry, no one's allowed back here."

Remy had half a notion to point out that he was back there, but she said instead, "I need to speak to my father, Frazier Jardin. It's urgent."

He hesitated, then drawled, "All right, but you wait here, Miss Jardin."

At another time, in a more puckish mood, she might have followed him, but tonight Remy simply wanted to get out of there. As she started to turn away, she caught sight of Gabe backstage. She nearly called out to him, but then she saw the man with him—Carl Maitland. She dropped the wineglass and covered her mouth with her hand, smothering a cry of shock as she backed up a step.

It had been Gabe with Maitland that night! Gabe, not Cole. She remembered now that she'd seen Cole with Maitland earlier—in the daylight. That had to be why the image of them together had been so sharp, so clear. But that night it had been Gabe. Gabe. How could she have gotten it so mixed up? Suddenly she could almost hear the French psychiatrist saying that her memory could return chronologically or . . . out of sequence, in random bits that made no sense.

Gabe saw her standing there. His mouth started to lift in a smile, then a stunned look claimed his face and he turned pale. He knew. He knew she remembered. And Maitland— he knew too. She felt the glare of his eyes, then saw him take a quick, angry step toward her. Gabe moved forward to stop him. Remy had a glimpse of Maitland shoving him aside as she turned to run, like an animal scenting danger, with flight her only defense.

She tried to lose herself in the crowd fringing the dance floor, but a quick glance over her shoulder showed Maitland cutting directly toward the main exit. She couldn't make it, not before he was there to block it.

Changing direction, Remy darted out a side exit into the warren of corridors that ringed the main auditorium. She hesitated. What now? She couldn't think. Her mind was reeling—no wonder Gabe hadn't wanted to go to the police about Charlie, no wonder he hadn't wanted charges brought against Maitland, his partner in crime, no wonder he'd wanted to hush the matter up with the insurance company, no wonder he'd been so eager to pin the blame on Cole.

Cole. She spied a bank of pay telephones tucked along the wall of a small alcove. She ran over to them and picked up the farthest one. She had no change, so she dialed his number and charged the call to her home phone.

"Please be there," she whispered, closing her eyes as she listened to the ring.

"Yes." That low, abrupt voice—it was Cole.

"Cole, it's Remy. I—" There was a sharp and very definite click on the other end. She jerked the receiver away from her ear to stare at it in shock. He'd hung up on her! She hesitated, then hurriedly tried again. When he answered, she spoke in a rush. "It was Gabe, not you. I didn't remember that until just now, when I saw him with Maitland. Please don't hang up. I was wrong. You weren't involved. I know that now."

"Your confession comes a little late, Remy."

"No," she choked on the word. "It can't be too late. They know I remember what really happened. And they know I know about Charlie Aikens. I think Maitland had him killed. Now he's looking for me. I can't go to the police. Gabe would convince them I'm crazy. The amnesia, the beating, he'd have them believing I'd become paranoid, schizoid, something. The beating, Cole, that was Maitland's warning for me to keep my mouth shut. My God, I'm babbling." She swallowed a hysterical laugh and tilted her head back, fighting down the panic.

"Where are you, Remy?"

"At the auditorium, the Comus ball."

"Stay there. I'm coming right over."

"I can't. He's looking for me—"

"And it would seem that he has found you," a voice said as her wrist was suddenly seized and the receiver ripped from her hand. Remy turned and had a moment to see Maitland's cold, cold eyes, magnified by the elegant gold-rimmed glasses he wore, then her arm was jerked behind her back and twisted high. She gasped at the paralyzing pain. "Don't scream, Remy," Maitland warned in a dry, confident voice. "I would hate to bruise that pretty face of yours, especially when the other marks are healing so nicely. And it would be embarrassing to carry you out of here because you passed out from drinking too much. You understand what I'm saying, don't you?"

"Yes," she gasped again.

"Good. Now, we're going to take a little walk—very calmly and very quietly. Right?"

Remy nodded. The tuxedoed security men on duty at the entrance to keep the "wrong" people from getting in to the ball—did he think he could walk her past them? How could he explain man-handling her this way? Or did he expect her to meekly walk at his side? If she could create just enough doubt in their minds, enough to make him turn her loose—regardless of any convincing lines he might tell them—she could run.

He steered her out of the alcove and back into the side corridor. He didn't turn her toward the entrance, though, but rather forced her in the opposite direction. Where were they going?

A short distance down the hall, Remy had her answer. There was a side exit—a fire door, the kind that opened from the inside but not from the outside. He propelled her toward it, then reached around and pushed down on the metal bar, swinging the door open, his grip on her tightening rather than loosening.

He pushed her through the doorway ahead of him, the cool night air sweeping over her as she stepped out into the deep shadows of the building. She heard the whoosh of the automatic closure pulling the door shut, and felt the press of his body against her.

"Where are you taking me?"

"I thought we might go for a ride."

The parking lot. There'd be people in the parking lot. But again, he didn't turn her in the anticipated direction. Instead, he made her keep in the building's shadows, staying parallel with the wall. She heard the jingle of car keys, then spied a black BMW parked close to the building's service entrance. Her heart sank.

As if sensing it, he murmured, "I never guessed how convenient it would turn out to be."

"You'll never get away with this," she said tightly.

There was a mocking click of his tongue. "Really, Remy, that sounds like a line from an old B movie or a bad TV script."

"You won't," Remy insisted, trying not to sound as desperate as she felt. "First Charlie, now me. Won't that look too suspicious?"

"Did you read yesterday's paper? There was an article in there about a young coed from LSU who died from a drug overdose. She was an honors student, came from a good middle-class family—not the kind of girl you'd think would get mixed up with cocaine. It was just a small story. When I read it, I couldn't help thinking how different it would have been if she had been the daughter of a wealthy, prominent family. It might have stirred the police to take action against these drug dealers."

"My family would never believe that."

"They wouldn't have any choice," he said curtly, then returned to a smoother tone. "Besides, the family is always the last to suspect their child's on drugs—until they're faced with irrefutable evidence."

"No," she whispered in protest.

"It won't be so bad, Remy. Think how high you'll be flying when you go."

She couldn't get into that car with him. Somehow she had

to get away. Then she realized that he'd either have to shift his hold on her or be forced to unlock the car with his left hand. In either case, that would be her chance—maybe her only chance.

He steered her to the passenger door and jerked her to a stop, then positioned her at right angles to the door. He wasn't going to switch hands; instead, he'd probably tighten his grip, as he'd done before. She'd have to block out the pain.

It stabbed through her shoulder as the keys jingled and he leaned toward the car. She sank her teeth into her lower lip and turned her head, focusing on his legs. She kicked as hard as she could, aiming for the side of his knee.

Remy felt his leg instantly buckle and heard his loud groan as his fingers loosened on her wrist. She spun free of him and broke into a run, grabbing up the front of her long taffeta skirt in one hand and ignoring the thousands of needles that seemed to be embedded in her other arm.

She heard him mutter, ''You bitch,'' and then the slam of the car door. She looked back and saw him hobbling after her, the light from an auditorium window glinting on the lens of his glasses—and on the metal barrel of a gun.

She ran blindly. There were cars on the street. Should she try to flag one down? Would it stop? Would they help—or speed away? If she tried, wouldn't that give Maitland a chance to catch up with her—to catch her? She looked back. He was still coming after her, still favoring his leg, still slowed by it, still carrying the gun. She had to get away.

The park, with its twisting, dimly lit paths, its thick shrubbery and quiet lagoons—she could hide there. She could lose him there.

She ran away from the streetlights, toward the gaping darkness of the park, sobbing with each breath. She plunged into its blanketing shadows, her heels immediately sinking in the grass. She stumbled and fell, her lungs, her side, her whole body on fire. For a brief moment she simply lay there, fighting for breath, not certain she could get back up. But she did, pausing long enough to slip off her high heels before pressing on, slower this time, hugging the shadows and holding her full skirt tightly around her to keep the taffeta from rustling so noisily.

Someone cursed long and low. Remy froze. It had sounded close. How close? Where? She searched the shadows and caught a movement. Someone was over there. There was a gap in the bushes behind her. She started to back into it, one quiet step at a time. Would he see her? Would he catch the faint shimmer of her sequined top in the darkness?

As a hand grabbed her from behind, she screamed and whirled around, striking out blindly to free herself. Both arms were seized.

"Stop it, Remy. Stop it," someone demanded, shaking her hard when she persisted in struggling. "Do you hear? Stop it."

Something penetrated—the sound of that voice, the sensation of the hands, the flashes of images in her mind. Remy paused to look at the man's face.

"You." She recoiled from the sight of her father. "You're the one who hit me. You're the one I was arguing with at the Espace Masséna." She moved her head slowly from side to side, not wanting to believe it, not wanting to remember. "Why?"

"I didn't mean to," he murmured. "But you wouldn't listen. You wouldn't understand. We would have lost everything. Wall Street . . . the real-estate deals that went sour in Texas . . . what money we had, we'd gambled on Maitland's offshore venture. When it failed too, he had to pay it back. That's all we did. Make sure he had the money to pay back what he owed. The extra was just . . . interest."

"'We'? You and Gabe. . . ." Then she remembered. "No, it was Marc and Lance too. It was all of you."

"For God's sake, no one got hurt."

"Only Charlie and Cole," she taunted.

"Buchanan's a cat. He'll land on his feet. Charlie . . . he was your fault."

"Oh, God." She bowed her head, unable to look at him as she strained to get as far away from him as possible.

The leaves whispered a warning. "Frazier," a voice said. Her father started to turn, relaxing his hold on her arm, and Cole stepped out of the shadows, his right hand swinging out of the darkness to clip Frazier Jardin's jaw. As her father reeled sideways, Cole caught her arm, his gray eyes smiling briefly at her. "I've wanted to do that for a long time." Then his hand was sliding around her waist, coaxing her along. "Come on. Let's get out of here."

"Maitland's out there somewhere. He has a gun, Cole."

The information elicited a few choice obscenities from him.

From a nearby street came the scream of police sirens. "Cole—"

"I called them before I left." He drew her with him as he moved slowly along the hedges. "Unfortunately, they're going to the auditorium. Maybe we can fool Maitland by doubling—"

At that moment Maitland stepped out of the bushes directly in front of them, the small but deadly-looking barrel of his gun leveled at them. "Look what we have here," he murmured coolly. "What do you suppose happened? A lovers' quarrel, maybe. In the rage of rejection, he shoots her, then commits suicide. Sounds plausible, doesn't it?"

Cole stepped a little ahead of Remy, placing himself between her and Maitland. "It's plausible *only* if you come close enough to leave powder burns. Why don't you do that, Maitland?" He wagged his fingers, urging him to come closer.

"Carl, no," came her father's strangled cry as he plunged out of the shadows a few feet from them, a frightened and panicked look on his face. "My God, she's my daughter. You can't do this."

"I suppose *you're* going to stop me," Maitland jeered in contempt. "How, Frazier, when you couldn't even stop her? I should have remembered that Jardins are notorious for never having the guts to finish what they start. Well, *I* do."

There was a noisy thrashing in the brush to his right. Maitland swung toward the sound and Cole lunged for the gun, driving his arm high in the air. A stab of flame shot from the barrel, accompanied by a small, explosive pop as Cole struggled to wrest the gun from Maitland. Gabe charged out of the bushes, and at the same second, Remy saw the gun arc through the air.

"Get it, Remy!" Cole shouted.

It landed somewhere in the grass. She ran to the spot where she thought it had fallen and frantically groped through the short, clipped grass. Then she felt the cool smoothness of metal beneath her fingers and quickly snatched it up. When she turned with the gun, Gabe was standing in front of her.

He hesitated a second, then held out his hand. "Give me the gun, Remy."

She took an uncertain step backward and shook her head.

"Dammit, Remy, I wouldn't have let him hurt you. I was trying to stop him. Now give me the gun."

Suddenly Cole was beside her, breathing hard and taking the revolver from her hand. Out of the corner of her eye, she caught the gleam of flashlights moving toward them: the police.

29

The cathedral rang the midnight hour, signaling the end of Mardi Gras and the beginning of the Lenten season, the time of fasting. Remy listened to it and shuddered faintly, staring heedlessly at the bare branches of a mimosa tree in the small brick-walled courtyard.

She heard a footstep on the flagstones and half turned as Cole stepped through the French doors and joined her on the private patio off his apartment. He silently offered her a glass of brandy. She took it and sipped it, then turned back to her contemplation of the night.

"I was coming to you. I was going to leave Nice the next morning," she said dully, the memory of it all now very clear. "When you accused my family of instigating this fraud and we argued so bitterly, I didn't believe you—even though I was nagged by the memory of that night when I saw Gabe's red Porsche parked on the levee road and stopped to see what he was doing there. I wanted to believe that the fresh water was for bathing and cooking. But when I confronted him—all of them—with it in Nice, they. . . ."

"I know," Cole said, studying the brandy in his own glass as he stood beside her.

"I listened to all their arguments—their justifications. The company was going to go bankrupt anyway, they said. And the way they looked at it, they had to get money out of it any way they could. They were destroying the Crescent Line—and they didn't care." She stopped in time to choke back a sob. "I thought I knew them, Cole. They're my family. To see them—to hear them . . . oh, God, it hurt."

"I know."

She breathed out a shaky sigh, realizing that it would never go away, that feeling of a faith betrayed—a trust, a love. "I . . . I knew I had to stop them. You and I had to take over the company. It was the only way to save it." She paused. "It still is."

"It won't be easy, Remy."

"*Easy.*" She laughed at the word. "It will be ugly. Very, very ugly. But it has to be done."

He watched her with a sidelong look, his gray eyes quiet and measuring. "Now you sound like a Donovan."

She smiled faintly. "Maybe I do."

"You know, you could work a deal with your family," he said. "In return for their signing over their proxies to you and resigning from the board, you could withdraw the charges you filed against them tonight."

"I thought about that," she admitted. "But once you start compromising, where do you stop, Cole? And what justification would I use? Would I say it was to avoid a fight for control? Or to avoid a messy scandal and protect the Jardin name? Charlie died helping a woman he knew as Remy Cooper—not Remy Jardin. It's time the Jardin name stopped meaning so much."

"Or maybe it's time for it to mean more."

She looked at him and smiled. "Maybe it is."

He touched his brandy glass to hers, then lightly curved his arm around her and drew her into the crook of his shoulder.

*Turn the page
for a
Special Bonus Chapter
of*

ASPEN GOLD

*by
Janet Dailey*

Just published by
LITTLE, BROWN AND CO.

A Learjet streaked across the crisp autumn air, its nose tipped down in a slow but steady angle of descent. Below, the Rockies loomed, mighty upthrusts of granite bristling with spruce. It was a wild land, an ageless land, harsh and beautiful by turns. Its unbridled grandeur was limitless, constantly challenging the strong and mocking the weak—and always indifferent to man's attempts to tame it.

Here, where great herds of elk once grazed the high mountain meadow, five hundred head of crossbred Hereford and Black Angus cattle trailed across the autumn yellow grass, flanked by a half dozen riders. On the right, a river of aspen gold tumbled down the stony breast of a mountain slope, crashed through a black-green wall of pine, and spilled its bright yellow flood onto the meadow.

Sunlight glinted on the jet's polished surface. Old Tom Bannon caught the flash of metal and threw back his head, directing his gaze skyward, away from the cattle being driven to the winter pasture near the headquarters of Stone Creek Ranch.

The ancient Stetson hat on his head was brown and weather-beaten like the eighty-two-year-old face it shaded. The big hands folded across the saddle horn were speckled with liver spots, and age had fleshed up his big-boned frame and shot his hair with gray.

His widely spaced and deep-set eyes looked out from beneath shaggy brows and searched the flawless October sky for the source of the light flash that had jarred him from his silent reminiscences of past autumn cattle drives. The sight of the sleek aircraft hurtling up the valley like a white arrow flying low—too low—brought his hard, square jaw together.

"Will you look at that blasted fool?" Old Tom flung a hand in the direction of the plane, directing the sharp-edged words at his son and namesake, Tom Bannon. "What in thunderation is going through his head to be flying that low? It's a damned fool stunt, that's what it is."

Following the line of his father's outstretched arm, Tom Bannon spotted the private jet. At thirty-six, he was a younger and leaner version of his father, with a face like the mountains, full of crags and hard surfaces, a face that wasn't handsome, yet one any woman would look at twice. Those who knew him well never called him Young Tom, or even Tom; he was simply Bannon. He'd been that from the first moment his father had set eyes on him and proclaimed, "He's a Bannon, right enough."

"What d'ya bet it's one of those idiots from Hollywood taking a scenic tour before landing in Aspen?" Old Tom challenged.

When Bannon saw the insignia of Olympic Pictures painted on the plane's white fuselage, he had an idea who was on board, but he didn't waste time on speculation. Instead his glance sliced to the cattle bunched in front of the open gate as the droning whine of the jet's engines began to make itself heard.

"Ned! Hank!" he shouted to the two riders on the flanks. "Push 'em through the gate!"

He spared one look to the rear of the herd, locating his nine-year-old daughter, Laura. She trailed behind, her head bobbing from side to side, her slim shoulders dipping and swaying, her fingers snapping to the beat of the rock music coming over her headset. Oblivious to everything but the song, she hadn't heard his shouted order.

Bannon whistled a shrill command to the two cowdogs trotting alongside her pinto. Like twin streaks, they shot after the herd, harrying them from the rear while Bannon pushed at the balking leaders, reluctant to leave the summer range. Ignoring their bawls of protest, he rode his buckskin against them, urging them forward with his voice and the slap of a coiled lariat against his thigh.

From the knoll, Old Tom watched as the first of the cows went through, stiff-legged and suspicious, heads lowered in distrust. But one look at the plane speeding through the sky and Old Tom knew they'd never get the rest of the herd through. The plane was so close he could see the pilot's dark aviator glasses and the faces pressed close to the cabin's porthole windows.

He yelled anyway: "Don't let 'em break. Don't let 'em break!"

The jet thundered by, a scant three hundred feet above the mountain's shoulder and the herd. The noise of its engines caught up with them, breaking across the cattle in a roar that vibrated the air and the ground. The aging red roan beneath Old Tom—a horse that never turned a hair at the blast of a thirty-ought-six between its ears —sank into a crouch, then spun in a half circle, joining the cattle that wheeled as one and bolted back across the meadow, their tufted tails raised high in panic.

For Old Tom, the sight of the stampeding herd and the racing riders was a patch from his youth, when half-wild cattle had run on the ranch. Caught up by the memory, he suddenly felt young again himself and spurred the roan after the herd.

Far ahead, Old Tom spotted his granddaughter sawing on the reins, regaining control of her frightened pinto. He took an instant pride in her skill. From her earliest talking days, he'd taught her to ride like that—loose and straight in the saddle yet always balanced, prepared for any sudden moves by her mount.

Then he saw the wall of aspens beyond, and she was forgotten. If the cattle made it into that dense timber, they'd scatter like leaves in the wind. It would take a day—maybe two—to gather them up again.

"Keep 'em in the meadow!" he shouted. "Don't let 'em get in those trees!"

But the fading rumble of the jet's engines and the loud drum of cloven and shod hooves drowned out his call. Then Old Tom saw that the warning had been needless. Bannon had seen the same thing, and had the buckskin stretched out flat, streaking to catch the leaders and turn them before they reached the timber.

Old Tom watched. There'd been a time when he and the old roan could have made a race of it, but no more. No more.

Inside the jet's lushly appointed cabin, Kit Masters sat on her knees, her shoes kicked off, her long legs tucked beneath her as she leaned across the back of the pewter velvet sofa to look out the window. A hand slid across her back, then settled with familiar ease on the rounded jut of a hipbone. Kit smiled, recognizing the touch of that hand. She glanced back, automatically tucking the loose tumble of honey blonde hair behind an ear as John Travis folded his six-foot-two-inch frame onto the plump sofa cushion, angling his body toward hers.

He flashed her one of his trademark smiles—quick,

crooked, and wicked—a smile that changed his face from merely sexy to dangerously charming.

"The pilot said we should be flying over your place shortly. Anything look familiar to you yet?" John Travis briefly peered out the window, the downward tip of his head bringing into view the sun-lightened streaks in his darkly gold hair.

"Nearly everything." Idly Kit studied his lean and faintly aristocratic face. It was a strong face, handsome with well-defined bones and a dimpled chin, a face made even more unique by its combination of charm and blatant sex appeal. A combination that had proved to be irresistible to the world at large ever since John Travis had burst onto the Hollywood scene fifteen years ago, soaring to almost instant stardom.

Looking at him, Kit was struck again by the illusory feeling that she'd known John Travis all her life, when, in fact, she'd met him for the first time just six short weeks ago, at a party she'd attended only days before auditioning for the female lead in his new, yet-to-be-filmed movie, *White Lies*. A role she'd ultimately won, with the shooting scheduled to begin in a matter of weeks.

Kit turned back to the window, smiling when she recalled the crazy roller-coaster ride her life had taken these last six weeks—a ride full of heart-stopping speed and surprises. She'd loved every minute of it. Yet at the same time, she looked forward to the chance to finally catch her breath.

"If it's all so familiar to you, tell me where we are?" John Travis arched a challenging look her way, a faintly ironic color to his blue-gray eyes.

"We're flying over Stone Creek," Kit replied easily, suppressing a slight twinge of pain, her nerves tensing at the sight of it.

"Stone Creek?" He peered out the window again. "I don't see any creek down there."

Her soft laugh drew a glance from Chip Freeman, the director and screenplay author of *White Lies*. But the instant his myopic eyes, aided by bottle-thick glasses, registered the blur of granite and gold mountains beyond the plane's windows, he turned back to the padded black-leather bar trimmed with chrome. The quick bobbing of his Adam's apple betrayed the fact he was a white-knuckle flier of the highest order.

Kit's agent, the stout and stubby Maury Rose, gave no indication that he'd heard her as he continued his nonstop hustling of publicist Yvonne Davis, determined to get Kit the lion's share of media attention at the charity dinner J. D. Lassiter, the billionaire owner of Olympic Pictures, was giving that night.

Paula Grant was the Learjet's one remaining passenger, a veteran soap actress who possessed that exotic combination of flaming red hair, porcelain skin, and green eyes—a hard and sleek kind of beauty that matched the bitchy characters she portrayed so well. She listened with only half an ear to the byplay between Kit and John Travis as she gazed out the window, intent on the mountain scenery, her deep leather cabin chair swiveled in a conversational mode toward the sofa.

"Stone Creek," Kit explained, "is the ranch that adjoins ours."

Ours. She sobered at her choice of pronouns. Silverwood could no longer accurately be called *ours.* After the death of her father eight months ago, ownership of the four-hundred-acre family ranch had passed solely to her.

The image of her father—the dark and handsome Clint Masters—came readily to her mind. She had recognized long ago that she'd inherited his blood, his recklessness, and his insatiable love of life.

She hadn't been back to the ranch since the funeral —not by choice, but by circumstance. She tried and failed to imagine the ranch house without him in it, without his laughter to fill it.

"Look at all those cows running across the meadow," Paula Grant announced to no one in particular. "And those cowboys chasing them. Good Lord, Kit, don't tell me the Old West is still alive?"

Kit spotted the stampeding herd and groaned in dismay. "Oh, no, we've spooked the cattle. Old Tom's going to have my head when he finds out."

"I take it Old Tom owns the cattle." This close to her, John Travis noticed the sweep of her lashes, the faint freckling across her nose, and the curve of her mouth.

"He does," she replied, her smile radiating that breezy friendliness that had first attracted him to her.

On the surface, Kit Masters seemed typical of thousands of blonde wannabes who possessed a kind of sunny and innocent California sexiness that had always had its place in Hollywood. Yet it was the unusual lake-blue color of her eyes that lifted her out of the commonplace, eyes with a depth that suggested many things. He wondered if he'd ever uncover all her layers as he breathed in the warm, teasing fragrance of her perfume. It had been a long time since he'd more than indifferently wanted a woman. But there was nothing indifferent about his feelings toward Kit Masters.

"They're moving the cattle down from the summer range," Kit offered in absent explanation. "When I was growing up, Dad and I went over to Stone Creek every spring and helped with the branding and ear-tagging, the vaccinating, culling, and castrating, then drove the herd up to the high country for the summer. In the fall, we'd help bring them down," she recalled, and thought of Bannon, who was so inextricably woven into all her memories of the past. The thought of him revived the old hurt—and the thready tension. She pushed them to the back of her mind. After ten years of practice, she'd become quite skilled at that.

"I simply cannot picture you punching cows, Kit," Paula Grant stated with a bemused shake of her head.

John Travis couldn't help agreeing with Paula Grant's observation, especially when he glanced at Kit, seeing the confident and self-assured tilt of her head.

Kit laughed at her friend's remark and immediately adopted a thick drawl. "Well, Paula honey, I'm plumb sorry you can't see me punching cows, but I did it just the same." She abandoned the accent. "Daddy had me on a horse before I learned to coo—to my mother's horror, I might add. By the time I was two years old, I had a pony of my own. At three, he gave me a miniature lariat and I drove the dogs and chickens crazy trying to rope them. When I was six, I was riding a full-sized horse." Her smile widened. "Of course, my mother countered all that by enrolling me in ballet class, making sure I took piano lessons, and dragging me off to concerts in the Music Tent and performances at the Wheeler Opera House. If I was going to be a cowgirl, she was determined to make me an *urbane* one."

"*Very* urbane," John Travis agreed, taking in the drops of chunky gold that dangled from her earlobes and mixed with strands of long blonde hair that ran faintly lawless back from her face. A trio of heavy gold bracelets circled her wrist and clashed with the bright coral jacket she wore over a grape-colored cashmere tunic and slacks. A gold flyaway coat, carelessly thrown over the arm of the sofa, completed the bold and thoroughly modern ensemble—an ensemble that few women had the flair to carry off with any degree of sophistication. Kit was one of them.

"Paula, John T. Look." She pressed closer to the window, her expression showing an excitement that made her appear much younger than thirty-two. "There's Silverwood. My home."

Picking up on the warmth in her voice, John Travis glanced out the window. Attachment to a place was something he'd never known growing up as he had on a succession of military bases scattered over half the globe. At seventeen, he'd run away to California rather than face another move to another base and another strange school. He'd taken up acting on a dare, trading one transient life for another.

With idle curiosity he studied the buildings nestled at the apex of a triangularly shaped valley, walled by two sprawling, snowcapped ridges of the Rocky Mountains. A picturesque barn, weathered gray by the elements, sat in the center with wood fences stretching to make square designs across the valley. In a grove of aspen trees stood a rambling, clapboard house with three gables and a porch that wrapped all four sides of the building.

"It looks positively rustic and quaint, Kit," Paula said on a note of rare approval.

"It does, doesn't it?" Kit murmured, caught up in the memories of the good times she'd had there—and the sad ones.

"It's the setting that does it," Paula stated. "The mountains rising behind it. The fabulous fall colors. I thought nothing could rival autumn in New England, but this" —she lifted a ringed hand to indicate the view from the jet's windows—"this is incredible."

Kit's gaze wandered from her childhood home to the mountains that autumn had painted with distilled sunshine. Drifts of canary yellow gleamed between solid ranks of spruce marching up a granite slope. Farther on, still more masses of slender white trunks rose from the forest floor, waving their crowns of saffron, lemon, amber, and topaz.

"I told you how glorious it would be at this time of year, Paula, but you wouldn't believe me," Kit said with a light trace of smugness. "You're such a cynic. You should have been born in Missouri instead of Vermont."

"Cynicism is necessary for survival in this business," Paula replied. "When you've been in it as long as I have, you'll find that out for yourself."

"So you've said. But you know me—I'm an incurable optimist." Kit shrugged in unconcern.

"It's a pity you aren't shooting your movie now instead of waiting for winter, John," Paula Grant remarked. "This scenery is spectacular."

"Careful, Paula," John Travis mocked. "You're starting to sound like a tourist."

"After the charity benefit tonight, that's exactly what I'm going to be for an entire month," she declared, fairly gloating. "No more early-morning calls, no more long days, no more endless pages of dialogue to learn, no more working six days a week. You can't possibly know how ecstatic I was when the writers decided it was time to kill off Rachel—"

"—and the producers had to buy out your contract," John Travis inserted.

"That, too," Paula admitted in a purr. "But after seven years on *Winds of Destiny*, I think I've earned a long and highly paid vacation. Don't you?"

"Pay no attention to John T.," Kit said. "He's spent the last two hours with Chip thinking like a producer instead of an actor."

"It shows." Paula turned back to the window. Something caught her eye and she edged closer to the pane. "That mountain," she murmured. "It looks like it's made of solid gold."

"Considering the price of real estate in Aspen, it might as well be," John Travis observed dryly.

Paula gave an absent nod. "I've heard the cost of even a small place is sinfully high."

Privately Kit hoped they were right, then immediately banished the thought and its overtones of greed.

"That's Aspen coming up, isn't it?" Paula asked.

Through the window, Kit watched the town take shape, spilling across the narrow valley of the Roaring Fork River and onto the shoulders of the walling Rocky Mountains.

Ski runs snaked down the slopes of Aspen Mountain where one hundred years ago black-faced miners trudged wearily home from their shifts in the silver mines. Ultraluxe, ultramodern mansions littered the mountainsides where once mining equipment stood guard over the entrances to the richest silver mines in the nation. Fashionable shops and trendy boutiques lined Durant Street, the former locale of Aspen's red-light district prior to the turn of the century. Here the rich and celebrated came to play where silver kings, railroad barons, and European royalty once visited.

Its tree-lined streets had known the rattle of horse-drawn streetcars, the rumble of freight wagons, the glitter of fancy carriages, the bleating of flocks of sheep, the tramp of ski-combat troops during the Second World War, the swish of skis and the purr of Mercedes Benzes.

Kit smiled when she considered the uniqueness of her hometown—from rough mining camp to silver boom-town to near ghost town to world-class-resort—a story Hollywood would have called *Cinderella Meets King Midas*. For once, they would have been accurate.

Hi from Branson, Missouri,

The old adage "Time flies" has never seemed more true. I feel as if I just finished writing MASQUERADE a few months ago and here you are holding the paperback edition from Little, Brown in your hands.

Even more astounding than that, Little, Brown has released the hardcover edition of my newest novel, ASPEN GOLD. I think you're going to love it. The setting is Aspen, Colorado, deep in the magnificent grandeur of the Rocky Mountains— the summer and winter playground of the mega-rich, mega-famous, and mega-powerful.

Once in a while, a writer gets lucky and creates a character he or she really admires. In ASPEN GOLD, I got mega-lucky. I created two: Kit Masters, a strong, laughter-loving woman on the verge of Hollywood stardom, and, Bannon, a man as rugged and enduring as the mountains he was raised in. Lovers once, but can they ever be again? I'm not telling. But you can begin to find out—the first chapter of ASPEN GOLD follows at the end of this edition of MASQUERADE!

Needless to say, another novel is in the works. This one will be set in Kentucky's Bluegrass country. Bill is hard at work pulling together all the research on it for me while I'm doing my thing with the plotting and characters.

And he's also hard at work finishing our new plantation-style home, Belle Rive, here in Branson, and adding the final touches to the landscaping. Without a doubt, this is our dream home and unlike some horror stories we've heard, Bill and I haven't had a single argument over it—yet. (He'll probably plant the roses in the wrong place now that I've said that.)

A few people have ribbed us about building a plantation-style home in the Ozarks of all places. But we have checked and, theoretically, we sit approximately forty miles *south* of the Mason-Dixon line—as the beautiful azaleas, rhododendrons, and magnolias in our garden will attest. Can you tell we love it here in Branson?

And before you ask, we have received letters from many of you who have visited Branson in the past, asking whether Bill and I are still involved in the country music scene here in Branson. The answer is—yes and no. No—we don't have our Country Music World theater anymore; it has been sold to Mickey Gilley. And—yes—Bill and I are still stockholders in the Roy Clark Celebrity Theater and Lodge of the Ozarks along with Jim and Joy Thomas. And I'm glad to say that my books, tee shirts, sweatshirts and other merchandise are available in the hotel's gift shop as well as—are you ready for this?—the Willie Nelson General Store and Museum in downtown Branson. Plus the Willie Nelson store has my pictures and various awards I've received hanging on the same wall with memorabilia from the likes of Willie Nelson, Elvis Presley, Johnny Cash, and David Allen Coe. That's some very exalted company for a writer.

What else is there to say except take care and—

Happy Reading!

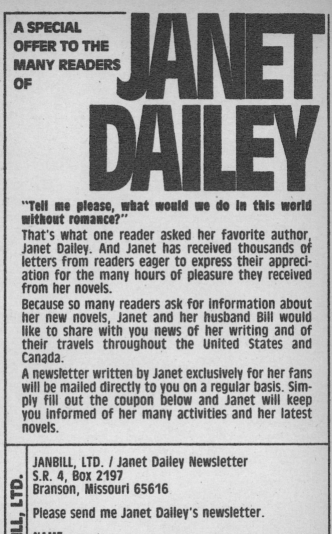